GEN
FIT

This book is due for return on or before the last date shown below.

PENELOPE FITZGERALD

Offshore
Human Voices
The Beginning of Spring

with an Introduction by
John Bayley

EVERYMAN'S LIBRARY
Alfred A. Knopf New York London Toronto

269

THIS IS A BORZOI BOOK
PUBLISHED BY ALFRED A. KNOPF

First included in Everyman's Library, 2003

Copyright information (UK):
Offshore: Copyright © Penelope Fitzgerald, 1979
First published in Great Britain by William Collins Sons and Co. Ltd.,
1979
Human Voices: Copyright © Penelope Fitzgerald, 1980
First published in Great Britain by William Collins Sons and Co. Ltd.,
1980
The Beginning of Spring: Copyright © Penelope Fitzgerald, 1988
First published in Great Britain by William Collins Sons and Co. Ltd.,
1988
Published by arrangement with HarperCollins Publishers

Copyright information (US):
Offshore: Copyright © 1979 by Penelope Fitzgerald
Human Voices: Copyright © 1980 by Penelope Fitzgerald
The Beginning of Spring: © 1988 by Penelope Fitzgerald
Published by arrangement with Houghton Mifflin Company

Introduction and Chronology Copyright © 2003 by Everyman's Library
Typography by Peter B. Willberg

All rights reserved under International and Pan-American Copyright
Conventions. Published in the United States by Alfred A. Knopf,
a division of Random House, Inc., New York, and simultaneously in
Canada by Random House of Canada Limited, Toronto. Distributed by
Random House, Inc., New York. Published in the United Kingdom by
Everyman's Library, Gloucester Mansions, 140A Shaftesbury Avenue,
London WC2H 8HD, and distributed by Random House (UK) Ltd.,
20 Vauxhall Bridge Road, London SW1V 2SA.

US website: www.randomhouse/everymans

ISBN: 1-4000-4125-2 (US)
1-85715-269-7 (UK)

A CIP catalogue reference for this book is available from the
British Library

Book design by Barbara de Wilde and Carol Devine Carson

Printed and bound in Germany by GGP Media, Germany

PENELOPE FITZGERALD

——

C O N T E N T S

———

Introduction	..	..	..	..	..	ix
Chronology	..	..	..	..	..	xvi
OFFSHORE	..	..	..	..	..	1
HUMAN VOICES	..	..	..	..	..	133
THE BEGINNING OF SPRING	..	..	..	273

INTRODUCTION

It is rare indeed to begin a literary career after the age of sixty, and then to achieve reputation and fame as a novelist during the next decade. But Penelope Fitzgerald was a highly unusual and original sort of writer. Before she turned to writing she had married and raised a family, worked during the war at the BBC (the setting of her fourth novel, *Human Voices*), run a bookshop (an experience that also provided a novel), and taught school, including a school for theatre and drama training.

Her first book was a study of the Victorian artist Edward Burne-Jones. She followed this with *The Knox Brothers*, a biography of her father Edmund Knox, the gifted and remarkable editor of *Punch*, and her equally talented set of uncles. That might well have been enough for most writers at her age, but it turned out to be in the nature of a prologue to her real career as a novelist.

In a cool modest way Fitzgerald was an experimenter, never repeating the same kind of novel twice. Her first, *The Golden Child*, plays engagingly with the forms of the mystery and detective story, but its real charm lies in the field of comedy: in this case the quirks and personalities of the staff who run the big museum which is housing a prize exhibit. This was followed by the lively and delightful story of *The Bookshop*, the prelude, as it might be said, to *Offshore*, her first assured masterpiece, nouvelle and almost miniature as in a sense it is. All her books have the quality, and the impact, that goes with a particular sort of brevity: their simplicity and their author's finely individual line of vision, unique in each particular case, makes them seem longer than they really are.

Offshore, which won the prestigious Booker Prize, to the surprise of some of the judges, and, indeed, to the amazement if not the chagrin of other, more heavyweight contenders, has a deceptive simplicity about it. It needs to be read at least twice before the reader grasps how subtle and how eventually rewarding are its method and effect.

As with Penelope Fitzgerald's other novels, a close analogy suggests itself with what happens to us when we meet new acquaintances in ordinary daily life. In such a situation we may soon realize that we know very little: our first impressions (to borrow the original title of Jane Austen's first novel) are probably not true, or even just, but in life itself we hardly have the opportunity, and seldom indeed the inclination, to enquire or to wonder much further. We are in that situation as we continue to encounter Nenna, the wife whose husband has left her, and who – in a muddled way, distracted as she is by everyday cares and problems – wishes he hadn't. The wholly disconcerting effect that the young can have, even – or perhaps indeed especially – on their parents, is suggested by a sentence about them so quietly laconic and unobtrusive that it seems almost absent-minded: 'The crucial moment when children realise that their parents are younger than they are had long since been passed by Martha.'

Martha and her sister Tilda are, in their unflamboyant way, a disconcerting pair, but readers have, as it were, too much to do with other people and other matters, with the boats and the personalities of their owners, with the absorbing nature of the odd and yet perfectly normal world they find themselves in, to worry much about the nature of the children. They are so obviously not worried themselves: and very little attention is paid to them by anybody. As their creator so economically remarks – and the uninsistent humour of the moment is typical of all Penelope Fitzgerald's fiction – children do indeed discover, or at least receive the impression, that – in the words of a wise old priest – there are no true adults in the world, and that they themselves are as old as they are ever likely to be. There is a kind of insecurity about the Fitzgerald world which makes it, as every page turns, so increasingly fascinating and challenging. She never attempts to analyse or to possess her characters in the way, for instance, that Henry James, another master of the nouvelle form, finds it too strong a temptation not to do.

And this odd fact may indeed give the clue to the way in which readers finds themselves hooked. Some mystery, some secret will surely emerge; and yet it does not. Her readers are no wiser about what the people they have been reading about are like at the end of the novel than they were at the beginning. *That* is not, as it were, the point of the exercise, as it would be, say, in a nouvelle by Henry James or a novel by George Eliot.

The same applies to story or plot. Penelope Fitzgerald's novels don't have plots, but they give a wonderful illusion of having them, by keeping the reader glued to the page, in anticipation of what's to come. In a sense nothing much is, because nothing much happens to the characters, but the last thing the reader feels is disappointment. (*Offshore* has indeed an astonishing climax and conclusion, but it gives us the pure pleasure of accomplished art, rather than the mere surprise of an unexpected ending.)

Although always unobtrusive, the moments of drama in the novel are, in their own way, devastating. No one has ever described a husband–wife 'quarrel' with such appallingly accurate charity as Fitzgerald gives us in the scene between Nenna, longing to have her husband back, and Edward, longing to be taken back, but finding himself, as men do, in an impasse of perverse pride and muddled vehemence. All she can say is 'please give' and when he angrily demands 'what', she can only say 'anything'. But she has managed, as he has not, to say that she wants him every moment and to remember that one of his few accomplishments is the ability to fold up a map properly, something she herself can never do.

Although the author never says so, it is clear that the boat itself, the *Grace* (meaningfully incongruous name), and the way of life on the river, have really come between them. The little girls love their life and everything about the Thames – the mud, and the mess, and the chances of finding even quite valuable broken tiles on the muddy foreshore. Again the author makes us see, without stating the fact, how and why they love it, and yet how impossible it has become as a life for their elders.

Offshore is in some ways a sad book as well as a searching one, although sadness, like so many other things in the novel, is mingled with a kind of accepting gaiety. In *Human Voices*, Fitzgerald takes up again her own style and form of comedy. It is a most amazing book and, like all her books, a charitable one, although it may have made a few faces blush at the BBC. As the river is the essential background of *Offshore*, so London in wartime is presided over by the sound of those cultivated voices mediating the war to the British public. It is tempting to wonder whether there is a sly reference in the title to the concluding lines of T. S. Eliot's 'The Lovesong of J. Alfred Prufrock':

> We have lingered in the chambers of the sea
> By sea-girls wreathed with seaweed red and brown
> Till human voices wake us, and we drown.

Penelope Fitzgerald had been a sea-girl herself, so to speak, in the offices of the Corporation; and she loved a subtle or oblique joke as much as anybody. As a critic pointed out when *Human Voices* was published, although the temptation is to read fast because the novel is so delightfully readable, it is better to go slowly so as not to miss the jokes. There are plenty of them below that demure surface.

The Beginning of Spring has all the fascination of its predecessors and much more beside. 'Open the doors,' runs a Russian proverb, quoted by Penelope Fitzgerald, 'here comes trouble.' It is a very Russian proverb, for Russians are convinced that since trouble will come anyway it should be greeted with an appropriate hospitality. There is plenty of trouble in this strangely magical and in some ways very Russian novel, but there are other things too, including the promise of spring, and indeed its beginning, when all the double windows in Moscow houses are taken out, in readiness for the few short months of summer. Not the least magical aspect of the book, as if it were a Russian fairy-tale mixed with the innocent sophistication of a story by Chckhov, is the way in which the author has, as it were, contrived to Russianize her imagination while leaving its inherent Englishness still in place. Quite how she has discovered, absorbed, and made her own use of so much Russian material remains her secret. Perhaps a Knox uncle or two may have been useful? – who knows.

So authentic is the feel of the book that we may be baffled, and even unsatisfied at first, as much by the tone as by the intention. Penelope Fitzgerald has always given the feeling, in her fiction, of the way things are muddled up in life, but here such an impression is more overwhelming than ever, and seems, too, more cunningly engineered by a sophisticated process of art. Almost as in her first novel, the 'mystery', and its solution, seem to lie in the fact that there was no mystery in the first place, only the appearance of one. In this case it is Nellie – Mrs Reid, wife of an English printer in Moscow – going away, and then at the end, returning. Why does she do it? We don't know – any more, we might feel, than a lot of things which are never to be known or understood: in Russia, or, indeed, in the world at large. But so far from being frustrating or disappointing this effect of the novel seems, in its own way, both logical and deeply satisfying.

The humour of the book, never laborious or attempting to show itself off, is one of its joys. Frank Reid's assistant at the printing works, Selwyn Crane, is perhaps the nearest Penelope Fitzgerald comes to creating a 'character', and a comic one at that. He is one of those people most of us have somewhere in our lives who invariably manage to occupy, as one might say, the moral high ground. When Reid's wife Nellie leaves home – and it may be for no other reason than that she finds life in Moscow, with an English husband born and bred there, too unnatural, indeed too exacting, for her – Selwyn is at once on hand to give his own peculiar variety of consolation. Poor Frank puts his head in his hands, feeling that 'he could bear anything rather than determined unselfishness'. Selwyn makes everyone else feel guilty, as Frank tells him in a burst of exasperation, and when things are sorted out Selwyn can think of nothing but 'his next charitable enterprise'. Now, 'with the terrible aimlessness of the benevolent, he was casting round for a new misfortune.' On top of all this, the part he has played in the decamping of Nellie Reid seems to be a puzzling or, even, an equivocal one.

Such things, however, don't greatly matter: indeed one of the strange things about this jewel of a book is how little things like that do seem to matter; and yet we are always gripped by what is happening, and pleasantly taken up with wondering what might happen next. This is in a sense the old atmosphere of fantasy and fairy-tale, brought up to date here and with its species of strangeness never far away, and yet always strictly and beautifully down to earth. Penelope Fitzgerald's children – Frank's Dolly, Ben and Annushka in *The Beginning of Spring*, like Nenna's Tilda and Martha in *Offshore* – seem so natural a part of their author's highly individual world that they are wholly pleasing and acceptable, even to those of us who would normally be highly suspicious of child characters in fiction.

As much a part of the suggestiveness and material imagination of the story is the young girl from the big shop, Lisa, employed by Frank on Selwyn's advice to help look after the three children. What part Lisa subsequently plays in Frank's own life – emotionally, even perhaps sexually – is all a part of the artful mystery of the book's development. Frank and a Russian friend go, at the friend's suggestion, to a fashionable Moscow teashop called Rusalochka's. In Russian mythology a Rusalka is a water-sprite, once human, who has drowned herself when forsaken by a human lover. Sometimes, as in Pushkin's magical poem, she has borne a daughter in her new transformation, in fact a Rusalochka, who will herself sexually tempt her mother's faithless lover. Penelope Fitzgerald's meticulous inventiveness is much too subtle to labour this legend, or for any of the normal signposts and suggestions of symbolism, but the relationship between Lisa and Selwyn, and Lisa and Frank and his vanished wife, teases the reader – not into a search for clues, but into the superior enjoyments of aesthetic questioning and wondering.

No wonder, too, that Anita Brookner, writing in the *Spectator*, was sure that the novel had 'mastered a city, a landscape and a vanished time' in producing a work of art which was 'part novel, part evocation', done with 'a calm confidence behind its apparent simplicity'. That confidence in handling material so far distant from the normal domestic field which English novelists have made so distinctively their own, from Jane Austen to Barbara Pym and Anita Brookner herself, is indeed a very special achievement of Penelope Fitzgerald; and *The Beginning of Spring*, when it appeared in 1988, was the surest example of a triumph that was to be repeated in her novels to come.

John Bayley

CHRONOLOGY

DATE	AUTHOR'S LIFE	LITERARY CONTEXT
1916	Penelope Fitzgerald born in Lincoln, 17 December, to Edmund Valpy Knox (editor of *Punch* 1932–45) and Christina Knox.	1916 Joyce: *Portrait of the Artist as a Young Man*.
		1917 Eliot: *Prufrock and Other Observations*.
		1918 Strachey: *Eminent Victorians*.
		R. Brooke (died 1915): *Collected Poems*.
		1919 Woolf: *Night and Day*.
		1921 Pirandello: *Six Characters in Search of an Author*.
		Huxley: *Crome Yellow*.
		1922 Joyce: *Ulysses*.
		Eliot: *The Waste Land*.
		Yeats: *Later Poems*.
		Woolf: *Jacob's Room*.
1924–30	Attends Deerhadden prep school in Eastbourne.	1924 Forster: *A Passage to India*.
		Shaw: *Saint Joan*.
		Ford: *Parade's End* (to 1928).
		1925 Fitzgerald: *The Great Gatsby*.
		Kafka: *The Trial*.
		1927 Woolf: *To the Lighthouse*.
		Proust: *A la recherche du temps perdu*.
		1928 Lawrence: *Lady Chatterley's Lover*.
		Yeats: *The Tower*.
		Woolf: *Orlando*.
		1929 Hemingway: *A Farewell to Arms*.
		Remarque: *All Quiet on the Western Front*.
1930–35	Continues her education at Wycombe Abbey.	1930 Coward: *Private Lives*.
		Waugh: *Vile Bodies*.
		1934 Scott Fitzgerald: *Tender is the Night*.

1916 Lloyd George becomes Prime Minister. Easter Rising in Dublin. Huge death tolls at the battles of Verdun and the Somme.

1917 The Russian Revolution.

1918 In January the Suffrage bill is passed, giving women over 30 the vote. Armistice Day, 11 November, marks the end of World War I.

1919 The Treaty of Versailles.
1921 Irish Free State established. Vaughan Williams composes Pastoral Symphony.

1922 Establishment of USSR. Stalin General Secretary of Communist Party Central Committee. Mussolini marches on Rome.

1924 First Labour government formed by Ramsay MacDonald. Death of Lenin. Baldwin becomes Prime Minister again after a Conservative election victory.

1925 Locarno conference. Hitler writes *Mein Kampf* vol. 1. *New Yorker* magazine started.
1926 The General Strike, 3–12 May.
1927 Film: *The Jazz Singer* with Al Jolson.

1928 Women's Suffrage extended to women over 21. Ravel: *Boléro*.

1929 Collapse of the New York Stock Exchange. A worldwide depression follows, and in Britain mass unemployment.

1930 France begins building Maginot line.

1934 Hitler becomes German Führer.

DATE	AUTHOR'S LIFE	LITERARY CONTEXT
1935	Her mother Christina Knox dies in April; in October she goes up to Somerville College, Oxford, where she is taught by J. R. R. Tolkien.	1935 Eliot: *Murder in the Cathedral*. Isherwood: *Mr Norris Changes Trains*. Odets: *Waiting for Lefty*. Greene: *England Made Me*. Wodehouse: *Blandings Castle*. 1936 Dylan Thomas: *Twenty-five Poems*. Auden: *Look, Stranger!* Eliot: *Collected Poems 1909–35*.
1938	Receives an applauded First Class Honours degree in English Literature.	1938 Greene: *Brighton Rock*. Beckett: *Murphy*. Orwell: *Homage to Catalonia*.
1938–9	Works briefly for the Ministry of Food.	1939 Joyce: *Finnegans Wake*. Steinbeck: *The Grapes of Wrath*. Auden: *Journey to a War*.
1939–45	Works as a Programme Assistant at the BBC for the rest of the war. Meets her future husband, Desmond Fitzgerald MC, an Oxford history graduate who is one year her junior.	
1941	Marries Desmond Fitzgerald, a union which lasts until his death 35 years later. They set up home in Squires Mount, Hampstead, where they have three children (a son and two daughters).	1941 Joyce and Woolf die. Brecht: *Mother Courage*. Scott Fitzgerald: *The Last Tycoon*. O'Neill: *Long Day's Journey into Night*. Compton-Burnett: *Parents and Children*. Coward: *Blithe Spirit*. 1945 Orwell: *Animal Farm*. Betjeman: *New Bats in Old Belfries*. Waugh: *Brideshead Revisited*. 1949 Greene: *The Third Man*. De Beauvoir: *The Second Sex*. Orwell: *Nineteen Eighty-Four*. Miller: *Death of a Salesman*. 1950 Lessing: *The Grass is Singing*. 1951 Salinger: *The Catcher in the Rye*.

CHRONOLOGY

HISTORICAL EVENTS

1935 Italy invades Abyssinia. Anti-Jewish Nuremberg laws passed in Germany. Hitchcock: *The Thirty-Nine Steps*.

1936 The death of George V is followed by the accession and abdication crisis of Edward VIII (who wants to marry a divorcee). Spanish Civil War begins.

1938 Germany annexes Austria. Munich crisis. Hitchcock: *The Lady Vanishes*.

1939 Spanish Civil War ends. Germany makes a pact with Russia and invades Poland: World War II begins.

1941 Hitler invades USSR; Siege of Leningrad begins (to 1944). Japanese attack Pearl Harbor. US joins war. Orson Welles: *Citizen Kane*.

1945 Unconditional surrender of Germany; Hitler commits suicide. Atomic bomb dropped on Hiroshima. United Nations founded.

1949 Foundation of NATO. Communist regime in Hungary. Film: *The Third Man*.

1950 Korean War (to 1953). McCarthy's Communist witch-hunts (to 1954).

1951 Defection of Burgess and Maclean.

DATE	AUTHOR'S LIFE	LITERARY CONTEXT
		1952 Beckett: *Waiting for Godot*.
		Waugh: *The Sword of Honour Trilogy* (to 1961).
*c.*1953/ 1954	The Fitzgeralds edit a political-cum-literary journal called *World Review*, but although its contributors include Sartre and Dylan Thomas, it is short-lived.	1953 Bellow: *The Adventures of Augie March*.
		Borges: *Labyrinths*.
		1954 Golding: *Lord of the Flies*.
		Amis: *Lucky Jim*.
		Murdoch: *Under the Net*.
		1955 Nabokov: *Lolita*.
		1956 Ginsberg: *Howl and Other Poems*.
1957	The Fitzgeralds move to Southwold, Suffolk, where Penelope works in a bookshop.	1957 Kerouac: *On the Road*.
		Pinter: *The Birthday Party*.
		Pasternak: *Doctor Zhivago*.
		Hughes: *The Hawk in the Rain*.
		1958 Murdoch: *The Bell*.
		1959 Burroughs: *Naked Lunch*.
		Lee: *Cider with Rosie*.
Early 1960s	The Fitzgeralds live on a houseboat on Chelsea Reach which sinks twice. Penelope teaches at the Italia Conti stage school.	1961 Heller: *Catch-22*.
		Naipaul: *A House for Mr Biswas*.
		Hemingway dies.
		1962 Nabokov: *Pale Fire*.
		Solzhenitsyn: *One Day in the Life of Ivan Denisovich*.
		Burgess: *A Clockwork Orange*.
		1963 Plath: *The Bell Jar*.
		Stoppard: *A Walk on Water*.
		Le Carré: *The Spy Who Came in from the Cold*.
1965–75	Whilst living in Clapham, Penelope works part-time at the Oxbridge crammers, Westminster Tutors and Queensgate School in Kensington, until she retires.	1965 Pinter: *The Homecoming*.
		1966 Rhys: *Wide Sargasso Sea*.
		1967 Márquez: *One Hundred Years of Solitude*.
		Carter: *The Magic Toyshop*.
		Weldon: *The Fat Woman's Joke*.
		1968 Solzhenitsyn: *Cancer Ward*.
		Stoppard: *The Real Inspector Hound*.
		Updike: *Couples*.
		1969 Drabble: *The Waterfall*.
		First Booker Prize awarded.
		1974 Larkin: *High Windows*.

CHRONOLOGY

1952 Accession of Elizabeth II. Eisenhower elected US President. Britain produces atomic bomb. Mau Mau active in Kenya.

1953 European Court of Human Rights set up in Strasbourg. Conquest of Everest.

1954 Vietnam War begins. Nasser gains power in Egypt. Film: *On the Waterfront*.

1955 Albert Einstein dies.
1956 Suez crisis. Hungarian uprising. Film: *My Fair Lady*.

1957 Macmillan becomes Prime Minister. Treaty of Rome: Common Market established. Film: *West Side Story*.

1959 Fidel Castro forms new government in Cuba.

1961 John F. Kennedy elected President in the US. Erection of Berlin Wall. Yuri Gagarin becomes first man in space.

1962 Cuban missile crisis. Benjamin Britten: *War Requiem*.

1963 Assassination of John F. Kennedy. Beatles' first LP comes out.

1965 Malcolm X assassinated.
1966 Mao launches 'Cultural Revolution' in China.
1967 Arab–Israeli Six-Day War. Nigerian Civil War.

1968 Student unrest throughout Europe and the US. Soviet-led invasion of Czechoslovakia. Assassination of Martin Luther King. Nixon US President.

1969 Americans land first man on the moon.

1974 Resignation of Nixon following Watergate scandal.

DATE	AUTHOR'S LIFE	LITERARY CONTEXT
1975	Retires. First book published, on the pre-Raphaelite painter Edward Burne-Jones.	1975 Drabble: *The Realms of Gold*. Levi: *The Periodic Table*. Ruth Prawer Jhabvala: *Heat and Dust*.
1976	Desmond Fitzgerald dies. Penelope moves in with her elder daughter Christina and later with her younger daughter, Maria, in Highgate.	1976 Nina Bawden: *Afternoon of a Good Woman*. Carver: *Will You Be Quiet, Please?*
1977	*The Knox Brothers*, a biographical study of her father and his brothers: Dillwyn, who worked on Enigma, Wilfred, a chaplain at Cambridge, and the youngest, Ronald, the famous Catholic convert and translator of the Bible. Her first novel, *The Golden Child*, is published in the same year. Originally written to entertain her dying husband, it came out of the notion that the lighting for the 1922 Tutankhamen exhibition in the British Museum was so dim because the mummy was a fake.	1977 Morrison: *Song of Solomon*. Drabble: *The Ice Age*. Cheever: *Falconer*. Desai: *Fire on the Mountain*. Márquez: *Autumn of the Patriarch*. Grass: *The Flounder*. Carter: *The Passion of New Eve*. Fowles: *Daniel Martin*. Nabokov dies. Hughes: *Gaudete*. Alan Bennett begins writing *The Old Country*.
1978	*The Bookshop*, shortlisted for the Booker Prize.	1978 Iris Murdoch: *The Sea, The Sea* (wins Booker Prize). Greene: *The Human Factor*.
1979	*Offshore*, which wins the Booker Prize.	1979 Calvino: *If on a winter's night a traveller*. Barth: *Letters*. Grass: *The Meeting at Telgete*. Naipaul: *A Bend in the River*.
1980	*Human Voices*.	1980 Desai: *Clear Light of Day*. Kundera: *The Book of Laughter and Forgetting*. Golding: *Rites of Passage*. 1981 Rushdie: *Midnight's Children*. Updike: *Rabbit Is Rich*. Carver: *What We Talk About When We Talk About Love* (stories).

CHRONOLOGY

1975 End of Vietnam War. USSR and Western powers sign Helsinki Agreement.

1976 Death of Mao Tse-Tung. Sadam Hussein becomes President of Iraq. Carter elected US President. Soweto massacre in South Africa.

1977 Carter US President. Military coup in Pakistan.

1978 P. W. Botha comes to power in South Africa.

1979 Margaret Thatcher first woman Prime Minister in UK. Carter and Brezhnev sign SALT-2. Soviet occupation of Afghanistan. Iran hostage crisis (to 1981).

1980 Indira Gandi wins election and returns to power. Lech Walesa leads strikes in Gdansk, Poland. Iran–Iraq war (to 1988).

1981 Ronald Reagan becomes US President. Mitterrand elected President of France. President Sadat of Egypt assassinated.

DATE	AUTHOR'S LIFE	LITERARY CONTEXT
1982	*At Freddie's.* Also edits an unpublished novel by William Morris: *Novel on Blue Paper.*	1982 Alice Walker: *The Colour Purple.* Levi: *If not Now, When?* Márquez: *Chronicle of a Death Foretold.* 1983 Weldon: *The Life and Loves of a She-Devil.*
1984	Writes biography of the poet Charlotte Mew.	1984 Carter: *Nights at the Circus.* Barnes: *Flaubert's Parrot.* Brookner: *Hotel du Lac.* Heaney: *Station Island.*
1986	*Innocence.*	1986 DeLillo: *The End Zone.* Levi: *The Drowned and the Saved.*
1988	*The Beginning of Spring,* shortlisted for the Booker Prize.	1988 Rushdie: *The Satanic Verses.* Carey: *Oscar and Lucinda.* Attwood: *Cat's Eye.* Wolfe: *The Bonfire of the Vanities.* Larkin: *Collected Poems.* 1989 Ishiguro: *The Remains of the Day.* M. Amis: *London Fields.* Barnes: *A History of the World in 10½ Chapters.* Winterson: *Sexing the Cherry.*
1990	*The Gate of Angels,* shortlisted for the Booker Prize.	1990 Byatt: *Possession* (wins Booker Prize). Updike: *Rabbit at Rest.* Kureishi: *The Buddha of Suburbia.* 1991 Márquez: *The General in his Labyrinth.* Okri: *The Famished Road.* 1992 Byatt: *Angels and Insects.* Ondaatje: *The English Patient.*
1995	*The Blue Flower,* Critics' Book of the Year.	1995 M. Amis: *The Information.* Desai: *Journey to Ithaca.* Murdoch: *Jackson's Dilemma.*
1996	Heywood Hill prize for lifetime's achievement.	1996 Attwood: *Alias Grace.* Byatt: *Babel Tower.* Drabble: *The Witch of Exmoor.*

CHRONOLOGY

1982 Falklands War between Britain and Argentina.

1984 Famine in Ethiopia.

1986 Gorbachev–Reagan summit. Benazir Bhutto returns to Pakistan. Nuclear explosion at Chernobyl.

1988 George Bush elected US President. Gorbachev announces big troop reductions suggesting end of Cold War. Benazir Bhutto Prime Minister of Pakistan. Terrorist bomb destroys Pan Am Flight 103 over Lockerbie.

1989 Collapse of Communist empire in Eastern Europe. Fall of the Berlin Wall. Tienanmen Square massacre in China. De Klerk becomes President of South Africa.

1990 Resignation of Margaret Thatcher. John Major becomes Prime Minister in UK. Iraq invades Kuwait.

1991 Nelson Mandela released from jail after 27 years' imprisonment. Gulf War.

1992 Bill Clinton elected US President. Civil war in former Yugoslavia.

1995 After signing agreement expanding Palestinian autonomy with Arafat in September, Rabin is assassinated.

1996 President Clinton re-elected.

DATE	AUTHOR'S LIFE	LITERARY CONTEXT
		1997 McEwan: *Enduring Love.* Arundhati Roy: *The God of Small Things.* Kennedy: *Original Bliss.*
1998	Penelope Fitzgerald judges the Booker Prize and becomes the first non-American to win the US National Book Critics Circle fiction award for *The Blue Flower.* All her novels are subsequently re-published by Houghton Mifflin in the US to great acclaim.	1998 Morrison: *Paradise.* McEwan: *Amsterdam.* Desai: *Fasting, Feasting.* Roth: *American Pastoral.* Hughes: *Birthday Letters.* Murdoch and Hughes die. Bennett: *Talking Heads* published (originally written for television). Weldon: *Big Women.*
2000	Penelope Fitzgerald dies, aged 83, on 28 April. In October, Flamingo and Houghton Mifflin publish *The Means of Escape,* a new collection of short stories, which Fitzgerald was correcting the month before she died. It includes stories previously only published in British periodicals. A corrected new edition of *The Knox Brothers* is published in the US by Counterpoint. A further collection of her essays and shorter prose is in preparation.	2000 Attwood: *The Blind Assassin.* Ishiguro: *When We Were Orphans.* M. Amis: *Experience.*

CHRONOLOGY

1997 Tony Blair elected British Prime Minister (first Labour government since 1979). Princess Diana killed in a car accident in Paris.

1998 Clinton orders air strikes against Iraq. *The Washington Post* discloses a sexual liaison between President Clinton and a White House intern. President Clinton denies the affair, but an investigation continues. On 8 October the House approves an impeachment vote. Northern Ireland Referendum in May accepts the Good Friday Agreement; an assembly is elected in September. Omagh Bomb in August kills 29 people, breaking the Good Friday Agreement.

2000 Putin succeeds Yeltsin as Russian President. Violence in Chechnya. Milosevic's regime in the former Yugoslavia collapses; Vojislav Kostunica declares himself President.

OFFSHORE

For Grace
and all who sailed in her

'che mena il vento, e che batte la pioggia,
e che s'incontran con sì aspre lingue.'

I

'ARE WE to gather that *Dreadnought* is asking us all to do something dishonest?' Richard asked.

Dreadnought nodded, glad to have been understood so easily.

'Just as a means of making a sale. It seems the only way round my problem. If all present wouldn't mind agreeing not to mention my main leak, or rather not to raise the question of my main leak, unless direct enquiries are made.'

'Do you in point of fact want us to say that *Dreadnought* doesn't leak?' asked Richard patiently.

'That would be putting it too strongly.'

All the meetings of the boat owners, by a movement as natural as the tides themselves, took place on Richard's converted *Ton* class minesweeper. *Lord Jim*, a felt reproof to amateurs, in speckless, always-renewed grey paint, over-shadowed the other craft and was nearly twice their tonnage, just as Richard, in his decent dark blue blazer, dominated the meeting itself. And yet he by no means wanted this respon-sibility. Living on Battersea Reach, overlooked by some very good houses, and under the surveillance of the Port of London Authority, entailed, surely, a certain standard of conduct. Rich-ard would be one of the last men on earth or water to want to impose it. Yet someone must. Duty is what no one else will do at the moment. Fortunately he did not have to define duty. War service in the RNVR, and his whole temperament before and since, had done that for him.

Richard did not even want to preside. He would have been happier with a committee, but the owners, of whom several rented rather than owned their boats, were not of the substance from which committees are formed. Between *Lord Jim*, moored almost in the shadow of Battersea Bridge, and the old wooden Thames barges, two hundred yards upriver and close to the

7

rubbish disposal wharfs and the brewery, there was a great gulf fixed. The barge dwellers, creatures neither of firm land nor water, would have liked to be more respectable than they were. They aspired towards the Chelsea shore, where, in the early 1960s many thousands lived with sensible occupations and adequate amounts of money. But a certain failure, distressing to themselves, to be like other people, caused them to sink back, with so much else that drifted or was washed up, into the mud moorings of the great tideway.

Biologically they could be said, as most tideline creatures are, to be 'successful'. They were not easily dislodged. But to sell your craft, to leave the Reach, was felt to be a desperate step, like those of the amphibians when, in earlier stages of the world's history, they took ground. Many of these species perished in the attempt.

Richard, looking round his solid, brassbound table, got the impression that everyone was on their best behaviour. There was no way of avoiding this, and since, after all, Willis had requested some kind of discussion of his own case, he scrupulously collected opinions.

'*Rochester? Grace? Bluebird? Maurice? Hours of Ease? Dunkirk? Relentless?*'

Richard was quite correct, as technically speaking they were all in harbour, in addressing them by the names of their craft. Maurice, an amiable young man, had realised as soon as he came to the Reach that Richard was always going to do this and that he himself would accordingly be known as *Dondeschiepolschuygen IV*, which was inscribed in gilt lettering on his bows. He therefore renamed his boat *Maurice*.

No one liked to speak first, and Willis, a marine artist some sixty-five years old, the owner of *Dreadnought*, sat with his hands before him on the table and his head slightly sunken, so that only the top, with its spiky crown of black and grey hair, could be seen. The silence was eased by a long wail from a ship's hooter from downstream. It was a signal peculiar to Thames river – I am about to get under way. The tide was making, although the boats still rested on the mud.

Hearing a slight, but significant noise from the galley, Richard courteously excused himself. Perhaps they'd have a little more to contribute on this very awkward point when he came back.

'How are you getting on, Lollie?'

Laura was cutting something up into small pieces, with a cookery book open in front of her. She gave him a weary, large-eyed, shires-bred glance, a glance whose horizons should have been bounded by acres of plough and grazing. Loyalty to him, Richard knew, meant that she had never complained so far to anyone but himself about this business of living, instead of in a nice house, in a boat in the middle of London. She went home once a month to combat any such suggestion, and told her family that there were very amusing people living on the Thames. Between the two of them there was no pretence. Yet Richard, who always put each section of his life, when it was finished with, quietly behind him, and liked to be able to give a rational explanation for everything, could not account for this, his attachment to *Lord Jim*. He could very well afford a house, and indeed *Jim* had been an expensive conversion. And if the river spoke to his dreaming, rather than to his daytime self, he supposed that he had no business to attend to it.

'We're nearly through,' he said.

Laura shook back her dampish longish hair. In theory, her looks depended on the services of many employees, my hairdresser, my last hairdresser, my doctor, my other doctor who I went to when I found the first one wasn't doing me any good, but with or without their attentions, Laura would always be beautiful.

'This galley's really not so bad, is it, with the new extractor?' Richard went on, 'A certain amount of steam still, of course . . .'

'I hate you. Can't you get rid of these people?'

In the saloon Maurice, who had come rather late, was saying something intended to be in favour of Willis. He was incurably sympathetic. His occupation, which was that of picking up men in a neighbouring public house, with which he had a working arrangement, during the evening hours, and bringing them back to the boat, was not particularly profitable. Maurice was not born to make a profit, but then, was not born to resent this, or anything else. Those who felt affection for him had no easy way of telling him so, since he seemed to regard friend and enemy alike. For example, an unpleasant acquaintance of his used part of Maurice's hold as a repository for stolen goods. Richard and Laura were among the few boat owners who did not know this. And yet Maurice appeared to be almost proud, because Harry was not a customer, but somebody who had demanded a favour and given nothing in return.

'I shall have to warn Harry not to talk about the leak either,' he said.

'What does he know about it?' asked Willis.

'He used to be in the Merchant Navy. If people are coming to look at *Dreadnought*, he might be asked his opinion.'

'I've never seen him speak to anyone. He doesn't come often, does he?'

At that moment *Lord Jim* was disturbed, from stem to stern, by an unmistakable lurch. Nothing fell, because on *Lord Jim* everything was properly secured, but she heaved, seemed to shake herself gently, and rose. The tide had lifted her.

At the same time an uneasy shudder passed through all those sitting round the table. For the next six hours – or a little less, because at Battersea the flood lasts five and a half hours, and the ebb six and a half – they would be living not on land, but on water. And each one of them felt the patches, strains and gaps in their craft as if they were weak places in their own bodies. They dreaded, and were yet painfully anxious, to get back and see whether the last caulking had given way. A Thames barge has no keel and is afloat in the first few inches of shoal water. The only exception was Woodrow, from *Rochester*, the retired director of a small company, who was fanatical in the maintenance of his craft. The flood tide, though it had no real terrors for Woodie, caused him to fret impatiently, because *Rochester*, in his opinion, had beautiful lines below water, and these would not now be visible again for twelve hours.

On every barge on the Reach a very faint ominous tap, no louder than the door of a cupboard shutting, would be followed by louder ones from every strake, timber and weatherboard, a fusillade of thunderous creaking, and even groans that seemed human. The crazy old vessels, riding high in the water without cargo, awaited their owners' return.

Richard, like a good commander, sensed the uneasiness of the meeting, even through the solid teak partition. He would never, if he had taken to the high seas in past centuries, have been caught napping by a mutiny.

'I'd better see them on their way.'

'You can ask one or two of them to stay behind for a drink, if you like,' Laura said, 'if there's anyone possible.'

She often unconsciously imitated her father's voice, and, like him, was beginning to drink a little too much occasionally, out of boredom. Richard felt overwhelmed with affection for her. 'I got *Country Life* today,' she said.

He had noticed that already. Anything new was noticeable on shipshape *Lord Jim*. The magazine was lying open at the property advertisements, among which was a photograph of a lawn, and a cedar tree on it with a shadow, and a squarish house in the background to show the purpose of the lawn. A similar photograph, with variations as to size and county, appeared month after month, giving the impression that those who read *Country Life* were above change, or that none was recognised there.

'I didn't mean that one, Richard, I meant a few pages farther on. There's some smaller places there.'

'I might ask Nenna James to stay behind,' Richard said. 'From *Grace*, I mean.'

'Why, do you think she's pretty?'

'I've never thought about it.'

'Hasn't her husband left her?'

'I'm not too sure what the situation is.'

'The postman used to say that there weren't many letters for *Grace*.'

Laura said 'used' because letters were no longer brought by the postman; after he had fallen twice from *Maurice*'s ill-secured gangplank, the whole morning's mail soaked away in the great river's load of rubbish, the GPO, with every reason on its side, had notified the Reach that they could no longer undertake deliveries. They acknowledged that Mr Blake, from *Lord Jim*, had rescued their employee on both occasions and they wished to record their thanks for this. The letters, since this, had had to be collected from the boatyard office, and Laura felt that this made it not much better than living abroad.

'I think Nenna's all right,' Richard continued. 'She seems quite all right to me, really. I don't know that I'd want to be left alone with her for any length of time.'

'Why not?'

'Well, I'm not quite sure that she mightn't burst into tears, or perhaps suddenly take all her clothes off.' This had actually once happened to Richard at Nestor and Sage, the investment counsellors where he worked. They were thinking of redesigning the whole office on the more modern open plan.

The whole meeting looked up in relief as he came back to the saloon. Firmly planted on the rocking boat, he suggested, even by his stance in the doorway, that things, however difficult, would turn out reasonably well. It was not that he was too sure of himself, simply that he was a good judge of the possible.

Willis was thanking young Maurice for his support.

'Well, you spoke up . . . a friend in need . . .'

'You're welcome.'

Willis half got up from the table. 'All the same, I don't believe that fellow was ever in the Merchant Navy.'

Business suspended, thought Richard. Firmly, but always politely, he escorted the ramshackle assembly up the companion ladder. It was a relief, as always, to be out on deck. The first autumn mists made it difficult to see the whole length of the reach. Seagulls, afloat like the boats, idled round *Lord Jim*, their white feathers soiled at the waterline.

'You'll probably have plenty of time to do something about your trouble anyway,' he said to Willis, 'it's quite a long

business, arranging the sale of these boats. Your leak's somewhere aft, isn't it? . . . you've got all four pumps working, I take
it . . . one in each well?'

This picture of *Dreadnought* was so wide of the mark that
Willis found it better to say nothing, simply making a gesture
which had something in common with a petty officer's salute.
Then he followed the others, who had to cross to land and tramp
along the Embankment. The middle Reach was occupied
by small craft, mostly laying up for the winter, some of them
already double lashed down under weather-cloths. These were
for fairweather people only. The barge owners had to go as far
as the brewery wharf, across *Maurice*'s foredeck and over a series
of gangplanks which connected them with their own boats.
Woody had to cross *Maurice*, *Grace* and *Dreadnought* to rejoin
Rochester. Only *Maurice* was made fast to the wharf.

One of the last pleasure steamers of the season was passing,
with cabin lights ablaze, on its way to Kew. 'Battersea Reach,
ladies and gentlemen. On your right, the artistic colony.
Folk live on those boats like they do on the Seine, it's the
artist's life they're leading there. Yes, there's people living on
those boats.'

Richard had detained Nenna James. 'I wish you'd have a
drink with us, Laura hoped you would.'

Nenna's character was faulty, but she had the instinct to see
what made other people unhappy, and this instinct had only
failed her once, in the case of her own husband. She knew, at
this particular moment, that Richard was distressed by the
unsatisfactory nature of the meeting. Nothing had been evalu-
ated, or even satisfactorily discussed.

'I wish I knew the exact time,' she said.

Richard was immediately content, as he only was when
something could be ascertained to the nearest degree of accuracy. The exact time! Perhaps Nenna would like to have a look
at his chronometers. They often didn't work well in small boats
– they were affected by changes of temperature – he didn't
know whether Nenna had found that – and, of course, by
vibration. He was able to give her not only the time, but the

state of the tide at every bridge on the river. It wasn't very often that anyone wanted to know this.

Laura put the bottles and glasses and a large plateful of bits and pieces through the galley hatch.

'It smells of something in there.'

There was the perceptible odour of tar which the barge owners, since so much of their day was spent in running repairs, left behind them everywhere.

'Well, dear, if you don't like the smell, let's go aft,' said Richard, picking up the tray. He never let a woman carry anything. The three of them went into a kind of snug, fitted with built-in lockers and red cushions. A little yacht stove gave out a temperate glow, its draught adjusted to produce exactly the right warmth.

Laura sat down somewhat heavily.

'How does it feel like to live without your husband?' she asked, handing Nenna a large glass of gin. 'I've often wondered.'

'Perhaps you'd like to fetch some more ice,' Richard said. There was plenty.

'He hasn't left me, you know. We just don't happen to be together at the moment.'

'That's for you to say, but what I want to know is, how do you get on without him? Cold nights, of course, don't mind Richard, it's a compliment to him if you think about it.'

Nenna looked from one to the other. It was a relief, really, to talk about it.

'I can't do the things that women can't do,' she said. 'I can't turn over *The Times* so that the pages lie flat, I can't fold up a map in the right creases, I can't draw corks, I can't drive in nails straight, I can't go into a bar and order a drink without wondering what everyone's thinking about it, and I can't strike matches towards myself. I'm well educated and I've got two children and I can manage pretty well, there's a number of much more essential things that I know how to do, but I can't do those ones, and when they come up I feel like weeping myself sick.'

'I'm sure I could show you how to fold up a map,' said Richard, 'it's not at all difficult once you get the hang of it.'

Laura's eyes seemed to have moved closer together. She was concentrating intensely.

'Did he leave you on the boat?'

'I bought *Grace* myself, while he was away, with just about all the money we'd got left, to have somewhere for me and the girls.'

'Do you like boats?'

'I'm quite used to them. I was raised in Halifax. My father had a summer cabin on the Bras d'Or Lake. We had boats there.'

'I hope you're not having any repair problems,' Richard put in.

'We get rain coming in.'

'Ah, the weatherboarding. You might try stretching tarpaulin over the deck.'

Although he tried hard to do so, Richard could never see how anyone could live without things in working order.

'Personally, though, I'm doubtful about the wisdom of making endless repairs to these very old boats. My feeling, for what it's worth, is that they should be regarded as wasting assets. Let them run down just so much every year, remember your low outgoings, and in a few years' time have them towed away for their break-up value.'

'I don't know where we should live then,' said Nenna.

'Oh, I understood you to say that you were going to find a place on shore.'

'Oh, we are, we are.'

'I didn't mean to distress you.'

Laura had had time, while listening without much attention to these remarks, to swallow a further quantity of spirits. This had made her inquisitive, rather than hostile.

'Where'd you get your Guernsey?'

Both women wore the regulation thick Navy blue sailing sweaters, with a split half inch at the bottom of each side seam. Nenna had rolled up her sleeves in the warmth of the snug, showing round forearms covered with very fine golden hair.

'I got mine at the cut price place at the end of the Queens-
town Road.'

'It's not as thick as mine.'

Laura leant forward, and, taking a good handful, felt the close
knitting between finger and thumb.

'I'm a judge of quality, I can tell it's not as thick. Richard, like
to feel it?'

'I'm afraid I can't claim to know much about knitting.'

'Well, make the stove up then. Make it up, you idiot!
Nenna's freezing!'

'I'm warm, thank you, just right.'

'You've got to be warmer than that! Richard, she's your
guest!'

'I can adjust the stove, if you like,' said Richard, in relief,
'I can do something to the regulator.'

'I don't want it regulated!'

Nenna knew that, if it hadn't been disloyal, Richard would
have appealed to her to do or say something.

'We use pretty well anything for fuel up our end,' she began,
'driftwood and washed-up coke and anything that'll burn.
Maurice told me that last winter he had to borrow a candle
from *Dreadnought* to unfreeze the lock of his woodstore. Then
when he was entertaining one of his friends he couldn't get his
stove to burn right and he had to keep it alight with matchboxes
and cheese straws.'

'It's bad practice to keep your woodstore above deck,' said
Richard.

Laura had been following, for some reason, with painful
interest. 'Do cheese straws burn?'

'Maurice thinks they do.'

Laura disappeared. Nenna had just time to say, I must be
going, before she came back, tottering at a kind of dignified
slant, and holding a large tin of cheese straws.

'Fortnums.'

Avoiding Richard, who got to his feet as soon as he saw
something to be carried, she kicked open the top of the Arctic
and flung them in golden handfuls onto the glowing bed of fuel.

'Hot!'

The flames leaped up, with an overpowering stink of burning cheese.

'Lovely! Hot! I've got plenty more! The kitchen's full of them! We'll make Richard throw them. We'll all throw them!'

'There's someone coming,' said Nenna.

Footsteps overhead, like the relief for siege victims. She knew the determined stamp of her younger daughter, but there was also a heavier tread. Her heart turned over.

'Ma, I can smell burning.'

After a short fierce struggle, Richard had replaced the Arctic's brass lid. Nenna went to the companion.

'Who's up there with you, Tilda?'

Tilda's six-year-old legs, in wellingtons caked with mud, appeared at the open hatch.

'It's Father Watson.'

Nenna did not answer for a second, and Tilda bellowed:

'Ma, it's the kindly old priest. He came round to *Grace*, so I brought him along here.'

'Father Watson isn't old at all, Tilda. Bring him down here, please. That's to say . . . '

'Of course,' said Richard. 'You'll have a whisky, father, won't you?' He didn't know who he was talking to, but believed, from films he had seen, that R.C. priests drank whisky and told long stories; that could be useful at the present juncture. Richard spoke with calm authority. Nenna admired him and would have liked to throw her arms round him.

'No, I won't come in now, thank you all the same,' called Father Watson, whose flapping trousers could now be seen beside Tilda's wellingtons against a square patch of sky. 'Just a word or two, Mrs James, I can easily wait if you're engaged with your friends or if it's not otherwise convenient.'

But Nenna, somewhat to the curate's surprise, for he seldom felt himself to be a truly welcome guest, was already halfway up the companion. It had begun to drizzle, and his long macintosh was spangled with drops of rain, which caught the reflections of the shore lights and the riding lights of the craft at anchor.

'I'm afraid the little one will get wet.'

'She's waterproof,' said Nenna.

As soon as they reached the Embankment Father Watson began to speak in measured tones. 'It's the children, as you must be aware, that I've come about. A message from the nuns, a message from the Sisters of Misericord.' He sometimes wondered if he would be more successful in the embarrassing errands he was called upon to undertake if he had an Irish accent, or some quaint turn of speech.

'Your girls, Mrs James, Tilda here, and the twelve-year-old.'

'Martha.'

'A very delightful name. Martha busied herself about the household work during our Lord's visits. But not a saint's name, I think.'

Presumably Father Watson said these things automatically. He couldn't have walked all the way down to the Reach from his comfortless presbytery simply to talk about Martha's name.

'She'll be taking another name at confirmation, I assume. That should not long be delayed. I suggest Stella Maris, Star of the Sea, since you've decided to make your dwelling place upon the face of the waters.'

'Father, have you come to complain about the girls' absence from school?'

They had arrived at the wharf, which was exceedingly ill-lit. The brewers to whom it belonged, having ideas, like all brewers in the 1960s, of reviving the supposed jollity of the eighteenth century, had applied for permission to turn it into a fashionable beer garden. The very notion, however, ran counter to the sodden, melancholy, and yet enduring spirit of the Reach. After the plans had been shelved, the whole place had been leased out to various small-time manufacturers and warehousemen; the broken-down sheds and godowns must still be the property of somebody, so too must be the piles of crates whose stencilled lettering had long since faded to pallor.

But, rat-ridden and neglected, it was a wharf still. The river's edge, where Virgil's ghosts held out their arms in longing for the farther shore, and Dante, as a living man, was refused passage by the ferryman, the few planks that mark the meeting point of land and water, there, surely, is a place to stop and reflect, even if, as Father Watson did, you stumble over a ten-gallon tin of creosote.

'I'm afraid I'm not accustomed to the poor light, Mrs James.'

'Look at the sky, father. Keep your eyes on the lightest part of the sky and they'll adapt little by little.'

Tilda had sprung ahead, at home in the dark, and anywhere within sight and sound of water. Feeling that she had given her due of politeness to the curate, the due exacted by her mother and elder sister, she pattered onto *Maurice*, and, after having a bit of a poke round, shot across the connecting gangplank onto *Grace*.

'You'll excuse me if I don't go any further, Mrs James. It's exactly what you said, it's the question of school attendance. The situation, you see, they tell me there's a legal aspect to it as well.'

How dispiriting for Father Watson to tell her this, Nenna thought, and how far it must be from his expectations when he received his first two minor orders, and made his last acts of resignation. To stand on this dusky wharf, bruised by a drum of creosote, and acting not even as the convent chaplain, but as some kind of school attendance officer!

'I know they haven't been coming to class regularly. But then, father, they haven't been well.'

Even Father Watson could scarcely be expected to swallow this. 'I was struck by the good health and spirits of your little one. In fact I had it in mind that she might be trained up to one of the women's auxiliary services which justified themselves so splendidly in the last war – the WRENS, I mean, of course. It's a service that's not incompatible with the Christian life.'

'You know how it is with children; she's well one day, not so well the next.' Nenna's attitude to truth was flexible, and more like Willis's than Richard's. 'And Martha's the same, it's only to be expected at her age.'

Nenna had hoped to alarm the curate with these references to approaching puberty, but he seemed, on the contrary, to be reassured. 'If that's the trouble, you couldn't do better than to entrust her to the skilled understanding of the Sisters.' How dogged he was. 'They'll expect, then, to see both your daughters in class on Monday next.'

'I'll do what I can.'

'Very well, Mrs James.'

'Won't you come as far as the boat?'

'No, no, I won't risk the crossing a second time.' What had happened the first time? 'And now, I'm afraid I've somewhat lost my sense of direction. I'll have to ask you my way to dry land.'

Nenna pointed out the way through the gate, which, swinging on its hinges, no longer provided any kind of barrier, out onto the Embankment, and first left, first right up Partisan Street for the King's Road. The priest couldn't have looked more relieved if he had completed a mission to those that dwell in the waters that are below the earth.

'I've got the supper, Ma,' said Martha, when Nenna returned to *Grace*. Nenna would have felt better pleased with herself if she had resembled her elder daughter. But Martha, small and thin, with dark eyes which already showed an acceptance of the world's shortcomings, was not like her mother and even less like her father. The crucial moment when children realise that their parents are younger than they are had long since been passed by Martha.

'We're having baked beans. If Father Watson's coming, we shall have to open another tin.'

'No, dear, he's gone home.'

Nenna felt tired, and sat down on the keelson, which ran from end to end of the flat-bottomed barge. It was quite wrong to come to depend too much upon one's children.

Martha set confidently to work in *Grace*'s galley, which consisted of two gas rings in the bows connected to a Calor cylinder, and a brass sink. Water came to the sink from a container on deck, which was refilled by a man from the boatyard once every twenty-four hours. A good deal of improvisation was necessary and Martha had put three tin plates to heat up over the hissing saucepan of beans.

'Was it fun on *Lord Jim*?'

'Oh, not at all.'

'Should I have enjoyed it?'

'Oh no, I don't think so. Mrs Blake threw cheese straws into the stove.'

'What did Mr Blake say?'

'He wants to keep her happy, to make her happy, I don't know.'

'What did Father Watson want?'

'Didn't he talk to you at all?'

'I daresay he would have done, but I sent him out to fetch you, with Tilda, she needed exercise.'

'So he didn't mention anything.'

'He just came down here, and I made him a cup of tea and we said an act of contrition together.'

'He wanted to know why you hadn't been to class lately.'

Martha sighed.

'I've been reading your letters,' she said. 'They're lying about your cabin, and you haven't even looked at most of them.'

The letters were Nenna's connection, not only with the land, but with her previous existence. They would be from Canada, from her sister Louise who would suggest that she might put up various old acquaintances passing through London, or find a suitable family for a darling Austrian boy, not so very much older than Martha, whose father was a kind of Count, but was also in the import-export business, or try to recall a splendid person, the friend of a friend of hers who had had a very, very sad story. Then there were one or two bills, not many because Nenna had no credit accounts, a letter-card from an old schoolfriend which started Bet you don't remember me, and two charitable appeals, forwarded by Father Watson even to such an unpromising address as *Grace*.

'Anything from Daddy?'

'No, Ma, I looked for that first.'

There was no more to be said on that subject.

'Oh, Martha, my head aches. Baked beans would be just the thing for it.'

Tilda came in, wet, and black as coal from head to foot.

'Willis gave me a drawing.'

'What of?'

'*Lord Jim*, and some seagulls.'

'You shouldn't have accepted it.'

'Oh, I gave him one back.'

She had been waiting on *Dreadnought* to watch the water coming in through the main leak. It had come halfway up the bunk, and nearly as far as Willis's blankets. Nenna was distressed.

'Well, it goes out with every tide. He'll have to show people round at low tide, and get them off before it turns.'

'Surely he can do some repairs,' said Martha.

'No, Fate's against him,' said Tilda, and after one or two forkfuls of beans she fell fast asleep with her head across the table. It was impossible, in any case, to bath her, because they were only allowed to let out the bathwater on a falling tide.

By now the flood was making fast. The mist had cleared, and to the north-east the Lots Road Power Station had discharged from its four majestic chimneys long plumes of white pearly smoke which slowly drooped and turned to dun. The lights dazzled, but on the broad face of the water there were innumerable V-shaped eddies, showing the exact position of whatever the river had not been able to hide. If the old Thames trades had still persisted, if boatmen had still made a living from taking the coins from the pockets of the drowned, then this was the hour for them to watch. Far above, masses of autumn cloud passed through the transparent violet sky.

After supper they sat by the light of the stove. Nenna was struck by the fact that she ought to write to Louise, who was married to a successful businessman. She began, Dear Sis, Tell Joel that it's quite an education in itself for the girls to be brought up in the heart of the capital, and on the very shores of London's historic river.

2

TILDA WAS up aloft. *Grace*'s mast was fifteen foot of blackened pine, fitted into a tabernacle, so that it could be lowered to the deck in the days when *Grace* negotiated the twenty-eight tideway bridges between Richmond and the sea. Her mizzen mast was gone, her sprit was gone, the mainmast was never intended for climbing and Tilda sat where there was, apparently, nowhere to sit.

Martha, whose head was as strong as her sister's, sometimes climbed up as well, and, clinging on about a foot lower down, read aloud from a horror comic. But today Tilda was alone, looking down at the slanting angle of the decks as the cables gave or tightened, the passive shoreline, the secret water.

Tilda cared nothing for the future, and had, as a result, a great capacity for happiness. At the moment she was perfectly happy.

She was waiting for the tide to turn. Exactly opposite *Grace* a heap of crates which had driven up through the bends and reaches, twenty miles from Gravesend, was at rest in the slack water, enchanted apparently, not moving an inch one way or the other. The lighters swung at their moorings, pointing all ways, helpless without the instructions of the tide. It was odd to see the clouds move when the water was so still.

She blinked twice, taking the risk of missing the right few seconds while her eyes were shut. Then one end of a crate detached itself from the crates and began to steal away, edging slowly round in a half circle. Tilda, who had been holding her breath, let it go. A tremor ran through the boats' cables, the iron lighters, just on the move, chocked gently together. The great swing round began. By the shore the driftwood was still travelling upriver, but in midstream it was gathering way headlong in the other direction. The Thames had turned towards the sea.

Willis had frequently told her that these old barges, in spite of their great sails, didn't need a crew of more than two men, in

23

fact a man and a boy could handle them easily. The sails had
been tan-coloured, like the earth and dressed with oil, which
never quite dried out. There were none left now. But *Grace*
wouldn't need them to go out to sea on the ebb tide.
She wouldn't make sail until she reached Port of London.
With her flat bottom, she would swim on the tide, all gear
dropped, cunningly making use of the hidden drifts. The six-
year-old boy knew every current and eddy of the river. Long
had he studied the secrets of the Thames. None but he would
have noticed the gleam of gold and diamonds – the ring on the
dead man's finger as his hand broke the surface. Farewell! He
recognised it as the hand of his father, missing now for countless
years. The *Grace*, 180 tons fully loaded, nosed her way through
the low arches by the Middlesex bank, where there was no
room for other craft, passing, or surpassing, all the shipping
there. At Tower Bridge if four-foot diameter discs bearing
black and white signal stripes are displayed fourteen foot to
landward of the signals, this is an indication that the bridge
cannot be raised from mechanical or other cause. Only *Grace*
could pass, not *Maurice*, not even *Dreadnought*, a sight never to
be forgotten. Men and women came out on the dock to watch
as the great brown sails went up, with only a six-year-old boy at
the winch, and the *Grace*, bound for Ushant, smelt the open sea.

There was a scratching at the heel of the mast. A cat, with her
mouth full of seagull feathers, was feebly trying to climb up, but
after a few feet her claws lost purchase and she slithered back by
gradual stages to the deck.

'Stripey!'

The ship's cat was in every way appropriate to the Reach.
She habitually moved in a kind of nautical crawl, with her
stomach close to the deck, as though close-furled and ready
for dirty weather. The ears were vestigial, and lay flat to
the head.

Through years of attempting to lick herself clean, for she had
never quite lost her self-respect, Stripey had become as thickly
coated with mud inside as out. She was in a perpetual process of
readjustment, not only to tides and seasons, but to the rats she

encountered on the wharf. Up to a certain size, that is to say the size attained by the rats at a few weeks old, she caught and ate them, and, with a sure instinct for authority, brought in their tails to lay them at the feet of Martha. Any rats in excess of this size chased Stripey. The resulting uncertainty as to whether she was coming or going had made her, to some extent, mentally unstable.

Stripey did not care to be fed by human beings, and understood how to keep herself warm in cold weather. She slept outside, on one or other of the stove pipes which projected out of the stacks on deck. Curled up on the pipe, she acted as an obstruction which drove the smoke down again into the barge, making it almost uninhabitable. In turn, Woodie, Willis, Nenna, Maurice and even his visitors could be heard coughing uncontrollably. But Stripey rarely chose to sleep in the same place two nights running.

From the masthead Tilda, having sailed out to sea with *Grace*, took a closer survey of the Reach. Her whole idea of the world's work was derived from what she observed there and had little in common with the circulation of the great city which toiled on only a hundred yards away.

No movement on *Lord Jim*. Willis was walking towards *Dreadnought* with the man from the boatyard, whose manner suggested that he was refusing to supply more tar, gas and water until the previous bill had been paid.

On *Rochester*, Woodie was getting ready to lay up for the winter. It seemed that he was not, after all, a true barge dweller. His small recording company, as he explained only too often, had gone into voluntary liquidation, leaving him with just enough to manage nicely, and he was going to spend the cold weather in his house in Purley. Managing nicely seemed an odd thing to do at the north end of the Reach. Woodie also spoke of getting someone to anti-foul his hull, so that it would be as clean as *Lord Jim*'s. The other barges were so deeply encrusted with marine life that it was difficult to strike wood. Green weeds and barnacles were thick on them, and whales might have saluted them in passing.

Maurice was deserted, Maurice having been invited, as he quite often was, to go down for the day to Brighton. But his deckhouse did not appear to be locked. A light van drew up on the wharf, and a man got out and dropped a large quantity of cardboard boxes over the side of the wharf onto the deck. One of them broke open. It was full of hair dryers. The man then had to drop down on deck and arrange the boxes more carefully. It would have been better to cover them with a tarpaulin, but he had forgotten to bring one, perhaps. He wasted no time in looking round and it was only when he was backing the van to drive away that his face could be seen. It was very pale and had no expression, as though expressions were surplus to requirements.

Willis, walking in his deliberate way, looked at the boxes on *Maurice*, paused, even shook his head a little, but did nothing. Nenna might have added to her list of things that men do better than women their ability to do nothing at all in an unhurried manner. And in fact there was nothing that Willis could do about the boxes. Quite certainly, Maurice did not want the police on his boat.

'Ahoy there Tilda! Watch yourself!' Willis called.

Tilda knew very well that the river could be dangerous. Although she had become a native of the boats, and pitied the tideless and ratless life of the Chelsea inhabitants, she respected the water and knew that one could die within sight of the Embankment.

One spring evening a Dutch barge, the *Waalhaven*, from Rotterdam, glittering with brass, impressive, even under power, had anchored in midstream opposite the boats. She must have got clearance at Gravesend and sailed up on the ebb. Of this fine vessel the *Maurice*, also from Rotterdam, had once been a poor relation. The grounded barges seemed to watch the *Waalhaven*, as prisoners watch the free.

Her crew lined up on deck as gravely as if at a business meeting. A spotless meeting of well-regarded businessmen in rubber seaboots, conducted in the harmonious spirit which had always characterised the firm.

Just after teatime the owner came to the rails and called out to *Maurice* to send a dinghy so that he could put a party ashore. When nothing happened, and he realised that he had come to a place without facilities, he retired for another consultation. Then, as the light began to fail, with the tide running very fast, three of them launched their own dinghy and prepared to sail to the wharf. They had been waiting for high water so that they could sail alongside in a civilised manner. It was like a demonstration in small boat sailing, a lesson in holiday sport. They still wore their seaboots, but brought their shoregoing shoes with them in an oilskin bag. The gods of the river had, perhaps, taken away their wits.

The offshore wind was coming hard as usual through the wide gap between the warehouses on the Surrey side. Woodie, observing their gallant start, longed to lend them his Chart 3 and to impress upon them that there was one competent owner at least at this end of the Reach. Richard, back from work after a tiresome day, stopped on the Embankment to look, and remembered that he had once gone on board the *Waalhaven* for a drink when she put in at Orfordness.

Past the gap, the wind failed and dropped to nothing, the dinghy lost way and drifted towards three lighters moored abreast. Her mast caught with a crack which could be heard on both sides of the river on the high overhang of the foremost lighter. The whole dinghy was jammed and sucked in under the stem, then rolled over, held fast by her steel mast which would not snap. The men were pitched overboard and they too were swallowed up beneath the heavy iron bottoms of the lighters. After a while the bag of shoes came up, then two of the men, then a pair of seaboots, floating soles upwards.

Tilda thought of this incident with distress, but not often. She wondered what had happened to the other pairs of boots. But her heart did not rule her memory, as was the case with Martha and Nenna. She was spared that inconvenience.

Willis called again, 'Ahoy there, Tilda! Don't shout down back to me!' Imagining her to be delicate, he was anxious for her not to strain her voice. Tilda and Martha both sang absolutely true, and Willis, who was fond of music, and always optimistic about the future of others, liked to think of them as concert performers. They could still manage *Abends, wenn wir schlafen gehen*, taught them by the nuns as a party piece, and then, indeed, they sounded like angels, though angels without much grasp of the words after the second line. More successful, perhaps, was *Jailhouse Rock*. But Tilda had taught herself to produce, by widening her mouth into the shape of an oblong, a most unpleasant imitation of a bosun's whistle, which could be heard almost as far as *Lord Jim*. The sound indicated that she was coming down the mast. Father Watson had been more than a little frightened by it, and had confided in the nuns that it was more like something produced by some mechanical contrivance, than by a human being. His words confirmed the opinion of the Sisters of Misericord that the two children, so clever and musical, were at risk on the boat, spiritually and perhaps physically, and that someone ought to speak much more seriously to Mrs James.

3

BELOW DECKS, *Grace* was shipshape, but after calling on *Lord Jim* Nenna always felt impelled to start cleaning the brightwork. They hadn't much – just the handholds of the companion, the locker hinges, and the pump–handle of the heads, which was part of the original equipment and was engraved with the date: 1905.

Nenna was thirty-two, an age by which if a blonde woman's hair hasn't turned dark, it never will. She had come to London after the war as a music student, and felt by this time she was neither Canadian or English. Edward and she had got married in 1949. She was still at the RSM then, violin first study, and she fell in love as only a violinist can. She didn't know if they had given themselves sufficient time to think things over before they married – that was the kind of question her sister Louise asked. Edward stayed in the Engineers for a bit, then came out and was not very successful in finding a job to suit him. That wasn't his fault, and if anyone said that it was, Nenna would still feel like poking a hole in them. They got a flat. People who asked her why she didn't make use of her talent and give singing lessons had perhaps not tried to do this while living in two rooms over a greengrocers, and looking after young children. But Edward was said by his friends to have business sense, and to be able to make things work. That was why the launderette was so evidently a good investment. It was quite a new idea over here, you didn't do your washing at home but brought it out to these machines, and the courteous manager greeted you and put in the soap powder for you, and had the clothes all ready for you when you came back, but wasn't alas, as it turned out, much of a hand at doing the accounts. The closing of the launderette had given rise to a case in the County Court, in which Edward and she had been held not to blame, but had been conscious of the contempt of their solicitor, who always seemed to be in a great hurry.

29

This, no doubt, was the reason that Nenna's thoughts, whenever she was alone, took the form of a kind of perpetual magistrates' hearing, in which her own version of her marriage was shown as ridiculously simple and demonstrably right, and then, almost exactly at the same time, as incontrovertibly wrong. Her conscience, too, held, quite uninvited, a separate watching brief, and intervened in the proceedings to read statements of an unwelcome nature.

'... Your life story so far, Mrs James, has had a certain lack of distinction. I daresay it seemed distinguished enough while you were living it – distinguished, at least, from other peoples' lives.'

'You put that very well, my lord.' She realised that the magistrate had become a judge.

'Now then ... in 1959 your husband came to the conclusion, and I am given to understand that you fully agreed, that it would be a sensible step for him to take employment for 15 months with a construction firm in Central America, in order to save the larger part of his salary ...'

Nenna protested that she had never exactly thought it sensible, it was the parting of lovers, which must always be senseless, but they'd both of them thought that David, Panama, would be a wretched place to take small children to. The words sounded convincing, the judge leaned forward in approbation. Encouraged, she admitted that she had been entrusted with their last £2,000, and had bought a houseboat, in point of fact, the barge *Grace*.

'The children missed their father?'

'The older one did. Tilda didn't seem to, but no one understands what she thinks except Martha.'

'Thank you, Mrs James, we should like you to confine yourself to first-hand evidence ... you wrote to your husband, of course, to explain the arrangements you had made in his absence?'

'I gave him our new address at once. Of course I did.'

'The address you gave him was 626 Cheyne Walk, Chelsea S.W.10?'

'Yes, that's right. That's the address of the boatyard office, where they take in the letters.'

' . . . giving him the impression, as indeed it would to anyone who did not know the district, that you had secured a well-appointed house or flat in Chelsea, at a very reasonable figure?'

'Well-appointed' was quite unfair, but Nenna's defence, always slow to move, failed to contest it.

'I didn't want to worry him. And then, plenty of people would give a lot to live on the Reach.'

'You are shifting your ground, Mrs James . . .'

'When I sent photographs to my sister in Canada, she thought it looked beautiful.'

'The river is thought of as romantic?'

'Yes, that's so!'

'More so by those who do not know it well?'

'I can't answer that.'

'They may be familiar with the paintings of Whistler, or perhaps with Whistler's statement that when evening mist clothes the riverside with poetry, as with a veil, and the poor buildings lose themselves in the dim sky, and the tall chimneys become campanili, and the warehouses are palaces in the night, and the whole city hangs in the heavens, and fairyland is before us – then the wayfarer hastens home, and Nature, who, for once, has sung in tune, sings her exquisite song to the artist alone, her son and her master – her son, in that he loves her, her master in that he knows her? . . . shall I read you that deposition again, Mrs James?'

Nenna was silent.

'Whistler, however, lived in a reasonably comfortable house?'

Nenna refused to give way. 'You soon get used to the little difficulties. Most people like it very much.'

'Mrs James. Did your husband, on his return to this country, where he expected to be reunited with his wife and family, like the houseboat *Grace* very much?'

'A number of these houseboats, or disused barges, including *Grace*, are exceedingly damp?'

'Mrs James. Do you like your husband?'

'Mrs James. Did your husband, or did he not, complain that the houseboat *Grace*, apart from being damp, needed extensive repairs, and that it was difficult if not impossible for you to resume any meaningful sexual relationship when your cabin acted as a kind of passageway with your daughters constantly going to and fro to gain access to the hatch, and a succession of persons, including the milkman, trampling overhead? You will tell me that the milkman has refused to continue deliveries, but this only adds weight to my earlier submission that the boat is not only unfit to live in but actually unsafe.'

'I love him, I want him. While he was away was the longest fifteen months and eight days I ever spent. I can't believe even now that it's over. Why don't I go to him? Well, why doesn't he come to us? He hasn't found anywhere at all that we could all of us live together. He's in some kind of rooms in the north-east of London somewhere.'

'42b Milvain Street, Stoke Newington.'

'In Christ's name, who's ever heard of such a place?'

'Have you made any effort to go and see the plaintiff there, Mrs James? I must remind you that we cannot admit any second-hand evidence.'

So now it was out. She was the defendant, or rather the accused, and should have known it all along.

'I repeat. Have you ever been to Milvain Street, which, for all any of us know, may be a perfectly suitable home for yourself and the issue of the marriage?'

'I know it isn't. How can it be?'

'Is he living there by himself?'

'I'm pretty sure so.'

'Not with another woman?'

'He's never mentioned one.'

'In his letters?'

'He's never liked writing letters very much.'

'But you write to him every day. That is perhaps too often?'

'It seems I can't do right. Everyone knows that women write a lot of letters.'

To the disapproval and distaste of the court she was shouting.

'I only want him to give way a little. I only want him to say that I've done well in finding somewhere for us to be!'

'You are very dependent on praise, Mrs James.'

'That depends, my lord, on who it's from.'

'You could be described as an obstinate bitch?' That was an intervention from her conscience but she had never been known for obstinacy in the past, and it was puzzling to account, really, for her awkward persistence about *Grace*. In calmer moments, too, she understood how it was that Edward, though generous at heart, found it difficult to give way. He was not much used to giving at all. His family, it seemed, had not been in the habit of exchanging presents, almost inconceivably to Nenna, whose childhood had been gift-ridden, with much atonement, love and reconciliation conveyed in the bright wrappings. Edward had no idea of how to express himself in that way. Nor was he fortunate as a shopper. He had realised, for instance, when Martha was born, that he would do well to take flowers to the hospital, but not that if you buy an azalea in winter and carry it on a bus and through a number of cold streets, all the buds will drop off before you arrive.

Nenna had never criticised the bloomless azalea. It was the other young mothers in the beds each side of her who had laughed at it. That had been 1951. Two of the new babies in the ward had been christened Festival.

'Your attention, Mrs James.'

The first exhibit in her case was a painful quarrel, laid out before the court in its naked entirety. Edward had not come back from the construction firm at David with anything saved up, but then, she had hardly expected him to. If he had saved anything he would have changed character and would hardly have been the man she loved. And, after all, they had *Grace*. Nenna, who was of hopeful temperament, intended to ask Edward's mother to look after Martha and Tilda for a while. She and Edward would be alone on *Grace*, and they could batten down and stay in bed for twenty-four hours if they felt like it.

'Mrs James, are you asking the court to believe that you were sincere in this? You know perfectly well that your husband's mother lives at a considerable distance, in point of fact in a suburb of Sheffield, and that she has never at any time offered to look after your children.'

Edward had made the same objection. And yet this particular quarrel, now that it was under rigorous scrutiny, hadn't arisen over that matter at all, but over something else entirely, the question of where Nenna could possibly have put his squash racquets while he was away. They had both of them thought that the climate of Panama would be bad for the racquets, although it turned out in the end that he could perfectly well have taken them with him. If Nenna had brought them with her to *Grace*, they must certainly have been ruined by the damp. But, worse still, they were not on *Grace*. Nenna was full of contrition. O my God, I am heartily sorry for having offended Thee. Thirty minutes of squash gives a man as much exercise as two hours of any other game. She had been entrusted with the racquets. They were, in a sense, a sacred trust. But she could not remember anything at all about them.

'You mislaid them deliberately?'

'I don't do anything deliberately.'

That seemed to be true. Some of her actions were defensive, others optimistic, more than half of them mistaken.

'On this occasion you lost your temper, and threw a solid object at Mr James?'

It had only been her bank book, and Edward had been quite right to say that it was not worth reading.

But then the exhibit, the quarrel, hateful and confusing in being exposed to other eyes, changed character and became after all, evidence for the defence. In mid-fury Edward had asked what day of the week she imagined it was, for at the time, in the highly coloured world of the argument, this detail had become of supreme importance.

'Look here, is it Wednesday or Thursday?'

'I don't know, Ed, whichever you like.'

Given so much free choice, he had melted immediately, and by good fortune they had several hours alone on the boat. The girls were at school, and no misery that Nenna had ever felt could weigh against their happiness which flowed like the current, with its separate eddies, of the strong river beneath them.

Perhaps the whole case was breaking down, to the disappointment of the advocates, who, after all, could hardly be distinguished from the prosecution on both sides. So little was needed for a settlement, and yet the word 'settlement' suggested two intractable people, and they were both quite humble. Nor was it true, as their accusers impartially suggested, that she or Edward preferred to live in an atmosphere of crisis. They both needed peace and turned in memory towards their peaceful moments together, finding their true home there.

When Nenna was not in the witness box, she sometimes saw herself getting ready for an inspection at which Edward, or Edward's mother, or some power superior to either, gave warning that they might appear – she could only hope that it would be on a falling tide – to see where she could be found wanting. Determined not to fail this test, she let the image fade into the business of polishing the brasses and cleaning ship. The decks must be clear, hatches fastened, Stripey out of sight, and above all the girls ought to be back in regular education.

'You're both going in to school on Monday, aren't you, Martha?'

Martha, like her father, and like Richard, saw no need for fictions. She gave her mother a dark brown, level glance.

'I shall go in, and take Tilda with me, when the situation warrants it.'

'We shall have Father Watson round again.'

'I don't think so, Ma. He missed his footing on the gangplank last time.'

'I'm so tired of making excuses.'

'You should tell the truth.'

In what way could the truth be made acceptable? Tilda had initiated the train of events, as, with her careless mastery of life, she often did. Pressed by the nuns to complete a kettle-holder in cross-stitch as a present for her father, she had replied that she had never seen her father holding a kettle and that Daddy had gone away.

The fact was that she had lost the six square inches of canvas allocated for the kettleholder when it was first given out to the class. Martha knew this, but did not wish to betray her sister.

Tilda had at first elaborated her story, saying that her mother was looking for a new Daddy, but her observation, quick as a bird's flight, showed her that this was going too far, and she added that she and her sister prayed nightly to Our Lady of Fatima for her father's return. Up till that moment Tilda, in spite of her lucid grey eyes, showing clarity beneath clarity, which challenged the nuns not to risk scandalising the inno-cent, had often been in disfavour. She was known to be one of the little ones who had filled in their colouring books irrever-ently, making our Lord's beard purple, or even green, largely, to be sure, because she never bothered to get hold of the best crayons first. Now, however, she was the object of compassion. After a private conference with Mother Superior, the Sisters announced that there would be a special rosary every morning, during the time set aside for special intentions, and that the whole Junior School would pray together that Martha and Tilda's Daddy should come back to them. After this, if the weather was fine, there would be a procession to the life-size model of the grotto of Lourdes, which had been built in the recreation ground out of a kind of artificial rock closely resem-bling anthracite. Sister Paul, who was the author of several devotional volumes, wrote the special prayer: Heart of Jesus, grant that the eyes of the non-Catholic father of Thy little servants, Martha and Matilda, may be opened, that his tepid soul may become fervent, and that he may return to establish himself on his rightful hearth, Amen.

'They are good women,' Martha said, 'but I'm not going to set foot in the place while that's going on.'

'I could speak to the nuns.'

'I'd rather you didn't, Ma. They might begin to pray for you as well.'

She glanced up, apparently casually, to see if Nenna had taken this too hard.

Tilda appeared with a ball of oozing clay in her arms which she flung down on the table. Apparently carrion, it moved and stretched a lean back leg, which turned out to be Stripey's.

'She's in voluntary liquidation,' said Martha, but she fetched a piece of old towelling and began to rub the cat, which squinted through the folds of white material like Lazarus through the grave-clothes.

'How did she get into this state?' Nenna asked. 'That isn't shore mud.'

'She was hunting rats on the wharf and she fell into a clay lighter, Mercantile Lighterage Limited, flag black diamond on broad white band.'

'Who brought her in, then?'

'One of the lightermen got off at Cadogan Stairs and walked back with her and gave her to Maurice.'

'Well, try to squeeze the water out of her tail. Gently.'

The clay rapidly set in a hard surface on the table and the floorboards underneath it. Martha mopped and scraped away for almost half an hour, long after Tilda had lost interest. During this time it grew dark, the darkness seeming to rise from the river to make it one with the sky. Nenna made the tea and lit the wood stove. The old barges, who had once beaten their way up and down the east coast and the Channel ports, grumbled and heaved at their cables while their new owners sat back in peace.

Without warning, a shaft of brilliant light, in colour a sickly mauve, shone down the hatchway.

'It must be from *Maurice*,' said Martha, 'it can't be a shore light.'

They could hear his footsteps across the gangplank, then a heavier one as he dropped the eighteen-inch gap onto *Grace*'s deck.

'Maurice can't weigh much. He just springs about.'

'Cat-like?' Nenna asked.

'Heaven forbid,' said Martha.

'*Grace!*' Maurice called, in imitation of Richard, 'perhaps you'd like to come and have a look.'

Nenna and the two girls shook off a certain teatime drowsiness and went back on deck, where they stood astounded. On the afterdeck of *Maurice*, which lay slightly at an angle to *Grace*, a strange transformation had taken place. The bright light – this was what had struck them first – issued from an old street lamp, leaning at a crazy angle, rather suggesting an amateur production of *Tales of Hoffmann*, fitted, in place of glass, with sheets of mauve plastic, and trailing a long cable which disappeared down the companion. On the deck itself were scattered what looked like paving stones, and the leeboard winch had been somewhat garishly painted in red, white, and gold.

The wash of a passing collier rocked both boats and the enormous reverberation of her wailing hooter filled the air and made it impossible for them to speak. Maurice stood half in the shadow, half brightly purple, and at last was able to say:

'It'll make you think of Venice, won't it?'

Nenna hesitated.

'I've never been to Venice.'

'Nor have I,' said Maurice, quick to disclaim any pretence to superiority, 'I got the idea from a postcard someone sent me. Well, he sent me quite a series of postcards, and from them I was able to reconstruct a typical street corner. Not the Grand Canal, you understand, just one of the little ones. When it's as warm as it is tonight, you'll be able to leave the hatch open and imagine yourselves in the heart of Venice.'

'It's beautiful!' Tilda shouted.

'You don't seem quite certain about it, Nenna.'

'I am, I am. I've always wanted to see Venice, almost more than any other place. I was only wondering what would happen when the wind gets up.'

What she must not ask, but at the same time mustn't be thought not to be asking, was what would happen when Harry came next. As a depot for stolen goods *Maurice*, surely, had to look as inconspicuous as possible.

'I may be going abroad myself quite soon,' said Maurice casually.

'Oh, you didn't tell us.'

'Yes, I met someone the other night who made a sort of suggestion about a possible job of some kind.'

It wasn't worth asking of what kind; there had been so many beginnings. Sometimes Maurice went over to Bayswater to keep up his skating, in the hopes of getting a job in the ice show. Perhaps it was that he was talking about now.

'Would you be selling *Maurice*, then?'

'Oh yes, of course, when I go abroad.'

'Well, your leak isn't nearly as bad as *Dreadnought*.'

This practical advice seemed to depress Maurice, who was trying the paving stones in various positions.

'I must ask Willis how he's getting on . . . there's so much to think about . . . if someone wanted a description of this boat, I suppose the Venetian corner would be a feature . . .'

He switched off the mauve light. None of the barge owners could afford to waste electricity, and the display was really intended for much later at night, but he had turned it on early to surprise and please them.

'Yes! I'll soon be living on land. I shall tell my friend to take all his bits and pieces out of my hold, of course.'

'Maurice is going mad,' said Martha, quietly, as they went back onto *Grace*.

4

MAURICE'S STRANGE period of hopefulness did not last long. Tenderly responsive to the self-deceptions of others, he was unfortunately too well able to understand his own. No more was said of the job and it rapidly became impossible to tell who was trying to please whom over the matter of the Venetian lantern.

'What am I to do, Maurice?' Nenna asked. She confided in him above all others. Apart from anything else, his working day did not begin till seven or eight, so that he was often there during the day, and always ready to listen; but there were times when his customers left early, at two or three in the morning, and then Maurice, somewhat exhilarated with whisky, would come over to *Grace*, magically retaining his balance on the gangplank, and sit on the gunwale, waiting. He never went below, for fear of disturbing the little girls. Nenna used to wrap up in her coat and bring out two rugs for him.

During the small hours, tipsy Maurice became an oracle, ambiguous, wayward, but impressive. Even his voice changed a little. He told the sombre truths of the lighthearted, betraying in a casual hour what was never intended to be shown. If the tide was low the two of them watched the gleams on the foreshore, at half tide they heard the water chuckling, waiting to lift the boats, at flood tide they saw the river as a powerful god, bearded with the white foam of detergents, calling home the twenty-seven lost rivers of London, sighing as the night declined.

'Maurice, ought I to go away?'
'You can't.'
'You said you were going to go away yourself.'
'No one believed it. You didn't. What do the others think?'
'They think your boat belongs to Harry.'

'Nothing belongs to Harry, certainly all that stuff in the hold doesn't. He finds it easier to live without property. As to *Maurice*, my godmother gave me the money to buy a bit of property when I left Southport.'

'I've never been to Southport.'

'It's very nice. You take the train from the middle of Liverpool, and it's the last station, right out by the seaside.'

'Have you been back since?'

'No.'

'If *Maurice* belongs to you, why do you have to put up with Harry?'

'I can't answer that.'

'What will you do if the police come?'

'What will you do if your husband doesn't?'

Nenna thought, I must take the opportunity to get things settled for me, even if it's only by chance, like throwing straws into the current. She repeated –

'Maurice, what shall I do?'

'Well, have you been to see him yet?'

'Not yet. But of course I ought to. As soon as I can find someone to stay with the girls, for a night or two if it's necessary, I'm going to go. Thank you for making my mind up.'

'No, don't do that.'

'Don't do what?'

'Don't thank me.'

'Why not?'

'Not for that.'

'But, you know, by myself I can't make my mind up.'

'You shouldn't do it at all.'

'Why not, Maurice?'

'Why should you think it's a good thing to do? Why should it make you any happier? There isn't one kind of happiness, there's all kinds. Decision is torment for anyone with imagination. When you decide, you multiply the things you might have done and now never can. If there's even one person who might be hurt by a decision, you should never make it. They tell you, make up your mind or it will be too late, but if it's really too late, we should be grateful. You know very well that we're two of the same kind, Nenna. It's right for us to live where we do, between land and water. You, my dear, you're half in love with your husband, then there's Martha who's half a child and half a girl, Richard who can't give up being half in the Navy, Willis who's half an artist and half a longshoreman, a cat who's half alive and half dead . . . '

He stopped before describing himself, if, indeed, he had been going to do so.

Partisan Street, opposite the Reach, was a rough place, well used to answering police enquiries. The boys looked on the Venetian corner as a godsend and came every day as soon as they were out of school to throw stones at it. After a week Harry returned to *Maurice*, once again when there was no one on the boat, took away his consignment of hair dryers, and threw the lantern and the paving stones overboard. Tilda, an expert mudlark, retrieved most of the purple plastic, but the pieces were broken and it was hard to see what could be done with them. Maurice appreciated the thought, but seemed not to care greatly one way or the other.

5

WILLIS DEEPLY respected Richard, whom he privately thought of, and sometimes called aloud, the Skipper. Furthermore, although he had been pretty well openly accused of dishonesty at the meeting, his moral standards were much the same as Richard's, only he did not feel he was well enough off to apply them as often, and in such a wide range of conditions, as the Skipper. It didn't, thank heavens, seem likely that a situation would ever arise in which there was no hope for Richard, whereas, on the other hand, Willis considered that for himself there was scarcely any hope at all if he could not sell *Dreadnought*. £2,000 would, according to his calculations, be more or less enough for him to go and spend the rest of his days with his widowed sister. He could hardly go empty-handed, and the benefits of the move had been pointed out to him often.

'My sister's place is on gravel soil. You don't feel the damp there. Couldn't feel it if you wanted to.'

Nor, however, did you see the river, and Willis would have to find something else to fill the great gap which would be left in his life when it was no longer possible to see the river traffic, passing and repassing. Like many marine painters he had never been to sea. During the war he had been an auxiliary coast-guard. He knew nothing about blue water sailing. But to sit still and watch while the ships proceeded on their lawful business, to know every class, every rig and every cargo, is to make inactivity a virtue, and Willis from *Dreadnought* and from points along the shore as far as the Cat and Lobster at Gravesend had honourably conducted the profession of looking on. Born in Silvertown, within sound of the old boat-builders' yards, he disliked silence. Like Tilda, he found it easier to sleep when he could hear the lighters, like iron coffins on Resurrection Day, clashing each other at their moorings all night, and behind that the whisper of shoal water.

Tilda, in spite of her lack of success with the convent's colouring books, wished to be a marine painter also. Her object was to paint exactly like Willis, and to put in all the rigging with a ruler, and to get everything right. She also wanted to have a Sunday dinner, whenever possible, in the style of Willis, who followed the bargemen's custom of serving first sultana pudding with gravy, and then the roast.

As an artist, he had always made an adequate living, and Willises, carefully packed in stiff board and oiled paper, were despatched – since a number of his patrons were in the Merchant Navy – to ports all over the world for collection. But these commissions, mostly for the originals of jokes and cartoons which Willis had managed in former times to sell to magazines, had grown fewer and fewer in the last ten years, as, indeed, had the drawings themselves. After the war the number of readers who would laugh at pictures of seasick passengers, or bosuns getting the better of the second mate, diminished rapidly.

A few distant correspondents, untouched by time, still asked confidently for a painting of a particular ship. *Dear Willis – As I am informed by those who ought to know that you have 'taken the ground' somewhere near London River, I expect you can tell me the whereabouts of the dear old* Fortuna, *built 1892, rigged when I last saw her in 1920 as a square foresail brigantine. Old ships never die and doubtless she is still knocking around the East Coast, though I suppose old Payne may have made his last port by now . . . I should be interested in an oil painting on canvas, or board (which I suppose would come a bit cheaper!!) showing her beating around the Foreland under sail in fairly heavy weather, say Force 6 . . .* Willis could only pray that the writers of such letters, stranded in ports which the war had passed by almost without notice, would never return, to be betrayed by so much change.

Willis sometimes took Tilda, in her character as an apprentice painter, to the Tate Gallery, about two and a half miles along the Embankment. There was no Tube then to Pimlico, and they proceeded by a series of tacks to Victoria. At Sloane Square Underground Station Willis pointed out the mighty iron pipe crossing high in the air above the passenger line.

'Look, that carries the River Westbourne, flowing down from Paddington. If that was to take and start leaking, we'd all have to swim for it.'

Tilda eyed the great pipe.

'Where does it come out?'

'The outfall? Well, it's one of the big sewers, my dear, I'll get the name right for you.' He made a note.

The other passengers drew back from the dishevelled river dwellers, so far out of their element.

Laura was doubtful whether the little girl ought to be allowed to go out like that alone with an old man, and not a very scrupulous one at that, for a whole afternoon. She told Richard a number of stories on the subject, some of them taken from the daily papers, and suggested that he might turn the matter over in his mind. But Richard said it wasn't necessary.

'You told me yourself that he was dishonest.'

'It isn't necessary.'

Willis and Tilda usually stopped on the way at a little shop in the Vauxhall Bridge Road, which seemed glad of any kind of custom, to buy a quarter of aniseed marbles. These were sold loose, but were put into a special paper bag overprinted with the words

COME ON, CHILDREN, HERE'S A NEW HIT!
FIRST YOU ROLL IT, THEN YOU CHEW IT.

Willis had never known many children, and until Nenna had come to the boats he had rather tended to forget there were such things. The very distinctive taste of the aniseed marbles, which were, perhaps, some of the nastiest sweets ever made, recovered time past for him.

Once at the Tate, they usually had time only to look at the sea and river pieces, the Turners and the Whistlers. Willis praised these with the mingled pride and humility of an inheritor, however distant. To Tilda, however, the fine pictures were only extensions of her life on board. It struck her as odd, for example, that Turner, if he spent so much time on Chelsea

Reach, shouldn't have known that a seagull always alights on the highest point. Well aware that she was in a public place, she tried to modify her voice; only then Willis didn't always hear, and she had to try again a good deal louder.

'Did Whistler do that one?'

The attendant watched her, hoping that she would get a little closer to the picture, so that he could relieve the boredom of his long day by telling her to stand back.

'What did he put those two red lights up there for? They're for obstruction not completely covered by water, aren't they? What are they doing there among the riding lights?'

'They don't miss much, do they?' the attendant said to Willis. 'I mean, your little granddaughter there.'

The misunderstanding delighted Tilda. 'Dear grandfather, are you sure you are not weary? Let us return to our ship. Take my arm, for though I am young, I am strong.'

Willis dealt with her admirably by taking almost no notice of what she said.

'Whistler was a very good painter. You don't want to make any mistake about that. It's only amateurs who think he isn't. There's Old Battersea Bridge. That was the old wooden bridge. Painted on a grey ground, you see, to save himself trouble. Tide on the turn, lighter taking advantage of the ebb.'

It was understood that on their return they would have tea on *Grace*.

'How old do you think I am, Mrs James?' Willis asked, leaning quietly forward. 'Don't tell me you've never thought about it. It's my experience that everybody thinks how old everybody else is.'

There was no help for it. 'Well, perhaps nearer seventy than sixty.'

Willis's expression never changed quickly. It seemed to be a considerable undertaking for him to rearrange the leathery brown cheeks and the stiff grey eyebrows which were apparently supported by his thick-lensed spectacles.

'I don't seem to feel my age while I'm on these little expeditions, or when I'm drawing.'

Now he wouldn't have time for either. Cleaning ship, and worrying about the visits of intending purchasers, occupied his entire horizon.

His ideas proceeded from simplicity to simplicity. If the main leak could be concealed by showing only at low tide, Willis thought that the equally serious problem of rain – for the weatherboards were particularly weak in one place – could be solved if he stood directly under the drip, wearing a sort of broad waterproof hat. He was sure he had one stowed away somewhere.

'He's no idea of how to sell anything except his drawings,' Woodie told Charles, 'and then I doubt whether he charges enough for them. I should describe him as an innocent.'

'He knows a fair amount about boats.'

'He lives in the past. He was asking me about some man called Payne who seems to have died years ago.'

Richard saw, with reservations, where his duty lay, and put *Dreadnought* on the market through the agency of an old RNVR friend of his, who had gone into partnership, on coming out of the forces, as an estate agent in Halkin Street. Perhaps 'acquaintance' would be a fairer description than 'friend', but the difference was clearer in peacetime than it had been during the war.

The agent was up-to-date and wished, as was fashionable in those years, to give an amusing turn to the advertisement, which he thought ought to appear, not where Willis had thought of putting it, in the *Exchange and Mart*, but in the A circulation newspapers.

'... Whistler's Battersea ... main water ... no? well, main electricity ... two cabins, one suitable for a tiny Flying Dutchman ... huge Cutty Sark type hold awaits conversion ... complete with resident Ancient Mariner ... might be persuaded to stop awhile if you splice the mainbrace ...'

The senior partner usually drafted these announcements himself, but all the partners felt that, given the chance, they could do it better.

'The *Cutty Sark* was a tea clipper,' Richard said. 'And I don't think there's any question of Willis staying on board. In fact, that's really the whole point of the transaction.'

'Did this barge go to Dunkirk?'

'A number of them were drafted,' Richard said. '*Grace* was, and *Maurice*, but not *Dreadnought*, I think.'

'Pity. It would have been a selling point. How would it be, Richard, if we were to continue this discussion over a very large pink gin?'

This remark, often repeated, had earned Richard's friend, or acquaintance, the nickname of Pinkie.

Since this meeting, Richard had had a further debate with his conscience. It was, of course, the purchaser's business to employ a surveyor, whether a house or a boat was in question, and Pinkie would not be offering *Dreadnought* with any kind of guarantee as to soundness, only, after all, as to quaintness. On the other hand, Pinkie seemed to have lost his head to a certain extent, perhaps at the prospect of making his mark by bringing in something novel in the way of business. Surely he hadn't been quite so irritating as a watchkeeping officer in the *Lanark*? But the weakest element in the situation – the one most in need of protection, towards which Richard would always return – the weakest element was certainly Willis. He had begun to neglect himself, Laura said. She had gone along once to pay a casual visit and found one of Nenna's youngsters, the little one, cooking some kind of mess for him in *Dreadnought*'s galley. Richard rather liked Willis's pictures, and had got him to do a pen and wash drawing of *Lord Jim*. He saw the old man as in need of what, by current standards, was a very small sum to enable him to wind up his affairs.

Richard was not aware that he was no longer reasoning, but allowing a series of overlapping images – the drawing of *Lord Jim*, Tilda cooking – to act as a substitute for argument, so that his mind was working in a way not far different from Maurice's, or Nenna's. But the end product would be very different – not indecisive and multiple, but single and decisive. Without this faculty of Richard's, the world could not be maintained in its present state.

Having explained carefully to Willis what he was about to do, Richard invited Pinkie out to lunch. This had to be at a restaurant, because the only club that Richard belonged to was Pratt's. He had got himself put up for Pratt's because it was impossible to have lunch there. There was, too, something unaccountable about Richard – perhaps the same wilfulness that induced him to live offshore although his marriage was in a perilous state – which attracted him to Pratt's because celebrations were only held there for the death of a king or queen.

The restaurant to which Richard invited Pinkie was one at which he had an account, and there was, at least, no difficulty in knowing what drinks to order. Pinkie sucked in his drink in a curious manner, very curious considering how many gins he must have in the course of the week, as though his glass was a blowhole in Arctic ice and to drink was his only hope of survival.

'By the way, Richard, when are you and Laura going to give up this nonsense about living in the middle of the Thames? This is the moment to acquire property, I'm sure you realise that.'

'Where?' Richard asked. He wondered why Pinkie mentioned Laura, then realised with sinking heart that she was no longer keeping her discontent to herself, and the echo of it must have travelled for some distance.

'Where? Oh, a gentleman's county,' Pinkie replied, wallowing through his barrier of ice, 'say Northamptonshire. You can drive up every morning easily, be in the office by ten, down in the evening by half-past six. I calculate you could spend about 60 per cent of your life at work and 40 per cent at home. Not too bad, that. Mind you, these Jacobean properties don't come on the market every day. We just happen to be more lucky at laying hands on them than most. Or Norfolk, of course, if you're interested in small boats.'

Richard wondered why living on a largish boat should automatically make him interested in small ones.

'Not Norfolk, I think.' A number of Laura's relations lived there, but he had not come to the Relais to discuss them. 'You wouldn't make a profit on *Lord Jim* anyway,' he added, 'I don't regard her as an investment.'

'Then what in the name of Christ did you buy her for?'

This was the question Richard did not want to answer. Meanwhile, the waiter put a warm plate printed with a name and device in front of each of them and, after a short interval, took it away again, this, presumably, representing the cover for which the restaurant made a charge. Subsequently he brought various inedible articles, such as bread dried to a crisp, and questionable pieces of shellfish, and placed these in front of them. Pinkie chewed away at a raw fragment.

'We might call him an old shellback, if you think that'd go down better, instead of an Ancient Mariner.'

'Who?'

'This Willis of yours. It doesn't do to be too literary.'

The waiter invited them to choose between coq au vin and navarin of lamb, either of which, in other circumstances, would have been called stew.

'Knows his job, that fellow,' said Pinkie. Richard felt inclined to agree with him.

The wine, though Richard was not the kind of person whom the sommelier kept waiting, was not particularly good. Pinkie said nothing about this because he was dazed by gin, and was not paying, and Richard said nothing because, after a little thought, he concluded that the wine was good enough for Pinkie.

After they had been given the coq au vin the waiter shovelled onto their plates, from a mysteriously divided dish, some wilted vegetables, and Richard recognised that the moment had come to make his only point.

'I really haven't any particular interest in the sale, except that I want to do the best that I can for this retired artist, Sam Willis,' he said. 'I regard him as a friend, and you remember that apart from all this local colour, I gave you the specifications of his boat.'

'Oh, I daresay. They'll have those in the office. The invaluable Miss Barker. Well, proceed.'

'There wasn't any mention, I think I'm right in saying, of a survey -- that rested with the purchaser.'

Another waiter brought round a trolley on which were a number of half-eaten gateaux decorated with a white substance, and some slices of hard apple resting in water, in a glass bowl. The idea of eating these things seemed absurd, and yet Pinkie asked for some.

'Well, these specifications. I'll have to go back to the shop, and check up on them, as I said, but I imagine you won't grudge me a glass of brandy first.'

Richard gave the order. 'There's something which I didn't mention, but I want to make it absolutely clear, and that is that I've reason to believe that this craft, the *Dreadnought*, leaks quite badly.'

Pinkie laughed, spraying a little of the brandy which had been brought to him onto the laden air. 'Of course she does. All these old boats leak like sieves. Just as all these period houses are as rotten as old cheese. Everyone knows that. But age has its value.'

Richard sighed. 'Has it ever struck you, Pinkie, what it would be like to belong to a class of objects which gets more valuable as it gets older? Houses, oak trees, furniture, wine, I don't care what! I'm thirty-nine, I'm not sure about you . . .'

The idea was not taken up, and half an hour later Richard signed the bill and they left the Relais together. Pinkie could still think quite clearly enough to know that he had very little prospect of a new commission. 'As you're fixed, Richard,' he said, half embracing his friend, but impeded by his umbrella, 'as you're fixed, and you're an obstinate bugger, I can't shake you, you're living nowhere, you don't belong to land or water?' As Richard did not respond, he added, 'Keep in touch. We mustn't let it be so long next time.'

The second or third lot of clients sent along by Pinkie, an insurance broker and his wife, who wanted somewhere to give occasional parties in summer, at high tide only, were very much taken with *Dreadnought*. It was raining slightly on the day of inspection, but Willis, who had not been able to lay hands on his waterproof 'tile', but made do with a deep-crowned felt hat, stood on duty under the gap in the weatherboards, while an unsuspecting clerk from the agency showed the rest of the boat. The galley was very cramped, but the ship's chests, still marked FOR 2 SEAMEN, and the deckhouse, from which Willis had watched the life of the river go by, both made a good impression.

'You'll have noticed the quality of the bottom planking,' said the clerk. 'All these ends are 2½ English elm for three strakes out from the centre, and after that you've got oak. That's what Nelson meant, you know, when he talked about wooden walls. Mind, I don't say that she hasn't been knocked about a bit . . . There may be some weathering here and there . . .'

After a few weeks which to Willis, however, seemed like a few years, the broker's solicitors made a conditional offer for the poor old barge, and finally agreed to pay £1,500, provided that *Dreadnought* was still in shipshape condition six months hence, in the spring of 1962.

Six months, Willis repeated. It was a long time to wait, but not impossible.

Richard suggested that the intervening time could well be spent in replacing the pumps and pump-wells, and certain sections of the hull. It was difficult for him to realise that he was dealing with, or rather trying to help, a man who had never, either physically or emotionally, felt the need to replace anything. Even Willis's appearance, the spiky short black hair and the prize-fighter's countenance, had not changed much since he had played truant from elementary school and gone down to hang about the docks. If truth were known, he had had a wife, as well as a perdurable old mother, a great bicyclist and supporter of local Labour causes, but both of them had died of cancer, no replacements possible there. The body must either repair itself or stop functioning, but that is not true of the emotions, and particularly of Willis's emotions. He had come to doubt the value of all new beginnings and to put his trust in not much more than the art of hanging together. *Dreadnought* had stayed afloat for more than sixty years, and Richard, Skipper though he was, didn't understand timber. Tinkering about with the old boat would almost certainly be the end of her. He remembered the last time he had been to see the dentist. Dental care was free in the 60s, in return for signing certain unintelligible documents during the joy of escape from the surgery. But when the dentist had announced that it was urgently necessary to extract two teeth Willis had got up and walked away, glad that he hadn't taken off his coat and so would not have to enter into any further discussion while he recovered it from the waiting-room. If one goes, he thought, still worse two, they all go.

'*Dreadnought* is good for a few years yet,' he insisted. 'And what kind of repairs can you do on oak?'

'Have you asked him about the insurance valuation?' Laura asked Richard.

'There isn't one. These old barges – well, they could get a quotation for fire, I suppose, but not against flood or storm damage.'

'I'm going home for a fortnight. It may be more than a fortnight – I don't really know how long.'

'When?'

'Oh, quite soon. I'll need some money.'

Richard avoided looking at her, for fear she should think he meant anything particular by it.

'What about *Grace*?' Laura went on.

'What about her?'

'Is *Grace* in bad condition?'

Richard sighed. 'Not as good as one would like. There the trouble is largely above the waterline, though. I've told Nenna time and again that she ought to get hold of some sort of reliable chap, an ex-Naval chippie would be the right sort, just to spend the odd day on board and put everything to rights. There aren't any partitions between the cabins, to start with.'

'Did Nenna tell you that?'

'You can see for yourself, if you drop in there.'

'What a very odd thing to tell you.'

'I suppose people have got used to bringing me their queries, to some extent,' said Richard, going into their cabin to take off his black shoes and put on a pair of red leather slippers, which, like all his other clothes, never seemed to wear out. The slippers made him feel less tired.

'There are more queries from *Grace* than from *Dreadnought*, aren't there?'

'I'm not sure. I've never worked it out exactly.'

'They're not worth talking about anyway. I expect they talk about us.'

'Oh, do you think so?'

'They say "There goes that Mrs Blake again. She turns me up, she looks so bleeding bored all day."'

Richard did not like to have to think about two things at once, particularly at the end of the day. He kissed Laura, sat down, and tried to bring the two subjects put to him into order, and under one heading. A frown ran in a slanting direction between his eyebrows and halfway up his forehead. Laura's problem was that she had not enough to do – no children, though she hadn't said anything about this recently – and his heart smote him because he had undertaken to make her happy, and hadn't. Nenna, on the other hand, had rather too much. If her husband had let her down, as was apparently the case, she ought to have a male relation of some kind, to see to things. In Richard's experience, all women had plenty of male relations. Laura, for instance, had two younger brothers, who were not settling very well into the stockbrokers' firm in which they had been placed, and numerous uncles, one of them an old horror who obtained Scandinavian au pairs through advertisements in *The Lady*, and then, of course, her Norfolk cousins. Nenna appeared to have no one. She had come over here from Canada, of course. This last reflection – it was Nova Scotia, he was pretty sure – seemed to tidy up the whole matter, which his mind now presented as a uniform interlocking structure, with working parts.

Laura was very lucky to be married to Richard, who would not have hurt her feelings deliberately for the whole world. A fortnight with her parents, he was thinking now, on their many acres of damp earth, must surely bring home to her the advantages of living on *Lord Jim*. Of course, it hadn't so far done anything of the kind, and he had to arrive at the best thing to do in the circumstances. He was not quite satisfied with the way his mind was working. Something was out of phase. He did not recognise it as hope.

'I want to take you out to dinner, Lollie,' he said.

'Why?'

'You look so pretty, I want other people to see you. I daresay they'll wonder why on earth you agreed to go out with a chap like me.'

'Where do you go when you take people out to lunch from the office?'

'Oh, the Relais, but that's no good in the evening. We could try that Provençal place. Give them a treat.'

'You don't really want to go,' said Laura, but she disappeared into the spare cabin, where, unfortunately, her dresses had to be kept. Richard took off his slippers and put on his black shoes again, and they went out.

6

MARTHA AND Tilda were in the position of having no spending money, but this was less important when they were not attending school and were spared the pains of comparison, and they felt no bitterness against their mother, because she hadn't any either. Nenna believed, however, that she would have some in the spring, when three things would happen, each, like melting ice-floes, slowly moving the next one on. Edward would come and live on *Grace*, which would save the rent he was paying on his rooms at present; the girls, once they were not being prayed for at the grotto, would agree to go back to the nuns; and with Tilda at school she could go out herself and look for a job.

Martha could not imagine her mother going out to work and felt that the experiment was likely to prove disastrous.

'You girls don't know my life,' said Nenna. 'I worked in my vacations before the war, wiping dishes, camp counselling, all manner of things.'

Martha smiled at the idea of these dear dead days. 'What did you counsel?' she asked.

The girls needed money principally to buy singles by Elvis Presley and Cliff Richard, whose brightly smiling photograph presided over their cabin. They had got the photograph as a fold-in from *Disc Weekly*. If you couldn't afford the original records, there were smaller ones you could buy at the Woolworths in the King's Road, which sounded quite like.

Like the rest of London's river children, they knew that the mud was a source of wealth, but were too shrewd to go into competition with the locals from Partisan Street for coins, medals and lugworms. The lugworms, in any case, Willis had told them, were better on Limehouse Reach. Round about *Grace* herself, the great river deposited little but mounds of plastic containers.

Every expedition meant crossing the Bridge, because the current on Battersea Reach, between the two bridges, sets towards the Surrey side. The responsibility for these outings, which might or might not be successful, had worn between Martha's eyebrows a faint frown, not quite vertical, which exactly resembled Richard's.

'We'll go bricking today,' she said. 'How's the tide?'

'High water Gravesend 3 a.m., London Bridge 4, Battersea Bridge 4.30,' Tilda chanted rapidly. 'Spring tide, seven and a half hours' ebb, low tide at 12.'

Martha surveyed her sister doubtfully. With so much specialised knowledge, which would qualify her for nothing much except a pilot's certificate, with her wellingtons over which the mud of many tides had dried, she had the air of something aquatic, a demon from the depths, perhaps. Whatever happens, I must never leave her behind, Martha prayed.

Both the girls were small and looked exceptionally so as they crossed the bridge with their handcart. They wore stout Canadian anoraks, sent them by their Aunt Louise.

Below the old Church at Battersea the retreating flood had left exposed a wide shelf of mud and gravel. At intervals the dark driftwood lay piled. Near the draw dock some long-shoremen had heaped it up and set light to it, to clear the area. Now the thick blue smoke gave out a villainous smell, the gross spirit of salt and fire. Tilda loved that smell, and stretched her nostrils wide.

Beyond the dock, an old wrecked barge lay upside down. It was shocking, even terrifying, to see her dark flat shining bottom, chine uppermost. A derelict ship turns over on her keel and lies gracefully at rest, but there is only one way up for a Thames barge if she is to maintain her dignity.

This wreck was the *Small Gains*, which had gone down more than twenty-five years before, when hundreds of barges were still working under sail. Held fast in the mud with her cargo of bricks, she had failed to come up with the rising tide and the water had turned her over. The old bricks were still scattered over the foreshore. After a storm they were washed back in dozens, but most of them were broken or half ground to powder. Along with the main cargo, however, *Small Gains* had shipped a quantity of tiles. At a certain moment in the afternoon the sun, striking across the water from behind the gas works, sent almost level rays over the glistening reach. Then it was possible for the expert to pick out a glazed tile, though only if it had sunk at the correct angle to the river bed.

'Do you think Ma's mind is weakening?' Tilda asked.

'I thought we weren't going to discuss our affairs today.' Martha relented and added – 'Well, Ma is much too dependent on Maurice, or on anyone sympathetic. She ought to avoid these people.'

The two girls sat on the wall of Old Battersea churchyard to eat their sandwiches. These contained a substance called Spread, and, indeed, that was all you could do with it.

'Mattie, who would you choose, if you were compelled at gunpoint to marry tomorrow?'

'You mean, someone off the boats?'

'We don't know anybody else.'

Seagulls, able to detect the appearance of a piece of bread at a hundred yards away, advanced slowly towards them over the shelving ground.

'I thought perhaps you meant Cliff.'

'Not Cliff, not Elvis. And not Richard, he's too obvious.'

Martha licked her fingers.

'He looks tired all the time now. I saw him taking Laura out to dinner yesterday evening. Straight away after he'd come back from work! Where's the relaxation in that? What sort of life is that for a man to lead?'

'What was she wearing?'

'I couldn't make out. She had her new coat on.'

'But you saw the strain on his features?'

'Oh, yes.'

'Do you think Ma notices?'

'Oh, everybody does.'

When the light seemed about right, striking fire out of the broken bits of china and glass, they went to work. Tilda lay down full length on a baulk of timber. It was her job to do this, because Martha bruised so easily. A princess, unknown to all about her, she awaited the moment when these bruises would reveal her true heritage.

Tilda stared fixedly. It was necessary to get your eye in.

'There's one!'

She bounded off, as though over stepping stones, from one object to another that would scarcely hold, old tyres, old boots, the ribs of crates from which the seagulls were dislodged in resentment. Far beyond the point at which the mud became treacherous and from which *Small Gains* had never risen again, she stood poised on the handlebars of a sunken bicycle. How had the bicycle ever got there?

'Mattie, it's a Raleigh!'

'If you've seen a tile, pick it up straight away and come back.'

'I've seen two!'

With a tile in each hand, balancing like a circus performer, Tilda returned. Under the garish lights of the Big Top, every man, woman and child rose to applaud. Who, they asked each other, was this newcomer, who had succeeded where so many others had failed?

The nearest clean water was from the standpipe in the churchyard; they did not like to wash their finds there, because the water was for the flowers on the graves, but Martha fetched some in a bucket.

As the mud cleared away from the face of the first tile, patches of ruby-red lustre, with the rich glow of a jewel's heart, appeared inch by inch, then the outlines of a delicate grotesque silver bird, standing on one leg in a circle of blue-black leaves and berries, its beak of burnished copper.

'Is it beautiful?'

'Yes.'

'And the dragon?'

The sinuous tail of a dragon, also in gold and jewel colours, wreathed itself like a border round the edge of the other tile.

The reverse of both tiles was damaged, and on only one of them the letters NDS END could just be made out, but Martha could not be mistaken.

'They're de Morgans, Tilda. Two of them at one go, two of them in one morning.'

'How much can we sell them for?'

'Do you remember the old lady, Tilda?'

'Did I see her?'

'Tilda, I only took you three months ago. Mrs Stirling, I mean, in Battersea Old House. Her sister was married to William de Morgan, that had the pottery, and made these kind of tiles, that was in Victorian days, you must remember. She was in a wheelchair. We paid for tea, but the money went to the Red Cross. We were only supposed to have two scones each, otherwise the Red Cross couldn't expect to make a profit. She explained, and she showed us all those tiles and bowls, and the brush and comb he used to do his beard with.'

'How old was she?'

'In 1965 she'll be a hundred.'

'What was her name?'

'Mrs Wilhemina Stirling.'

Tilda stared at the brilliant golden-beaked bird, about which there was something frightening.

'We'd better wrap it up. Someone might want to steal it.'

Sobered, like many seekers and finders, by the presence of the treasure itself, they wrapped the tiles in Tilda's anorak, which immediately dimmed their lustre once again with a film of mud.

'There's Woodie!'

Tilda began to jump up and down, like a cork on the tide.

'What's he doing?'

'He's getting his car out.'

There were no garages near the boats and Woodie was obliged to keep his immaculate Austin Cambridge in the yard of a public house on the Surrey side.

'I'm attracting his attention,' Tilda shouted. 'He can drive us home, and we can put the pushcart on the back seat.'

'Tilda, you don't understand. He'd have to say yes, because he's sorry for us, I heard him tell Richard we were no better than waifs of the storm, and we should ruin the upholstery, and be taking advantage of his kindness.'

'It's his own fault if he's kind. It's not the kind who inherit the earth, it's the poor, the humble, and the meek.'

'What do you think happens to the kind, then?'

'They get kicked in the teeth.'

Woodie drove them back across the bridge.

'You'll have to look after yourselves this winter, you know,' he said. 'No more lifts, I'm afraid, I shall be packed up and gone till spring. I'm thinking of laying up *Rochester* in dry dock. She needs a bit of attention.'

'Do you have to manage all that packing by yourself?' Tilda asked.

'No, dear, my wife's coming to give me a hand.'

'You haven't got a wife!'

'You've never seen her, dear.'

'What's her name?'

'Janet.' Woodie began to feel on the defensive, as though he had made the name up.

'What does she look like?'

'She doesn't much care for the river. She spends the summer elsewhere.'

'Has she left you, then?'

'Certainly not. She's got a caravan in Wales, a very nice part, near Tenby.' Although Woodie had given this explanation pretty often, he was surprised to have to make it to a child of six. 'Then in the winter we go back to our house in Purley. It's an amicable arrangement.'

Was there not, on the whole of Battersea Reach, a couple, married or unmarried, living together in the ordinary way? Certainly, among the fairweather people on the middle Reach. They lived together and even multiplied, though the opportunity for a doctor to hurry over the gangplank with a black bag, and, in his turn, fall into the river, had been missed. *Bluebird*, which was rented by a group of nurses from the

Waterloo Hospital, had been at the ready, and when the birth was imminent they'd seen to it that the ambulance arrived promptly. But, apart from *Bluebird*, the middle Reach would be empty by next week, or perhaps the one after.

Martha, who had decided to stop thinking about the inconvenience they were causing, asked Woodie not to stop at the boats; they would like to go onto the New King's Road.

'We want to stop at the Bourgeois Gentilhomme,' she said, with the remnants of the French accent the nuns had carefully taught her.

'Isn't that an antique shop, dear?'

'Yes, we're going to sell an antique.'

'Have you got one?'

'We've got two.'

'Are you sure you've been to this place before?'

'Yes.'

'I shall have to pull up as near as I can and let you out,' said Woodie. He wondered if he ought to wait, but he wanted to get back to *Rochester* before she came afloat. He watched the two girls, who, to do them justice, thanked him very nicely, they weren't so badly brought up when you came to think about it, approach the shop by the side door.

On occasions, Martha's courage failed her. The advantages her sister had in being so much younger presented themselves forcibly. She sharply told Tilda, who had planted herself in a rocking-chair put out on the pavement, that she must come into the shop and help her speak to the man. Tilda, who had never sat in a rocker before, replied that her boots were too dirty.

'And anyway, I'm old Abraham Lincoln, jest sittin and thinkin.'

'You've got to come.'

The Bourgeois Gentilhomme was one of many enterprises in Chelsea which survived entirely by selling antiques to each other. The atmosphere, once through the little shop-door, cut down from a Victorian billiard table, was oppressive. Clocks struck widely different hours. At a corner table, with her back turned towards them, sat a woman in black, apparently doing some accounts, and surrounded by dusty furniture; perhaps she had been cruelly deserted on her wedding day, and had sat there ever since, refusing to have anything touched. She did not look up when the girls came in, although the billiard table was connected by a cord to a cow-bell, which jangled harshly.

'Where's Mr Stephen, please?'

Without waiting for or expecting a reply, Martha and the reluctant Tilda walked through into the back office. Here no conversion had been done to the wretched little room, once a scullery, with two steps down to a small yard stacked high with rubbish. Mr Stephen, sitting by a paraffin heater, was also writing on pieces of paper, and appearing to be adding things up. Martha took out the two tiles and laid them in front of him.

Well used to the treasures of the foreshore, the dealer wiped the gleaming surfaces free, not with water this time, but with something out of a bottle. Then, after carefully taking off his heavy rings, he picked each of the tiles up in turn, holding them up by the extreme edge.

'So you brought these all this long way to show me. What did you think they were?'

'I know what they are. I only want to know how much you can pay me for them.'

'Have you any more of these at home?'

'They weren't at home.'

'Where did you find them, then?'

'About the place.'

'And you're sure there aren't any more?'

'Just the two.'

Mr Stephen examined the gold and silver bird through a glass.

'They're quite pretty tiles, dear, not anything more than that.'

'Then why did you take your rings off so carefully?'

'I'm always careful, dear.'

'These are ruby lustre tiles by William de Morgan,' said Martha, 'with decoration in gold and silver – the "starlight and moonlight" lustre.'

'Who sent you in here?' Mr Stephen asked.

'Nobody, you know us, we've been in before.'

'Yes, but I mean, who told you what to say?'

'Nobody.'

'Mrs Wilhemina Stirling,' Tilda put in, 'ninety-seven if she's a day.'

'Well, whoever you're selling for, I'm sorry to disappoint you, but these tiles can't be by de Morgan. I'm afraid you just don't know enough about it. I don't suppose you looked at what's left of the lettering on the reverse. NDS END. William de Morgan had his potteries in Cheyne Walk, and later he moved his kilns to Merton Abbey. This is not the mark for either one of those.'

'Of course it isn't. These are part of a very late set. His very last pottery was at Sands End, in Fulham. Didn't you know that?'

Dignity demanded that the dealer should hand the tiles back with a pitying smile. But he could not resist holding the bird up to his desk lamp, so that the light ran across the surface and seemed to flow over the edges in crimson flame. And now Martha and he were united in a strange fellow feeling, which neither of them had expected, and which they had to shake off with difficulty.

'Well, I think perhaps we can take these. The bird is much the finer of the two, of course – I'm only taking the dragon to make a pair with the bird. Perhaps you'd like to exchange them for something else in my shop. There are some charming things out there in front – some very old toys. Your little sister here . . . '

'I hate very old toys,' Tilda said. 'They may have been all right for very old children.'

'A Victorian musical box . . . '

'It's broken.'

'I think not,' said the dealer, leaving the girls and hastening out front. He began to search irritably for the key. The woman sitting at the table made no attempt to help him.

'Tilda, have you been tinkering about with the musical box?'

'Yes.'

Martha saw that discovery, which could not be long delayed, would reduce her advantage considerably.

'We're asking three pounds for the two de Morgan lustre tiles. Otherwise I must trouble you to hand them back at once.'

Tilda's respect for her sister, whom she had never seen before in the possession of so much money, reduced her almost to silence; in a hoarse whisper she asked whether they were going to get the records straight away.

'Yes, we will, but we ought to get a present for Ma first. You know Daddy always used to forget to give her anything.'

'Did she say so?'

'Have you ever actually seen anything that he's given her?'

They walked together down the King's Road, went into Woolworths, and were dazzled.

7

THE SAME flood tide that had brought such a good harvest of tiles heaped a mass of driftwood onto the Reach. Woodie looked at it apprehensively. He wouldn't, of course, as he usually did, have to spend the months in Purley worrying about *Rochester*, and wondering whether she was getting knocked about by flotsam in his absence. There were only a few weeks now before she went into dry dock. Perhaps he half realised that the absence of worry would make his winter unendurable. As though clinging to the last moments of a vanishing pleasure, he counted the baulks of timber edging darkly towards the boats.

His wife had already arrived from Wales. He had in prospect a time of truce, while Janet, an expert manager, in a trouser suit well adapted to the task, gave him very real help with the laying-up, but at the same time made a series of unacceptable comparisons between the caravan and *Rochester*. These comparisons were never made or implied once they were both back in Purley. They arose only in the short uneasy period passed between land and water.

As he crossed *Grace*'s deck Woodie looked up with astonishment at *Dreadnought*, which was a bigger boat, and, having much less furniture on board, rode higher in the water. In the lighted deckhouse he could not only see old Willis, fiddling about with what looked like tins and glasses, but Janet, wearing her other trouser suit.

'It's a celebration,' said Nenna, coming up to the hatch, 'they're only waiting for you to come. It's because Willis has sold *Dreadnought*.'

'A provisional offer, I should call it. Still, it's not my object to spoil things. Aren't you going to come?'

'No, it's our turn tomorrow. The deckhouse only holds four.' And Woodie could see now that Maurice was in there as well. He never quite knew what to make of Maurice. Mrs James seemed to talk to him by the hour, in the middle of the night, sometimes, he believed, and so did the children. 'I left your two at an antique shop in the King's Road,' he said. 'They seemed to know exactly what they wanted.'

Nenna put on her jacket. She knew the Bourgeois Gentil-homme, and always feared that one day Martha might get into difficulties. If they weren't there, they were pretty sure to be in Woolworths. She started out to meet them.

Willis had noticed Woodie's return, and could be seen gesturing behind the window of the deckhouse, expressing joy, pointing him out to Janet, and waving to him to come on in.

Woodie was not feeling very sociable, as he had had, of course, to return his car to the Surrey side and walk home across the bridge. But the deckhouse was certainly cosy, and the door, as he pulled it to behind him, cut out, to a considerable extent, the voices of the river. It was the only door on *Dreadnought* which could be considered in good repair. Even the daylong scream of the gulls was silent in here, and the hooters and sound signals arrived only as a distant com-plaint. For Willis, indeed, it was rather too quiet, but useful this evening when he had guests. 'We want to be able to make ourselves heard,' he said. Evidently he had toasts in mind.

In preparation, he had opened several bottles of Guinness, and one of the cans, which contained Long Life – the lady's drink – in compliment to Mrs Woodie. But he was distressed that he had no glasses.

'I shouldn't let Janet have a glass anyway,' cried Maurice, never at a loss. He explained that the lager was manufactured by the Danes, an ancient seafaring people, to be drunk straight out of the can, so that the bubbles would move straight up and down in the stomach to counteract the sideways rocking movement of the boat. To Woodie's surprise his wife laughed as though she couldn't stop. 'You never told me it was so social on the boats,' she said. He tried hard to get into the spirit of the thing. Why should a boat be less social than a caravan, for heaven's sake? He'd never seen Janet drinking out of a can before, either. But he mustn't forget that it was a great occasion for old Willis, who must be getting on for sixty-five, ready to take the knock any day now.

'It's good of you to come at such short notice, very good,' said Willis. 'I'd like to call you all shipmates. Is that passed unanimously? And now I'd like to ask how many of you go regularly to the fish shop on Lyons Dock?'

At this moment the electricity failed, no surprise on *Dreadnought* where the wiring was decidedly makeshift. They were all in the dark; only the river lights, fixed or passing, wavered over cans, bottles and faces.

'A bit unfortunate,' said Woodie.

'Forty years ago we wouldn't have said that!' Willis exclaimed. 'Not with the right sort of woman in the room! We'd have known what to do!'

Once again Janet and Maurice laughed uproariously. The place was becoming Liberty Hall. Woodie put his hand at once, as he invariably could, on his set of pocket screwdrivers, but before he felt that it was quite tactful to offer help, Willis had lit an Aladdin, which presumably he always kept ready, no wonder. Fixed in gimbals, the lamp gradually extended its radiant circle into every corner of the deckhouse.

Maurice sprang to his feet, slightly bending his head, so as to avoid stunning himself on the roof. Although the four of them were practically knee to knee, he made as if speaking in a vast auditorium. 'Can everybody see me clearly? . . . you at the back, madam? . . . can I take it, then, that I'm heard in all parts of the house?'

Willis opened more bottles. His spectacles shone, even his leathery cheeks shone.

'Now, I was saying something about the fish shop on Lyons Dock. If you don't ever go there, you won't have had the chance of sampling their hot mussels. They boil them in an iron saucepan. Must be iron.'

'The river's oldest delicacy!' Maurice cried.

'Oh no, they're quite fresh. I've got some boiling down below. They should be just about done now.'

'Surely mussels aren't in season?' Woodie asked.

'You're thinking of whitebait, there's no season for mussels.'

'I'm under doctor's orders, to some extent.'

'First time I've heard of it,' Janet cried.

'Mussels are at their best in autumn,' said Maurice, 'that's what they continually say in Southport.'

Encouraged, Willis offered to fetch the mussels at once, and some plates and forks and vinegar, and switch on the radio while he was gone, to give them a bit of music. Woodie was surprised to learn that there were any plates on *Dreadnought*. 'May I have the first dance, Janet?' Maurice asked, up on his feet again. Couldn't he see that there was hardly room to sit?

As Willis went to the afterhatch it struck him that *Dreadnought* was rather low in the water, almost on a level with *Grace*. He looked across to see if he could catch a glimpse of Nenna and the girls, and ask them what they thought about it, but everybody seemed to have gone ashore.

The hold was very dark, but not quite as dark as Willis had expected. In fact, it was not as dark as it should be. There were gleams and reflections where none could possibly be. Halfway down the companion he stopped, and it was as though the whole length of the hold moved towards him in a body. He heard the faintest splash, and was not sure whether it was inside or out.

'What's wrong?' he thought.

Then he caught the unmistakable dead man's stench of river water, heaving slowly, but always finding, no matter what the obstacle, the shortest way home.

How bad was it?

Another step down, and the water was slopping round his ankles. His shoes filled. He bent down and put a hand in the water, and swore when an electric shock ran through his elbow and shoulder. Now he knew why the lights were out. A pale blue light puzzled him for a moment, until he realised that it was the Calor gas stove in the galley. He could just make out the bottom of the iron saucepan in which the mussels were still boiling for his guests.

The main leak had given way at last. And Willis had it in his heart to be sorry for old *Dreadnought*, as she struggled to rise against the increasing load of water. It was like one of those terrible sights of the racecourse or the battlefield where wallowing living beings persevere dumbly in their duty although mutilated beyond repair.

There was a box of matches in his top pocket, but when he got them out his hands were so wet that he could not make them strike. The only hope now was to reach the hand-pump in the galley and see if he could keep the level within bounds. About a foot below the outwale there was a pretty bad hole which he'd never felt concerned him, it was so far above the waterline. He could see the shore lights through it now. If *Dreadnought* went on sinking at the present rate, in ten minutes the hole wouldn't be above the waterline, but below.

Willis set out to wade through the rolling wash. Something made for him in the darkness and struck him a violent blow just under the knee. Half believing that his leg was broken, he stooped and tried to fend the object off with his hands. It came at him again, and he could just make out that it was part of his bunk, one of the side panels. That, for some reason, almost made him give up, not the pain, but the familiar bit of furniture, the bed he had slept in for fifteen years, now hopelessly astray and, as it seemed, attacking him. Everything that should have stood by him had become hostile. The case of ice that weighted him down was his best suit.

He lost his footing and went right under. Totally blinded, his spectacles streaming with water as he bobbed up, he tried to float himself into the galley. Then he realised that there was no chance of finding the hand-pump. The flood was up to the top of the stove already, and as the gas went out the saucepan went afloat and he was scalded by a stream of boiling water that mixed with the cold. There was no hope for *Dreadnought*. He would be lucky to get back up the companion.

Above in the deck-cabin the guests, for a while, noticed nothing, the music was so loud, and Maurice was so entertaining. It was said by his acquaintances in the pub that he gave value for money, but there was a touch of genius in the way he talked that night. With a keener sense of danger than the others, and finding it exhilarating, as they certainly would not, he had noticed at once that something was wrong, even before he had rubbed a clear patch on the steamy windows and, looking out into the night, had seen the horizon slowly rising, inch by inch. He made a rapid calculation. Give it a bit longer, we're all enjoying ourselves, he thought. Maurice had never learned to swim, but this did not disturb him. If only there was a piano, I could give them 'Rock of Ages' when the time comes, he said to himself.

Woodie's complaints had died down somewhat. 'Don't know about these shellfish. Taking his time about it, isn't he?'

'Never mind!' Maurice cried. 'It'll give me time to tell both your fortunes. I just glanced at both your hands earlier on, just glanced, you know, and I seemed to see something quite unexpected written there. Now, you won't mind extending your palm, will you, Janet? You don't mind being first?'

'Do you really know how to do it?'

Maurice smiled radiantly.

'I do it almost every night. You'd be surprised how many new friends I make in that way.'

'I've got a copper bracelet on, that I wear for rheumatism,' she said, 'will that affect your reading?'

'Believe me, it won't make the slightest difference,' said Maurice.

The door opened, and Willis stood there, like a drowned man risen from the dead, his spectacles gone, water streaming from him and instantly making a pool at his feet. *Dreadnought*'s deck was still a foot or so above the tide. He was able to escort his guests, in good order, across *Grace* for Maurice, while the Woodies retreated over the gangplank to *Rochester*.

It is said on the river that a Thames barge, once she has risen with the tide, never sinks completely. But *Dreadnought*, let alone all her other weak places, had been holed amidships by a baulk of timber, and before long the water poured into her with a sound like a sigh and she went down in a few seconds.

The loss of *Dreadnought* meant yet another meeting of the boat owners on *Lord Jim*, more relaxed in atmosphere than the former one, because it seemed that Mrs Blake was away, but hushed by the nature of Willis's misfortune. And yet this too had its agreeable counterpart; their boats, however much in need of repair, had not gone down.

One glass of brown sherry each – the best, there was no second best on *Lord Jim* – restored the impression of a funeral. Richard consulted a list. He wrote lists on special blank pages at the end of his diary, and tore them out only when they were needed, so that they were never lost. With care, there was no need to lose anything, particularly, perhaps, a boat. The disaster having taken place, however, the meeting must concern itself only with practical remedies.

Grace had already taken in all that could be salvaged of Willis's clothing, for drying and mending. The nuns, Nenna's nuns, what a very long time ago it seemed, in a class known as plain sewing, had taught her bygone arts, darning, patching, reinforcing collars with tape, which at last found their proper object in Willis's outmoded garments. Richard congratulated *Grace*. Nenna thought: I'm pleased for him to see that I can make a proper job of something. Why am I pleased?

Far greater sacrifices were required from *Rochester*, who volunteered to take Willis in as a lodger. At a reasonable rent, Richard suggested – but the Woodies wanted no payment. It would, after all, only be for a week or so, after that they were due back at Purley.

'That seems satisfactory, then – he can go straight to you after he comes out of hospital,' – Willis had been admitted to the Waterloo, where it was exceedingly difficult to get a bed, once more with the help of the nurses on *Bluebird*.

'And now, if you'll excuse me, I'm going onto the worst problem of the lot – Willis's financial position . . . Not the sort of thing any of us would usually discuss in public, but essential, I'm afraid, in the present case. I've been onto the P.L.A. and they confirm that *Dreadnought* has been officially classed as a wreck, and what's worse, I'm afraid, is that she's lying near enough to the shipping channels for them, to quote their letter, to exercise their statutory powers and remove her by means of salvage craft.'

'Will that matter?' Woodie asked. 'She'll never be raised again,' and Maurice suggested that Willis would be much better off if he didn't have to look at the wreck of *Dreadnought* at every low tide.

'I quite accept that, but, to continue, all expenses of salvage and towage will be recoverable from the owners of the craft. I'm not too sure, to be quite honest with you, that Willis will be able to pay any, let alone all, of these expenses. I can't see any way out but a subscription list, to be organised as soon as possible. If there are any other suggestions . . .'

There were none, and it being obvious who would have to head the subscribers, Richard wound up the meeting by reading aloud a letter from Willis, delivered by way of *Bluebird*, in which, addressing them all as shipmates, he sent them all a squeeze of the hand and God bless. The words sounded strange in Richard's level unassuming voice, which, however quiet, always commanded attention. The catastrophe had evidently relaxed Willis's habitual control, and he had spoken from the heart, but who could tell how much else survived?

Three days later, Richard came along to *Grace* early in the morning, and told her that there was a call for her. The only telephone on the Reach was on *Lord Jim*. If this was inconvenient, Richard did not say so, although to be called to the telephone, or wanted on the telephone, as Richard put it, always seemed a kind of reproach in itself. More awkward still, since Laura was not on board, he was obliged to lock up before going to the office, and had to wait on board, with his briefcase and umbrella, determinedly not listening, while Nenna went down to the saloon.

Nenna felt sure that there was no one that it could be but Edward. Although it was very unlikely, he must have got the number from the boat company.

'Hullo, Nenna! This is Louise! Yes it's Louise!'

'Louise!'

'Didn't you get my last letter?'

'I don't think so. They get lost sometimes.'

'How come?'

'People fetch them from the office and mean to take them round, and then they get lost or dropped in the water.'

'That's absolutely absurd, Nenna dear.'

'What does it matter anyway? Where are you, Louise, can I come right over and see you?'

'Not right now, Nenna.'

'Where are you calling from?'

'From Frankfurt on the Rhine. We're over here on a business trip. Too bad you didn't read my letters. Has Heinrich arrived?'

'God, Louise, who is Heinrich?'

'Nenna, I know all your intonations as well as I know my own, and I can tell that you're in a very bad state. Joel and I have a suggestion about that which we're going to put to you as soon as we get to London.'

'I'm quite all right Louise. You're coming here, then?'

'And Edward. Exactly what is the position in regard to your marriage. Is Edward still with you?'

Nenna was a child again. She felt her responsibilities slipping away one by one, even her marriage was going.

'Oh, Louise, do you still have lobster sandwiches at Harris's?'

'Now, this boat of yours. What number is this I'm calling you on, by the way? Is that the yacht club?'

'Not exactly . . . it's a friend.'

'Well, this boat you and the children are living on. I understand very well how people live year round in houseboats on the Seine, but not on the Thames, isn't it tidal?'

'Why, yes, it is.'

'And this boat of yours — is she crewed, or is it a bareboat rental?'

'Neither really. I've bought her.'

'Where do you sail her then?'

'She never sails, she's at moorings.'

'We were reading in the London *Times* that some kind of boat was sunk on the Thames the other day. In one of the small paragraphs. Joel reads it all through. He says it's so long since he saw you and the girls that he won't know you. In any case, as I said, we have certain plans which we'd like to put before you, and in the meantime I want you to say hello from us to young Heinrich.'

'Louise, don't ring off. Whatever it's costing. I've never met young Heinrich.'

'Well, neither have we, of course. Didn't you get my letter?'

'It seems not, Louise.'

'He's the son of a very good business friend of ours, who's sent him to school at Sales Abbey, that's with the Benedictines, and he's currently returning home, he has permission to leave school early this term for some reason and return home.'

'Does he live in Frankfurt on the Main?'

'On the Rhine. No, not at all, he's Austrian, he lives in Vienna. He just requires to spend one night in London, he's due to catch a flight to Vienna the next day.'

'Do you mean that he expects to come and stay on *Grace*?'

'Who is Grace, Nenna?'

'What's the name of this boy?' Nenna asked.

'His parents are a Count and Countess, in business as I told you, of course all that doesn't mean anything now, but they're in very good standing. He should have been with you last Friday.'

'Well, he wasn't. There must have been a misunderstanding about that . . . Oh, Lou, you don't know how good it is to hear your voice . . . '

'Nenna, you're becoming emotional. Wouldn't you agree it's just about time that somebody helped you to restore some kind of order into your life?'

'Oh, please don't do that!'

'I hate to cut you short,' said Richard from the hatch, 'it's only that I can hardly expect my staff to be in time if I'm late myself.'

His voice was courteous to the point of diffidence, and Nenna, giving way a little, let herself imagine what it would be like to be on Richard's staff, and to be directed in everything else by Louise, and to ebb and flow without volition, in the warmth of love and politeness.

'Goodbye Louise. As soon as you get to England. – Forgive me, Richard, it was my sister, I don't know how she got your number, I haven't seen her in five years.'

'I sensed that she wasn't used to being contradicted.'

'No.'

'She was very firm.'

'That's so.'

'Are you sure she's your sister?'

'As far as he's concerned, I'm just a drifter,' Nenna thought, smiling and thanking him. Richard patted himself to see that he had some matches on him, a gesture which appealed to Nenna, and walked off up the Embankment to call a taxi.

I won't go down without a struggle, Nenna thought. I married Edward because I wanted to live with him, and I still do. While she ironed Willis's stiff underclothes which, aired day after day, never seemed to get quite dry, the accusations against her, not inside her mind but at some point detached from it, continued without pause. They were all the more tedious because they were reduced, for all practical purposes, to one question: why, after everything that has been put forward in this court, have you still made no attempt to visit 42b Milvain Street? Nenna wished to reply that it was not for the expected reasons – not pride, not resentment, not even the curious acquired characteristics of the river dwellers, which made them scarcely at home in London's streets. No, it's because it's my last chance. While I've still got it I can take it out and look at it and know I still have it. If that goes, I've nothing left to try.

She told Martha that she would be going out that evening and would quite likely not be back until the following day.

'Well, where do we stay?'

'On *Rochester*. I'll ask them.'

In less than a week the impeccable *Rochester* had been transformed into a kind of boarding-house. Nenna would never have dreamed before this of asking them to look after the girls. Willis, on his return from hospital, had taken up his quarters there, though he was no trouble, remaining quietly in the spare cabin without even attempting to watch the river's daily traffic. He had not come up on deck when the P.L.A. tug arrived, and the poor wreck had been towed away, still under water, but surfacing from time to time as though she had still not quite admitted defeat.

'That's just a launch tug,' said Tilda, 'under forty tons. It didn't take much to move *Dreadnought*.'

The salvage men returned what they could, including the iron saucepan, but Willis's painting materials were past repair. Nothing was said about his next move, except that he could hardly expect his sister to take him in now, and that he was unwilling, under any circumstances, to move to Purley. Therefore the daily life of the Woodies, which had depended almost entirely on knowing what they would be doing on any given day six months hence, fell into disrepair. They had to resort to unpacking many of the things which they had so carefully stowed away. They repeated, however, that Willis was no trouble.

When Nenna told them that she had urgent business on the other side of London and that she would have to ask whether Martha and Tilda could stay the night, *Rochester* accepted without protest, and they went over, taking with them their nightdresses, Cliff records, the Cliff photograph and two packets of breakfast cereals, for they did not like the same kind. Tilda, who had been vexed at missing the actual shipwreck, went straight down to Willis's cabin to ask him if he would draw her a picture of it. Martha confronted her mother.

'You're going to see Daddy, aren't you?'

'I might be bringing him back with me. Would you like that?'

'I don't know.'

8

BETTER TAKE a cheap all–day ticket, the bus conductor advised, if Nenna really wanted to get from Chelsea to Stoke Newington.

'Or move house,' he advised.

Although as she changed from bus to bus she was free at last of the accusing voices, she had time for a number of second thoughts, wishing in particular that she had put on other clothes, and had had her hair cut. She didn't know if she wanted to look different or the same. Her best coat would perhaps have been better because it would make her look as though she hadn't let herself go, but on the other hand her frightful old lumber jacket would have suggested, what was true enough, that she was worried enough not to care. But among all these doubts it had not occurred to her that if she got as far as 42b Milvain Street, and rang the bell, Edward would not open the door.

It was the b, perhaps, that was the trouble. b suggested an upstairs flat, and there was only one bell at 42. The yellowish-grey brick houses gave straight onto the street, which she had found only after turning out of another one, and then another. On some doorsteps the milk was still waiting to be taken in. She still missed the rocking of the boat.

He might be in or he might be out. There was a light on in the hall, and apparently on the second floor, though that might be a landing. Nenna struggled against an impulse to rush into the fish and chip shop at the corner, the only shop in the street, and ask them if they had ever seen somebody coming out of number 42b who looked lonely, or indeed if they had ever seen anyone coming out of it at all.

The figure turning the corner and walking heavily down the road could not under any circumstances have been Edward, but at least it relieved her from the suspicion that the street was uninhabited. When the heavily-treading man slowed down at number 42, she couldn't believe her luck. He had been out and was coming in, although the way he walked suggested that going out had not been a great success, and that not much awaited him at home.

As he stopped and took out two keys tied together, neither of them a car key, Nenna faced him boldly.

'Excuse me, I should like you to let me in.'

'May I ask who you are?'

The 'may I ask' disconcerted her.

'I'm *Grace*. I mean, I'm Nenna.'

'You don't seem very sure.'

'I am Nenna James.'

'Mrs Edward James?'

'Yes. Does Edward James live here?'

'Well, in a way.' He dangled the keys from hand to hand. 'You don't look at all how I expected.'

Nenna felt rebuked.

'How old are you?'

'I'm thirty-two.'

'I should have thought you were twenty-seven or twenty-eight at most.'

He stood ruminating. She tried not to feel impatient.

'Did Edward say what I looked like, then?'

'No.'

'What *has* he been saying?'

'As a matter of fact, I very rarely speak to him.'

Nenna looked at him more closely, trying to assess him as an ally. The cuffs of his raincoat had been neatly turned. Somebody must be doing his mending for him, as she was doing Willis's, and the idea gave her a stab of pain which she couldn't relate to her other feelings. She stared up at his broad face.

'We can't stand here all night on the pavement like this,' he said, still with the two keys in his hand.

'Then hadn't you better let me in?'

'I don't know that that would be quite the right thing to do.'

'Why not?'

'Well, you might turn out to be a nuisance to Edward.'

She mustn't irritate him.

'In what way?'

'Well, I didn't care for the way you were standing there ringing the bell. Anyway, he's out.'

'How can you tell? You're only just coming in yourself. Do you live here?'

'Well, in a way.'

He examined her more closely. 'Your hair is quite pretty.'

It had begun to rain slightly. There seemed no reason why they should not stand here for ever.

'As a matter of fact,' he said, 'I do remember you. My name is Hodge. Gordon Hodge.'

Nenna shook her head. 'I can't help that.'

'I have met you several times with Edward.'

'And was I a nuisance then?'

'This isn't my house, you see. It belongs to my mother. My mother is taking your husband in, at considerable inconvenience, as a kind of paying guest.'

'He's the lodger?'

'She only agreed to it because I used to know him at school.'

Abyss after abyss of respectability was opening beneath her. How could Edward be living in a house belonging to somebody's mother, and, above all, Gordon Hodge's mother?

'Why do you very rarely speak to him?'

'We're just living here quietly, with my mother, two quiet chaps working things out for ourselves.'

A wave of cold discouragement closed over her. The disagreement about where they were to live had come to seem the only obstacle. But perhaps Edward was altogether better without her. Perhaps he knew that. He must have heard her at the door.

'Well,' said Gordon, 'you'd better come inside, I suppose.' Once the key was in the lock, he pushed forward with both hands, one on the front door, one on Nenna's back, so that in the end she was propelled into no. 42. Gordon's mother had an umbrella stand and a set of Chinese temple bells in her hall.

'Carry on up.' They passed two landings, Gordon following her with majestic tread, but faster than one might expect, since although he had lost time in hanging up his raincoat in the hall, he reached the door first, and opened it without any kind of announcement, and Edward was standing, with his back to them at first, thinner and smaller than she remembered, but then she always made the mistake when she hadn't seen him for a bit – he turned round, protesting, and it was Edward.

Who else, after all, could it have been? But in her relief Nenna forgot the quiet reasonable remarks which she had rehearsed at the bus stops, and in the buses, all the way to Stoke Newington.

'Darling, darling.'

Edward looked at her with grey eyes like Tilda's, but without much expectation from life.

'Darling, aren't you surprised?'

'Not very. I've been listening to you ringing the bell.'

'How did you know it was me?'

'Nenna. Have you come all this way, after all this time, to try to get me to live on that boat?'

Nenna had forgotten about Gordon, or rather she assumed that he must have gone away, but he had not. To her amazement, he was still planted just behind her.

'Edward, Nenna. You two seem to be having a bit of a difference of opinion. Yes, let's face it, you're in dispute. And in these matters it's often helpful to have a third party present. That's how these marriage counsellors make their money, you know.'

This must have been a joke, as he laughed, or perhaps any mention of marriage was a joke to Gordon, who walked past Nenna and settled himself between them in a small chair, actually a nursing chair, surviving from some earlier larger family home and much too low for him, so that he had to try crossing his legs in several positions. He creaked, as he settled, as a boat creaks. Had he really been at the same school as Edward? His feet were now stuck out in front of him and Nenna could read the word EXCELLA on the soles of each of his new shoes.

'Get out!'

Gordon sat quite still for a few seconds, then uncrossed his legs and went out of the room, a room in his own house, or rather his mother's. Because it was theirs, he knew how to shut the door, although it did not fit very well, without any irritating noise.

'You've always known how to get rid of my friends,' Edward muttered.

Nenna was no more able to deny this than any other woman.

'He's hateful!'

'Gordon's all right.'

'We can't talk while he's around.'

'His mother has been very good to me.'

'That's ridiculous! To be in a position where you have to say that someone's mother has been very good to you – that's ridiculous! Isn't it?'

'Yes.'

'Where did you meet these Hodges anyway? I never remember you ever talking about them.'

'I had to go somewhere,' Edward said.

They had plenty of time, and yet she felt that there was almost none.

'Eddie, I'll tell you what I came to say. Why won't you come over to us for a week, or even for a night?'

'That boat! It's not for me to come to you, it's for you to get rid of it. I'm not quarrelling with you about the money. If you don't want to sell it, why can't you rent it out?'

'I don't know that I can, right away.'

'Why, what's wrong with it?'

'She's a thought damp. It would be easier in the spring.'

'Didn't I see something in the paper about one of them sinking? I don't even know if they're safe for the children!'

'Some of them are beautiful. *Lord Jim*, for instance, inside she's really better than a house.'

'Who lives on *Lord Jim*?' Edward asked with the discernment of pure jealousy, the true lover's art which Nenna was too distraught to recognise.

'I don't know, I don't care. Well, the Blakes do. Richard and Laura Blake.'

'Have they got money?'

'I suppose so.'

'They live on a boat because they think it's smart.'

'Laura doesn't.'

'What's this Richard Blake like?'

'I don't know. He was in the Navy, I think, in the war, or the RNVR.'

'Don't you know the difference?'

'Not exactly, Eddie.'

'I bet he does.'

Things were going as badly as they could. From the room immediately beneath them, somebody began to play the piano, a Chopin nocturne, with heavy emphasis, but the piano was by no means suitable for Chopin and the sound travelled upwards as a hellish tingling of protesting strings.

'Eddie, is this the only room you've got?'

'I don't see anything wrong with it.'

She noticed now that there was a kind of cupboard in the corner which was likely to contain a washbasin, and a single bed, tucked in with a plaid rug. Surely they'd do better making love on board *Grace* than on a few yards of Mackenzie tartan?

'You can't expect us to come here?'

It must be Gordon playing downstairs. There were pauses, then he banged the keys plaintively, going over the passages he hadn't been able to get right, then suddenly he put on a record of the Chopin and played along with it, always two or three notes behind.

'Eddie, what do you want? Why are you here? Why?'

He replied reluctantly, 'My job's up here.'

'I don't even know what you do. Strang Graphics! What are they?'

They were both still standing up, facing each other, at about the same height.

'Strang is an advertising firm. It's small, that's why it's up here, where the rents are low. They hope to expand later, then

they'll move. I'm not going to pretend anything about my job.
It's clerical.'

Edward's references from the construction firm when he left
Panama had not been very good. Nenna knew that, but she was
sure it couldn't have been Edward's fault, and at the moment
she couldn't be bothered with it.

'You don't have to stay there! There's plenty of jobs! Anyone
can get a job anywhere!'

'I can't.'

He turned his head away, and as the light caught his face at
a certain angle Nenna realised in terror that he was right and
that he would never get anywhere. The terror, however, was
not for herself or for the children but for Edward, who might
realise that what he was saying was true. She forgot whatever
she had meant to tell him, went up close and took him tenderly
by both ears.

'Shut up, Eddie.'

'Nenna, I'm glad you came.'

'You are?'

'Curious, I didn't mean to say that.'

She clung to him hard, she loved him and could never
leave him. They were down on the floor, and one side of
her face was scorched by Gordon's mother's horrible gas fire,
in front of which there was a bowl of tepid water. He stroked
her face, with its one bright red cheek, one pale.

'You look as ugly as sin.'

'Wonderful.'

There was a tapping, just audible above the piano. 'Excuse
me, Mrs James, I'm Gordon's mother, I thought I'd just look
in, as I haven't had the pleasure of meeting you.'

Nenna got to her feet, trying to pull down her jersey.

'I hope you don't find the gas fire too high,' said Mrs Hodge,
'it's easily lowered. You just turn the key down there on the
right-hand side.'

Not receiving any response, she added, 'And I hope
the music doesn't disturb you. Gordon is something of a
pianist.'

'No, he isn't,' said Nenna.

The mother's face crumpled up and withered, then corrected itself to the expression of one who is in the right. She withdrew. Nenna was ashamed, but she couldn't make amends, not now. In the morning she would beg sincerely for forgiveness, less sincerely praise Gordon as a pianist, offer to help pay to have the piano seen to.

Then she looked at Edward and saw that he was furious. 'You've only come here to hurt these people.'

'I didn't. I never knew they existed. Forgive!'

'It's not a matter of forgiveness, it's a matter of common politeness.'

They were quarrelling, but at first they were not much better at it than Gordon was at Chopin.

'I want you, Eddie, that's the one and only thing I came about. I want you every moment of the day and night and every time I try to fold up a map.'

'You're raving, Nenna.'

'Please give.'

'Give you what? You're always saying that. I don't know what meaning you attach to it.'

'Give anything.'

She didn't know why she wanted this so much, either. Not presents, not for themselves, it was the sensation of being given to, she was homesick for that.

And now the quarrel was under its own impetus, and once again a trial seemed to be in progress, with both of them as accusers, but both figuring also as investigators of the lowest description, wretched hirelings, turning over the stones to find where the filth lay buried. The squash racquets, the Pope's pronouncements, whose fault it had been their first night together, an afternoon really, but not much good in either case, the squash racquets again, the money spent on *Grace*. And the marriage that was being described was different from the one they had known, indeed bore almost no resemblance to it, and there was no one to tell them this.

'You don't want me,' Edward repeated. 'If you did, you'd have been with me all this time. All you've ever cared about is being approved of, like a little girl at a party.'

He must have forgotten what Tilda's like, she thought, and she felt frightened. But Edward went on to tell her that she didn't really care for the children, she only liked to think she did, to make herself feel good.

So far neither of them had raised their voices, or only enough to be heard above Gordon's din. But when she made a last appeal, and told him, though feeling it was not quite true, that Martha had asked her to bring her father back, and then, very unwisely, referred again to Mrs Hodge, and the house, and the single bed, and even the temple bells, and asked him why he didn't come to his senses and whether he didn't think he'd be happier living with a woman, whether she was on a boat or not, he turned on her, upsetting the bowl of water in front of the gas fire, and shouted:

'You're not a woman!'

Nenna was outside in the street. In leaving the room, swelling for the first time with tears, she had collided awkwardly with Gordon's mother, who supposed she could stand where she liked in her own house, and even if Edward had called after her, she would not have been able to hear him. She walked away down Milvain Street as fast as it was possible for her feet to hit the ground. The fish and chip shop was still lighted and open. She had expected to spend that night with Edward and wake up beside him, the left-hand side, that had become a habit and it was a mistake, no doubt, to allow marriage to become a matter of habit, but that didn't prove that she was not a woman.

She walked down street after street, always turning to the right, and pulled herself up among buses, and near a railway bridge. Seven Sisters Road. It was late, the station was shut. Her hands were empty. She realised now for the first time that she had left her purse behind in Edward's room. That meant that she had no money, and the all-day bus ticket was of course also in the purse.

Nenna set out to walk. A mile and a half down Green Lanes, half a mile down Nassington Green Road, one and a half miles the wrong way down Balls Pond Road, two miles down Kingsland Road, and then she was lost. As is usual in such cases her body trudged on obstinately, knowing that one foot hurt rather more than the other, but deciding not to admit this until some sort of objective was reached, while her mind, rejecting the situation in time and space, became disjointed and childish. It came to her that it was wrong to pray for anything simply because you felt you needed it personally. Prayer should be beyond self, and so Nenna repeated a Hail Mary for everyone in the world who was lost in Kingsland Road without their bus fares. She had also been taught, when in difficulty, to think of a good life to imitate. Nenna thought of Tilda, who would certainly have got onto a late-night bus and ridden without paying the fare, or even have borrowed money from the conductor. Richard would never have left anything behind anywhere, or, if he had, he would have gone back for it. Louise would not have made an unsuccessful marriage in the first place, and she supposed her marriage must be unsuccessful, because Edward had told her that she was not a woman.

Nenna had no more than an animal's sense of direction and distance, but it seemed to her that the right thing to do would be to try to reach the City, then, once she got to Blackfriars, she knew where the river was, and though that would be Lambeth Reach or King's Reach, a long way downstream of the boats, still, once she had got to the river she would be on the way home. She had worked in an office in Blackfriars once, before Tilda came.

That meant turning south, and she would have to ask which way she was headed. She began to look, with a somewhat dull kind of hopefulness, for somebody friendly, not too much in a hurry, walking the opposite way, although it would be more reasonable, really, to ask somebody walking the same way. Handfuls of sleet were beginning to wander through the air. Radio shop, bicycle shop, family planning shop, funeral parlour, bicycles, radio spare parts, television hire, herbalist, family planning, a florist. The window of the florist was still lit and entirely occupied by a funeral tribute, a football goal, carried out in white chrysanthemums. The red ball had just been introduced into soccer and there was a ball in the goal, this time in red chrysanthemums. Nenna stood looking into the window, feeling the melted hail make its way down the gap between the collar of her coat and her body. One shoe seemed to be wetter than the other and the strap was working loose, so, leaning against the ledge of the shop window, she took it off to have a look at it. This made her left foot very cold, so she twisted it round her right ankle. Someone was coming, and she felt that she couldn't bear it if he, because it was a man, said, 'Having trouble with your shoe?' For an unbalanced moment she thought it might be Gordon Hodge, pursuing her to see that she would not come back, and make a nuisance of herself to Edward.

The man stood very close to her, pretended to look in the window, advanced with a curious sideways movement and said –

'Like flowers?'

'Not at the moment.'

'Fixed up for the night?'

Nenna did not answer. She was saddened by the number of times the man must have asked this question. He smelled of loneliness. Well, they always moved off in the end, though they often stayed a while, as this one did, whistling through their teeth, like standup comics about to risk another joke.

He snatched the shoe out of her hand and hurled it violently away from her into the Kingsland Road.

'What you going to do now?'

Nenna shook off her other shoe and began half walking and half running as fast as she could, not looking behind her, Laburnum Street, Whiston Street, Hows Street, Pearson Street, a group at the end of Cremers Street who stood laughing, probably at her. One foot seemed to be bleeding. I expect they think I've been drinking.

Where the Hackney Road joins Kingsland Road a taxi drew up beside her.

'You're out late.'

'I don't know what the time is.'

'A bit late for paddling. Where are you going?'

'To the river.'

'Why?'

'Why not?'

'People jump in sometimes.'

Nenna told him, without much expecting to be believed, that she lived on Battersea Reach. The driver twisted his arm backwards to open the door.

'You'd like a lift, wouldn't you?'

'I haven't any money.'

'Who said anything about money?'

She got into the warm interior of the taxi, reeking of tobacco and ancient loves, and fell asleep at once. The taxi-man drove first to Old Street, where there was a garage open all night for the trade, and bought a tankful of petrol. Then he turned through the locked and silent City and towards the Strand, where the air first begins to feel damp, blowing up the side streets with the dawn wind off the river.

'We can go round by Arthur's in Covent Garden and get a sandwich, if you want,' he said. 'That won't break the bank.'

Then he saw that his fare was asleep. He stopped and had a cup of tea himself, and explained to the Covent Garden porters, who wanted to know what he'd got in the back, that it was the Sleeping Beauty.

The taxi drew up opposite the Battersea Bridge end of the boats. Only the driver's expression showed what he thought of the idea of living in a place like that. But it might suit some people. Carefully, as one who was used to such endings, he woke Nenna up.

'You're home, dear.'

The he made a U turn and drove away so rapidly that she could not make out his number, only the red tail light diminishing, at more than legal speed, down the deserted Embankment. She was, therefore, never able to thank him. Although it must be three or four in the morning, there were still lights showing on *Lord Jim*. Richard was standing on the afterdeck, wearing a Naval duffle coat, Arctic issue.

'What are you doing, Nenna, where are your shoes?'

'What are you doing, Richard, standing there in your greatcoat?'

Neither of them was speaking sensibly.

'My wife's left me.'

She must have done, Nenna thought, or he wouldn't call Laura 'my wife'.

'Surely she's only gone to stay with her family. You told me so.'

Although it was very unlikely that they could be disturbing anyone they both spoke almost in whispers, and Nenna's last remark, which scarcely deserved an answer, was lost in the air, drowned by the wash of high tide.

'I haven't liked to say anything about it, but you must have noticed, that evening you stayed to have a drink with us, that my wife wasn't quite herself.'

'I thought she was,' said Nenna.

Richard was startled. 'Don't you like her?'

'I can't tell. I should have to meet her somewhere else.'

'You probably think I'm an obstinate swine to make her live here on *Lord Jim*. I couldn't really believe she wouldn't like it. I'm afraid my mind doesn't move very fast, not as fast as some people's. I wanted to get her right away from her family, they're a disrupting factor, I don't mind telling you.'

'Do they play the piano?' Nenna asked. She could no longer feel her feet, but, glancing down at them, not too obviously for fear Richard should feel that he ought to do something about them, she saw that both of them were now bleeding. A hint of some religious association disturbed her. In the convent passage the Sacred Heart looked down in reproach. And suppose she had left marks on the floor of the taxi?

'Of course I wouldn't have suggested taking her to live anywhere that was below standard. I had a very good man in to see to the heating and lighting, and the whole conversion was done professionally. But I suppose that wasn't really the point. The question really was, did being alone with me on a boat seem like a good idea or not?'

'She'll come back, Richard.'

'That won't alter the fact that she went away.'

Richard evidently felt that memory must keep to its place, otherwise how could it be measured accurately?

'Nenna, you've hurt your foot!'

Overwhelmed by not having noticed this earlier, by his failure of politeness, observation and helpfulness, all that had been taught him from boyhood up, Richard proceeded at the double onto the Embankment, to escort her onto *Lord Jim*.

'They're all right, honestly, Richard. It's only a scrape.' That was the children's word. 'Just lend me a handkerchief.'

Richard was the kind of man who has two clean handkerchiefs on him at half-past three in the morning. From the hold, where everything had its proper place, he fetched a bottle of TCP and a pair of half-wellingtons. The boots looked very much too big, but she appreciated that he wouldn't have liked to lend a pair of Laura's. Or perhaps Laura had taken all her things with her.

'Your feet are rather small, Nenna.'

Richard liked things to be the right size.

'Smaller than standard, I think.' He seated her firmly on one of the lights, and, without mistake or apology, put each of her feet into one of the clean boots. Each foot in turn felt the warmth of his hands and relaxed like an animal who trusts the vet.

'I don't know why you're wandering about here in the dark anyway. Nenna, have you been to a party?'

'Do you really think I go to parties where everyone leaves their shoes behind?'

'Well, I don't know. You lead a bit of a Bohemian existence, I mean, a lot more Bohemian than I do. I mean, I know various people in Chelsea, but they don't seem very different from anyone else.'

'I've come from a bit farther than Chelsea tonight,' Nenna said.

'Please don't think I'm being inquisitive. You mustn't think I'm trying to find out about your private affairs.'

'Richard, how old are you?'

'I was born on June 2nd 1922. That made me just seventeen when the war broke out.' Richard only estimated his age in relationship to his duties.

Nenna sat moving her feet about inside the spacious wellingtons. It was the river's most elusive hour, when darkness lifts off darkness, and from one minute to another the shadows declare themselves as houses or as craft at anchor. There was a light wind from the north-west.

'Nenna, would you like to come out in the dinghy?'

Too tired to be surprised by anything, Nenna looked at the davits and saw that the dinghy must have been lowered away already. If everything hadn't been quite in order he wouldn't, of course, have asked her.

'We can go up under Wandsworth Bridge as far as the Fina Oil Depot and then switch off and drift down with the tide.'

'Were you going to go anyway?' asked Nenna. The question seemed of great importance to her.

'No, I was hoping someone might come along and keep me company.'

'You mean you'd left it to chance?' Nenna couldn't believe this.

'I was hoping that you might come.'

Well, thought Nenna.

They had to go down the rope side-ladder, Richard first. Her feet hurt a good deal, and she thought, though not wishing to be ungrateful, that she might have done better without the boots. However, she managed to step in amidships without rocking *Lord Jim*'s dinghy by an inch.

'Cast off, Nenna.'

She was back for a moment on Bras d'Or, casting off, coiling the painter up neatly, approved of by her father, and by Louise.

It had been a test, then, she remembered, of a day's success if the outboard started up first time. Richard's Johnson, obedient to the pressed button, came to life at once, and she saw that it had never occurred to him that it mightn't. Small boats develop emotions to a fine pitch, and she felt that she would go with him to the end of the world, if his outboard was always going to start like that. And indeed, reality seemed to have lost its accustomed hold, just as the day wavered uncertainly between night and morning.

'I've been wanting to tell you, Nenna, that I very much doubt whether you're strong enough to undertake all the work you do on *Grace*. And some of the things you do seem to me to be inefficient, and consequently rather a waste of energy. For example, I saw you on deck the other morning struggling to open the lights from the outside, but of course all your storm fastenings must be on the inside.'

'We haven't got any storm fastenings. The lights are kept down with a couple of bricks. They work perfectly well.' Now she felt furious. 'Surely you don't watch me from *Lord Jim*.'

Richard considered this carefully.

'I suppose I do.'

She had been unjust. She knew that he was good, and kept an eye on everybody, and on the whole Reach.

'I shouldn't be any happier, you know, if everything on *Grace* worked perfectly.'

He looked at her in amazement.

'What has happiness got to do with it?'

The dinghy followed the left bank, passing close to the entrance to Chelsea creek. They scanned the misty water, keeping a watch-out for driftwood which might foul up the engine.

'Do you talk a great deal to Maurice?' Richard asked.

'All day and half the night, sometimes.'

'What on earth do you talk about?'

'Sex, jealousy, friendship and music, and about the boats sometimes, the right way to prime the pump, and things like that.'

'What kind of pump have you got?'

'I don't know, but it's the same as Maurice's.'

'I could show you how to prime it any time you like.' But he was not satisfied. 'When you've finished saying all that you want to say about these things, though, do you feel that you've come to any definite conclusion?'

'No.'

'So that, in the end, you've nothing definite to show for it?'

'About jealousy and music? How could we?'

'I suppose Maurice is very musical?'

'He's got a nice voice and he can play anything by ear. I've heard him play Liszt's Campanello with teaspoons, without leaving out a single note. That wasn't music, but we had a good time . . . and then, I don't know, we do talk about other things, particularly I suppose the kind of fixes we're both in.'

She stopped, aware that it wouldn't be advisable for Richard to know about Harry's visits. The crisis of conscience and duty would be too painful. Yet she would have very much liked to keep nothing back from him.

'That leads up to what I've really often wanted to ask you,' Richard went on. 'It seems to me you find it quite easy to put your feelings into words.'

'Yes.'

'And Maurice?'

'Yes.'

'I don't. I'm amazed at the amount people talk, actually. I can't for the life of me see why, if you really feel something, it's got to be talked about. In fact, I should have thought it lost something, if you follow me, if you put it into words.'

Richard looked anxious, and Nenna saw that he really thought that he was becoming difficult to understand.

'Well,' she said, 'Maurice and I are talkative by nature. We talk about whatever interests us perhaps for the same reason that Willis draws it and paints it.'

'That's not the same thing at all. I like Willis's drawings. I've bought one or two of them, and I think they'll keep up their value pretty well.'

Beyond Battersea Bridge the light, between grey and silver, cast shadows which began to follow the lighters, slowly moving round at moorings.

At a certain point, evidently prearranged, for he didn't consult Nenna and hardly glanced at the banks, Richard put about, switched off the engine and hauled it on board. Once he had fitted in the rudder to keep the dinghy straight against the set of the tide he returned to the subject. A lifetime would not be too long, if only he could grasp it exactly.

'Let's say that matters hadn't gone quite right with you, I mean personal matters, would you be able to find words to say exactly what was wrong?'

'I'm afraid so, yes I would.'

'That might be useful, of course.'

'Like manufacturers' instructions. In case of failure, try words.'

Richard ignored this because it didn't seem to him quite to the point. On the whole, he disliked comparisons, because they made you think about more than one thing at a time. He calculated the drift. Satisfied that it would bring them exactly down to the point he wanted on the starboard side of *Lord Jim*, he asked –

'How do you feel about your husband?'

The shock Nenna felt was as great as if he had made a mistake with the steering. If Richard was not at home with words, still less was he at home with questions of a personal nature. He might as well capsize the dinghy and be done with it. But he waited, watching her gravely.

'Aren't you able to explain?'

'Yes, I am. I can explain very easily. I don't love him any more.'

'Is that true?'

'No.'

'You're not making yourself clear, Nenna.'

'I mean that I don't hate him any more. That must be the same thing.'

'How long have you felt like this?'

'For about three hours.'

'But surely you haven't seen him lately?'

'I have.'

'You mean tonight? What happened?'

'I insulted his friend, and also his friend's mother. He gave me his opinion about that.'

'What did your husband say?'

'He said that I wasn't a woman. That was absurd, wasn't it?'

'I should imagine so, yes. Demonstrably, yes.' He tried again. 'In any ordinary sense of the word, yes.'

'I only want the ordinary sense of the word.'

'And how would you describe the way you feel about him now?' Richard asked.

'Well, I feel unemployed. There's nothing so lonely as unemployment, even if you're on a queue with a thousand others. I don't know what I'm going to think about if I'm not going to worry about him all the time. I don't know what I'm going to do with my mind.' A formless melancholy overcame her. 'I'm not too sure what to do with my body either.'

It was a reckless indulgence in self-pity. Richard looked steadily at her.

'You know, I once told Laura that I wouldn't like to be left alone with you for any length of time.'

'Why did you?'

'I don't know. I can't remember what reason I gave. It must have been an exceptionally stupid one.'

'Richard, why do you have such a low opinion of yourself?'

'I don't think that I have. I try to make a just estimate of myself, as I do of everyone else, really. It's difficult. I've a long way to go when it comes to these explanations. But I understood perfectly well what you said about feeling unemployed.'

They were up to *Lord Jim*. With only the faintest possible graze of the fender, the dinghy drifted against her.

'Where shall I tie up?'

'You can make fast to the ladder, but give her plenty of rope, or she'll be standing on end when the tide goes down.'

Nenna knew this perfectly well, but she felt deeply at peace.

As Richard stood up in the boat, he could be seen to hesitate, not about what he wanted to do, but about procedures. He had to do the right thing. A captain goes last onto his ship, but a man goes first into a tricky situation. Nenna saw that the point had come, perhaps exactly as she tied up, when he was more at a loss than she was. Their sense of control wavered, ebbed, and changed places. She kicked off the wellingtons, which was easy enough, and began to go up the ladder.

'Is the hatch open?' she asked, thinking he would be more at ease if she said something entirely practical. On the other hand, it was a waste of words. The hatch on *Lord Jim* was always locked, but Richard never forgot the key.

9

NENNA'S CHILDREN neither showed any interest in where she had been nor in why she did not come back until next morning. Back again on *Grace*, Tilda was messing about at the foot of the mast with a black and yellow flag, one of the very few they had.

'We haven't much line either,' she said. 'I shall have to fly it from the stays.'

'What's it mean, Tilda dear?'

'This is L, *I have something important to communicate*. It was for you, Ma, in case you were out when we got back.'

'Where were you going, then?'

'We're going to take him out and show him round.'

'Who?'

'Heinrich.'

Martha came up the companion, followed by a boy very much taller than she was. Nenna was struck by the difference in her elder daughter since she had seen her last. Her hair was out of its fair pony tail and curled gracefully, with a life of its own, over her one and only Elvis shirt.

'Ma, this is Heinrich. He was sixteen three weeks ago. You don't know who he is.'

'I do know. Aunt Louise told me, but there was some kind of confusion in that she told me that he was due last Friday.'

'The date was altered, Mrs James,' Heinrich explained. 'I was delayed to some extent because the address given to me was 626 Cheyne Walk, which I could not find, but eventually the river police directed me.'

'Well, in any case I'd like to welcome you on board, Heinrich, hullo.'

'Mrs James. Heinrich von Furstenfeld.'

Heinrich was exceptionally elegant. An upbringing designed to carry him through changes of regime and frontier, possible

99

loss of every worldly possession, and, in the event of crisis, protracted stays with distant relatives ensconced wherever the aristocracy was tolerated, from the Polish border to Hyde Park Gate, in short, a good European background, had made him totally self-contained and able with sunny smile and the formal handshake of the gymnase to set almost anybody at their ease, even the flustered Nenna.

'I hope Martha has shown you where to put your things.'

Martha looked at her impatiently.

'There's no need for him to unpack much, he's got to go to the airport tomorrow. He arrived here very late, and they had to find a bunk for him on *Rochester*. Willis was much more cheerful and said it reminded him of a boarding-house in the old days.'

'I must go and explain to Mrs Woodie.'

'Oh, it's quite unnecessary. And I've shown Heinrich all round *Grace*. He understands that he can only go to the heads on a falling tide.'

'I am not so very used to calculating the tides, Mrs James,' said Heinrich in a pleasant conversational tone. 'The Danube, close to where I live, is not tidal, so that I shall have to rely for this information upon your charming daughters.'

'What's your house like in Vienna?' Tilda asked.

'Oh, it's a flat in the Franciskanerplatz, quite in the centre of things.'

'What kind of things are you used to doing in Vienna?' said Nenna. 'If you've only got one day in London, we shall have to see what we can arrange.'

'Oh, Vienna is an old city – I mean, everybody remarks on how many old people live there. So that although my native place is so beautiful, I am very much looking forward to seeing Swinging London.'

'Heinrich has to stand here on the deck while you drone on,' said Tilda. 'He ought to be given a cup of coffee immediately.'

'Oh, hasn't he had breakfast?'

'Ma, where are your shoes?' asked Martha, drawing her mother aside and speaking in an urgent, almost tragic undertone. 'You look a mess. From Heinrich's point of view, you hardly look like a mother at all.'

'I don't know what his mother's like. I know his father's an old business acquaintance of Auntie Louise and Uncle Joel.'

'His mother is a Countess.'

Tilda had taken Heinrich below, and put a saucepan of milk on the gas for his coffee. To his dying day the young Count would not forget the fair hand which had tended him when none other had heeded his plight.

'Why is your mother barefoot?' Heinrich asked. 'But I won't press the query if it is embarrassing. Perhaps she is Swinging.'

'Oh, you'll get used to her.'

A diplomat by instinct, Heinrich considered which of his twenty or thirty smaller European cousins Tilda most resembled. The Swiss lot, probably. His tone became caressing and teasing.

'I shall have to take you back with me to Vienna, dear Tilda, yes, I'm sorry, I shan't be able to manage without you, fortunately you're so small they won't miss you here and I can take you for a Glücksbringer.'

Here he went astray, for Tilda did not at all like being so small. 'Get outside this,' she said, slamming the tin mug of coffee in front of him, and sawing away energetically at the loaf.

With a faint smile the young Count turned to thank his saviour, while some colour stole back into his pale cheeks.

On deck, Martha and Nenna had been joined by Maurice, who had decided to consider himself on holiday, and had not been to the pub for several nights.

'Who's the boyfriend?' he asked Martha.

'He is the son of the friend of my aunt.'

'Have it your own way. Pretty face, at all events.'

'Maurice,' said Martha. 'Help me. I'm trying to get my mother to dress and behave properly.'

It was just ten minutes to nine, and Richard walked by on his way up to World's End to catch a bus to the office. Nenna thought, if he doesn't look my way I'll never speak to him

again, and in fact I'll never speak to any man again, except
Maurice. But as he drew level with *Grace* Richard gave her a
smile which melted her heart, and waved to her in a way
entirely peculiar to himself, halfway between a naval salute
and a discreet gesture with the rolled umbrella.

Maurice folded his arms. 'Congratulations, Nenna.'

'Oh, don't say that.'

'Why not?'

'God made you too quick-witted. I don't know what's
happening to me exactly.'

'Weak-mindedness.'

'Self-reproach, really.'

'What's that, dear?'

Martha left them, and went down the companion. Armed at
all points against the possible disappointments of her life, conscious of the responsibilities of protecting her mother and sister,
worried at the gaps in her education, anxious about nuns and
antique dealers, she had forgotten for some time the necessity
for personal happiness. Heinrich at first seemed strange to her.

The three children sat round the table and discussed how
they were to spend the day. Tilda, unwatched by the other two,
shook out the packets of cereal, at the bottom of which small
plastic tanks, machine-guns and images of Elvis had been
concealed by the manufacturers. When she had found the
tokens she shovelled back the mingled wheat and rye, regard-
less, into the containers.

'You have no father, then, it seems, Martha,' Heinrich said
quietly.

'He's left us.'

This was no surprise to Heinrich. 'My father, also, is often
absent at our various estates.'

'You're archaic,' said Martha. Heinrich, while continuing to
eat heartily, took her hand.

'I really came to bring you a telegram,' Maurice said. 'I fetched
it from the boatyard office.'

'Did you, well, thank you, Maurice. I seemed to have missed some mail lately, my sister kept asking me whether I hadn't received her letters.'

'They have to take their chance with wind and tide, my dear, like all of us.'

The telegram was from Louise. They'd arrived in London. They were at the Carteret Hotel and Nenna was to call her there as soon as possible.

'Hullo, can I speak with Mrs Swanson? Hullo, is that Mr Swanson's room? Louise, it's Nenna.'

'Nenna, I was just about to ring you on that number I called before, from Frankfurt.'

'I'd as soon you didn't ring there, Louise.'

'Why, is there anything wrong?'

'Not exactly.'

'Is Edward with you, Nenna?'

'No.'

'That's what I anticipated. We want you to come and have lunch with us, dear.'

'Look, Louise, why don't I come over and see you both right away?'

'Lunch will be more convenient, dear, but after that we've put the whole of the rest of the day aside to have a thorough discussion of your problems. There seems to be so much to be settled. Joel is of one mind with me about this. I mean of course about yourself and the little girls, the possibility of your returning to Halifax.'

'It's the first time you've ever even mentioned this, Louise.'

'But I've been thinking about it, Nenna, and praying. Joel isn't a Catholic, as you know, but he's told me that he believes there's a Providence not so far away from us, really just above our heads if we could see it, that wants things to be the way they're eventually going. Now that idea appeals to me.'

'Listen, Louise, I went to see Edward yesterday.'

'I'm glad to hear it. Did he see reason?'

Nenna hesitated. 'I'm just as much to blame as he is and more. I can't leave him with nothing.'

'Where is he living?'

'With friends.'

'Well, he has friends, then.'

'Louise, you mustn't interfere.'

'Look, Nenna, we're not proposing anything so very sensational. I think we have to admit that you've tried and failed. And if we're offering you your passage home, you and the children, and help in finding your feet once you get there, and a good convent school for the girls, so that they can go straight on with the nuns and won't really notice any difference, well, all that's to be regarded as a loan, which we're very glad to offer you for an extended period, in the hopes of getting you back among caring people.'

'But there are people who care for me here too, Lou. I do wish you'd come and see *Grace*.'

'We must try and make time, dear. But you were always the one for boats – I'm always thankful to remember how happy that made Father, the way you shared his feeling for boats and water. Tell me about your neighbours. Do you ever go and visit any of them?'

'We haven't any money,' said Martha, 'so you'll have to share our limited notion of entertainment.'

'There is nothing to be ashamed of in being poor,' said Heinrich.

'Yes, there is,' Martha replied, with a firmness which she could hardly have inherited either from her father or her mother, 'but there's no reason why we shouldn't go and look at things. Looking is seeing, really. That's what we do most of the time. We can go this afternoon and look at the King's Road.'

'I should like to visit a boutique,' said Heinrich.

'Well, that will be best about five or six, when everybody leaves work. A lot of them don't open till then.'

Tilda had lost interest in what was being said and had gone to fetch Stripey, who was being pursued across *Maurice* by a rat. Maurice was constantly being advised by Woodie and Richard to grease his mooring-ropes, so that the rats could not get across them, but he always forgot to do so.

Later in the day they prepared for their expedition into Chelsea. 'And your mother?' enquired Heinrich.

'You're always asking about her!' Martha cried. 'What do you think of her?'

'She is a very attractive woman for her years. But on the Continent we appreciate the woman of thirty.'

'Well, she's gone to talk things over with Aunt Louise, who's also an attractive woman for her years, but a good bit older, and quite different. She lives in Nova Scotia, and she's wealthy and energetic.'

'What do they talk over?'

'I expect Ma's arranging to take us out to Canada. She hasn't said so, but I should think it's that.'

'Then I shall see you often. We have relations both in Canada and in the United States.'

Martha tried not to wish, as they set out, that they could leave Tilda behind. She hardly remembered ever feeling this before about her ragged younger sister.

Without the guidance of the nuns, Tilda seemed to have lost her last vestige of moral sense. Partisan Street, the first street on the way up from the boats, was, as has been said, considered a rough place – a row of decrepit two-up two-down brick houses, the refuge of crippled and deformed humanity. Whether they were poor because they were lame, or lame because they were poor, was perhaps a matter for sociologists, and a few years later, when their dwellings were swept away and replaced by council flats with rents much higher than they could afford, it must be assumed that they disappeared from the face of the earth. Tilda, who knew them all, loved to imitate them, and hobbled up Partisan Street alternately limping and shuffling, with distorted features.

'Your sister makes me laugh, but I don't think it's right to do so,' Heinrich said.

Martha pointed out that everybody in the street was laughing as well. 'They've asked her to come and do it at their Christmas Club,' she said. 'I wish I could still laugh like that.'

They turned into World's End, and opened the door into the peaceful garden where the faithful of the Moravian sect lie buried.

'They're buried standing, so that on Judgement Day they can rise straight upward.'

'Men and women together?'

'No, they're buried separately.'

Shutting the door in the wall, they walked on, Martha conscious, through every nerve in her body, of Heinrich's hand under her elbow. She asked him what was the first sentence he had ever learned in English.

'I am the shoemaker's father.'

'And French?'

'I don't remember when I learned French. It must have been at some time, because I can speak it now. I can also get along in Polish and Italian. But I don't know that I shall ever make much use of these languages.'

'Everything that you learn is useful. Didn't you know that everything you learn, and everything you suffer, will come in useful at some time in your life?'

'You got that from Mother Ignatius,' Tilda interrupted. 'Once, in the closing years of the last century, a poor woman earned her daily bread by working long hours at her treadle sewing machine. Work, work, ah it was all work I'm telling you in them days. Up and down, up and down, went that unwearying right foot of hers. And so by incessant excercise, her right foot grew larger and broader, while the other remained the same size, and at length she feared to go out in the streets at all, for fear of tripping and falling flat. Yet that woman, for all her tribulations, had faith in the intercessions of our Lady.'

'Tilda,' said Martha, stopping suddenly and taking her sister by the shoulders, 'I'll give you anything you like, within reason, to go back to the boats and stay there.'

Between the sisters there was love of a singularly pure kind, proof against many trials. Martha's look of request, or appeal, between her shadowing lashes, was one that Tilda would not disregard. Her protests were formal only.

'There's a lot more of that sewing-machine story.'

'I know there is.'

'I shall be all by myself. Ma's gone into London.'

'You must go to *Rochester*.'

'I've just been there.'

'Mrs Woodie told me she never finds the little ones a worry.'

'Perhaps she wishes she hadn't said that.'

'Willis will be there.'

Tilda alternately nodded her head and shook it violently from side to side. This meant consent.

'You must promise and vow to go straight to *Rochester*,' Martha told her. 'You must swear by the Sacred Heart. You know you like it there. You don't like it in the King's Road, because they won't let you into the boutiques, and you're too young to try on the dresses.'

Tilda darted off, hopping and skipping.

In this, its heyday, the King's Road fluttered, like a gypsy encampment, with hastily-dyed finery, while stage folk emerged from their beds at a given hour, to patrol the long pavements between Sloane Square and the Town Hall. Heinrich and Martha went in and out of one boutique after another, Dressing Down, Wearwithal, Wearabouts, Virtuous Heroin, Legs, Rags, Bags. A paradise for children, a riot of misrule, the queer-looking shops reversed every fixed idea in the venerable history of commerce. Sellers, dressed in brilliant colours, outshone the purchasers, and, instead of welcoming them, either ignored them or were so rude that they could only have hoped to drive them away. The customers in return sneered at the clothing offered to them, and flung it on the ground. There were no prices, no sizes, no way to tell which stock was which, so that racks and rails of dresses were transferred as though by a magic hand from one shop to another. The doors stood open, breathing out incense and heavy soul, and the spirit was that of the market scene in the pantomine when the cast, encouraged by the audience, has let the business get out of hand.

Heinrich and Martha walked through this world, which was fated to last only a few years before the spell was broken, like a prince and princess. At Wearwithal, Heinrich tried on a pair of pale blue sateen trousers, which fitted tightly. Martha, guarding his jeans while he changed, admired him more for deciding against them than if he had bought them.

'Won't they do?' she asked.

'Such trousers are not worn on the Continent.'

'I thought perhaps you hadn't enough money.'

Heinrich in fact had plenty of money, and his own cheque-book, but his delicacy, responding to Martha's pride, prevented him from saying so.

'We will go to a coffee bar.'

These, too, were something new in London, if not in Vienna. The shining Gaggia dispensed one-and-a-half inches of bitter froth into an earthenware cup, and for two shillings lovers could sit for many hours in the dark brown shadows, with a bowl of brown sugar between them.

'Perhaps they'll be annoyed if we don't have another cup.'

Heinrich again put his fine, long-fingered hand over hers. She was amazed at its cleanliness. Her own hands were almost as black as Tilda's.

'You must not worry. I am in charge. How does that suit you?'

'I'm not sure. I'll tell you later,' said Martha, who wished one of her school friends would come in and see her. They'd tell Father Watson and the nuns, but what did that matter, they must know why she was absent from school anyway.

'I expect, living here in Chelsea, you go out a great deal.'

'How can I? I've no one to go out with.'

'I think you would like the cake-shops in Vienna, also the concerts. I should like to present you to my mother and great-aunts. They take subscription tickets every winter for all the concerts, the *Musikverein*, anything you can name. You're fond of music?'

'Of course,' said Martha impatiently. 'What music do your great-aunts like?'

'Mahler. Bruckner . . .'

'I hate that. I don't want to be made to feel all the time.'

Heinrich put his head on one side and half closed his eyes.

'You know, I think that you could be heading for a very serious depression.' Martha felt flattered. It seemed to her that she had never been taken seriously before.

'You mean I could break down altogether?'

'Listen, Martha, the best thing would be for you to tell me about your worries. They are probably those with which your catechism class does not help. The nuns will not understand the physiological causes of your restlessness and priests do not know everything either. Perhaps you would rather I did not speak like this.'

'It's all right, Heinrich, go on.'

'I, too, have many problems at school. About that you wouldn't understand very well, Martha. We are all of us youths between sixteen and eighteen years of age, and for month after month we are kept away from women. I, personally, have the number of days pasted up on the inside of my locker. All this can produce a kind of madness.'

'What do your teachers say?'

'The monks? Well, they comprehend, but they can't cover all our difficulties. A good friend of mine, in the same set for physics and chemistry, grew so disturbed that he took some scissors and cut all round the stiff white collars, which we have to wear on Sundays, and made them into little points.'

'Like a dog in a circus,' said Martha, appalled.

'He wanted to make himself grotesque. He has left school, but I received an air-letter from him recently. Now he is anxious to join the priesthood.'

'But are you happy there?'

Henrich smiled at her consolingly. 'I shall not allow sex to dominate my life, I shall find a place for it, that is all . . . But, my dear, we are here to talk about you.'

She could see that he meant it, and knew that there might never again be such an opportunity.

'There's a great deal of sin in me,' she began rapidly. 'I know that a great part of me is darkness, not light. I wish my father and mother lived together, but not because I care whether they're happy or not. I love Ma, but she must expect to be unhappy because she's reached that time of life. I want them to live together in some ordinary kind of house so that I can come and say, how can you expect me to live here! But I shall never lead a normal life because I'm so short – we're both short – that's why Tilda stands on the deck half the day, it's because somebody told her that you only grow taller while you're standing up. And then I don't develop. We had a class composition, My Best Friend, and the girl who was describing me put up her hand and asked to borrow a ruler because she said she'd have to draw me straight up and down.'

'That is not friendship,' said Heinrich.

'There might be something wrong with me. I might be permanently immature.'

'I am sure you aren't, my dear. Listen, you are like the blonde mistress of Heine, the poet Heine, *wenig Fleisch, sehr viel Gemüt*, little body, but so much spirit.' He leaned forward and kissed her cheek, which, from being cold when they entered the coffee bar, was now glowing pink. This was quite the right thing to do in a coffee bar in the King's Road. But afterwards they became, for the time being, rather more distant.

'It has been very pleasant to spend the day here, Martha, and to see your boat.'

'Yes, well, at least that's something you haven't got in Vienna.'

Heinrich's father was a member of the Wiener Yacht Club.

'Certainly, not such a large one.'

Outside the boutiques were still aglow with heaps of motley flung about the feet of the disdainful assistants. The music grew louder, the Chelsea Granada welcomed all who would like to come in and watch the transmission of *Bootsie and Snudge*. They wandered on together at random.

'Two people can become close in a very short time,' Heinrich said. 'It is up to them not to let circumstances get the better of them. It is my intention, as I think I told you, to shape my own life.'

Tilda had not gone straight onto *Rochester*. Aware of the not quite familiar atmosphere which had surrounded Martha and Heinrich and detached her sister, she felt, for the first time, somewhat adrift. Jumping defiantly onto *Grace*'s deck, she gathered up the surprised Stripey and hugged her close. Then she examined her more attentively.

'You've got kittens on you.'

Depositing the cat, who flattened out immediately into a gross slumber, she swarmed up the mast. Low tide. A tug passed, flying a white house flag with the red cross of St George, and with a funnel that might have been either cream or white.

'Thames Conservancy. She oughtn't to be as far downriver as this. What's she doing below Teddington?'

On *Maurice*, fifteen feet below her, Harry, in the owner's absence, was unusually busy. He was wiring up the main hatch above the hold, in such a way that showed he was certainly not an electrician by trade, with the intention of giving a mild electric shock to anyone who might try to get into it.

Tilda did not understand what he was doing, but she stared at him from the height of the mast until he became conscious of her, and turned round. He put down his pliers and looked up at her. His eyes were curious, showing an unusual amount of the whites.

'Want some sweeties?'

'No.'

'Want me to show you a comic?'

'No.'

'Come on, you can't read, can you?'

'I can.'

'You could get over here, couldn't you? You can come and sit on my knee if you like and I'll show you a comic.'

Tilda swung to and fro, supported by only one arm round the mast.

'Have you got *Cliff Richard Weekly*?'

'Oh, yes, I've got that.'

'And *Dandy*?'

'Yes, I've got that too.'

'This week's?'

'That's right.'

'I don't need showing.'

'You haven't seen the things I've got to show you.'

'What are they like?'

'Something you've never seen before, love.'

'You've no right on that boat,' Tilda remarked. 'She belongs to Maurice.'

'Know him, then?'

'Of course I do.'

'Know what he does for a living?'

'He goes out to work.'

'I'll show you what he does, if you like. You won't find that in a comic.'

Tilda persisted. 'Why are you putting up wires on *Maurice*?'

'Why? Well, I've got a lot of nice things in here.'

'Where did you get them from?'

'Don't you want to know what they are?'

'No, I want to know where you got them from.'

'Why?'

'Because you're a criminal.'

'Who told you that, you nasty little bitch?'

'You're a receiver of stolen goods,' Tilda replied.

She watched him sideways, her eyes alight and alive. After all, there were only two ways that Harry could come onto *Grace*, the gangplank across from *Maurice*, on which Stripey lay digesting uneasily, or back to the wharf and round by the afterdeck.

Harry bent down and with one hand lifted the gangplank so that it hung in mid-air. Stripey shot upwards, sprang, and missed her footing, falling spreadeagled on the foreshore.

'Your kitty's split open, my love.'

'No, she's not. She's been eating a seagull. If she was open you'd see all the feathers.'

Harry had a bottle in his hand.

'Are you going to get drunk?'

'The stuff in this bottle? Couldn't drink that. It would burn me if I did. It'd fucking well burn anybody.'

It was spirits of salt. He looked at her with the points of his eyes, the whites still rolling. The bottle was in his right hand and he swung it to and fro once or twice, apparently judging its weight. Then he moved towards the wharf, coming round to meet her on *Grace*.

Tilda clambered over the washboard, and clinging on by fingers and toes to the strakes, half slithered and half climbed down the side, gathered up the cat and skimmed across to *Rochester*. The side-ladder was out, as she very well knew.

'Oh, Mrs Woodie, will you look after me? Martha told me to come here. I came here straight away.'

'What's that you're carrying?' asked Mrs Woodie, resigned by now to almost anything.

'She's my pet, my pet, the only pet I've been allowed to have since I was a tiny kiddie.'

Mrs Woodie looked at the distended animal.

'Are you sure, dear, that she's not . . . '

'What do you mean, Mrs Woodie? I believe that there's an angel that guards her footsteps.'

The hold of *Rochester* had changed, in the last few weeks, from below decks to a cosy caravan interior. There was a good piece of reversible carpet put down, and Tilda seated herself, open-mouthed, in front of the television, where *Dr Kildare* flickered. Mrs Woodie began to cut sandwiches into neat squares. 'Where are you?' she called to her husband.

Woodie appeared, somewhat put out. 'I'll take a cup to Willis. He's still dwelling too much on the past, in my opinion.'

'Tell him Tilda's here.'

Willis came in quietly and sat beside the child on the locker, covered with brand-new flower-patterned cushions.

'Where's your sister?'

'Out with Heinrich.'

'With the German lad? Well, he seems nice enough. He wouldn't remember the war, of course.'

Tilda began to tell him exactly what had been happening in *Dr Kildare*, so far. She said nothing about Harry, because, for the time being, she had forgotten all about him.

Richard came back from work that evening later than he had hoped. Disappointed that there were no lights showing on *Grace* – it had never occurred to him that Nenna would not be there tonight – he was turning to walk along the Embankment to *Lord Jim* when he caught sight of a stranger on *Maurice*. He therefore changed direction and went along the wharf.

'I'm a friend of the owner's,' he said. 'Good evening.'

There was no reply, and he noticed that the gangplank was down between *Maurice* and *Grace*. Something was not quite right, so without hesitation he dropped down onto the deck.

Harry did not look up, but continued paying out the flex until he rounded the corner of the deck-house and could see Richard without bothering to turn his head. He put down the pair of pliers he was holding and picked up a heavy adjustable spanner.

'What are you doing on this boat?' Richard asked.

'Who made you God here?' said Harry.

The light was fading to a point where the battlements of the Hovis tower could only just be distinguished from the pinkish-grey of the sky. When Richard came a couple of steps nearer – it would never have occurred to him to go back until the matter was satisfactorily settled – Harry, looking faintly surprised, as though he couldn't believe that anything could be quite so simple, raised the adjustable spanner and hit him on the left side of the head, just below the ear. Richard fell without much sound. He folded up sideways against the winch, and immediately tried to get up again. It would have been better if he had been less conscientious, because he had broken one of his ribs against the handle of the winch and as he struggled to his feet the sharp broken edge of the bone penetrated slightly into his lung. Harry watched him fall back and noted that a considerable quantity of blood was coming away at the mouth. He wiped the spanner and put it away with his other tools. He was reflecting, perhaps, that this had been an easier job than the electrical wiring. Carrying the bag of tools, he disappeared up the wharf towards Partisan Street and the King's Road.

Heinrich and Martha were walking back to the Reach hand in hand. 'That's Maurice's pub,' she told him, 'he'll be in there now,' and, as they got nearer, 'I wish the Venice lantern was still there, it looked nice at night,' but in reality there was no need to say very much.

The foreshore was dark as pitch, but the corner street lamps palely illuminated the deck of *Maurice*. The body of a man lay across the winch, with an arm dropped over the side.

'Martha, don't look.'

Often, as the night drew on, a number of people were seen to lie down in odd places, both in Partisan Street and on the Embankment. Maurice's customers, too, were unpredictable. But none of them lay still in quite this way.

'Perhaps it's Harry,' Martha said. 'If it is, and he's dead, it'll be a great relief for Maurice.'

They walked steadily nearer, and saw blood on the deck, looking blackish in the dim light.

'It's *Lord Jim*,' she whispered.

The sight of a lord, knocked out by criminals, exactly fitted in with Heinrich's idea of Swinging London.

'It's Mr Blake,' said Martha.

'What should we do?'

Martha knew that with any luck the police launch would be at *Bluebird*. 'They go there to fetch the nurses on night shift and give them a lift down to hospital.'

'That would not be permitted in Vienna.'

'It's not permitted here.'

They were both running along the Embankment. Loud music, complained of by the neighbours on shore, thumped and echoed from cheerful *Bluebird* on the middle Reach. You could have told it a mile away. The river police duty-boat, smart as a whistle, was waiting alongside.

In this way Richard, still half-alive, was admitted to the men's casualty ward of the Waterloo hospital. One of the young probationers from *Bluebird* was on the ward, and came in with an injection for him, to help him to go to sleep.

'Isn't it Miss Jackson?' Richard said faintly. He had been trained to recognise anybody who had served under him, or who had helped him in any way. Miss Jackson had assisted with the removal of Willis. But Richard's polite attempt to straighten himself and to give something like a slight bow made the damage to his lung rather worse.

They patched him up, and he dozed through the night.

The long pallid hospital morning passed with interruptions from the nursing, cleaning, and auxiliary staff, all of whom gravitated to the bed, where they were received by the nice-looking Mr Blake, who was in terrible pain, with grave correctness. The probationers told him to remember that every minute he was getting a little better, and Ward Sister told him not to make any effort, and not to try to take anything by the mouth. 'I'm afraid I'm being a bit of a nuisance,' Richard tried to say. 'You're not supposed to talk,' they said.

When he was left to himself his mind cleared, and he began to reflect. He remembered falling, and the deck coming up to hit him, which brought back the sensation – although it hadn't done so at the time – of the moment just before the torpedo hit *Lanark*. He also remembered the look of the adjustable spanner, and it seemed to him appropriate that having been knocked down with a spanner his whole body was now apparently being alternately wrenched and tightened. There must surely be some connection of ideas here, and he would get better quickly if he could be certain that everything made sense.

Next, having reviewed, as well as he could, his work at the office, and made a courageous but unsuccessful attempt to remember whether there was any urgent correspondence he hadn't dealt with, he let his thoughts return to Nenna. Yesterday, or was it the day before yesterday, or when was it, he had gone first up the ladder onto *Lord Jim*, but Nenna had gone first into the cabin. Thinking about this, he felt happier, and then quite at peace. It was rather a coincidence that she was wearing a dark blue Guernsey exactly like Laura's, with a neck which necessitated the same blindfold struggle to get it off. About the whole incident Richard felt no dissatisfaction and certainly no regret. He could truly reflect that he had done not only the best, but the only thing possible.

At the end of the morning a very young doctor made his rounds and told Richard on no account to talk, he was only making a routine check-up. 'You can answer with simple signs,' he said reassuringly. 'We'll soon have you out of here and on four wheels again.' Less sensitive than the nurses, he evidently took Richard for a quarrelsome garage proprietor.

'No bleeding from the ears?'

The young houseman appeared to be consulting a list, and Richard, anxious to help a beginner, tried to indicate that he would bleed from the ears if it was the right thing to do. As to the exact locality of the pain, it was difficult to convey that it had grown, and that instead of having a pain he was now contained inside it. The doctor told him that they would be able to give him something for that.

'And absolute quiet, no police as yet. We had an officer here wanting you to make a statement, but he'll have to wait a couple of days. However,' he added unexpectedly, 'we're going to bend the regulations a little bit and let you see your children.'

From the no-man's land at the entrance to the ward, where the brown lino changed to blue, Tilda's voice could be heard, asking whether she and her sister might be allowed to bring Mr Blake a bottle of Suncrush.

'Is he your Daddy, dear?'

'He is, but we haven't seen him for many, many years, for more than we can remember.'

'Well, if Dr Sawyer's given permission . . . '

Tilda advanced, with Martha lingering doubtfully behind, and swept several plants from the loaded windowsill to make room for the Suncrush.

'Do you remember us, Daddy dear?'

Ward Sister was still complaining that children were not allowed to see the patients unattended. By good fortune, however, another visitor arrived; it was Willis, who took charge at once of the two girls. Richard's catastrophe had brought him to himself. Gratitude, felt by most people as a burden, was welcome to the unassuming Willis.

'Well, Skipper, it's sad to see you laid low. Not so long since I was in here myself, but I never dreamed . . . '

Willis had not quite known what to bring, so he'd decided on a packet of Whiffs. In his ward at the Waterloo they'd been allowed to smoke for an hour a day. 'But I can see it's different in here,' he said, as though this, too, was a mark of the superiority of Skipper. Richard did not smoke, but Willis had never noticed this.

'I think he wants to write something for you, dear,' the nurse said to Martha. Tilda, unabashed, was out in the pantry, helping the ward orderlies take the lids off the supper trays. Richard looked at Martha and saw Nenna's puzzled eyes, though they were so much darker. He painfully scrawled on the piece of paper which had been left for him: HOW IS YOUR MOTHER?

Martha wrote in turn – it didn't occur to her to say it aloud, although Richard could hear perfectly well – BUSY, SHE'S PACKING.

WHAT FOR?

WE'RE GOING TO CANADA.

WHEN?
But this Martha could not answer.

Laura was sent for, and arrived back in London the following afternoon. She dealt easily and efficiently with Richard's office, with the police, with the hospital. There she spoke only to Matron and the lung specialist. 'It's no use talking to the ward staff, they're so overworked, poor dears, they can't tell one case from another!' The Ward Sister had actually drawn her aside and asked her whether she did not think it would be a good idea to let her husband see his children more often in the future.

Richard was still not allowed to speak – he was not recovering quite so fast as had been expected – and he could make little reply when Laura told him that this was exactly the kind of thing she had expected all along, and that she would see about disposing of *Lord Jim* immediately. Her family, applied to, began to scour the countryside for a suitable house, within reasonable commuting distance from London, in good condition, and recently decorated, so that she could move Richard straight there as soon as he was discharged from hospital.

10

Nenna felt that she could have made a better hand at answering Louise if only Edward had taken the trouble to return her purse. It wasn't only the money, but her library card, her family allowance book, the receipt from the repair shop without which she couldn't get her watch back, creased photographs, with Edward's own photograph among them, her address book, almost the whole sum of her identity.

After all, she thought, if she did go away, how much difference would it make? In a sense, Halifax was no further away than 42b Milvain Street, Stoke Newington. All distances are the same to those who don't meet.

Halifax was equally far from the Norfolk border, to which Laura had removed Richard. The FOR SALE notice nailed to *Lord Jim*'s funnel saddened her and if possible she approached *Grace* from the other direction. If she had told Richard about Harry, and about *Maurice*'s dubious cargo, he wouldn't have had to lie in a pool of blood waiting for her own daughter to rescue him. But curiously enough the regret she felt, not for anything she had done but for what she hadn't, quite put an end to the old wearisome illusion of prosecution and trial. She no longer felt that she needed to defend herself, or even to account for herself, there. She was no longer of any interest to Edward. The case was suspended indefinitely.

As Louise seemed unwilling to come to the boats, Nenna was obliged to take the girls to tea at the luxurious Carteret. It was an anxious business to make them sufficiently respectable. On the twelfth floor of the hotel, from which they could just get a view of the distant river, they were delighted with their prosperous-looking aunt. Taller, stronger, not so blonde but much more decisive than their mother, she still seemed perpetually astonished by life.

'Martha! Tilda! Well I'll be! I haven't seen you both for such a long time, and you're both of you just! Well, how are you going to like us in Canada?'

'Louise, that depends on such a number of things. We have to sell *Grace*, to begin with.'

'What would happen if I pressed that bell?' Tilda asked.

'Well, somebody would come along, one of the floor waiters, to ask if we wanted tea, or cakes, or any little thing like that. Go on, you can press it, honey.'

Tilda did so. The bell was answered, and their order arrived.

'Is that right, dear?'

'Yes, those are the things Martha and I like. Are there any boats in Canada?'

'No shortage of boats, no shortage of water.'

Tilda's mind was made up in favour of the New World.

'But I'm not sure that we ought to leave Maurice, though,' she said, licking each finger in turn. 'Now that he won't have Ma to talk to, and there's no Mr Blake to get up a subscription if he goes down, I'd say he might lose heart altogether. And then the police are always coming round to interrogate him.'

'Who's Maurice, dear?' asked her aunt rather sharply.

'Maurice is on *Maurice*, just like the Blakes were on *Lord Jim*.'

'Ah, yes, Richard Blake, he called me up.'

'How could he?' Nenna cried.

'You remember, he's the one I had to call his number to get you, that's when we were in Frankfurt. I told him then that when we came to England we'd be staying at this hotel. It suits us all right, although Joel keeps saying that the service was so much better before the war.'

'But what did he say?'

Nenna's question caused confusion, which Louise gradually sorted out. What had this Richard Blake said, well, she got the impression that he was counting on coming to a series of Transatlantic insurance conferences in the spring, and he was either coming to Montreal first, or to New York, she couldn't remember which order it was, search me, said Louise, she hadn't thought it mattered all that much.

'I don't know whether it does or not,' said Nenna. 'He was going to show me how to fold up a map properly.'

'Joel can do that for you, dear.'

'We shan't be able to take Stripey,' said Tilda, continuing the course of her own thoughts. 'She won't leave *Grace*. Mrs Woodie bought her a basket, a very nice one made by the blind, but she wouldn't get into it.'

'Mrs Woodie?'

'A kindly lady, somewhat advanced in years.'

'She'll enjoy being back at school with girls of her own age,' Louise quietly observed to Nenna.

Mr Swanson came in, greeted everybody, and ordered a rye.

'Well, von Furstenfeld called me today, their boy's arrived safely in Vienna, and they're more than pleased, Nenna, with the spirit of hospitality you and your family extended to him. I owe you a debt of gratitude there.'

Martha smiled, perfectly tranquil.

Joel Swanson did not understand, nor did he ever expect to understand, exactly what was going on, but the kind of activity he seemed to be hearing about, in snatches only, was more or less exactly what he'd expect from his wife's relatives. He smiled at them with inclusive good will.

With *Lord Jim* and *Grace* both on his books, Pinkie felt doubtful about his chance of selling either. Of course, they were at the opposite ends of the price range. But the market would be affected, particularly as the disappointed broker hadn't hesitated to tell everyone how lucky he'd been not to drop a packet on *Dreadnought*, which had gone straight to the bottom like a stone in a pond. It was awkward, too, from the sales point of view, that Richard had been aboard one of these barges when he got knocked over the head. Thank heavens he hadn't got to try and sell that one. Poor old Richard, torpedoed three times, and then finished off, near as a toucher, with an adjustable spanner. Pinkie consulted the senior partner.

'Not everyone's buy. But if someone's looking for an unusual night spot . . .'

On *Grace* there was, after all, not so very much to be done. The barges, designed to be sailed by one man and a boy, could be laid up in a few days. Only the mast gave trouble. Not all Woodie's efforts could succeed in lowering it. 'I've another idea about your mast,' he said every morning, coming brightly across, but the thick rust held it fast. As to the packing, Mrs Woodie, eager to give a hand, was disappointed to find so little to do. The James family seemed to have few possessions. Mrs Woodie felt half inclined to lend her some, so as to have more to sort out and put away.

Unperturbed, Stripey gave birth. The warm hold of *Rochester* was chosen by the sagacious brute, and Willis, always up very early, found her on the ruins of the new locker cushions, with five mud-coloured kittens. Martha presented all but one to Father Watson. The presbytery needed a cheerful touch, he had so often hinted at this. But the priest, who had a strong instinct of self-preservation, transferred the litter of river-animals to the convent, as prizes in the Christmas raffle. With relief, he discussed the emigration of the James family with the nuns; so much the best thing – if there was no chance of a reconciliation – all round.

The night before Nenna and her two daughters were due to leave England, storm weather began to blow up on the Reach. There had been a good deal of rain, the Thames was high, and a north-westerly had piled up water at the river's mouth, waiting for a strong flood tide to carry it up. Before dark the wind grew very strong.

A storm always seems a strange thing in a great city, where there are so many immoveables. In front of the tall rigid buildings the flying riff-raff of leaves and paper seemed ominous, as though they were escaping in good time. Presently, larger things were driven along, cardboard boxes, branches, and tiles. Bicycles, left propped up, fell flat. You could hear glass smashing, and now pieces of broken glass were added to the missiles which the wind flung along the scoured pavement. The Embankment, swept clean, was deserted. People came out of the Underground and, leaning at odd angles to meet the wind, hurried home from work by the inner streets.

Above the river, the seagulls kept on the wing as long as they could, hoping the turbulence would bring them a good find, then, defeated and battered, they heeled and screamed away to find refuge. The rats on the wharf behaved strangely, creeping to the edge of the planking, and trying to cross over from dry land to the boats.

On the Reach itself, there could be no pretence that this would be an ordinary night. Tug skippers, who had never before acknowledged the presence of the moored barges, called out, or gave the danger signal – five rapid blasts in succession. Before slack tide the police launch went down the river, stopping at every boat to give fair warning.

'Excuse me, sir, have you checked your anchor recently?'

The barge anchors were unrecognisable as such, more like crustaceans, specimens of some giant type long since discarded by Nature, but still clinging to their old habitat, sunk in the deep pits they had made in the foreshore. But under the ground they were half rusted away. *Dreadnought*'s anchor had come up easily enough when the salvage tug came to dispose of her. The mud which held so tenaciously could also give way in a moment, if conditions altered.

'And how much anchor chain have you got? The regulation fifteen fathoms? All in good condition?'

Like many questions which the police were obliged to put, these were a formality, it being clear that the barge owners couldn't answer them. It could only be hoped that the mooring-ropes were in better case than the anchors. The visit was, in fact, a courteous excuse to leave a note of the nearest Thames Division telephone number.

'Waterloo Pier. WAT 5411. In all emergencies. Sure you've got that?'

'We'd have to go on shore to telephone,' said Woodie doubtfully, when his turn came. He was thinking of taking *Rochester*'s complement straight to Purley in the car, whether Willis agreed or not.

'What do you think of this weather, officer?'

The sergeant understood him, as one Englishman to another. The wind had ripped the tarpaulin off some of the laid-up boats, and huge fragments of oilcloth were flying at random, wrapping themselves round masts and rails.

'You want to look out for those,' he said. 'They could turn nasty.'

The Thames barges, built of living wood that gave and sprang back in the face of the wind, were as much at home as anything on the river. To their creaking and grumbling was added a new note, comparable to music. As the tide rose, the wind shredded the clouds above them and pushed a mighty swell across the water, so that they began to roll as they had once rolled at sea.

Nenna and Martha had absolutely forbidden Tilda to go above decks. Banished to the cabin, she lay there full of joy, feeling the crazy desire of the old boat to put out once again into mid-stream. Every time *Grace* rose on the swell, she was aware of the anchor chain tightening to its limit.

'We're all going ashore,' Nenna called, '*Rochester*'s gone already. We're just taking a bag, we'll come back for the rest when the wind's gone down.'

Tilda put on her anorak. She thought them all cowards. No one knew that Maurice was on board ship, because there were no lights showing. Certainly not a habitual drinker, he was nevertheless sitting that night in the darkness with a bottle of whisky, prepared for excess.

It wasn't the uncertain nature of his livelihood that worried him, nor the police visits, although he had twice been invited to accompany the officers to the station. So far they hadn't applied for a search warrant to go over the boat, but Maurice didn't care if they did. Still less did he fear the storm. The dangerous and the ridiculous were necessary to his life, otherwise tenderness would overwhelm him. It threatened him now, for what Maurice had not been able to endure was the sight of the emptying Reach. *Dreadnought*, *Lord Jim*, now *Grace*. Maurice, in the way of business, knew too many, rather than too few, people, but when he imagined living without friends, he sat down with the whisky in the dark.

When he heard steps overhead on deck, he switched on the light. Making two shots at it before he could manage the switch, he wondered if he'd better not drink any more. Of course, that rather depended on who was coming; he didn't know the footsteps. Someone was blundering about, didn't know the boat, probably didn't know about boats at all, couldn't find the hatch. Maurice, always hospitable, went to open it. His own steps seemed enormous, he floated up the steps, swimming couldn't be so difficult after all, particularly as he'd become weightless. Reaching the hatch at the same time as the stranger outside, he collided with it, and they fell into each other's arms. Not a tall man, quite young and thin, and just as drunk, to Maurice's relief, as he was.

'My name's James.'

'Come in.'

'This is a boat, isn't it?'

'Yes.'

'Is it *Grace*?'

'No.'

'Pity.'

'You said your name was James?'

'No, Edward.'

'Never mind.'

Edward took a bottle of whisky out of his pocket and, unexpectedly, two glasses. The glasses made Maurice sad. They must have been brought in the hope of some celebration to which the way had been lost.

'Clever of you to come on the right night,' he said.

He was absorbed, as host, in the task of getting his guest safely below decks. Fortunately he had had a good deal of practice in this. As he filled the glasses his depression emptied away.

Edward, sitting down heavily on the locker, said that he wanted to explain.

'Doctors tell you not to drink too much. They're very insistent on this. They're supported by teams of physiologists and laboratory researchers.'

He steered his way round these words much as he had negotiated the deck.

'What these so-called scientists should be doing is to study effects. Take my case. If one whisky makes me feel cheerful, four whiskies ought to make me feel very cheerful. Agreed?'

'I'm with you.'

'They haven't. I've had four whiskies and I feel wretched. Bloody wretched. Take that from me. And now I'd like to leave you with this thought...'

'Do you have to make many speeches in the course of your work?' Maurice asked.

For an instant Edward sobered up. 'No, I'm clerical.'

The barge took a great roll, and Maurice could hear the hanger with his good suit in it, waiting for the job which never came, sliding from one end of its rail to the other.

'I came to give Nenna a present,' Edward said. Out of the same pocket which had held the glasses he produced a small blue and gold box.

'There's a bottle of scent in this box.'

'What kind?'

'It's called L'Heure Bleue.'

'Do you mind if I write that down?' Maurice asked.

'Certainly. Have my biro.'

'It's the Russian for "pen", you know.'

'Hungarian.'

'Russian.'

'A Hungarian invented them.'

'He would have made a fortune if.'

'What's so special about this scent? You brought it for Nenna. Does she wear it?'

'I don't know. I think perhaps not. I haven't much sense of smell.'

'I don't think Nenna uses scent at all.'

'Do you know her, then?'

They both emptied their glasses.

'The mother whose man I live of the house in suggested it,' said Edward.

'What?'

'Wasn't that clear? I'm afraid I'm losing my fine edge.'

'Not a bit of it.'

'Gordon said I ought to bring her some scent.'

From directly above them came a noise like an explosion in a slate quarry. Something heavy had been torn away and, bouncing twice, landed flat on the deck directly over their heads. The deck timbers screamed in protest. Edward seemed to notice nothing.

'I've brought her purse.'

This too he dragged and tugged out of his pocket, and they both stared at it as though by doing so they could turn it into something else.

'Do you think she'll take me back?'

'I don't know,' Maurice said doubtfully. 'Nenna loves everybody. So do I.'

'Oh, do you know Nenna, then?'

'Yes.'

'You must know her pretty well, living on the same boat.'

'The next boat.'

'I expect she sometimes comes to borrow sugar. Matches, she might borrow.'

'We're both borrowers.'

'She's not easy to understand. You could spend a very long time, trying to understand that woman.'

There was about a quarter of the bottle left, and Edward poured it out for both of them. This time the movement of the boat helped him, and *Maurice* rocked the whisky out in two curves, one for each glass.

'Do you understand women?'

'Yes,' said Maurice.

With a great effort, holding his concentration as though he had it in his two hands, he added:

'You've got to give these things to her. Give them, that's it, give them. You've got to go across to *Grace*.'

'How's that done?'

'It's not difficult. Difficult if you're heavy. Luckily we haven't any weight this evening.'

'How do I go?'

It was worse than ever getting up the companion, much worse than last time. The whole boat plunged, but not now in rhythm with the staggering of Maurice and Edward. They managed three steps. The hatch in front of them flew open and the frame, tilted from one side to the other, gave them a sight of the wild sky outside. A rat was sitting at the top of the companion. A gleam of light showed its crossed front teeth. Edward struggled forward.

'Brute, I'll get it.'

'It's one of God's creatures!' cried Maurice.

Edward hurled all that he had in his hands, the purse, the scent, which struck the rat in the paunch. Hissing loudly, it swivelled on its hind legs and disappeared, the tail banging like a rope on the top step as it fled.

'Did the scent break?'

'I can smell it, I'm afraid.'

'I came here to give her a present.'

'I know, James.'

'What do I give her now?'

Edward sat empty-handed on the companion. Maurice, who still hadn't exactly made out who he was, suddenly cared intensely about the loss.

'Another present.'

'What?'

'Hundreds. I've got hundreds.'

Clinging together they followed the line of the keelson to the forward hatch.

'Hundreds!'

Record-players, electric guitars, transistors, electric hair-curlers, electric toasters, Harry's hoard, the strange currency of the 1960s, piled on the floor, on the bunks, all in their new containers, all wrapped in plastic. Maurice snatched out a pile and loaded them onto the reeling Edward.

'She'll find these useful on *Grace*.'

'How do I get there?'

How had they got back on deck? As the battering wind seized them they had to stoop along in the darkness, fighting for handholds, first the base of the old pulley, then the mast. Three toasters sailed away like spindrift in the gale. It was still blowing hard north-west. The gangplank to *Grace* was missing. The crash above their heads had come when it was lifted bodily and flung across the deck.

'There's still the ladder.'

Maurice had a fixed iron ladder down the port side.

'Is that *Grace*?' Edward shouted above the wind.

'Yes.'

'Can't see any lights.'

'Of course you can't. It's dark.'

'I hadn't thought of that. Don't know much about boats.'

Edward was much more confused than Maurice and needed all the help he was getting as Maurice manhandled him to the top of the ladder. Maurice was still sober enough to know that he was drunk, and knew also that the water between the boats was wilder than he had ever seen it. That something was dreadfully wrong was an idea which urgently called his attention, but it wavered beyond his grasp. It was to do with getting over to *Grace*.

'This isn't the usual way we go.'

Edward had dropped the whole cargo of gifts by the time he had got down the twenty iron rungs of the ladder. As he reached the bottom the whole boat suddenly heaved away from him, so that the washboard at the top rolled out of sight and a quite new reach of sky appeared.

'Look out!'

Maurice was half-collapsed over the gunwale. Even like that, hopelessly drunk and quite tired out, there was about him an appealing look of promise, of everything that can be meant by friendship.

'You must come again when the weather's better!'

He leaned out, perilously askew, just to catch a sight of Edward's white face at the bottom of the ladder. Edward shouted back something that the wind carried away, but he seemed to be saying, once again, that he was not very used to boats.

With that last heave, Maurice's anchor had wrenched clear of the mud, and the mooring-ropes, unable to take the whole weight of the barge, pulled free and parted from the shore. It was in this way that *Maurice*, with the two of them clinging on for dear life, put out on the tide.

HUMAN VOICES

INSIDE BROADCASTING House, the Department of
Recorded Programmes was sometimes called the Seraglio,
because its Director found that he could work better when
surrounded by young women. This in itself was an understandable habit and quite harmless, or, to be more accurate,
RPD never considered whether it was harmless or not. If he
was to think about such things, his attention had to be
specially drawn to them. Meanwhile it was understood by
the girls that he might have an overwhelming need to confide
his troubles in one of them, or perhaps all of them, but never
in two of them at once, during the three wartime shifts in
every twenty-four hours. This, too, might possibly suggest the
arrangements of a seraglio, but it would have been quite
unfair to deduce, as some of the Old Servants of the Corporation occasionally did, that the RP Junior Temporary Assistants had no other duties. On the contrary, they were in
anxious charge of the five thousand recordings in use every
week. Those which the Department processed went into
the Sound Archives of the war, while the scrap was silent
for ever.

'I can't see what good it would be if Mr Brooks did talk to me,'
said Lise, who had only been recruited three days earlier, 'I
don't know anything.'

Vi replied that it was hard on those in positions of responsibility, like RPD, if they didn't drink, and didn't go to
confession.

'Are you a Catholic then?'

'No, but I've heard people say that.'

Vi herself had only been at BH for six months, but since she
was getting on for nineteen she was frequently asked to explain
things to those who knew even less.

'I daresay you've got it wrong,' she added, being patient with Lise, who was pretty, but shapeless, crumpled and depressed. 'He won't jump on you, it's only a matter of listening.'

'Hasn't he got a secretary?'

'Yes, Mrs Milne, but she's an Old Servant.'

Even after three days, Lise could understand this.

'Or a wife? Isn't he married?'

'Of course he's married. He lives in Streatham, he has a nice home on Streatham Common. He doesn't get back there much, none of the higher grades do. It's non-stop for them, it seems.'

'Have you ever seen Mrs Brooks?'

'No.'

'How do you know his home is nice, then?'

Vi did not answer, and Lise turned the information she had been given so far slowly over in her mind.

'He sounds like a selfish shit to me.'

'I've told you how it is, he thinks people under twenty are more receptive. I don't know why he thinks that. He just tries pouring out his worries to all of us in turn.'

'Has he poured them out to Della?'

'Well, perhaps not Della.'

'What happens if you're not much good at listening? Does he get rid of you?'

Vi explained that some of the girls had asked for transfers because they wanted to be Junior Programme Engineers, who helped with the actual transmissions. That hadn't been in any way the fault of RPD. Wishing that she didn't have to explain matters which would only become clear, if at all, through experience, she checked her watch with the wall clock. An extract from the Prime Minister was wanted for the midday news, 1'42" in, cue *Humanity, rather than legality, must be our guide*.

'By the way, he'll tell you that your face reminds him of another face he's seen somewhere – an elusive type of beauty, rather elusive anyway, it might have been a picture somewhere or other, or a photograph, or something in history, or something, but anyway he can't quite place it.'

Lise seemed to brighten a little.

'Won't he ever remember?'

'Sometimes he appeals to Mrs Milne, but she doesn't know either. No, his memory lets him down at that point. But he'll probably put you on the Department's Indispensable Emergency Personnel List. That's the people he wants close to him in case of invasion. We'd be besieged, you see, if that happened. They're going to barricade both ends of Langham Place. If you're on the list you'd transfer then to the Defence Rooms in the sub-basement and you can draw a standard issue of towel, soap and bedding for the duration. Then there was a memo round about hand grenades.'

Lise opened her eyes wide and let the tears slide out, without looking any less pretty. Vi, however, was broad-minded, and overlooked such things.

'My boy's in the Merchant Navy,' she said, perceiving the real nature of the trouble. 'What about yours?'

'He's in France, he's with the French army. He *is* French.'

'That's not so good.'

Their thoughts moved separately to what must be kept out of them, helpless waves of flesh against metal and salt water. Vi imagined the soundless fall of a telegram through the letter-box. Her mother would say it was just the same as last time but worse because in those days people seemed more human somehow and the postman was a real friend and knew everyone on his round.

'What's his name, then?'

'Frédé. I'm partly French myself, did they tell you?'

'Well, that can't be helped now.' Vi searched for the right consolation. 'Don't worry if you get put on the IEP list. You won't stay there long. It keeps changing.'

Mrs Milne rang down. 'Is Miss Bernard there? Have I the name correct by the way? We're becoming quite a League of Nations. As she is new to the Department, RPD would like to see her for a few minutes when she comes off shift.'

'We haven't even gone on yet.'

Mrs Milne was accustomed to relax a little with Vi.

'We're having a tiresome day, all these directives, why can't they leave us to go quietly on with our business which we know like the back of our hand. Tell Miss Bernard not to worry about her evening meal, I've been asked to see to a double order of sandwiches.' Lise was not listening, but recalled Vi to the point she had understood best.

'If Mr Brooks says he thinks I'm beautiful, will he mean it?'

'He means everything he says at the time.'

There was always time for conversations of this kind, and of every kind, at Broadcasting House. The very idea of Continuity, words and music succeeding each other without a break except for a cough or a shuffle or some mistake eagerly welcomed by the indulgent public, seemed to affect everyone down to the humblest employee, the filers of Scripts as Broadcast and the fillers-up of glasses of water, so that all in turn could be seen forming close groups, in the canteen, on the seven floors of corridors, beside the basement ticker-tapes, in the washrooms, in the studios, talking, talking to each other, and usually about each other, until the very last moment when the notice SILENCE: ON THE AIR forbade.

The gossip of the seven decks increased the resemblance of the great building to a liner, which the designers had always intended. BH stood headed on a fixed course south. With the best engineers in the world, and a crew varying between the intensely respectable and the barely sane, it looked ready to scorn any disaster of less than *Titanic* scale. Since the outbreak of war damp sandbags had lapped it round, but once inside the bronze doors, the airs of cooking from the deep hold suggested more strongly than ever a cruise on the *Queen Mary*. At night, with all its blazing portholes blacked out, it towered over a flotilla of taxis, each dropping off a speaker or two.

By the spring of 1940 there had been a number of castaways. During the early weeks of evacuation Variety, Features and Drama had all been abandoned in distant parts of the country, while the majestic headquarters was left to utter wartime instructions, speeches, talks and news.

Since March the lifts below the third floor had been halted as an economy measure, so that the first three staircases became yet another meeting place. Few nowadays were ever to be found in their offices. An instinct, or perhaps a rapidly acquired characteristic, told the employees how to find each other. On the other hand, in this constant circulation much was lost. The corridors were full of talks producers without speakers, speakers without scripts, scripts which by a clerical error contained the wrong words or no words at all. The air seemed alive with urgency and worry.

Recordings, above all, were apt to be mislaid. They looked alike, all 78s, aluminium discs coated on one side with acetate whose pungent rankness was the true smell of the BBC's war. It was rumoured that the Germans were able to record on tapes coated with ferrous oxide and that this idea might have commercial possibilities in the future, but only the engineers and RPD himself believed this.

'It won't catch on,' the office supervisor told Mrs Milne. 'You could never get attached to them.'

'That's true,' Mrs Milne said. 'I loved my record of Charles Trenet singing *J'ai ta main*. I died the death when it fell into the river at Henley. The public will never get to feel like that about lengths of tape.'

But the Department's discs, though cared for and filed under frequently changing systems, were elusive. Urgently needed for news programmes, they went astray in transit to the studio. Tea-cups were put down on them, and they melted. Ferried back by mobile units through the bitter cold, they froze, and had to be gently restored to life. Hardly a day passed without one or two of them disappearing.

Vi was now looking for Churchill's *Humanity, rather than legality, must be our guide* with the faint-hearted help of Lise. It was possible that Lise might turn out to be hopeless. They'd given up For Transmission, and were looking in what was admittedly the wrong place, among the Processed, whose labels, written in the RPAs' round school-leavers' handwriting, offered First Day of War: Air-Raid Siren, False Alarm: Cheerful

Voices with Chink of Tea-Cups: Polish Refugees in Scotland, National Singing, No Translation. 'You won't find anything in that lot,' said Della, brassily stalking through, 'that's all Atmosphere.'

'It's wanted in the editing room. Do you think Radio News Reel went and took it?'

'Why don't you ask the boys?'

Three of the Junior RPAs were boys, and RPD, though fond of them, felt less need to confide in them. As the Department expanded more and more girls would be taken on. 'What a field that's going to give us!' said Teddy, relaxing in the greasy haze of the canteen with Willie Sharpe. Willie only paid twopence for his coffee, because he was a juvenile.

'I don't grudge you that in any way,' Teddy went on. 'It's a mere accident of birth. I just wonder how you reconcile it with what you're always saying, that you expect to be in training as a Spitfire pilot by the end of 1940.'

'My face is changing,' Willie replied. 'Coming up from Oxford Circus on Wednesday I passed a girl I used to know and she didn't recognise me.'

Teddy looked at him pityingly.

'They're still asking for School Certificate in maths,' he said.

'Pretty soon they mayn't mind about that, though. They'll be taking pilots wherever they can get them.'

'They'll still want people who look a bit more than twelve.'

Willie was rarely offended, and never gave up.

'Hitler was a manual worker, you know. He didn't need School Cert to take command of the Nazi hordes.'

'No, but he can't fly, either,' Teddy pointed out.

The boys' ears, though delicately tuned to differences of pitch and compression, adapted easily to the frightful clash of metal trays in the canteen. Unlike the administrative staff, they had no need to shout. Teddy sat with his back to the counter, so that he could see the girls as they came in – Della, perhaps, although there was nothing doing there – and at the same time turned the pages of a yank mag, where white skin and black lace glimmered. These mags were in short supply. Vi's merchant seaman, who was on the Atlantic run, had passed it on.

'You know, Willie, I need money for what I want to do. Honestly, the kind of woman I have in mind is unattainable on £378 a year.'

'Your mind's tarnished, Teddy.'

'I'm not responsible for more than one-eighth of it,' Teddy protested.

'No, but you can increase the proportion by concentrated will-power. As I see it, in any case, after the conflict is over we shan't be at the mercy of anything artificially imposed on us, whether from within or without. Hunger will be a thing of the past because the human race won't tolerate it, mating will follow an understandable instinct, and there'll be no deference to rank or money. We shall need individuals of strong will then.'

Neither Teddy nor anyone else felt that Willie was ridiculous when he spoke like this, although they sometimes wondered what would become of him. Indeed, he was noble. His note-book contained, besides the exact details of his shift duties, a new plan for the organisation of humanity. Teddy also had a notebook, the back of which he kept for the estimated meas-urements of the Seraglio.

'I'd put this Lise Bernard at 34, 25, 38. Are you with me?'

'I'm not too sure,' said Willie doubtfully. 'By the way, she cries rather a lot.'

'She's mixed a lot with French people, that would make her more emotional.'

'Not all foreigners are emotional. It depends whether they come from the north or the south. Look at Tad.'

Taddeus Zagorski, the third of the junior RPAs (male), had arrived in this country with his parents only last October. How had he managed to learn English so quickly, and how, although he wasn't much older than the rest of them and was quite new to the Department, did he manage to dazzle them with his efficiency and grasp?

'I can't seem to get to like him,' said Teddy. 'He's suffered, I know, but there it is. He wants to be a news reader, you know.'

'I daresay he'll get on,' Willie replied, 'in the world, that is, as it's at present constituted. It's possible that we're jealous of him. We ought to guard against that.'

Tad, in fact, was emerging at the head of the counter queue, where, with a proud gesture, he stirred his coffee with the communal spoon tied to the cash register with a piece of string. He must have been doing Messages from the Forces.

'My auntie got one of those messages,' said Willie. 'It was my uncle in the Navy singing *When the Deep Purple Falls*, but by the time it went out he was missing, believed killed.'

'Was she upset?'

'She never really heard it. She works on a delivery van.'

The young Pole stood at their table, cup of coffee in hand, brooding down at them from a height.

'You should have been off ten minutes ago,' said Teddy.

Tad sat down between them, precisely in the middle of his chair, in his creaseless white shirt. The boys felt uneasy. He had an air of half-suppressed excitement.

'Who is that fellow?' he asked suddenly.

Willie looked up, Teddy craned round. A man with a pale, ruined-looking face was walking up to the bar.

Tad watched him as he asked quietly for a double whisky. The barman seemed unnerved. In fact, the canteen had only obtained a licence at the beginning of the year, on the under-standing that the news readers should not take more than two glasses of beer before reporting for work, and the shadow of disapproval still hung over it. Higher grades were expected to go to the Langham for a drink, but this one hadn't.

'I ask you about that fellow,' said Tad, 'because it was he who just came into Studio LG14. I was clearing up the Messages preparatory to returning them to registry, and I asked him what he was doing in the studios, as one cannot be too careful in the present circumstances. He replied that he had an administrative post in the BBC, and, as he seemed respectable, I explained the

standard routine to him. I think one should never be too busy
to teach those who are anxious to learn.'

'Well, you set out to impress him,' said Teddy. 'What did
you tell him?'

'I told him the rules of writing a good news talk – "the first
sentence must interest, the second must inform". Next
I pointed out the timeless clock, which is such an unusual
feature of our studios, and demonstrated the "ten seconds
from now".'

The familiar words sounded dramatic, and even tragic.

'What did he do?'

'He nodded, and showed interest.'

'But didn't he say anything?'

'Quite quietly. He said, "Tell me more." '

Tad's self-assurance wavered and trembled. 'He does not
look quite the same now as he did then. Who is he?'

'That's Jeffrey Haggard,' Willie said. 'He's the Director of
Programme Planning.'

Tad was silent for a moment. 'Then he would be familiar
with the ten-second cue?'

'He invented it. It's called the Haggard cue, or the Jeff,
sometimes.' Teddy laughed, louder than the din of crockery.

'God, Tad, you've made me happy today. Jeepers Creepers,
you've gone and explained the ten-second cue to DPP . . . '

Their table rocked and shook, while Tad sat motionless,
steadying his cup with his hand.

'Doubtless Mr Haggard will think me ludicrous.'

'He thinks everything's ludicrous,' said Willie hastily.

Teddy laughed and laughed, not able to get over it, meaning
no harm. He wouldn't laugh like that if he was Polish, Willie
thought. However, in his scheme of things to come there
would no frontiers, and indeed no countries.

The Director of Programme Planning ordered a second double
in his dry, quiet, disconcerting voice. Probably in the whole of
his life he had never had to ask for anything twice. The barman,
knowing, as most people did, that Mr Haggard had run through

three wives and had lost his digestion into the bargain, wondered what he'd sound like if he got angry.

The whisky, though it had no visible effect, was exactly calculated to raise DPP from a previous despair far enough to face the rest of the evening. When he had finished it he went back to his office, where he managed with no secretary and very few staff, and rang RPD.

'Mrs Milne, I want Sam. I can hear him shouting, presumably in the next room.'

On the telephone his voice dropped even lower, like a voice's shadow. He waited, looking idly at the schedules that entirely covered the walls, the charts of Public Listening and Evening Meal Habits, and the graphs, supplied by the Ministry of Information, of the nation's morale.

RPD was put through.

'Jeff, I want you to hear my case.'

DDP had been hearing it for more than ten years. But, to do his friend justice, it was never the same twice running. The world seemed new created every day for Sam Brooks, who felt no resentment and, indeed, very little recollection of what he had suffered the day before.

'Jeff, Establishment have hinted that I'm putting in for too many girls.'

'How can that be?'

'They know I like to have them around, they know I need that. I've drafted a reply, saying nothing, mind you, about the five thousand discs a week, or the fact that we provide a service to every other department of the Corporation. See what you think of the way I've put it – I begin quite simply, by asking them whether they realise that through the skill of the recording engineer sound can be transformed from air to wax, the kind of thing which through all the preceding centuries has been possible only to the bees. It's the transference of pattern, you see – surely that says something encouraging about the human mind. Don't forget that Mozart composed that trio while he was playing a game of billiards.'

'Sam, I went to a meeting today.'

'What about?'

'It was about the use of recordings in news bulletins.'

'Why wasn't I asked?'

But Sam was never asked to meetings.

'We had two Directors and three Ministries – War, Information, Supply. They'd called it, quite genuinely I think, in the interests of truth.'

The word made its mark. Broadcasting House was in fact dedicated to the strangest project of the war, or of any war, that is, telling the truth. Without prompting, the BBC had decided that truth was more important than consolation, and, in the long run, would be more effective. And yet there was no guarantee of this. Truth ensures trust, but not victory, or even happiness. But the BBC had clung tenaciously to its first notion, droning quietly on, at intervals from dawn to midnight, telling, as far as possible, exactly what happened. An idea so unfamiliar was bound to upset many of the other authorities, but they had got used to it little by little, and the listeners had always expected it.

'The object of the meeting was to cut down the number of recordings in news transmissions – in the interests of truth, as they said. The direct human voice must be used whenever we can manage it – if not, the public must be clearly told what they've been listening to – the programme must be announced as recorded, that is, Not Quite Fresh.'

Sam's Department was under attack, and with it every recording engineer, every RPA, every piece of equipment, every TD7, mixer and fader and every waxing and groove in the building. As the protector and defender of them all, he became passionate.

'Did they give specific instances? Could they even find one?'

'They started with Big Ben. It's always got to be relayed direct from Westminster, the real thing, never from disc. That's got to be firmly fixed in the listeners' minds. Then, if Big Ben is silent, the public will know that the war has taken a distinctly unpleasant turn.'

'Jeff, the escape of Big Ben freezes in cold weather.'

'We shall have to leave that to the Ministry of Works.'

'And the King's stammer. Ah, what about that. My standby recordings for his speeches to the nation – His Majesty without stammer, in case of emergency.'

'Above all, not those.'

'And Churchill. . . . '

'Some things have to go, that was decided at a preliminary talk long before I got there. Otherwise it's just a general directive, and we've lived through a good many of those. It doesn't affect the total amount of recording. If you want to overwork, you've nothing to worry about.' Sam said that he accepted that no one present had had the slightest understanding of his Department's work, but it was strange, very strange, that there had been no attempt whatever, at any stage, to consider his point of view.

'If someone could have reasoned with him, Jeff. Perhaps this idea that's come to me about the bees. . . . '

'I protested against any cuts in your mobile recording units. I managed to save your cars.'

'Those Wolseleys!'

'They're all you've got, Sam.'

'The hearses. I've been asking for replacements for two years. They're just about fit to take a Staff Officer to a lunch party, wait till he collapses from over-indulgence, then on to the graveyard. And I've had to send two of those out to France. . . . Jeff, were you asked to break this to me?'

'In a way.' As they left the meeting one of the Directors had drawn him aside and had asked him to avoid mentioning the new recommendations to RPD for as long as possible.

Sam was floundering in his newly acquired wealth of grievances.

'Without even the commonplace decency . . . no standbys . . . my cars, well, I suppose you did your best there . . . my girls. . . . '

'In my opinion you can make do with the staff you've got,' Jeff said. 'One of your RPAs was talking to me in the studio just now, and I assure you he was very helpful.'

*

When he had done what he could Jeff walked out of the building. It was scarcely necessary for him to show his pass. His face, with its dark eyebrows, like a comedian's, but one who had to be taken seriously, was the best known in the BBC. He stood for a moment among the long shadows on the pavement, between the piles of sandbags which had begun to rot and grow grass, now that spring had come.

DPP was homeless, in the sense of having several homes, none of which he cared about more than the others. There was a room he could use at the Langham, and then there were two or three women with whom his relationship was quite unsentimental, but who were not sorry to see him when he came. He never went to his house, because his third wife was still in it. In any case, he had a taxi waiting for him every night, just round the corner in Riding House Street. He hardly ever used it, but it was a testimony that if he wanted to, he could get away quickly.

RPD seemed to have forgotten how to go home. Mrs Milne suggested as much to him as she said goodnight. Her typewriter slumbered now under its leatherette cover. He gave no sign of having heard her.

Long before it was dark men in brown overalls went round BH, fixing the framed blackouts in every window, circulating in the opposite direction to the Permanents coming downstairs, while the news readers moved laterally to check with Pronunciation, pursued by editors bringing later messages on pink cards. Movement was complex, so too was time. Nobody's hour of work coincided exactly with the life-cycle of Broadcasting House, whose climax came six times in the twenty-four hours with the Home News, until at nine o'clock, when the nation sat down to listen, the building gathered its strength and struck. The night world was crazier than the day world. When Lise Bernard paused in doubt at the door of RPD's office, she saw her Head of Department pacing to and fro like a bear astray, in a grove of the BBC's pale furniture, veneered with Empire woods. He wore a tweed jacket, grey trousers and one of the BBC's frightful house ties, dark blue embroidered with thermionic valves in red. Evidently he put on whatever came to hand first. Much of the room was taken up with a bank of turntables and a cupboard full of clean shirts.

When he recognised who she was he stopped pacing about and took off his spectacles, changing from a creature of sight to one of faith. Lise, the crowded office, the neatly angled sandwiches, the tray with its white cloth suitable for grades of Director and above, turned into patches of light and shade. To Lise, on the other hand, looking at his large hazel eyes, the eyes of a child determined not to blink for fear of missing something, he became someone who could not harm her and asked to be protected from harm. The effect, however, was quite unplanned, he produced it unconsciously. All the old lechers and yearners in the building envied the success which he seemed to turn to so little account.

'He just weeps on their shoulders you know,' they said. 'And yet I believe the man's a trained engineer.'

'Sit down, Miss Bernard. Have all these sandwiches. You look hungry.' When he had put his spectacles on again he couldn't pursue this idea; Lise was decidedly overweight. 'I like to get to know everyone who comes to work for me as soon as possible – in a way it's part of the responsibility I feel for all of you – and the shortest way to do that, curiously enough, I've found, is to tell you some of the blankly incomprehensible bloody idiotic lack of understanding that our Department meets with every minute of the day.'

Lise sat there blankly, eating nothing. He picked up the telephone, sighing.

'Canteen, I have a young assistant here, quite new to the Corporation, who can't eat your sandwiches.'

'That's National Cheese, Mr Brooks. The manufacturers have agreed to amalgamate their brand names for the duration in the interest of the Allied war effort.'

'I believe you've been waiting to say that all day.'

'I don't want anything, Mr Brooks, really I don't,' whimpered Lise.

'Not good enough for you.' He looked angrily at the window, unable to throw them out because of the blackout. Then he sat down opposite to the girl and considered her closely. 'You know, even though I only saw you for a few minutes at the interview, I was struck by the width between your eyes. You can see something like it in those portraits by – I'm sure you know the ones I mean. It's a sure index of a certain kind of intelligence, I would call it an emotional intelligence.' Lise wished that there was a looking-glass in the room.

'Some people might find what I have to say difficult to grasp, because I let my ideas follow each other just as they come. But people whose eyes are as wide apart as yours won't have that difficulty.' He took her hand, but held it quite absent-mindedly.

'You may find Broadcasting House rather strange at first, but there's nothing unusual about me. Except for this, I suppose – it just so happens that all my energies are concentrated, and always have been, and always will be, on one thing, the recording of sound and of the human voice. That doesn't make for an easy life, you understand. Perhaps you know what it's like to have a worry that doesn't and can't leave room in your mind for anything else and won't give you peace, night or day, for a single moment.'

Now something went not at all according to programme. Lise began to sob. These tears were not of her usual manageable kind, and her nose turned red. Having no handkerchief with her she struggled to her feet and heaved and streamed her way out of the room.

'Bad news?' asked Teddy, meeting her in the corridor. Set on her way to the Ladies, she only shook her head. RPD's gone for one of them at last, he thought. Jeez, I don't blame him. But Della, expert in human behaviour, thought this impossible.

'Why?' Teddy asked. 'He's capable.'

'If it was that, she wouldn't be crying.'

When Lise did not come back, Sam was at first mildly puzzled, and then forgot about her. But he was still oppressed with the injustice that had been done to him in the name of truth, in the name of patriotism too, if you thought of the cheese sandwiches, and the added injustice of being abandoned without a listener. In the end he had to turn to Vi, too busy and perhaps too accustomed to his ways to be quite what he wanted, but not tearful, and always reliable. By this time, however, having been sorting out administrative and technical problems since five in the morning, he was exhausted. He put his head on her shoulder, as he was always rumoured to do, took off his spectacles, and went to sleep immediately.

Twenty minutes passed. It was coming up for the nine o'clock news.

'Aren't you exceeding your duties?' said one of the recording engineers, putting his head round the door. 'You've got a situation on your hands there.'

'If that's a name for cramp,' said Vi.

2

THE SECOND year of the war was not a time when the staff of BH gave very much thought to promotion. But, even so, it seemed odd that Jeff Haggard and Sam Brooks, who, though they could hardly be termed Old Servants, had been bitterly loyal for more than ten years, should be nothing more than DPP and RPD. True, nobody else could have done their jobs, and then again Sam always seemed too overworked to notice, and Jeff too detached to care. One might have assumed that they would be there for ever.

But if they were either to move or to leave, it would have to be together. Without understanding either their warmly unreasonable RPD, or their sardonic DPP, the BBC knew that for a fact. The link between them was consolingly felt as the usefulness of having Haggard around when Brooks had to be got out of trouble. This was enough for practical purposes, but Jeff would have liked to have been able to explain it further. By nature he was selfish. He had left his first wife because he had found his second wife more attractive, and his second wife had left him because, as she told her lawyers, she could never make him raise his voice. It was, therefore, going against his nature, a most unsafe proceeding, to put himself out to help a friend, worse still to do so for so long. Their long relationship looked like an addiction – a weakness for the weak on Jeff's part – or a response to the appeal for protection made by the defenceless and single-minded. Of course, if this appeal were to fail entirely, the human race would have difficulty in reproducing itself.

Perhaps if Sam had ever been able to foresee the result of his actions, or if he had suspected for one moment that he was not entirely self-sufficient, the spell might have been broken, or perhaps there was a fixed point in the past when that might have been done.

'I ought to have stopped in 1938,' Jeff thought. 'With Englishry.' At the time of the Munich Agreement a memo had been sent round calling, as a matter of urgency, for the recording of our country's heritage.

It was headed *Lest we forget our Englishry*. Sam had disappeared for over two weeks in one of the Wolseleys, pretty infirm even at that time, with an engineer and an elderly German refugee, Dr Vogel – Dr Vogel, cruelly bent, deaf in one ear, but known to be the greatest expert in Europe on recorded atmosphere.

There was not much hope of commonsense prevailing. Dr Vogel, in spite of his politeness and gentle *ganz meinerheits*, was an obsessive, who had been seen to take the arms of passers-by in his bony grip and beg to record their breathing, for he wished to record England's wheezing before the autumn fogs began. 'Have the goodness, sir, to cough a little into my apparatus.' Sam thought the idea excellent.

The expedition to the English countryside arrived back with a very large number of discs. The engineer who had gone with them said nothing. He went straight away to have a drink. It was probably a misfortune that the Controllers were so interested in the project that they demanded a playback straight away. Usually there was a judicious interval before they expressed any opinion, but not this time.

'What we have been listening to – patiently, always in the hope of something else coming up – amounts to more than six hundred bands of creaking. To be accurate, some are a mixture of squeaking and creaking.'

'They're all from the parish church of Hither Lickington,' Sam explained eagerly. 'It was recommended to us by Religious Broadcasting as the top place in the Home Counties. What you're hearing is the hinges of the door and the door itself opening and shutting as the old women come in one by one with the stuff for the Harvest Festival. The quality's superb, particularly on the last fifty-three bands or so. Some of them have got more to carry, so the door has to open wider. That's when you get the squeak.'

'Hark, the vegetable marrow comes!' cried Dr Vogel, his head on one side, well contented.

For several weeks the Recorded Programme Department was in danger of complete reorganisation, for the BBC could form and re-form its elements with ease. It was put to DPP, in consultation, that although RPD was successfully in charge of hundreds of thousands of pounds' worth of equipment, and no fault could be found with his technical standing. . . .

'You feel that he's too interested in creaking doors,' Jeff said.

'He's irresponsible.'

'Oh, I wouldn't say so.'

'There was a considerable financial investment in this project, and Brooks was well aware that copies of the recordings were to be buried certain fathoms in the earth as a memorial for future generations.'

'You could still do that,' Jeff replied. 'There mayn't be any doors that creak by then. Mine doesn't now.' All the doors in BH were fitted with self-closing devices of an irritating nature.

It was not Jeff's habit to soothe, but as usual the case he made for his friend, only just over the borderline of detachment, and gradually becoming more serious, proved effective. Sam never heard of these discussions. He continued like a sleepwalker, who never knows what obstacles are removed, and by what hands, from his path.

And Sam was not the only member of the Corporation who confided in Jeff. That was surprising, in view of the imperturbable surface he presented, which gave back only a stony resonance, truthful and dry, to the complaints of others. But his advice was excellent, and he could be relied upon, as so few could, not to wait for a convenient opening to start on his own grievances. Perhaps he hadn't any, certainly he admitted to none. His calmness was really recklessness, as of a gambler who no longer felt anything was valuable enough to stake. That in turn was not likely to make him popular. Those who valued his cold judgement when they needed it, very naturally resented it when they didn't. To see the Director of

Programme Planning miscalculate might have been a relief, but during the first nine months of the war no hint of such a thing arose – never, until the affair of General Pinard.

'You'll get your boy back, then,' said Della to Lise. A strong line was best, in her opinion. Everyone knew that Lise considered herself engaged and that Frédé was some kind of electrician with the French 1st Army. The way things were going they'd have to bring the French over here, there was nowhere else for them to go.

'But that will be quite impossible,' said Tad, demonstrating with his map. 'You underestimate the obstacle of the English Channel.'

'In that case, if you want my advice, you'd do best to forget him,' said Della. 'After all, he never gave you a ring, did he?'

Lise had not proved any better at her work than Della, which made some sort of bond between them.

Vi's merchant seaman wrote making apparent references to home leave, but a good deal of his letter had been blacked out by the censor. What a job having to go through other people's personal letters, Vi thought, they must feel uncomfortable, you had to pity them.

On June 10 1940 the French Government admitted that Paris could not be defended, and left for Bordeaux. Between the *débandade* and de Gaulle's arrival on the 17th, there was a bizarre moment of hope when the Government learned that General Georges Pinard had escaped to London, flying his own light aircraft, and bringing with him nothing but a small valise and one junior officer. He went straight to the Rembrandt Hotel.

Historians have not yet decided – or rather, they have decided but not agreed – as to who sent the General on his desperate mission. Certainly no one could have been more welcome. Whereas de Gaulle was practically unknown in Britain, Pinard was instantly recognisable, with his coarse silvery moustache, the joy of worn-out cartoonists, and his nose broken by a fall from a horse and flattened out of its

French sharpness. His name was one of the few that the public knew well and it created its own picture.

The General was a peasant's son from the flattest, wettest and most unpicturesque part of France, where the provinces of Aisne and Somme join. Born in 1869, he grew up with the Prussian occupation; the army rescued him from hoeing root vegetables, and he rose at a moderate speed through the ranks. Improbable as it seemed, he was a romantic, a Dreyfusard and a devotee of the aeroplane – indeed, his lectures on the importance of airpower delayed his promotion by several years. However, he cared nothing for Empire, nothing for impossible ambitions, only for the stubborn defence of the solid earth of his country. In the Great War, he was with one of the only two divisions not affected by the mutiny of 1917. He always slept excellently, and it was said that he had to be wakened by his orderly before every battle.

When the Ecole Supérieure de Guerre was reopened in 1919, Pinard was one of the first to be appointed, and was looked upon as a sound man, a counterweight, with his peasant blood, to the impossible de Gaulle. In 1940, in spite of his advanced age, he had managed to get himself the command of the 5th Armoured Division, which, in the middle of May, had made a last counterattack against the German advance.

A romantic, then, though limited by earth and sky, but nothing in his military career explained his curious fondness for the English. This could be traced to his shrewd marriage with a very rich woman, addicted, as Pinard was himself, to racehorses. Between the wars he had become a familiar figure at bloodstock sales, and at Epsom and Ascot. Much photographed at every meeting, he was always cheerful, and, most important of all, nearly always a loser. That was the foundation of his great popularity over here, something he had never attained in France. On his wife's money, he became an Anglophile. He learnt to love because he was loved, for the first time in his life.

At half-past eight on the 14th of June the Director General's office told DPP that General Pinard was going on the air as soon as it could be arranged. 'He wants to broadcast to the English nation and it seems it's a matter of great urgency. It's all been agreed.'

'Well, the evening programmes must shove over a bit,' said Jeff. 'I'll see to it.'

'It's more than that. We want you down in the studio.'

'What for?'

'Don't you speak fluent French?'

'Well?'

'He wants you there when Pinard comes.'

'He speaks perfectly good English, with a strong French accent, which is exactly what you want.'

'The point is this – the War Office is sending someone and so is the F.O., and the DG and DDG don't think it will look well if we can't produce a French speaker from our top level in BH.'

'What do you want me to say?'

'Oh, it might be a few sentences of greeting. Some hospitality may be considered appropriate. I suppose there'd better be some absinthe, isn't that what they drink?'

'The General prefers cognac,' Jeff said.

'Have you met him, then? That might be extremely useful.'

'I met him in a dugout, behind a village called Quesnoy en Santerre, twenty-three years ago.'

'I've never heard you talk about your war experiences before, Haggard.'

'This wasn't an experience. We were supposed to be taking over from the French, then it turned out that we were retreating. I was Mess Officer and I stayed to see if the French had left any brandy behind, they did sometimes. Pinard came back with exactly the same idea in mind. He was a captain then. I don't flatter myself that he'll remember this incident, by the way.'

'I see, well, that isn't really . . . did he seem to be a good speaker?'

'He didn't say very much on that occasion.'

'In a sense it hardly matters whether he is or not. It's a morale talk, he's expected to fly on to Morocco to organise the resistance there, he'll want to encourage himself as well as us.'

General Pinard arrived brushed and shining, to the relief of the Talks Producer, who believed, in the old way, that appearances were projected through the microphone. His silent young aide wished to accompany him into the studio, but was detained in the rather crowded continuity room. Pinard sat down behind the glass panel, his eyes resting for a moment upon everybody present.

'He won't wear headphones,' the Talks Producer told Jeff. 'It seems he doesn't like them. He prefers to go ahead on a hand cue.'

'I don't think we should grudge him anything.'

The canteen's brandy, Martell 2 Star, left over from Christmas, was brought out. The General raised his hand in a gesture of mild, but emphatic, refusal. That meant that no one could have any – a disappointment to everybody except Talks, whose allocation for the month had already run out. The brandy would now do for the Minister of Coastal Defence, due later that evening. But these considerations faded as the General's presence was felt. He waited in immaculate dignity. Behind him lay France's broken armies.

A piece of paper was put in front of him. He looked at it, then moved it to one side.

In the continuity studio it was hardly possible to move. The War Office's Major, the Foreign Office's liaison man, sat awkwardly on high stools. The young French aide stood warily on guard. The Acting Deputy Director General suddenly came in through the soundless door to join them. DPP leant in a corner, looking up at the ceiling.

'Don't forget it's your duty to put everyone at their ease,' he said to the talks producer.

'He didn't look at my notes and suggestions. We need a run-through.'

'You've no time. I did what I could for you, but we can't alter the nine o'clock. You're on in forty-three seconds.'

The producer pressed his switch.

'How would you like to be introduced, General?'

'I don't know,' Pinard replied. 'I am in uniform, but I am a soldier without a post, an officer without authority, and a Frenchman without a country.'

'The English people know your name quite well, sir.'

'Use it if you wish. But make it clear that I am speaking to them as an individual. I have something to say from the heart.'

'How long is this going to take?' asked the programme engineer. No one knew, it was open-ended. The PE's face tightened with disapproval.

'My dear friends,' General Pinard said, 'many persons who have occupied the stage of history have been forgiven not only their mistakes, but their sins, because of what they did at one moment only. I pray that for me, this will prove to be the moment.'

It was a quiet, moving, old man's voice, with a slight metallic edge.

'It gives me a strange feeling to speak to you this evening, and even stranger, after all that has happened in the past few weeks, to think that I should be speaking the truth, and that so many of you should be willing to hear it. Old soldiers like to tell stories, and old generals most of all. That kind of story is called a *giberne*.'

The producer passed a note: *Should we translate at the end?* ADDG wrote: *I think a few untranslated French words give the right atmosphere.* Jeff wrote: *Don't worry, he's not going to tell it anyway.*

'This evening I am not here to indulge myself with a *giberne*. I have come to tell you what I saw yesterday, and what you must do tomorrow.

'But perhaps you will say to yourselves, "I am listening to a Frenchman." He is French, and I am English and I don't trust him, any more than I would have done these past five hundred years, let them make what alliances they will. And today above all I don't trust him, this evening I don't trust him, because his country has been defeated. You know that every road leading to the south is impassable, every road is crowded not only with troops in retreat, but with families on the move, the old, the weak and the very young, the bedding, the cooking-pots, the scenes to which we have become so terribly accustomed since Poland fell.'

'What's this about cooking-pots?' said the engineer to his JPE. 'He may be going to break down. Watch the level.'

'So, to repeat, you will think: I shan't trust this man. . . . And we French, do we trust the English? The answer is: not at all. In the past weeks, most of all in the past twenty-four hours, I have heard you called many hard names, I don't only mean by colleagues in the Conseil de Guerre but every soldier and every little shopkeeper on the road. They say that you led us unprepared into war with Germany and that having done so you have deserted us. And perhaps "in the misfortunes of our friends there is something not displeasing to us". Well, in that case you must be satisfied. We are ruined, and we blame it on you.

'Why then when I began to speak to you did I call you "friends"? That is a word that means so much that I understand no language is without it. I use it to you, and I mean it. The truth is that I am here this evening, in spite of all I have said, because I care deeply for England and the English.

'Well, is this nonsense, or is the old man weak in the head? No more unsuitable task could be imagined than for a general, worse still, an aged general, to show his feelings. And those who hold power in France at the moment did not wish me to come. They tried to prevent me, but I came.'

Without warning, General Pinard's voice rose to the level of the parade ground, and the engineer, caught on the hop, allowed it to blast fifteen million listeners.

'But, believe me, I am not here to flatter you! That would not be the duty of friendship. Dear listeners, dear Englishmen and -women, dear people of the green fields, the streets and the racecourses that I know so well – I have seen my nation lose hope, and I say to you now that there is no hope for you either, *ne vous faîtes pas aucune illusion*, you have lost your war. I tell you – do not listen to your leaders – neither those who are ready, as they always have been, to depart from these shores to Canada, nor to the courageous drunkard whom you have made your Prime Minister.'

The talks producer stared round from face to face, his hand on the censor switch, waiting for orders. The Foreign Office confronted the War Office.

'Who's going to stop him?'

'I don't know who authorised him to speak. I understand it was the War Cabinet.'

'I'll get on to the PM's office,' said the Assistant Deputy Director General.

'Don't barricade yourselves in, dear English people, do not take down your rusty shotguns. The French are a nation who have always cared about their army, while you have never cared about yours. Be sure that it won't protect you now, and most certainly you cannot protect yourselves. When the Germans arrive, and at best it will be in a few weeks, don't think of resistance, don't think of history. Nothing is so ungrateful as history. Think of yourselves, your homes and gardens which you tend so carefully, the sums of money you have saved, the children who will live to see all this pass and who will know that all governments are bad, and Hitler's perhaps not worse than any other. I tell you out of affection what France has learnt at the cost of terrible sacrifice. Give in. When you hear the tanks rolling up the streets of your quarter, be ready to give in, no matter how hard the terms. Give in when the Boche comes in. Give in.'

A terrible fit of coughing overwhelmed the microphone.

'He's overloading,' said the programme engineer, in agony.

'*Messieurs, brisons là . . . je crève . . .*'

'What does he mean by that?' asked the producer, unnerved, seizing DPP by the arm.

'What do you think he means?' said Jeff. 'He's not feeling well.' The General's right hand, lying on the table in front of him, opened and shut. He tried to force himself to stay sitting upright, but could not. His face, with its heavy silver moustaches, had turned bluish red.

The young aide was almost in tears. He had remained silent, no French junior officer speaks in the presence of his superior, clearly now he was at the end of his endurance. Jeff, who could move very quickly, picked up the bottle of Martell and taking the aide with him went into the other studio, emptied the BBC's glass of water onto the floor and filled it with brandy for the poor trembling old man. With a very different gesture now, the hand rejected it.

'*Surtout pas ça.*'

The duty officer rang through. There had been many complaints. For the past ten minutes there had been total silence on the Home network. The fifteen million listeners had heard nothing. But their reaction was not surprise so much as a kind of relief, the interruption of their programmes being exactly the kind of thing which everyone had expected from the moment war was declared, but which had failed to happen, holding the listeners' attention in a super-saturated solution which had failed month by month to crystallise. The public put even greater confidence in the BBC, because for ten minutes it had failed to speak to them.

'Of course I pulled the plugs on the General,' said Jeff. 'I felt that what he was going to say wouldn't, on the whole, be helpful to the nation at this particular juncture.'

'How in God's name did you know what he was going to say?' ADDG asked, jolted and disturbed to the very depths of his Old Servantship.

'I didn't know. I guessed.'

'I don't get it. He seemed quite all right to me when he arrived.'

'I didn't think so.'

'Why not?'

'It was something he said to me in the corridor, just before he got to the studios.'

'I didn't notice, I came down later.'

'He did recognise me, after all. I ought to have realised that generals always do remember faces, otherwise they don't become generals.'

'What did he say?'

'He said: I am going to repeat my former advice.'

'Meaning what?'

'I told you about the St Quentin front and the cognac. There was plenty left but it wasn't drinkable, it had got mixed up with dead Germans. I was going to see what I could salvage just the same, but Pinard stopped me. He said, "*Soyons réalistes*".'

'And you went ahead, entirely on your own initiative, because of that?'

'It's time to be realistic . . . I thought I'd better be on the safe side.'

'If you call it that. Why in the name of God didn't you consult me? In ordinary circumstances you wouldn't have been in the studio at all. Of course, I admit that as things turned out we've been saved from a very dangerous incident, it might have caused I don't know what despondency and panic, furthermore it would have given the M.O.I. and the War Office exactly the chance they've been looking for to step in and threaten our independence and press for governmental control – I grant you all that, I suppose in a sense one ought to congratulate you, perhaps you're expecting to be congratulated. . . . ' He paused. Jeff had never been known to expect anything of the kind. 'Leaving that aside, you acted without authority, and as a member of the administrative staff meddling with the equipment you've risked a strong protest from the unions. I don't know what to say to you. Heads will roll. He was a privileged speaker. Do you intend to do this sort of thing often?'

'I hope we shan't often be within measurable distance of invasion.'

'I don't like that, Haggard.'

'I don't mind withdrawing "measurable".'

ADDG had judged the reactions of the Ministries correctly. No one, it was true, could deny that to let General Pinard's appeal, so wretched, so heartfelt, go out to the unsuspecting public would have been a setback. Equally, it was no one's business, now that the General had been taken seriously ill, to decide what kind of a setback it might have been. This left more scope for attack. The BBC, in face of the grave doubts of the Services, who felt the less said the better on every occasion, persisted obstinately in telling the truth in their own way. But their own way was beginning to look irresponsible to the point of giddiness. And if directors of departments were to take a hand in decision-making of this order, what guarantee could there be that other French leaders who might cross the Channel in the hope of continuing the struggle would not be cut off in their turn? This last remark was part of a combined directive from the Ministries, which also suggested a formula: Haggard might be complimented on his presence of mind and packed off to one of the Regions for the duration. A new post could surely be created if necessary.

The BBC loyally defended their own. As a cross between a civil service, a powerful moral force, and an amateur theatrical company that wasn't too sure where next week's money was coming from, they had several different kinds of language, and could guarantee to come out best from almost any discussion. Determined to go on doing what they thought best without official interference, they spoke of their DPP's artistic tempera-ment which could not be restrained without risk, and when asked why they'd put this freakish impresario in charge of planning, they referred to his rigid schedules and steely devo-tion to duty. Then, after a few days, it became known that the Prime Minister had heard the whole story and thought it was excellent. He'd particularly liked the phrase 'to pull the plugs on someone', which he hadn't, apparently, come across before.

The Pinard affair was closed. But it did nothing to lessen that distance or difference between DPP and some of his colleagues, which they felt as an atmosphere of faint coldness even when they needed his help. Jeff Haggard was useful because if he felt a matter was worth taking up he didn't mind what he said or who he said it to. Look at what he'd done, over the years, for Sam

Brooks! Undoubtedly, also, he was clever. But they felt, perhaps out of a sense of self-preservation, that no one can be good and clever at the same time.

ADDG, with the leniency of someone who has been unjust in the first place, considered that Haggard's nerves might have been overtaxed. The planning of the complete Home and Forces programmes, in all their delicate bearings, couldn't be undertaken with impunity.

'I think I'll advise him to read a few chapters of *Cranford* every night before he retires to bed. I've been doing that myself ever since Munich. I think, you know, that Mrs Gaskell would have been glad to know that.'

The whole notion was comforting, but in fact Jeff had never been nervous and was now arguably the calmest person in the whole building. He didn't regard himself as either lucky, or in disgrace, but, if he was either, the feeling was quite familiar.

On the night of the 16th of June General Pinard died in the King Edward VII Hospital for Officers. It was impossible to send the body back to German-occupied territory and an awkward funeral took place at Notre Dame de France, off Leicester Square. The BBC sent a wreath, with a card on which Jeff had written *À Georges Pinard: mort pour la civilisation.* On the 17th of June de Gaulle arrived in this country.

Like Pinard, he had brought only a small suitcase. He was lodged in the Rubens Hotel and given permission to broadcast and to raise his own army.

There were French sailors camping at Aintree, French airmen in South Wales, two battalions of légionnaires at Tufnell Park, French gunners, chasseurs and signals at Alexandra Park. 'You'll never find him,' Vi said to Lise, 'we'll all do our best, though. What does your family think?' But Lise's father, who had been a cashier at Barclay's Lyons branch, had brought his family back to England in January and was now a cashier in Southampton. He wasn't favourable to the idea of Frédé and never had been.

'Well, does he know your London address?'

Lise wasn't sure, and it wouldn't do anyway. She had a room in a Catholic hostel attached to a convent near Warren Street.

'How do you know he'll turn up at all?' asked Teddy. Lise replied that she was psychic, with the result that she had a certain sensation in the points of her breasts when Frédé was near at hand.

'Who'd be a woman?' Teddy thought.

All this time Lise had remained steadily in low spirits. RPD had made only a half-hearted attempt to tell Mrs Milne that Miss Bernard was very unusual, probably talented, should not on any account be overworked, and so forth. His heart was not in it. She was less responsive than the deadened walls of the studios. But now her sluggish energies seemed to revive, at least to the extent of asking other people to do something for her.

The mobile unit had been sent by Archives to capture the scene at de Gaulle's new headquarters in Westminster. Here, in a dusty bare room, those who had made the decision to join France Libre signed their names, and afterwards drank a pledge to Victory from a barrel of red wine in the passage. 'Not much of a sound picture there,' said the recording engineer, who had flatly refused to let Dr Vogel accompany him. 'You've just got them taking this oath, footsteps coming and going on the bare boards, a nice bit of echo there, your wine coming out of the tap and a few more words, nothing in English, though.'

'Did you see anyone who looked like a sapper?' Lise asked him with dazed, heavy persistence.

'Search me, sweetheart.'

'He's bound to come there one day. He's sure to want to stay in England.'

'Well, we're going back tomorrow to see if we can get some more atmosphere. With luck, one of them might smash a glass.' The RE told Willie Sharpe that Lise seemed pretty well idiotic. 'You don't make allowances for human hope,' Willie replied.

And yet, out of the two hundred thousand French troops brought over here and quartered at random, in the miraculously fair weather, wherever a space could be found, they did come across Frédé.

They were out for a breather in Kensington Gardens – Della and Vi, with Lise, who had made them go there in the first place, dragging behind. You often saw French soldiers in the gardens, detachments of *français libres* and of the vastly greater number who had not signed on and were waiting to go back home as soon as they got the chance. There wasn't much for them to do in a park, but then, there wasn't much for them to do anyway.

Della never went out looking less than her best. She wore a striped silk blouse with a deeply suggestive V-neckline under her red linen costume; on the lapels of this she pinned, on alternate weeks, her RAF wings, naval crown, Free Polish, Free Czech, Free Norwegian, Free Dutch and Free Belgian flashes and the badges of Canadian and New Zealand regiments. Her hair was gallantly swept back in sparkling ridges and she advanced on high heels, ready to receive or repel any opening shots in the way of glances, remarks, or hard cheek. Under persuasion, Lise had also bought a pair of strapped high-heeled shoes. Della felt almost professionally insulted at the idea of a friend trying to meet her fiancé, if that was what he was, without tarting herself up at least a little. Vi looked her usual self in a cotton dress she had made on her mother's machine. It was all right, but no more than that.

Kensington's leafy glades were full of lovers and, at a discreet distance, workers off work, each with their own thermos. The girls passed close enough to the anti-aircraft battery to hear and take no apparent notice of the long whistle that followed them. At last they chose to sit on the ground at the edge of the dingle, with a good view of the Peter Pan statue. 'I expect the man who made that died young,' Della said. It was odd for them, after eight hours in BH, to sit on the grass, picking off bits of grass and chewing them, under the lazing clouds.

When the French soldiers appeared they came in two groups, and from opposite directions, a few *français libres* to begin with, idling across from Hyde Park. They stopped at the bridge and looked at the water, not as if they knew each other very well as yet. Someone had given them cigarettes and they had evidently stopped by previous arrangement to hand round the packets and allow themselves one each. Quite a few of them had légionnaires' chinstrap beards and Della, who had never seen these before, kept pointing. Vi jerked her elbow down. Without a word Lise heaved herself to her feet and began to stumble forward on her strappies, but the other way, towards the Round Pond.

There the summer turf of the gardens was dotted with more French soldiers coming over the ridge, who suddenly all sat or lay down, like a herd on a fine day. They were determined not to go any farther. A refreshment van, driven by a middle-aged woman in a navy-blue beret, pulled up and parked itself among them. On its side you could read, painted in white, the words ANGLO-FRENCH AMENITIES COMMITTEE. She opened up the side of her van and began to count out rolls of bread and paper cups. Nobody took any notice of her.

Lise gracelessly panted up the slope to within speaking distance. A man got to his feet. True, she'd never told them exactly what this Frédé looked like, but this one was short, and not even dark. It was deeply disappointing, and at the same time confusing – Lise made an awkward grab and then lost her footing, then righted herself and clung on to him, taller than he was and much heavier. She seemed to be wrestling with the dishevelled khaki creature.

'I wouldn't have thought she'd got it in her,' said Della. Stir it up, she thought. She only wanted for Lise what she'd have liked for herself.

'Yes but those aren't Free French,' said Vi. 'He's got into the wrong lot.' She was frightened. Against the protests of Frédé and his cronies Lise was crying out in French, and when she did that she seemed to turn into another person, or let out the one she had been all along. This made the girls feel queer.

By now the FLs on the bridge had finished their cigarettes and put the stubs away inside their caps. Sighting the others on the opposite slope only two hundred yards away, they warily advanced through Peter Pan's dingle. Then some of them began to run in ragged formation, like boys anxious to get into a football game, the small, neat and elegant ones in front, as though trained, others in the rear beating up clouds of dust with their boots from the dry earth. Lise and Frédé disappeared from sight as the hostile forces engaged, the front runners gesturing, with one fist clenched and one stiffened arm pointing beyond the horizon of the park. They shouted something, as hoarse as rooks, then their voices pitched higher into uproar. The people who had come for a nice afternoon in the gardens stood where they were and stared.

'They're having a political altercation,' said a man with his children. 'Where's their NCOs?'

There was a sound of something flat hitting something flat – say a wet cloth on a kitchen table. It was a slap on the face. Just for a moment the girls could see Frédé staggering and holding his jaw in his hand like toothache, with thick blood running through the fingers, but it wasn't Lise who'd hit him, she was still half up and half down, but nowhere near him any more. It was one of the FLs, and now they were all going down in twos and threes, rolling on the ground in squalor, with banging heads and seams splitting, showing a flash of whitish-grey pants.

'The soldiers!' Della cried. 'They're fighting! They can't do that!'

Those who were on their feet snatched up the rolls from the counter of the refreshment van and the summer air was streaked with missiles. The woman in the navy-blue beret was running away towards the Round Pond. Money fell from her bag onto the grass. The food she had prepared was trodden to a pulp and thrust and plastered into angry faces. There was nothing to laugh at, the sight of the homesick boys battering away at each other was like the naked spirit of hate itself.

The torn bread lay scattered everywhere. 'They're not English, you can't expect them to understand the shortages,' Vi thought. 'Thank God there's Lise.' She was making her way towards them, looking swollen and ugly.

'Where's Frédé?'

Two policemen were approaching in the distance, followed by five or six corporals, who had perhaps been absent without leave in the wine-bars of Kensington. The riot died down, the culprits began to explain themselves.

'He won't stay,' Lise sobbed, 'he doesn't want me any more. They hit him. He wants to go back to Lyons.'

'We'll have to take her with us, Della. She can't go back to that convent place looking like that. She's distraught.'

But Della was going out dancing at the Lyceum. 'I've got to go and get into my black, but it isn't that that takes the time, it's ringing up to see if anyone can lend me some pearls or a white collar. If you're going to wear black you have to have some little touches.'

Vi did not contest this. 'You can come home with me for a bit,' she said to Lise. 'My mother won't mind.'

They took a bus to Hammersmith. Vi paid both their fares, as although Lise had succeeded in hanging on to her bag she seemed, as often, to have no money with her. But it was a mercy she hadn't lost her BBC pass and identity card.

They walked up a quiet side road, simmering in the late afternoon heat.

The gate of Vi's home hung open among shaggy evergreens.

'Don't shut it, it's always open.'

'It's a big house,' said Lise.

'It has to be. There's nine of us.'

She went into the dark hall, lit by stained glass, with the air of an eldest child who expects to restore order, and listened for a moment to the noises from radios, hammers, pulled lavatory chains, taps running and a piano banging to identify who was at home, and whether they were more or less doing what they ought to be.

'You can't come across the hall, it's the English Channel,' said a small boy who was sitting on the stairs.

'Where's Dad?'

'Still at the shop.'

'Where's Mum, then?'

She was thought to be putting on the kettle. To oblige the child they retreated through the front door and walked round

by the lawn, dug up and planted with vegetables, the one rose-
bed, the rabbit-hutches, coal-shed and coke-shed, and entered
the kitchen by the back scullery.

'You want to put these in water at once, Mum,' said Vi,
lifting a pile of crimson ramblers out of the sink. 'This is Lise
Bernard, from work.'

Mrs Simmons was a broadly-based woman in an overall, not
at all disconcerted by Lise's appearance. Having revived her
memories of 1914, she in fact expected girls to be in tears. There
was no question as to where Vi's kind heart came from. At
home, however, one of her duties was to moderate its excesses.

'Sit down, Lizzie,' cried Mrs Simmons, who didn't get names
right. 'You needn't mind showing your feelings. I daresay
tea will help. But I can't pretend it'll alter the fact that he's
far away.'

'He's in Kensington Gardens,' said Vi.

She kept remembering Frédé's face, dark and mad, with the
blood oozing through his fingers.

'Perhaps Lise could share my room for a bit. She could
manage ten shillings a week on what we get, couldn't you,
Lise?'

In both Mrs Simmons's mind and Vi's the three-year-old's
cot moved out of Vi's room and one of the boys went onto the
lounge sofa and to compensate for this Chris, the merchant
seaman, was asked to bring him something special by way of a
souvenir. There was no need for either of them to explain
further. It would be no trouble at all.

Lise appeared to be glad to leave the convent, but who could
tell what she really thought? She seemed to have relapsed into
her old sloth. One would say that she had given up the power of
choice. Yet ten days later she left her job at Broadcasting House
without saying goodbye. She did not come back to Hammersmith either, and Mrs Simmons couldn't think what to do with
her few things. Finally Vi forbade her to mention the subject
more than twice at any one suppertime.

3

'Jeff,' shouted Sam, 'do you remember that French general that came to the studio and died?'

'Yes.'

'Has anyone told you that you buggered up the whole thing?'

'Not in so many words.'

'But just tell me this, have you faced the fact that we didn't record him, not one single word? Nothing in the can, nothing to process for Archives. If you'd got to mess about with the transmission you could at least have put him on to closed circuit. Nobody bothered to tell me this, of course. It's only just been brought to my notice.' Jeff felt relieved. If Sam had indignantly offered to go to his defence, or even realised that some defence might be necessary, the situation would have been so disturbed that he'd have felt sea-sick. Nations fall, relationships have a duty to stay firm.

Sam's rage subsided into a regretful, eager anxiety. 'We've no decent French atmosphere, those Free French signing on were very disappointing, I've had Vogel in to listen to them and he just kept shaking his head. The wine coming out of the barrel isn't satisfactory.'

'We might try substituting white for red, perhaps.'

Sam ignored him.

'And now they say they're bringing Eddie Waterlow back from Drama to do some programme, *France Fights On* was the provisional title, sixty minutes of transcriptions I bloody well shouldn't wonder.'

'They're not exactly bringing him back, it's only that he wrote them such a very sad letter. He doesn't understand life in Manchester. He's never lived north of Regent's Park before. I don't suppose his programme will ever come to anything.'

'The point is that I oughtn't to be harassed about pro-gramme material at all – I oughtn't even to be consulted – the only thing that's of interest to me at the moment, the only thing I can think about and talk about, that is whenever I'm lucky enough to find anyone in this place who has the slightest comprehension of what I'm saying, the thing that's so much more important to me than happiness or health or sanity, is the improvement I'm hoping to make to the standard microphone windshield. The windshield, I mean, for the mobile units in battle areas. Whatever they choose to say, Directors, DG, Higher Command, War Cabinet, Prime Minister, you name it, I'm not sending my units back into Europe without a better windshield than the one they've got.'

'When do you envisage this new invasion taking place?' asked Jeff with interest.

'Not for six months. I'll have it ready by then. They'll have to wait till then.'

They had been on the telephone, but Jeff now went down to the third floor. Sam was sitting with a scale drawing in front of him. Mrs Milne was just leaving the room, and remarked: 'I've just been saying to RPD that by the end of the present emer-gency none of us will feel inclined to trust foreigners again.' But she could scarcely be heard above the deafening sound of *The Teddy Bears' Picnic* which was playing at high volume on one of the turntables. *Today's the day they're having the Teddy Bears' Picnic.* . . . It was the engineers' favourite testing record, with its curious changes from low level to high. Jeff lifted the needle and switched off.

'Don't do that!' cried Sam.

'You know I'm not interested in your box of tricks.'

'I'm obliged, in the face of criticism, and my present state of under-manning, to do two things at once.'

'I think you ought to come out for a bit.'

'Out? Out?' Sam took off his glasses and gazed with his child's eyes.

His expression changed and he spoke humbly.

'Perhaps I don't lead a very healthy life. If ever I do go out of BH I hope I don't look different from other people, but I feel different.'

'Do you mean you're getting afraid to leave the place at all?'

'They don't seem to encourage me to go out with the cars any more. I don't know why that is.'

'I didn't mean that. I was thinking of your own place, Streatham Drive, isn't it, I came to dinner there last summer, perhaps you remember.'

'I'd like to ask you again, but I don't quite know if anyone's there.'

'Who knows if you don't?'

'My wife's evacuated herself, you know, to the country.'

'You haven't mentioned it.'

Sam pondered.

'She's learning to drive a tractor, which I rather think she's always wanted to do. A friend of hers is married to a farmer, they're producing Vegetables for Victory. Plums, too, I think, all this is near Pershore.'

'How many acres?'

'How many acres do people have? What are you talking about? You don't know anything about farming anyway. We were discussing the Archives. They're threadbare. It's not only omissions through mismanagement, like your general. For example, we've no Stukas. When we're asked for dive-bombing we have to borrow from Pathé Gazette.'

Jeff envied Sam the number of things he didn't notice, and even more his absorption in a fairy-tale world of frequency responses, a land of wire and wax where *The Teddy Bears' Picnic* was the password and the Fool could walk protected by his own spell. It was less envy, though, after all, than playing with envy, but it reminded him that when he himself had got out of the army and finished at Cambridge he had certainly not intended to be an administrator. Perhaps even now he could scarcely be called that, as his system depended so largely on considering his own comfort. Even his refusal to have a secretary was a kind of luxury, enabling him to ignore at least half his correspondence as not worth a reply. The Old Servants, though they had never been able to fault his methods, could not accept them. 'DPP will hardly be able to do without a secretary if tea-rationing is introduced,' Mrs Milne had begun to say, 'and it's threatened.'

On the 20th June Jack Barnett of Transport, Supply and Equipment asked if DPP could spare him a few minutes.

'Mr Haggard, do you still want that taxi to wait for you every night in Riding House Street?'

'Why, is the driver objecting?' asked Jeff. 'I should have thought he might have come and talked to me himself. He often does.'

'Not as far as I know. Of course, you're paying for his time yourself so he doesn't come onto my account. But I was thinking that perhaps you're not aware that since the news got so bad you're entitled as a Departmental Director to the use of an armoured car every evening on standby until further notice. Of course we're leaving it to your public spirit to share the car whenever possible.'

'Jack, you want my taxi for somebody else. Who is it?'

'Well, we've been notified that a very distinguished American newscaster is going to turn up here. He's just made his own way out of France, and NBS have asked us to give him transport facilities. We don't know how long he'll be over here, but he's said to be one of Britain's firmest friends, and believe me, Mr Haggard, we need them now.'

'He can have my armoured car.'

'I'm afraid I haven't made my point clear, Mr Haggard. He wants a cab with a Cockney driver who's a bit of a character. That's what journalists like, and that's what he is, newscaster's just their word for it. And you seem to be the only member of staff that can get a cab to wait regularly.'

'What's he called?'

'Something McVitie.'

DPP looked somewhat moved, you could almost call it pleased, but all he said was: 'If it's Mac, it will do him good to walk.'

The door seemed to explode inwards. It was fortunate that the desk was always kept clear, because the man who came in immediately piled it high with tin hats, webbing belts, mess-tins, three cameras, a Press arm-band, a bedroll, French wines, French cheeses, a holster, a .45 automatic and a pair of officer's field-glasses.

'Take all this junk out of here,' said Jeff.

Mac flung down a large sack of oranges and threw his arms round Jeff, as when brave and reluctantly friendly paleface meet. Barnett was taken aback. He'd never seen anybody, man, woman or child, attempt to embrace DPP and he could hardly credit it now.

'These are times of stress, times of decision,' growled Mac in a deeply rich New Jersey accent. 'I find you sitting here.'

'That's all I'm required to do until the Germans cross the Channel,' Jeff replied. 'I expect to get further instructions then.'

'Let's go on a real beat-up,' said Mac. 'You too, kid,' he added, turning to Barnett.

Barnett excused himself. His duties in regard to the important American correspondent were at an end. DPP and he were evidently as thick as thieves and could decide for themselves about the taxi. Meanwhile it was time to address himself to his next problem. The newly-installed French section didn't like the grade 3 mid-green carpets which he'd supplied with such difficulty. It was a moral issue, it seemed, they wanted to bivouac in the simplest possible conditions and to purify themselves through suffering, London being their new front line until victory was in sight. Now he was left with three carpets on his hands.

Up till 1939 Mac had been stationed in London rather more often than in other parts of the world, and on routine visits to BH he had got to know Jeff as well perhaps as anybody did. He loved Jeff because he saw him as a human being not over-impressed by the world, less so in fact than anyone he knew except his own grandmother who'd always refused to leave Stony Ridge, Vermont. Hence when Jeff had had to go to New

York on the BBC's business or his own, he had always stayed with the McVitie family, out on Long Island.

Now Mac's unexpected arrival and generous progress through Broadcasting House was like a gust of warm wild air, exposing its thin places. At his approach Barnett had become a kid, while the office, ready for a forward planning meeting, had turned into a dump for left luggage. Even the well-tried national defence of expecting the worst, in which Jeff shared because it suited him temperamentally, had to give way and let through the impatient pioneer. Everything seemed possible, except to leave things as they were.

The two of them crossed the road together in the sunlight for a drink at the Langham. The vast hotel, rented by the BBC, gave the impression of being too proud to submit to its new occupants. The cathedral-like apse, the colossal Corinthian pillars branching into gilded foliage, the antique iron fire escapes, the pendants of Lalique glass glimmering from the high ceilings, all suggested many cycles of art and civilisation, now put to baser uses and menaced by war. Upstairs, most of the bedrooms had been converted with hardboard partitions into offices; turning left through the mighty glass doors you came to a bar which the BBC had furnished with timid cocktail stools.

Mac drove his way through the clearings between the tables.

'My cut-through to New York's at seven. We've got half an hour. Do they have anything to drink here?'

'Give them time,' said Jeff. 'When you come into the war they'll lay in some root beer for you.'

'What do you want me to fight your war for?' Mac asked. He took a bottle of bourbon out of his coat pocket and offered the barman a drink in exchange for the loan of two clean glasses. 'What's the idea, why are you so anxious to survive?'

'Habit,' said Jeff.

'You ought to think about it very carefully. You'd get to be sixty or seventy, and then what are you going to do with yourself?'

'I shall care about less things.'

'As it happens my father's sixty-three today,' Mac went on. 'That makes me feel pretty young. Who was that character anyway, that one who was talking with you and couldn't come out? I'd hoped to ply him with liquor, I'd imagined he'd be the better for being plied.'

'He was consulting me about a taxi, but I rather think he was going on to the question of carpets.'

For the first time Mac's creased affectionate face was completely serious.

'You take on the hell of a lot too much of this advice and assistance. You're weakening these people. In times like these we've got to forgo luxuries and that includes the obligation to help others. Probably you ought to be doing something totally else.'

Over the different accents and languages at almost every table of the Langham Mac's lazily purring voice could be distinctly heard.

'Anyway, I'm told you've been in trouble.'

Jeff was not disconcerted, he didn't mind when heads turned round to look at him from a wide circle of tables, but he was surprised.

'When did you hear that?'

Mac, pouring out the bourbon, said that he'd been to see all his contacts as soon as he landed. He'd come over just before dawn in a Breton fishing boat.

'Breton fishermen at dawn are the equivalent of Cockney taxi-drivers,' said Jeff. 'You'll choke yourself on local colour.'

'Let's get this right, I was told you were in trouble,' Mac persisted. 'Nobody said you were now. But your trouble-making capacity is God's gift, Jeff. You'll have to render an account some day of what the hell you did with it and the quality of the trouble you made. Don't tell me you're giving up just when you're getting your hand in.'

Jeff looked at him meditatively. 'Do you mean to say you went round all your contacts with that load of cheeses?'

'No, I dropped off quite a few of them as I went by. They were gifts.'

'What about all that stuff in my office?'

'Gifts, gifts. That's one of the things that's wrong with you, Jeff. You don't recognise a giver.'

Mac's call to New York came through on time and an hour later he flew home, either to get a clean shirt or to find a shirt that would fit him, there were two versions. He said he'd be back in September. That would be about the right time, according to his sources. Before leaving he had scattered oranges, which were unobtainable in England, and it wasn't clear where he could have got them in France, throughout the offices of BH. The strange fruit glowed from the bottom of in-trays and out-trays; a dozen of them were rolling about the deserted music library. The Recorded Programmes Assistants received three between the four of them who were left – Tad had gone to train as a fitter with the Free Polish Air Force. Willie and Vi waited until two minutes to fourteen hours, when Teddy and the yawning Della turned up on shift, while they were due to go off. The division of the oranges was a serious matter, since the shortages had produced in the whole population a delicate and bizarre sense of justice. The only sharp knives were in Packing and Despatch – the canteen had none – and Willie undertook to get hold of one.

They laid the three oranges on a copy of the *Radio Times*. It is difficult to know what to do with scarce items in wartime and David was no doubt right, when his servants risked their lives to bring him water, to pour it out on the ground as an offering to the Lord. For the RPAs, it came to three-quarters of an orange each. They were, of course, much too old to be greedy. Vi made a sensible calculation that it wouldn't be worth taking hers home to share it with so many. Willie picked up the packers' knife.

'Ten seconds from now.'

'Poor old Tad, I miss him,' said Teddy. 'I'd like to send him his slice.' None of them mentioned Lise.

'How are you going to work it out?' asked Della. 'One of them's smaller than the others.'

'That's a point.'

'. . . Aah, the Three Oranges . . . I am the Magician Tehe-lio . . .' sang a thin, disturbing tenor from the corridor. A lean and silvery figure sidled past.

'It's Mr Waterlow,' said Vi. 'He was down here before, when I first came, in January.' Surely he couldn't want a piece?

'I believe there's plenty of oranges in the other departments, Mr Waterlow,' snapped Della. But of course, he scarcely belonged to a department. He'd drifted back to London to do Heaven knows what.

'Ah, my dear, I have never brought myself to touch one . . .' he drifted on, and they could hear him start singing again, further down the passage.

Willie drew the sharp edge of the blade across the brilliant, delicately pitted skin of the first orange, and let it slide through the pith. Like a firework it sprayed up and burst into fragrance. The best moment. They sat licking and lingering, wondering if it was worth planting the pips, the heating would be on in BH next winter, but they wouldn't thrive, plants always knew the difference.

Della finished some time after the others. She was reading a General Circulation memo headed Christmas Arrangements 1940. The BBC, like most British organisations, thought about these in June. It began *Although it is not possible to forecast what shape this year's Christmas Programmes will take, or to give any assurance as to whether His Majesty will broadcast to the nation as he did in 1939, all Departments are asked to send in their suggestions as soon as possible. The Corporation also feels that it is not too early to warn staff, particularly in the Drama and Variety Departments, that all presents offered to them by the outside public, particularly money, jewellery, and alcoholic drinks, should be refused or returned as soon as possible, without comment.*

'I'm going to apply for a transfer,' said Della.

They stared at her, with the limp empty quarters of peel in their hands.

'If Eddie Waterlow can come down from Drama, I don't see why I shouldn't go up there. It's a free country.'

'Jewellery!' Teddy exclaimed.

'You know I've always wanted to do something with my singing. I can't get anyone to audition me here. I believe I'd meet with understanding in Drama.'

'Everyone understands you down here,' said Vi.

'I've had my voice described as dark brown velvet,' Della said.

Teddy jumped up, putting the peel in his pocket, and told her that they'd be late if they didn't look out.

Mrs Milne's confidential crony, the Secretary of Assistant Director (Establishment), spoke to her without reserve. AD(E) simply didn't think that RPD knew how to select his staff. That last RPA, the half-French girl who snivelled, had left without even handing in her BBC pass and had left no forwarding address. And now he'd lost another one, although of course Zagorski, T., couldn't be blamed for joining his country's armed forces.

'What do you suggest, then? We're very short-handed.'

'It might be a much better plan to try for a sensible middle-aged woman, I mean someone a few years older than ourselves. Of course the job and the pay are on a junior scale, but that mightn't matter if she was just augmenting her husband's income. It's been demonstrated time and again that older women are less prone to tears and hysteria. I could show you our reliability charts. There's no reason at all why they shouldn't handle the discs efficiently, and if it came, as I believe it does, to holding RPD's hand when he feels under the weather, then one would imagine that they'd have had considerably more practice.'

'That, I think, is rather a delicate area where RPD has been very much misunderstood,' replied Mrs Milne. 'RPD likes to chat quietly about day-to-day problems of the Department and it's very unfortunate that my hours of work make it impossible for me to listen to him as often as in his heart of hearts he would like.'

The two women were simply aiding and abetting each other to disband the Seraglio. Mrs Milne had allowed herself to take another step forward into illusion, and her friend, also an Old Servant, had not dissuaded her. AD(E) had insisted that this time a small panel should interview the applicants for the job of RPA, to avoid any repetition of mistakes. Both secretaries would attend it, and Mrs Milne thought that if they could guarantee to get through the business quickly, DPP might be prevailed upon to come too. She knew that he was devoted to RPD's interests, in spite of his sour manner; well, if not sour, you could hardly call it encouraging. However, she personally believed that DPP's main function – although he did his own job exceedingly well, no one denied that – was to encourage RPD and to help him over those moments of depression which come to even the best of us.

The question of Lise's replacement also weighed heavily on RPD himself. For Establishment to count her as one of the girls he'd used up was a characteristic injustice. He had put her on his Emergency List, and told Mrs Milne that she was a somewhat unusual person, and surely needed special consideration, but only in a half-hearted manner, and before he had got to know her at all, she had simply disappeared.

'You might, perhaps, consider someone who would stay a little longer,' said Jeff. AD(E) had privately told him in advance that he'd have to assist in conducting the interview this time and see that a sensible appointment was made or there'd be nothing doing.

'They claim that in the present situation all the girls are needed for Coastal Defence,' said Sam, 'but that's ludicrous. I see girls walking about everywhere.'

'Do you mean you've actually been out?'

Sam ignored this. He was hurt and puzzled. 'Jeff, they want to surround me with old women. You know, there's a good deal of sagging on the late night shift, just when hopefulness is needed, and firmness, and roundness, and readiness to be pleased, and so on.'

'Have you mentioned this to Mrs Milne?'

'What's she got to do with it? I couldn't carry on if I didn't know that she was going to leave every day at half past five. And you know I've always had the best possible relationships with the junior members of my Department. I consider myself as morally responsible for them all and I can honestly say that I know their troubles as well as I do my own.'

Jeff felt that that was saying a good deal. He waited silently.

'Then there's another thing, I'm not sure I've made myself absolutely clear about my wife. Leaving London was her idea, not mine. I don't want you to think she's in any way out of the picture, just because she's never here. She sent me a photograph of the tractor, quite a good one. She seems to be occupied with the War Agricultural Committee which gets rather in the way of things, and then they all have coffee in each other's houses for some reason, and she's in the Red Cross with some friends of hers, splendid women, she tells me. The truth is that other things being equal she really prefers women to men.'

'So do you, Sam,' said Jeff.

He arranged for a recruitment interview at the end of the following fortnight.

4

It was reassuring to see the interviews and provisional Christmas arrangements going ahead and looking as they always had done while Broadcasting House reached its final state of War Emergency. The defence rooms were shut off by iron doors, armed guards patrolled the sub-basement, and the lists of Indispensable Personnel, except for Sam's, were complete. After repeated consultations Sam still hesitated as to who might be asked to accompany him, perhaps for weeks on end, behind the barricades. Meanwhile all departments were asked to find volunteers for the Red Cross Certificate Course.

Accommodation put the now unused concert-hall at the disposal of the Red Cross classes. The canvas-seated chairs, drawn up too close together for comfort just beneath the platform, conjured up the rapt ghosts of the BBC's old invited audiences. The lighting, designed for the orchestras now stranded in Bristol, was not too well suited to the lecturer, a harassed doctor from the nearby Middlesex Hospital who had probably expected younger listeners. Some of them, it was true, didn't look much more than children, but among them were departmental heads and even an Assistant Controller with folded arms, unused to sitting on a chair without a conference table in front of him. All ranks had been mingled to learn elementary first-aid. The BBC had always been liable to these sudden appealing manifestations of the democratic spirit, derived from both its moral and its veteran-theatrical sides, reminding both highest and lowest that they shared the same calling and, at the moment, the same danger.

'In cases of emergency,' muttered the lecturer, 'an umbrella, walking-cane or broomstick is sure to be handy, and will furnish an excellent splint.' Unashamedly reading out of a handbook, he went on: 'When a fracture has taken place the object is to bring the ends of the broken bone as nearly as possible to the position they were in previous to the accident. In order to do this, the part nearest to the body must be steadied by someone, while that furthest removed is gently stretched out, the sound limb being uncovered and observed as a guide. . . . For God's sake, ladies and gentlemen, don't dream of doing any of these things. Leave the patient exactly as he is, and if you have to move him take him straight round to Casualties. However, my object, as I understand it, is to see that by the end of six weeks you can be passed competent in bandaging, simple and compound fractures, first and second degree burns, lesions, cramp, poisoning, intoxication, snake-bite . . . no need to take all these down, they're simply some of the chapter headings. . . . '

As soon as he decently could the doctor passed on to practical work, asking them to envisage the scene after a general attack from the air, but to assume, for the sake of convenience, that all the casualties were broken bones. DPP, sitting at the extreme edge of a row to make room for his long legs, was summoned to the front to take the part of an incident. Unruffled and resigned, labelled Multiple Injuries and Compound Fractures, he was laid out prone on one of a long line of stores trolleys. While the other incidents settled themselves he passed the time by smoking a cigar, which is difficult when both arms are immobilized.

'Perhaps you'd like me to copy out my notes for you as I go along, Mr Haggard,' said Willie Sharpe, bent over him and prodding him with a pencil, 'you'll probably miss a number of important points while you're lying here.' He scribbled rapidly. 'I've got you down as both femurs, both collarbones and right patella.'

Jeff emitted a faint cloud of smoke. The lecturer glanced at him in understandable annoyance. The cause of realism wasn't served by a multiple fracture smoking a cigar.

'Please will the incidents remember not to make signs or convey information of any kind to the class.'

Willie, however, had understood that DPP wanted the ash tipped off his cigar. He did so, then, not wishing to waste

an opportunity, he drew up a chair, sat down near the
trolley, and leant forward eagerly, half confiding, half
appealing.

'We mustn't grudge the time we're spending on this Red
Cross course, Mr Haggard. In fact, personally speaking, I'm
very glad of the training because it contributes in a small way
to one of my general aims for all humanity. I mean the maintenance of health both in mind and body. Education will be
a very different thing in the world of tomorrow. It will start
at birth, or even earlier. It won't be a petty matter of School
Certificate, the tedious calculations of facts and figures
which hold many a keen and hopeful spirit back today. It
will begin as we're beginning now, Mr Haggard, you and
I and all these others here this evening, with a knowledge of
our own bodies and how they can be kept fighting trim –
fighting, I mean, needless to say, for the things of the spirit.
Yes, we shall learn to read our bodies and minds like a book
and know how best to control them. Oh boy, will the teachers
be in for a shock. Don't think, either, that I'm saying that
physical desires must be entirely subdued. On the contrary,
Mr Haggard, they have their part to play if every individual is
to develop his potentialities to the full. And the point I want to
make is how very little pounds, shillings, and pence have to
do with all this. Yes, sir, out in the fresh air and sunlight,
with your chosen mate by your side, you'll have little need
for money.'

Carried away, glowing and translated into a generous
future, Willie tucked away his notebook and pencil and
passed on to the next trolley. As soon as he decently could
the doctor hurried away, leaving two of his hospital nurses to
carry on. At half-time, incidents and students were asked
to change places. Jeff was released, and Willie became a
shock case.

The following week a message was posted on all notice boards
for the attention of volunteers for Red Cross training. The
classes had been amalgamated with other local courses, and they

were asked to attend in future at Marylebone Town Hall. Accommodation, it turned out, needed the concert-hall for a dormitory. In the event of an attack, the notice explained, personnel would be unable to get home, shift workers found it difficult already, and it hadn't escaped Accommodation's notice that a number of the staff never seemed to leave the building at all. In this connection, it should be emphasised that the new bathrooms on the fifth floor were for the use of grades of Assistant Controller and above. But in future the Corporation would provide beds for those who had earned them, strictly allocated on a ticket basis.

Quantities of metal bunks were dragged into Broadcasting House. Piled outside the concert-hall, they made an obstruction on the grand scale. Even the news readers, whose names and voices were known to the whole nation, were held up on their way to the studios. Even John Haliburton, assigned to read in case of enemy landing, with a voice of such hoarse distinction that if the Germans took over BH and attempted to impersonate him the listeners could never be deceived for a moment – even the beloved Halibut fell over a consignment of iron frames and himself became an incident. But the work went on with the exalted remorselessness characteristic of anyone who starts moving furniture. The bunks were fitted on top of each other in unstable tiers, and the platform, including the half-sacred spot where the grand piano had once stood, was converted into cubicles. Eddie Waterlow, insanely fond of music, was seen walking away from the sight with his head in his hands, a pantomime of grief. The fitters didn't mind, feeling that he acknowledged the importance of their work. If Broadcasting House had been built like a ship, it now had quarters for a crew of hundreds.

At length a cord was stretched across the great hall, dividing it in half, and grey hospital blankets were draped over it in place of a curtain. Barnett and his staff thought this part of the job by no means up to standard.

'It'll provide privacy for the ladies, which is the main point. But I don't like to see a job left like that.'

And might not the makeshift nature of the blankets lead to moral confusion? There were a lot of very young people among the temporary staff. Barnett was asked whether he thought there'd be goings on?

'Surely not while England's in danger,' he replied.

Everyone went to look at the arrangements. 'So near and yet so far,' Teddy said. At the end of the week the RPAs' tickets arrived with their time-sheets. They were relieved, all of them, to think they wouldn't have to queue any more for the all-night buses.

When Vi got home that afternoon a little brother, lying flat on his back on the lawn where the cabbage beds had become torpedoes, and he was drowned and floating, told her that someone had rung her up. When she went into the hall the telephone rang again.

'Vi, it's Lise.'

'Where are you? Are you coming back to work?'

'Vi, I want you to help me. I haven't anywhere to live.'

'Why don't you go home? Southampton's a defence zone, but of course it'll be all right for you if your parents live there.'

'I can't get on with them. I don't feel as though I'm their child at all. I don't want to hear what they say about Frédé. When my father starts up about Frédé I feel like doing him an injury.'

'Well, Lise, we're full up here at the moment, I'm sorry. I don't know whether . . .'

'Listen, it isn't for long, only for a night or so. I haven't any money, but I'm going to get a job, then I shall have money. Listen, Vi, is it true they've got places to sleep now in Broadcasting House?'

'Have you been back there, then?'

'No, I read it in the *Daily Mirror*.'

'Well, we get the *Mirror*, but I missed that.'

'It was headed THIS IS THE NINE O'CLOCK SNOOZE.'

'I didn't see it.'

'Vi, please get me a ticket, I've still got my pass, they'll recognise me at Reception and they'll never know I've left. It's only for a very short time.'

Vi considered. There was an extra ticket, it had been sent by mistake for Della, and should have been given back immediately to Mrs Milne. Of course, if Lise was found out it would be awkward, but on the whole it wasn't likely. They would think she'd been away in one of the regions, or on a training course, which heaven knows she'd needed badly enough.

'I can get you a ticket, Lise, but where shall I send it to?'

'Leave it at Reception in an envelope with my name on it. I'll pick it up. You needn't have anything more to do with it, you needn't see me or talk to me.'

Although she found the pathos of this last remark irritating, Vi was dissatisfied with herself. What she had been saying fell short of the truth. The house, by her family's standards, wasn't full up; the other bed in her room was free. But looking back over the last six weeks or so she thought of Lise in a state of doleful shapelessness, only half listening while her job was explained to her, then collapsing into tears it seemed, when RPD was doing no more than beginning to talk to her – and after all nobody in BH worked harder than he did – then the unpleasantness about Frédé and Lise's dampening presence in the house, Dismal Lizzie the little ones had called her and had to be threatened into silence, and finally even her mother having one or two things to say when she disappeared without explanation. Vi had been able to tell from one look at her mother's back, as she started the washing-up, that she was hurt. Surely that was justification enough for not having Lise back.

And then, she was expecting Chris on leave, pretty well certainly this time. 'I hope he keeps strong for you,' said Teddy gloomily, a spectator of experience, always on the wrong side of the windowpane. Sometimes he went down to the BH typing pool to see if any of the girls would like to come out, say to the pictures, or for a cup of tea at Lyons. Their heads, dark and fair, rose expectantly as he came in, then, although he was quite nice-looking, sank down again over their work. Nor was Teddy very popular with the Old Servant who supervised the pool.

The Department was getting a new girl as a replacement, but what use was that? He'd read an article by a psychologist in some magazine or other which explained rather well how owing to Nature's Law of Compensation girls in wartime, if they weren't fixed up already, were practically bound to fall in love with older men. That was a scientific analysis, and you couldn't fly in the face of science.

All the same, he allowed himself a mild interest in the newcomer. During his tea-break he went and hung about the second floor. The corridor, like all the others, curved mysteriously away, following the lines of the outer walls, and leading to sudden shipboard meetings, and even collisions, as the door opened. Most of Administration was there, and you could usually find out what was going on. While the tape machines in the basement ticked in the world's news from outside and radio gathered it from the air, the second floor generated the warm internal rumours of BH. There, through one of the filing clerks, a very plain girl, unfortunately, Teddy learned that they were considering an RPA application from Birmingham.

5

ANNIE ASRA was the kind of girl to whom people give a job, even when they didn't originally intend to. Her name sounded foreign, but wasn't. She came from Birmingham.

Annie was a little square curly-headed creature, not a complainer. Certainly, at seventeen, she would never have complained about her childhood. She had spent the part of it which was most important to her on the move, trotting round beside her father, who was a piano tuner. In the city of a thousand trades, he had seen his own decline, but he still had quite enough work to live on. He was a widower, and it was felt in the other houses in their terrace that he wouldn't be able to manage, but he did.

It was a curious existence for a child. Winter was the height of the piano-tuning season, and she became inured at an early age to extreme temperatures. The pianos that were considered good enough to tune were in little-used front parlours and freezing parish rooms, sometimes in the church itself where on weekdays a tiny Vesuvius struggled with the frost's grip, its stovepipe soaring high into the aisle vaulting. She didn't have to go, the neighbours would have minded her, but that didn't suit Annie. She knew all their regulars, who her father would have to speak to and where he had to hang up his coat. The pianos stood expectantly, some with the yellowed teeth of old age, helpless, once their front top was unscrewed, awaiting the healer's art. There were two Bechsteins on their round, one belonging to a doctor, the other to a builder's merchant, but Mr Asra didn't prefer them to the others. To each according to their needs.

It often seemed a very long time before the actual tuning began. The ailing pianos had to be put in good order first, cracks wedged up, the groaning pedals eased with vaseline. Annie was allowed to strike every key in turn to see if any of them stuck. If so, a delicate shaving of wood had to be pared away. Sometimes the felts needed loosening, or even taken right off, to be damped and ironed in the kitchen or the church vestry. They smelled like wet sheep under the iron, and lying all together on the board they looked like green or red sheep. Then they had to be glued back onto the hammers, and Mr Asra never did anything either quickly or slowly.

When at last he took out his hammer and mutes, ready to tune, his daughter became quite still, like a small dog pointing. While he was laying the bearings in the two middle octaves she waited quietly, though not patiently, watching for him to get the three C's right, tightening the strings a little more than necessary and settling them back by striking the keys, standing, bending, tapping, moving his hammer gently to and fro round the wooden pins, working through the G's, the D's and the A's until he came to middle E. When middle E was set Annie left the spot where he had put her, the warmest place, close to the stove, and stood at his elbow, willing him to play the first trial chord. It was a recurrent excitement of her life, like opening a boiled egg, the charm being not its unexpectedness but its reliability. And Mr Asra struck the chord of C.

'But the E's sharp, Dad,' she said.

That too was in order, she always said it. To please her, he lowered the E a little, and sounded the perfect chord, looking round at her, an unimpressive man in his shirtsleeves and waistcoat, able to share with her the satisfaction of the chord of C major. But he couldn't leave it like that, she knew. The E must be sharpened again, all the thirds must be a little bit sharp, all the fifths must be a little bit flat, or the piano would never come right. At this point he quite often gave her a boiled sweet from a paper bag in the pocket of his waistcoat.

When he reached the treble Mr Asra worked entirely by ear. The treble for Annie was entering a region of silver or tin, the wind through the keyhole, walking with due care over the ice, sharpening gradually until the uttermost tones at the top of the keyboard. With the bass she felt more at ease. There was danger, in that if a string broke it couldn't be replaced and had to be spliced there and then, but the tuning itself was easier, the strings ran easily and willingly over the bridges, and their warm growl took her downwards into a region of dark fur-covered animals crowned with gold who offered their kindly protection to the sleepy traveller. Annie, in fact, when she was very young, often fell asleep during the bass, even though she loved it best. The torrent of chromatic scales which signified the final testing, and which the householders thought of as the tuner (who'd probably once hoped to be a concert performer) letting himself go at last, didn't interest either of them nearly so much.

While her father was putting away his things into the familiar leather bag, worn threadbare round the edges, they were often brought a cup of tea, with two lumps of sugar put ready in the saucer. The owner, coming hesitantly out of some other room, looked at their piano, with everything screwed back and in order, as if it was a demanding relative newly come out of hospital. 'The Queen of the Home', Mr Asra called it, when a remark of this kind seemed necessary. Sometimes there was a vibration of distress, which Annie deeply felt. 'If you're going to give singing lessons, madam, you really ought to have it tuned to concert pitch. I could do that if you want, but it may mean replacing a few strings,' and the pale-coloured woman could be seen to shrink, anxiety adding to her embarrassment over handing him the right money.

Annie became self-contained, a serious tranquil believer in life and in the time ahead when she would know what was most important to her. She went to school with her brown curling hair in decent pigtails. Her aunt, her dead mother's eldest sister, came in from next door every day to do it for her. At the end of her first morning at Church School, when the teacher told them to go out for their second play, she half got up and then sat down again quickly, feeling her head dragged painfully back by a cruel weight. Dick Dobbs, the boy sitting behind her, had tied her pigtails to the back of her chair, perhaps with her aunt's new ribbon, perhaps with string. She sat there perfectly still until the teacher, who had gone out to patrol the yard, came back and found her sitting stiff and serious as a little idol. 'Why didn't you tell me as soon as class was done?' she asked, relieved that there were no tears.

'I wouldn't give him that satisfaction.'

At the end of the Christmas term there was a letter-box in the corner of the classroom. It was made from a dustbin covered with red crepe paper; the handles sticking out each side spoiled the illusion to some extent, but the teacher put a cardboard robin on each. In the box the children posted cards to one another, bought at Woolworths, carefully inscribed the night before, and brought to school in their cases that morning in an atmosphere of jealous secrecy. Some got few or no cards. The teacher could do nothing about this, the box was opened at mid-morning and she was unable to get at it in time to redress the balance. Annie, however, had plenty. When she was eight years old she received a large snow scene covered with glitter, beautiful, and from the expensive box. The rest of the class gathered round to admire until she slowly put it away in her case.

'I put that in the box for you,' said Dick Dobbs.

'It's a pretty card.'

The teachers asked her why, at Christmas time, she couldn't say something more friendly.

'He's a dirty devil,' Annie replied calmly. She accepted that people couldn't be otherwise than they were, good, bad, and middling, but one ought to be allowed to take them or leave them.

She kept seeing Dick, because although he didn't come on to grammar school with her friends, he sang in the same church choir as she did, at St Martin's. When she was twelve and a half he caught her behind the vicarage bicycle sheds, took a firm grip of her and pressed her back hard against the wall.

'I expect you think it's wrong to do this,' he said, unbuttoning her coat.

'I don't think it's wrong,' Annie replied. 'I daresay I'd do it if I liked it.'

He was disconcerted, hesitated and lost hold. Annie walked away, but not in a hurry, she stopped to do up the six buttons of her coat. There were one or two boys she liked at school, but not Dick. She'd not do any better for Dick by pretending. Luckily his voice was breaking.

Annie did well at her lessons, and would have liked to please the music teacher, who wanted her to start piano, but for reasons that were not clear to her, and therefore caused her annoyance, she didn't care to learn. Her father could have found the money, but he never made her do anything she didn't want to.

When she was nearly sixteen, Mr Asra fell ill. He asked Annie to make the round of the customers and tell them that unfortunately he wouldn't be coming. When she rang the bell-pulls which she hadn't been able to reach as a little girl, and saw through the front windows the familiar pianos, and the silver-framed photos on them that had to be moved away when the tuner called, she knew for certain that her father was going to die. The doctor couldn't make out what was wrong, but that was no surprise to their neighbours in the terrace, who were well aware that doctors don't know everything. Mr Asra didn't have to be sent away to hospital to die. Annie managed pretty well, sleeping on two chairs in the passage outside his room. He was with them one night and gone in the morning, when she got up to fetch him the medicine which the district nurse had left.

Her aunt, who lived next door, asked her to move in for the time being, and no one could fault the arrangements. But they were not surprised, either, when in spite of the emergency Annie went off to try her luck in London. That was on the 8th of July, the day they announced the tea-rationing, two ounces per person per week.

Annie left her luggage and umbrella at Paddington and took the Underground, hoping, as the result of this, that she'd never have to travel in it again. The windows of the trains, following regulations, were painted black, with a tiny square of glass left to peer through and to make out the name of the station. This presumably meant that the Tube came above ground some time, but it didn't do so before she got out at Oxford Circus.

The passers-by were quick to tell her that she couldn't miss Broadcasting House, because it looked like a ship with the wrong sort of windows. She walked right and left between the sandbags that masked the entrance and realised, from the way the sentry looked at her, that she'd done right to put on her white blouse and navy-blue skirt.

The entrance hall of BH worried her not at all. It reminded her of the Midland Hotel, where once or twice, when a friend had been taken ill, her father had been called in to tune the concert grand. In its size and height she recognised the need to impress. People had to feel they'd arrived somewhere. She remembered, too, that they hadn't much wanted a child running around the hotel, so they'd told her to go and look at some comics in a little room upstairs, much like the room where she went for her interview now.

There were two middle-aged women who identified themselves as Mrs Milne and Mrs Staples, from Establishment. They were in charge, and yet she felt they needed approval from the man sitting rather apart from them, at the corner of the table, who wasn't much like anyone Annie had ever met. He was both pale and dark, and had the sort of face that they used to say would make a fortune on the halls; perhaps, indeed, he had. At the moment he was half lying back and looking at the ceiling, which made Annie wonder why he had come to interview her at all. It must be an advantage, she thought, to be like that, and not to bother.

'You don't need to be musical,' Mrs Milne explained, 'or to have any kind of technical knowledge – just complete accuracy in following instructions, punctuality and reliability. We've got the references from your Vicar and your head teacher . . . and then you've had a Saturday job as well, haven't you?'

'At Anstruthers,' said Annie. 'I was on the loose sweets counter to start with, then they moved me to hosiery. We'd instructions to let the old folks help themselves to a few sweets if they wanted to,' she added.

'Their letter was satisfactory too,' murmured Mrs Staples.

'The job is largely chasing the recordings and seeing that they're available at the right time, and for the right programmes.'

'A straightforward service job,' said Mrs Staples.

Mrs Milne changed colour a little.

'Service, yes, but of a particularly important nature. The Department is quite indispensable to the Corporation as a whole. The name of your Director, by the way, if you were selected for this position, would be Mr Seymour Brooks. But you would be working on shift – you'll have to take that into account, by the way, when you're finding somewhere to live – and you're not likely to have much direct contact with Mr Brooks.'

Annie didn't miss the change from *you would* to *you will*, and she observed with compassion that Mrs Milne looked downright tired. Probably she'd been interviewing for hours and there'd been very few hopefuls.

Meanwhile the man stretched his legs and shifted in his chair as though he was thinking of going, causing an equal but contrary movement in the two women. Then he said, in a voice almost too quiet to catch: 'My name is Jeffrey Haggard. I have nothing to do, really, with your appointment, I'm the Director of Programme Planning . . . You're from Birmingham, Miss Asra?'

They'd all said that, seeming to think it was rather surprising for her to come. However far away did they think it was?

'I've been through it often enough, but I've never stopped there. Tell me, just as a point of geographical interest, would you call Birmingham north or south?'

He smiled, and for the first time since she'd passed the soldier at the door, Annie smiled back.

'It's neither.'

'I imagine that perhaps there's only one way to settle it. Are there pork butchers, separate from the ordinary butchers?'

'Of course there are, Mr Haggard.'

'Then it must be north.'

*

Annie was wrong in thinking that there hadn't been many hopefuls among the applicants. There had been none at all. She had been right, however, in detecting, as she did, that her interviewers were not quite of one mind. Mrs Milne was thinking of RPD, Mrs Staples was thinking of AD(E), and Jeff wanted to get away.

'I think we might as well appoint her at once,' Mrs Milne said, straightening her back, when she was left alone with her friend. 'Of course, she'll have to go through the college, but I hardly anticipate. . . . '

By this she meant that the BBC would have to ascertain that Annie had never been a member of the Communist Party. But, in view of the understaffing in Recorded Programmes, they thought it safe to issue her with a temporary pass, and tell her to report for work on Monday.

The next problem, of course, was where the girl was to live. It was no use leaving things to chance, she might slip back to Birmingham. Mrs Milne had hostels in mind, but Vi, with Lise still on her conscience, went with Annie to Paddington to pick up the luggage and then brought her back to Hammersmith on that very first evening. Mrs Simmons, who was generous enough to learn nothing from experience, welcomed a new lodger. She was bottling plums, and not ever remembering a year like it for plums. Hitler had given out that Britain would capitulate by August, she added, or rather he'd said it some time ago, but she'd only just read it off an old *Mirror* that she'd used to spread under the jars.

'Did you share a room before?' Vi asked, taking Annie upstairs.

'Not really, because I hadn't brothers and sisters.'

'Do children worry you, then?'

Annie shook her head.

'My little brothers don't need much,' Vi went on. 'Just fall down when they machine-gun you, halfway will do if we're at table.'

'I can manage that.'

'Well, I'll show you where to put your things. You'll have to make do with just a bit of the cupboard, because we've got all our winter things in there, and these two and a half drawers over here. How will that do?'

And after all, Annie had not brought much.

'What my mother meant, starting off about Hitler, and the jars, and everything, was that if there's any trouble you'd be better off in a house like this, where there's a lot of us.' She sat down on her own bed. 'Do you want to use the phone? Will they be worrying about you at home?'

'Writing will do,' said Annie stiffly. 'I don't think my aunt will be at her house. I think she's going to let it.'

Vi perceived that they had come to the end of that subject.

6

RPD HAD hit a snag in his design for lightweight recording equipment with an adequate – that was all he asked, heaven knew, that it should simply be adequate – windshield. At the moment he paid attention to nothing else, and nobody except the engineers had access.

'You'll have to await your summons,' said Teddy, sitting back, world weary, surveying Annie. 'That's what you have to expect in a Seraglio.'

Annie was annoyed at herself at first for not knowing what the word meant. She'd thought it was a kind of opera.

The first job she was called upon to undertake by herself was to check the whole series of de Gaulle's speeches, mark them up, and take them to the studio for the run-through of Eddie Waterlow's dramatic feature *France Fights On*. The programme had been scheduled some time ago and had changed its name several times during the German advance. Director (Home) thought that as the cast had been booked and a certain amount of money spent already, the whole thing had better be recorded before something happened to make further alterations necessary. Annie was afraid when she first got through the door with her armful of discs, because no one was there but Mr Waterlow, dancing quietly round the restricted space in the control studio. They'd told her that there were Old Servants in Broadcasting House, but not that there were mad Old Servants. It was the Hesitation Waltz he was doing. He paused and looked at her searchingly.

'You've come early.'

'I wanted to make sure that everything was all right, Mr Waterlow.'

He asked her name, then remarked: 'I don't think I've seen you before. You are my Recorded Programmes Assistant for this afternoon?'

'Yes, Mr Waterlow.'

'When did you join the Corporation?'

'Last Monday, Mr Waterlow.'

'You appear bewildered.'

'Well, Mr Waterlow, it's my first time on duty.'

He peered at her. 'I don't know if you're addressing me in this respectful way as a jest.'

'They told me upstairs that was your name.'

'It is. I have no intention of asking you what else they said. I may be too sensitive. I fancied that after only a few days you had joined the conspiracy against me.'

He'd stopped dancing, except for a few steps forward and back.

'I'm not surprised in the least that the most inexperienced Recorded Programmes Assistant in the building has been assigned to me. If my abilities were ever highly valued by the Corporation, they are certainly not so now. Nevertheless I've been put in charge of a not unimportant programme, a tribute to the country without which Europe could hardly be termed civilised. And yet, in asking me to do this, they may have asked too much. Somewhere along the way I've lost the one quality necessary to preserve the glitter and the illusion, not only of the theatre – even in wartime I put that first – but of life. I mean confidence. All mine is gone. And from your expression at the moment, I fear you have none either.'

'I've got plenty of confidence, Mr Waterlow,' said Annie. 'It's just that you talk so daft.'

She put her records neatly in the producer's rack. You couldn't help liking him. Exhausted by his tirade, he watched her dreamily.

'I think you must come from Birmingham. . . . What made you come to Broadcasting House?'

'I wanted to do my bit.'

'Ah, you can stand there and say that! I couldn't say it without the deepest embarrassment. The deepest! I envy you.'

A Junior Programme Engineer stuck his head round the door, saw Annie, and whistled.

'Got the running order, sweetheart?'

'Yes, it's announcement, narrator one minute twelve, cross-fade Marseillaise thirty seconds, fade out. . . . '

'Yep, that's what I came to tell you, Eddie,' said the JPE casually, 'European wanted me to remind you. You can't fade the Marseillaise, not for the duration, to avoid offence to our Allies.'

Mr Waterlow sank down in picturesque despair. 'My timing. . . . '

'Yep, the whole two minutes of it. All or nothing. You'll have to substitute.'

'Heartless, heartless children. . . . '

'Don't give way, Mr Waterlow,' Annie cried. 'It'll not take me a minute to go up to the Gram Library and get you a commercial. They showed me where it was on my tour of the building.'

'A spark. . . . '

'But what would you like me to get?'

'Anything . . . ' His voice strengthened a little. 'Anything but the song-cycles of Hugo Wolf. The Gramophone Library seem to have an unending supply of them, just as the canteen never runs out of digestive biscuits . . . my dear, fetch me something that is not by Hugo Wolf . . . let it at least be French.'

When Annie returned with a commercial of *Ma Normandie*, which she'd been told could be faded out anywhere, the situation in the studio had changed. The JPE had left, but someone else had come, a little old man, not looking at all well, but with a fierce air of not letting himself go, and of having dressed for the occasion. He had on a yellow checked waistcoat and a blue suit, the trousers pressed like blades.

'Who are you? Who? Who?' cried Eddie Waterlow.

'The agent told me what time to come along.'

'Why? At whose prompting? Did they tell you that, regard-
less of what rehearsals may have been called and what confirm-
ations may have been sent by Bookings, anyone and everyone
is welcome at Eddie Waterlow's productions?'

'I've got my letter from Bookings,' said the old man. 'I'll take
a chair if I may.'

He sat down with difficulty. 'I'm a bit stiff, you might say
I've one leg and a swinger. I don't do much dancing nowadays.'

Annie wondered if she oughtn't to fetch him something. He
looked bad; in fact, they both did.

'I've got my cast list here,' said Eddie, trying to maintain
authority.

'What is your name?'

'Fred Shotto.'

'I have that on my list, certainly, but there must be a mistake
of some kind. *Spotlight* gives him as twenty-nine years old,
Shakespeare and classic comedy, specialises in French accent.'

'That'll be my son,' said the old man. 'He's with the forces
now. He's Fred Shotto, junior. You can bill me as the old block
he's a chip of.'

Encouraged by Eddie's silence, he went on: 'The booking
was in my name, all right. You can't contest that, it's legal. I'm
all right myself once I've got my confidence.'

He took out a roll of sheet music.

'I've brought my material.'

Eddie had chosen to sink his face into his left hand, while his
right arm hung down helplessly towards the ground. Annie,
feeling that someone must, took the music, from which other
pieces of paper covered with writing fluttered to the ground.

'*That's* my material. The other's my opening number.'

'Annie! What has he brought me!'

Annie smoothed it out.

'It's the *I've Got the You Don't Know the Half of It, Dearie Blues*,
Mr Waterlow.'

The JPE thrust forcefully in again, this time winking broadly.

'How's it coming, curly? We're going to record in ten
minutes.'

Annie went to the door.

'Mr Waterlow seems to be in difficulties. Do you think he's all right?'

'Live in hopes.'

But *France Fights On* was cancelled, shelved to make room for the mounting defence instructions. Perhaps, indeed, it had never been planned for; only DPP was likely to be able to give an answer to that.

Eddie Waterlow had considerable difficulty in getting rid of Fred Shotto. The old man, who had started out as a clog-dancer at the age of four, had learned persistence in a harder school, as he pointed out, than Hitler's war, and beyond that he had some idea that by getting work he was keeping the place warm for his son. Long after the cast had been dismissed he clung to his chair, and Eddie was obliged in the end to make a recording of the *I've Got the You Don't Know the Half of It, Dearie Blues*, cracked and trembling, which might have become a collectors' piece if it had not been consigned at once to scrap. Dislodged at last, and given a farewell drink, Fred Shotto became affectionate in the theatre's old way, telling everyone in sight that Mr Waterlow had made him a happy man, and advising them to lean on Jesus till the clouds rolled by. It turned out that he'd done some hard years, too, as a revivalist.

After his programme was lost, Eddie drifted round the building, assisting a little here and there, a pensioner of the arts such as Broadcasting House, even in wartime, could not bring itself to discourage. He was told that *France Fights On* 'might have involved falsification'; the BBC remained loyal to the truth, even when they stretched it a little to spare the feelings of their employees.

As an institution that could not tell a lie, they were unique in the contrivances of gods and men since the Oracle of Delphi. As office managers, they were no more than adequate, but now, as autumn approached, with the exiles crowded awkwardly into their new sections, they were broadcasting in the strictest sense of the word, scattering human voices into the darkness of Europe, in the certainty that more than half must be lost, some for the rook, some for the crow, for the sake of a few that made their mark. And everyone who worked there, bitterly complaining about the short-sightedness of their colleagues, the vanity of the news readers, the remoteness of the Controllers and the restrictive nature of the canteen's one teaspoon, felt a certain pride which they had no way to express, either then or since.

7

SAM BROOKS asked Mrs Milne whether she'd noticed that there was a new Recorded Programmes Assistant.

'Perhaps one ought to keep a check on these things,' he said.

'She was interviewed by myself and a representative of Establishment,' replied Mrs Milne. 'DPP was also present.'

'Whatever for?'

'Her name is Annie Asra – I suppose Anne, I have put her on the register as Anne.'

'I don't quite see why I wasn't consulted. But I must have a word with her as soon as I can.'

Annie settled in easily with the Simmonses. She gave no feeling of upset, rather of solidity and peace. Vi loved her mother, but was too much like her not to get irritated after fifteen minutes. She lent a hand whenever she was at home, but in her own way. To Annie, who had been reared by her widowed father, and brought to her present excellent state of health entirely on fish and chips and tins, there was a charm in helping Mrs Simmons around the garden and kitchen. It was unpatriotic now not to sort the rubbish into pigfood, henfood, tinfoil (out of which, it seemed, battleships could be partly made), paper, cardboard and rags. At the same time Mr Simmons worked late at the shop, sorting the coupons from the customers' ration books. The nation defended itself by counting large numbers of small things into separate containers. But beyond this there were the old repetitive tasks of the seasons, the parts which, in the end, seem greater than the whole. Annie sat on the back doorstep and shelled peas with Mrs Simmons. She had never done it before.

'You've only just come, and yet you're the only one in this house that does it with a sense of what's fair,' said Mrs Simmons.

'The others just take all the ones with the large peas in and then go away and leave me with the awkward ones.'

The pods were almost autumnal, and striped with paler colour. The hard late peas fell with a light percussion into the colander, then, as the pile covered the bottom, the sound changed to a rustle.

'I still think that's an unusual name, Asra,' Mrs Simmons went on. 'Vi's mentioned to me not to ask you about it, but if I always did whatever she tells me I'd never know anything. Is it Jewish, or Spanish, or what?'

'I don't think it's either,' Annie replied, 'but I don't mind your asking.'

'Well, I suppose you get all sorts of names in a big manufacturing place. Perhaps it's taken out of the Bible.'

'My last head teacher told me it was the name of a tribe,' said Annie. 'I thought that was going a bit far.'

'Well, you'll change it one day. If you're a girl, you've always got that to look forward to.'

Vi had told her not to say that kind of thing, either. They sat there together calmly, their minds full of the July garden. After the peas, they'd have to do something about the runners.

'Look, there's seven peas in this one,' said Annie.

They both felt unreasonably happy. It wasn't much longer than any of the other pods, and yet none of them had had more than five.

Vi had come home, looking tired out.

'They'll be too hard to eat even when they're cooked,' she said, but not unkindly, looking at the whitish green heap.

'Well, these are the last we'll do this year.'

Annie got up, shook the bits of leaf and tendril off her lap into the pig bucket, and took the colander into the kitchen.

'She'll want to find something a bit more entertaining than sitting here helping me,' said Mrs Simmons, who always felt strangely impelled to talk about anyone who had just gone away. 'You could take her to the Palais one evening when you're both off work together. The management's bought more than a thousand pairs of shoes, you know, so that the servicemen can change out of their boots.'

'Well, I'll think about it when Chris gets back. But Annie's all right, Mum, she's only been at BH a week and there's plenty of boys would like to take her out. Teddy would, to start with.'

'Isn't that the one who talked to me so interestingly about the world to come?'

Mrs Simmons didn't know why it was that when Vi was at home and she particularly wanted to demonstrate her intelligence and power of memory, they both had to desert her at once. Of course, she'd confused Teddy with Willie Sharpe, who'd looked so young when he came to tea that she'd felt he ought to be out playing round the cabbage beds. But there was no need, really, for her daughter to correct her. All she needed was a little time to think.

On her second Monday, when Annie was passing RPD's office on her way to filing, the door opened and he looked out and shouted: 'Come in here!'

She knew him already, of course, by sight, but had no one much to compare him with as an employer except the head buyer at Anstruthers, and that was not much help. The buyer had always been peaked with worry, whereas even at a distance from RPD she felt herself on the edge of a crazy enthusiasm, like a ring of magic fire; he looked to be as wrapped up in what he was doing as Vi's little brothers. As she went in and shut the door he retreated backwards and snatched up a new recording.

'Spirit of the Earth, come to my call,' he read from the handwritten label.

'Do you want me, Mr Brooks?' enquired Annie.

'They made this in Bristol yesterday and sent it up to me on the van. It's got nothing to do with any of our programmes here, it's music, baritone and orchestra, but they wanted me to hear it at once.'

'I don't know the song, I'm afraid.'

He looked at her impatiently. 'It doesn't matter what you know! I only want someone with two ears.' The waste of even a moment was unbearable.

'Sit down, sit down, for God's sake.'

He checked the pickup of his turntable and put on the record. Annie sat with her hands in her lap and listened, as he did, without shifting or stirring while the record played through twice.

'Well? Well?' shouted Sam.

'I liked the song, as far as that goes.'

'The song! What do I care if you liked it or not? I called you in here because you were the first person I caught sight of in the corridor and I wanted you to share my experience. Nothing is an experience unless it's shared. When I've got something in my hands that's as near perfection as we can hope for in wartime conditions my first reaction is, someone else must have the chance to listen to this. I oughtn't to have played it at all before it was dubbed. I know that. If my RPEs were here they'd want to grind me into powder. Above all I shouldn't have played it back to you twice as I did just now. But I wanted you to know once and for all what's meant by the term "quality" and the term "balance", and on top of that, there was the singer.'

'I'm very glad to learn about quality and balance,' said Annie quietly, 'but the singer was flat.'

'I don't understand you.'

'His first phrase he started out with was C E flat B flat D. He was in tune till the D, then he was a twelfth of a tone flat and didn't get back till his last bar but one.'

'Do you claim to be particularly musical?' Sam asked with dangerous calm.

'No, they asked me that at my interview, and I told them not.'

Sam began to pace about.

'Perhaps I should explain that while the performance and the recording are of course two different and independent things, my whole training and working life suggest that I might fairly be considered as a judge of both. What's more, at this interview of yours, about which I was given no prior information, by the way, they may have made it clear to you – if not, indeed, you may realise it for yourself when you've been here rather longer – that I'm in charge of a department of which you too have become a part...feel that, please feel that and think about it...and in order to be sure that the strain doesn't become unendurable I have to look for a good deal of co-operation and human understanding and delicacy from my staff, all things that come naturally, I'm glad to say, to girls of your age.'

He took off his spectacles, and Annie met his defenceless gaze.

'It was flat, Mr Brooks.'

RPD asked Mrs Milne whether she'd noticed that the new RPA girl seemed rather different from anyone they'd ever had in the Department before.

'She does exactly the same hours as the others, Mr Brooks, and so far I've heard nothing to suggest that she's overworked, or that she doesn't get enough to eat, or that she needs any special consideration. She's fixed herself up with Violet Simmons's family, she's got a room in their house in Hammersmith. And if you're going to ask me whether she looks like some picture or portrait you've seen somewhere, I might as well tell you, in order to save time, that in my opinion she's a very usual-looking girl from the Midlands.'

Sam glanced up at his secretary in mild surprise.

'As it happens, her face does remind me of a portrait, but I can't quite place it. It might be Shelley. Did he have curly hair?'

'Everyone had curly hair in those days,' said Mrs Milne. 'It was the Spirit of the Age.'

'Where's the Picture Reference Library these days?'

'It was evacuated in the first week of the war, Mr Brooks.'

She waited for further instructions, but Sam said: 'I don't want that girl on my Indispensable Personnel List.'

The list by this time had worked itself down to the middle of the Defence Instructions file. Mrs Milne concealed her amazement by taking it out and moving it somewhere nearer the top.

'She's rather too sure of her opinions,' Sam went on. 'It would be unkind to call her obstinate, so let's say that I don't think she knows how to adapt. To see a girl of that age who can't adapt is ridiculous, or perhaps it's sad, I don't know which.'

He shook himself, as though he was emerging from cold water. But his dissatisfaction remained, not less so when he had a chance of a word with Dr Vogel. The doctor had been on a tour of the regional centres, where, in spite of his goodwill, he had caused as much distress as any other perfectionist.

'It's a trivial matter, I suppose, Josef, but I found it inexplicable. What it came to, really, was that she chose to set up her sense of hearing against mine. I hardly knew what to say to her. After all, perfect pitch is something you're born with, like a sense of humour. You're with me, Josef?'

Dr Vogel nodded.

'Certainly, Sam. You yourself were born with neither. But you are a fine man, a good man.'

This was the first time in his life – since Dr Vogel was accepted as infallible – that Sam Brooks had ever been obliged to change his opinion of himself. The experience did not make him less self-centred, but the centre of gravity shifted. He now declared that he had no ear at all for music, and couldn't be expected to have, he was an engineer and an administrator, nothing more than that. But generosity and selfishness are not incompatible, and his need to give and share would not quite settle down with the knowledge that he had been unjust to Annie. After all, where could his juniors, those beginners in life, look for a moral example, if not to him? It was strange that Sam, who forgot unacceptable incidents with such rapidity and skill, could not quite get over this one. Mrs Milne, for example, thought it strange.

Annie, on the other hand, remembered how RPD had looked without his glasses, and wished that she hadn't been obliged to say that the singer had been flat from the E onwards, though, really, there'd been no help for it. It didn't upset her that she seemed to be in disgrace; it was just that without his glasses it seemed cruel, and even wrong, to take him aback.

'You did right to say what you thought, though,' Vi told her. 'It's no use making yourself a doormat, like Lise Bernard.'

The two of them had been on late shift. They were lying on their metal bunks, one up, one down, in the concert-hall. It was not much use trying to get to sleep. Total blackout was Security's rule, and since the tickets didn't bear numbers, and couldn't have been read if they had, newcomers clambered and felt about in search of an empty corner, swarming across the others like late returners to a graveyard before cockcrow. Time, indeed, was the great concern. The sleepers were obscurely tormented by the need to be somewhere in five, ten, or twenty minutes. Awakened, quite often, by feet walking over them, they struck matches whose tiny flames wavered in every corner of the concert-hall, and had a look at their watches, just to be sure. Yet some slept on, and the walls, designed to give the best possible acoustics for classical music, worked just as well for snoring. Accommodation, who had provided so much, had never thought of this. No barracks or dormitory in the country produced snoring of such broad tone, and above that distinctly rose the variations of the overwrought, the junior announcers rehearsing their cues, correcting themselves and starting again, continuity men suddenly shouting: ' . . . and now, in a lighter mood . . . ', and every now and then a fit of mysterious weeping.

'I often wonder if Lise ever came in here or not,' said Vi. Annie craned over from the top bunk. In the next tier a middle-aged secretary began to sing in her sleep. Perhaps, like Della, she had always wanted to do so. The concert-hall encouraged such dreams.

'Why are you always on about her?' Annie whispered. 'This Lise, I mean. From all you've told me, if she finds things hard again she'll get hold of you quick enough.'

Vi acknowledged this, but it was troublesome about the missing CH ticket. They were asking for it back, and, if she had to tell lies, she didn't particularly want them to be for Lise's sake.

It worried her also that RPD seemed to have taken against Annie. Who was to eat the double cheese sandwiches now, and to listen to his woes? Annie was a real help both at home and at work, but in this one respect her coming had made no difference, worse than none. The whole Seraglio's task still lay on Vi's shoulders.

Vi, however, resembled her mother, and made her mother's mistakes, in calculating only from what she had known so far. Indeed, there is always a kind of comfort in doing this. But overnight, or so it seemed, the continuity was broken and the Department changed.

The juniors, Willie and Teddy as well as the girls, had been used to a patriarchal tyranny, where they might be summoned at any time by the thunder of their Director, but were conscious of his direct protection, always within touch of his hand. Suddenly, RPD ceased to take any notice of them. He recalled that he had, like everyone else of his grade except DPP, assistant administrators and executives of various kinds, who had got used to functioning almost entirely on their own. Now they were flattered by consultations, and by two meetings within one week. The engineers had always been close to his heart, but now members of staff who had never been asked for an opinion before, and scarcely knew that they had one, were called upon to give it. They sent in suggestions for reorganising the work, which Mrs Milne filed. Meanwhile the crazy nursery-tale atmosphere, the bear turned prince who could be led only by a maiden or a child, had disappeared, perhaps for ever.

The effect on the RPAs, reduced to their own tiny world, was curious. They were overawed. For the first time they looked at their Director from a distance and realised, almost with disbelief, how much he really had to do. Toiling up and down the first three floors of BH, humble servants of the discs, they were conscious of how far the work stretched beyond them. There were the mobile units in Egypt, there were the tireless wax cylinders which recorded the world's broadcasts, a hundred and fifty thousand words to be monitored every day. All of these depended on Sam Brooks, who not so long ago had been glad to go to sleep on Vi's shoulder.

'You'll never really get to know RPD now,' Willie told Annie. They were in a little room like a cupboard behind the ticker-tapes, which seemed not to be used for anything; he had brought a chair in there, and was cutting her hair. Willie believed that it was his duty to learn to do these things – the Red Cross Certificate had been only the first on his list – against the day when Broadcasting House was in a state of siege. At the moment he was not much of a hairdresser. A haze of snipped curls lay on the floor, and Annie's hair looked somewhat ragged.

'It doesn't matter, it'll find its own level,' she told him reassuringly.

She minded the withdrawal of RPD less than the others. After all, she'd only spoken to him the once.

Annie was absorbed, too, in those first weeks, with the discovery made by so many of those whom the chances of war swept into Broadcasting House; there was music everywhere, just for the asking. You could borrow records from the Library and find somewhere to play them, or walk into a studio and find someone else playing them. At any moment of the twenty-four hours you could listen. Round every corner Schubert sang, or Debussy murmured on the horizon, or Liszt descended in a shower of sparkling drops. Annie had heard scarcely any of this before. Sometimes she hardly wanted to go back to Hammersmith; she felt as though she was drowning.

'Didn't you get any music in Birmingham?' asked Eddie Waterlow.

'There's a greater variety of concerts than in any place in England,' said Annie stoutly, 'but my aunt didn't care for them, and my father never took me, except to *Messiah* at Christmas and *Elijah* in summer.'

'Couldn't you go on your own?'

'I hadn't the sense. I'm beginning to see that now.'

'Didn't you sing, Annie?'

'Only in choir.'

Eddie opened her mouth caressingly with the end of a chinagraph pencil.

'Untrained! You will sing the high E for me, Trilby, Treel-bee!'

Annie wasn't put out by his ways any longer. She thought he was probably a bit too much on his own.

'What were you going to play? Oh, Dvaw-aw-rzhak.' He liked to imitate the Pronunciation Section. 'No, my dear, I don't think so. Perhaps one should be grateful that there haven't been any peasants in England for centuries, and if there had been they wouldn't have sung and danced. Let me look at the Mood Label, " . . . the dance grows wilder and wilder, and at length the Devil laughs, with sinister effect . . . ", no, no, my dear, put it by. Refine yourself a little every day, that is my rule. I want you to learn how to listen to a whisper. Less is more! Annie, listen to less with me.'

He sent Dvořák spinning into a bin. They sat down to hear Fauré's Dolly Suite, two pianos nodding together through the afternoon, and the perpetually moving sadly unemphatic white sounds of Satie's *Socrate*.

'Have you ever shaken a concert pianist's hand when he comes off the platform?' Eddie asked her.

Annie shook her head.

'There's no strength left in that hand at all! It hangs down like this from the wrist! All used up, all!'

He was half disappointed when she asked him to play the Satie again, but at this stage of her life Annie liked everything. Most seriously he warned her that emotion must never intrude. If she ever had any strong feelings, let us say strong personal affection, she mustn't let that attach itself to the music. The subject of music was music, he told her.

The other juniors were also fond of music, and Teddy was an ambitious trumpet-player, but Annie's intoxication was rather beyond them.

'She's single-minded,' suggested Willie, who was unusual in appreciating his own qualities in other people.

'That ought to make her understand RPD,' said Vi.

'He's changed,' said Teddy. 'That's a frequent phenomenon with men in middle life. Religion sometimes does it.'

Yet Sam Brooks had not changed. He enjoyed playing at being what he really was, and in altering the Department's routine he was playing directors. But he retained the great accumulation of grievances which was in fact one of his sources of nourishment, arising, as it did, not from envy but from indignation at the blindness and deafness of all around him. The new RPA had, perhaps, not been quite deaf enough, but he didn't intend to think about that again. It was almost the only annoyance that he did not mention to DPP.

Jeff was now in the front line of the BBC's defence against the Ministries, Civil Defence, Supply, Economic Warfare, Food, Salvage, who riddled the Corporation with demands for more time on the air. Before the Home News they fell back, knowing it to be hallowed ground, but every other programme, and particularly those that might entertain the listeners, were required to give way at once. Poor Eddie Water-low's *France Fights On* was only the first of the fallen. Instructions to the public and hints – for example, towards saving tea, by using the tea-leaves twice – should, the Ministries felt, take precedence over all. The Director of Programme Planning might, in fact, have been felt to be fully employed, and yet Jeff was not surprised when Sam burst into his office.

'Jeff, I want to put this to you, as one of my oldest friends.'

'Surely you must have older friends than I am,' Jeff protested. Their life in BH had become so secluded and so strange that it was difficult to remember at times where wives or friends could come from. However, Sam was just old enough to have been shipped out to France at the end of 1917. What had become of his cronies from the last war? But Sam, unlike every other contemporary, couldn't remember much about the trenches. He'd devised a double spring for the Company's gramophone, he knew that, so that records would play twice as long; the

Commanding Officer had been delighted, but then, they had had only one record, *A Little Bit of Fluff*, the three cracks endlessly holding it up in the same three places, and blame for the tedium, Sam thought, had most unjustly been transferred to him. The Company had passed a vote of thanks to the Germans when the gramophone was caught by shrapnel.

'I've never seen one like it before or since,' Sam remarked. 'It had something in common with the Blattnerphone.'

Still, why were they talking about the last war? Experience must be shared, and he believed his oldest friend would want to enter into his new distress. He had been at long last to inspect the Indispensable Emergency Personnel Quarters and found that his Department had been allocated something not much bigger than a coop. They would have to share washing facilities with Stores, Bookings and Long Term Contracts, but that would only mean a few reasonable adjustments. The point he wanted to make was that there was no provision for his four turntables. Room must be found; perhaps, after all, all this washing wasn't necessary.

'Have you spoken to Accommodation?'

'I'm not satisfied with their replies. What's more, I'm being kept in the dark again. The bells!'

In the event of an enemy landing, church bells would warn the nation. Silent now for many months, they would be rung out in case of danger from every parish. The BBC had decided that it would be enough to supplement them with ordinary commercial recordings. Jeff thought that it would be better to tell Sam about this some other time.

8

SUDDENLY SAM Brooks's designs came right, both for the forty-pound mobile recording equipment and the microphone windshield. It was almost as if the war was won. All the four juniors were summoned. Their Director was going to celebrate, he was going to take them out to dinner.

'It's impossible for all of them to be off duty together, Mr Brooks,' Mrs Milne pointed out. 'You're aware of that, naturally.'

'Tell Spender to find out what their duties are and look after the discs for a couple of hours, about eight till ten this evening.'

'Mr Spender is a Permanent, Grade 3.'

'Well, it won't hurt him. It will familiarise him with the juniors' work.'

Mrs Milne reminded him that Spender had been an RPA himself for several years before reaching his present position.

'That'll make it all the easier for him,' said Sam.

Mrs Milne could hardly have explained, even to herself, why she was opposed to the whole scheme, or why, now that it appeared inevitable, she had to concern herself so much with the details.

'Lyons in Piccadilly would do very nicely for them, Mr Brooks. They serve a cold baked potato there now, you know, instead of bread, to beat the shortages. Sometimes you have to queue for a while, but a baked potato is very filling.'

'Book me a table at Prunier's,' Sam replied.

He disappeared immediately with his drawings, surrounded by engineers.

At the two o'clock changeover Mrs Milne summoned the RPAs to her office, to learn of their good fortune.

'This is a very well-known restaurant, a French restaurant, and you must all of you consider your appearance.'

217

She was falling imperceptibly into the tone of a Victorian housekeeper inspecting the slaveys.

'Of course, some people think that, with Hitler at our gates, there shouldn't be any of this luxurious and rather ostentatious eating out, particularly perhaps in the evening. We're all of us asked to economise in our own way. The Governors were served with dried egg pasty at their last Board Meeting.'

'They got whisky, too,' said Teddy. 'I saw it going up.'

'I wish you were coming with us, Mrs Milne,' Annie said, turning, on an impulse, towards her. Mrs Milne saw that she meant it, and if any one of the others had made the suggestion it would have been quite gratifying. They, after all, were in a sense children of the regiment, they had come before the cold winter of 1939 and were known all over the building; the boys, not really fully grown yet, were patted on the head and given small coins by Dr Vogel. Then she reminded herself, but not because she had forgotten it, that Annie Asra had been her own appointment. Mary Staples had referred to it only the other day, as a proof of how well things could be managed if all the interviewing was left to the two of them.

Before leaving the office, Mrs Milne always arranged a candle and a box of matches, half open, with one match taken out and laid diagonally across the box, on RPD's desk. This was in case the power failed and he needed a light in a hurry. She had never managed to get him to take very much interest in the arrangement, but it was the last thing she had to do before she left. Willing to extend her control for a little longer, she traced RPD to the fifth floor and asked what he intended to do about transport.

'Tell DPP I'll need his taxi,' said Sam impatiently.

DPP's taxi-driver allowed all five of them to get inside, Willie being small, and destined to provide exceptions. Regent Street was closed to traffic while the shop fronts were being re-inforced, so they went round by Marble Arch. There had been showers all day. In Green Park the barrage balloons were going up in a flock through the tepid evening sky, while inside the taxi a pastoral atmosphere also reigned, the juniors content with their newly restored guardian.

'They cost £500 each, you know, Mr Brooks,' said Willie, gazing at the silver-fleeced balloons, which seemed to be fixed and grazing in the upper air. 'It's going to be a serious matter if we lose two or three of those.'

In St James's they got out and waited on the pavement while the taxi was paid off, then entered the grand restaurant through whose doors came a whiff of the lost smell of Paris. Inside the brownish glitter of the two mirrored walls reflected a heroic display which rejected the possibility of change. Even the diners, many of them in uniform, seemed to have escaped time. Some of them could have sat opposite Clemenceau or Robert St Loup, and one, with his great starched napkin at the ready, might almost have been General Pinard.

Willie lingered rather behind the others, talking to the sedate commissionaire in his *chocolat au lait*-coloured uniform. Then he came confidently over to their corner table.

'Mrs Milne thought we wouldn't know how to behave in a place like this,' he observed.

'I'm not sure that you do,' Vi said quietly. 'What were you talking about to that man at the door?'

'I was asking him if he'd seen Frédé. I described him as well as I could from what you told me. After all, a chap like that must see a lot of Frenchmen come and go.'

'Frédé wouldn't ever come to a place like this, it's expensive.'

'French people spend a remarkably high proportion of their income on food,' said Willie seriously.

'Well, he's not spending it over here, anyway. You didn't see him. He couldn't wait to get rid of Lise and be off.'

Teddy was talking to RPD about wine, and, by a method as old as Socrates, was made to feel that he had chosen the champagne which they eventually ordered. Annie looked at de Gaulle's proclamations, pasted to the walls of the beautiful shadowy room. I'm beginning to know those by heart, she thought.

Prunier's were inclined to think that it must be a First Communion outing. There was a spirit of indulgence suitable to a godfather in the way the host demanded the best there was, and then, as it happened, Annie was wearing a white dress. It was, in fact, one she'd been obliged to get for choir competitions, in a style not likely to have been chosen by anyone but the Vicar's wife, with a view to Christmas and to further competitive events, and made in white silk from Anstruthers' Fabric Hall. She wouldn't have put it on if Mrs Simmons hadn't taken it out, and exclaimed, and insisted that it would only take her ten minutes to iron it, though in fact it came to much more like half an hour. Of course, she had to wear it then. The white dress caused the head waiter to place her on Mr Brooks's right.

Boiled lobsters came, and the table was almost hidden by the fringed sea creatures, resting between their cracked tails. None of the juniors liked the taste of them fresh. Seaweed and a taste of drains, thought Vi. But they bent their faces low, their sensations must not be guessed, and Sam, who deceived himself so often, was easily deceived by these children. They worked together as though following an unseen cue, one of them talking while the others concealed the bits and pieces, with tactful haste, under the lobster's carapace on their plates.

'They plunge them head first into boiling salted water,' declared Willie. 'That instantly destroys life.'

'I've done it often enough with shrimps,' said Vi, 'but it's hard to tell whether they've gone in head first or not.'

She had intended to check Willie when they got to the restaurant, but by now she felt that it wasn't worth while. Champagne is bought and drunk to lead to such changes of mind, and Vi had drunk three-quarters of a glass. So too had Teddy.

'I want you to know that I'll always treasure this moment,' he said suddenly. 'Land, sea, or air, I don't know where, But when the sad thought comes to you, Be sure that I'm remembering too.' While Teddy half-rose to his feet, toasting his own certainty of living for ever, the debris on the table was swept away and replaced by a beautiful red currant tart.

The waiter described a flourish with his tongs over the melting crust. Like all good waiters he was a fine adjuster of relationships, particularly when children were to be served, and he estimated the RPAs as that. Children had to be addressed with an eye on the adult who was paying for them, but directly, too, as from one who had a family to support at home.

'You are the youngest, you do not mind being served last?' he asked, poised over Willie with a fatherly smile.

'Perhaps, since you've put that question, you'd like my considered opinion,' Willie replied, 'I don't just mean on the comparatively trivial matter of eldest and youngest. When peace comes I think it shouldn't be too difficult to get the governments of the world to consent to my scheme of alternative roles for all human beings. It's generally accepted already that if everyone were to eat one day and have nothing at all on the next we could ensure world plenty. But I'd like to see more than that. Those who serve and those who are served would also change places in strict rotation, so that tomorrow evening, for example, you in your turn would be waited upon.'

Vi roused herself. 'I shouldn't like to be here when you're doing the serving, Willie. There'd be long delays all round.' She added, as kindly as she could, 'You shouldn't go on like that, he's got other tables to look after.'

Willie turned red. 'I can be thoughtless at times,' he said.

Their Director gave them all a little more champagne, ignoring the just perceptible hint not to do this, sketched by the retreating waiter. The infants are getting over-excited, his shoulders said. And now Sam, leaning back in his chair and filling such a noticeable space, began to exert a natural power which few people had ever seen, but which answered in human terms to his ability with electrical equipment. Some of the same qualities are needed to organise people and things, and though Sam did not understand his juniors, he knew how to make them happy. Without even noticing Willie's embarrassment of a few moments ago, he conjured it away. He told them stories, delaying as he drew near to an end so that they were on the verge of seeing too well what was going to happen next, then pausing and asking them if they'd like to finish for him, but they were under a spell, and could not. In these engrossing tales Eddie Waterlow appeared, and the Director General, and the last-minute removal of drunken commentators from the microphone, and the sad deafening of Dr Vogel as he knelt down to record the opening batsman at Old Trafford. Lured into the circle of words, knowing how much he was putting himself out, they felt themselves truly his guests, ready to do anything for him. Teddy's laughter must have been some of the loudest ever heard at Prunier's.

Annie's eyes were bright and her attention was almost painful, but she did not laugh as much as the others. It was not her way. That would not quite do for Sam, and without leaving the rest of them he turned to his right and concentrated his whole attention for a moment on her. She looked back at him fearlessly, sitting solid and composed in her peculiar white dress.

'Are you enjoying yourself?'

Annie nodded, but that was not enough for him.

'You know, I've remembered now what it is, I mean who it is, you remind me of, Annie. It's a French picture by Monet, or Manet, it doesn't really matter which, a girl, or perhaps a boy, dressed in white, and sitting at a café table, all in shade, under a striped awning, but there's very bright sunshine beyond that, and there's some older people at the table too, with glasses of something in front of them, wine I suppose, but none of them are really looking at each other.'

'I'm sorry you don't know whether it was a boy or a girl,' said Annie mildly. He saw that she had not given in.

'You haven't been with us as long as the others. I should like....' He was improvising. 'I should like to give you a present. The best! There's no point at all in a present unless it's the best one can give.'

'I don't know what the best would be, Mr Brooks.' She was not worried.

It was a game.

'I shall give you a ring.'

They had all of them been with him in the studio and knew how dexterous he was, but none of them would have believed that he could take the inch of gold wire still dangling from the champagne bottle, pierce the end through one of the red currants and give it three twists or flicks so that the currant was transfixed, a jewel on which the blond light shone. His broad fingers held the wire as neatly as a pair of pliers.

'Well, Annie.'

Annie had been keeping her hands under the table, but now she spread them out on the stiff-feeling tablecloth. They were pinkish and freckled, but delicate, not piano-player's hands, not indeed as practical as one would have expected, thin and tender. After some hesitation, as though making a difficult selection, Sam Brooks picked up the left hand and most ingeniously put the currant ring onto the third finger, compressing it to make it fit exactly.

The others watched in silence. Annie did not know what to say or do, so she said nothing, and left her hand where it was on the table. Something inside her seemed to move and unclose.

At that precise moment, while the juniors were eating their dessert at Prunier's, Annie fell in love with RPD absolutely, and hers must have been the last generation to fall in love without hope in such an unproductive way. After the war the species no longer found it biologically useful, and indeed it was not useful to Annie. Love without hope grows in its own atmosphere, and should encourage the imagination, but Annie's grew narrower. She exerted the utmost of her will-power to this end. She never pictured herself trapped in the main lift with Mr Brooks above the third floor, or of rescuing him from a burning building or a Nazi parachutist or even a mad producer armed with a shotgun. He existed, and so did she, and she had perhaps sixty years left to put up with it, although her father died at fifty-six. She was in love, as she quite saw, with a middle-aged man who said the same thing to all the girls, who had been a prince for an evening which he'd most likely forgotten already, who had given her a ring with a red currant in it and who cared, to the exclusion of all else, for his work. As a result, it was generally understood, Mrs Brooks had left him, and the thought of his loneliness made her heart contract as though squeezed by a giant hand; but then you couldn't really pretend that he *was* lonely, and so Annie didn't pretend. This, of course, meant that she suffered twice, and she failed to reckon the extra cost of honesty.

The truth was that she was almost too well trained in endurance, having drawn since birth on the inexhaustible fund of tranquil pessimism peculiar to the English Midlands. Her father's friends, who came round evenings and sat in their accustomed chairs, speaking at long intervals, said 'We're never sent more than we can bear', and 'You begin life helpless, and you end it helpless', and 'Love breaks the heart, porridge breaks the wind', and when she worked at Anstruthers' hosiery counter they hadn't asked the customers whether they wanted plain knit or micromesh, but 'Do you want the kind that ladders, or the kind that goes into holes?' These uncompromising alternatives were not intended to provide comfort, only self-respect.

Annie – although she also knew that those who don't speak have to pay it off in thinking – was resolved on silence. Whatever happened, and after all she was obliged to see Mr Brooks two or three times every day, though she by no means looked forward to it, feeling herself more truly alive when she could picture him steadily without seeing him – whatever happened, he needn't know how daft she was. But words were scarcely necessary in the closeness of the RPA room. They all knew how it was with her there.

Vi wanted to be of help, but it was difficult to find facts which Annie had not already faced.

'He's old, Annie,' she ventured at last.

'He is,' Annie replied calmly, 'he's forty-six: I looked him up in the BBC Handbook, and it's my opinion that he's putting on weight. I daresay he wouldn't look much in bed.'

'But what do you expect to come of it?'

'Nothing.'

Vi felt troubled. She was conscious, as she sometimes was when Willie Sharpe was talking, of a sort of wrong-headed dignity, and she had a conviction, too, that relationships could not be altered to such an extent as this, and that RPD was simply not there to be fallen in love with. 'It's not right,' she thought, feeling guilty, at the same time, of her own good luck in life. A few nights ago, just when Annie happened to be on night shift and she had her room to herself, Chris had turned up. He had docked at Liverpool with forty-eight hours' leave, got the train as far as Rugby, been shunted off into a siding because of an air-raid warning and told they would stay there till morning, taken a lift with an army convoy to Luton, another one to Woolwich, and a third on a potato lorry to Covent Garden, and then, since it was in the small hours, walked the last eight miles to Hammersmith, climbed up the back of the house by way of the coal-shed, opened her window, got in under the sheets and when she'd nearly jumped out of her skin said, in quite the old way: 'There's no need to be surprised, you're quite a nice-looking girl.' Next morning her mother, when told Chris had arrived for breakfast, had made no comment, and it struck Vi that this too might have been much the same in 1914.

Why couldn't things be as simple as that for everybody? Teddy suggested that they might consult the Readers' Problems in the *Mirror*. The answers column, conducted by the Two Old Codgers, he'd been told, had saved many from desperation and worse. He'd just set out the problem clearly, altering the names, of course, and the ages, and the addresses, and where they worked, and what they did. Vi had no patience with him sometimes.

Willie, saddened by the experience in which Annie seemed to be trapped without escape, took her to task.

'It's wrong, because your situation isn't natural. I've worked that out to my own satisfaction.'

'I can't get it to go away, though. Doesn't that make it natural?'

They were checking each other's time sheets before going down to tea.

'Love is of the body and the spirit,' Willie told her earnestly, 'and there's no real difference between them.'

'If you say that, you can't ever have seen anyone die,' said Annie. And indeed at this time he never had.

Mrs Milne, to whom no one had given any kind of hint, must have learned through listening to the air itself what she would never have been willingly told. The Old Servants had developed a sixth sense in these matters. It occurred to her that it was her duty to speak to RPD.

Speaking, in this sense, was undertaken only at a ceremonial time, when the day's letters were brought in for signature, and there was also a set rhetorical form, beginning with observations of general and even national interest and coming gradually to the particular. Mrs Milne, therefore, rustling in at five o'clock, began by asking whether he'd heard that members of the Stock Exchange had opened a book and were quoting odds on how many enemy aircraft were shot down each day, and what kind of mentality, when you came to think of it, did that show, and whether he'd noticed the acute shortage of kippers which made it well-nigh impossible to offer traditional hospitality to over-night visitors. It was different, of course, for those who could afford to frequent restaurants. These subjects were singularly ill-chosen and showed Mrs Milne to be in a state of nervous tension. Sam made no pretence of listening until she said:

'Mr Brooks, I should like to have a word with you about Miss Asra.'

'I can't think why. When I tried to talk to you about her before you told me she was a very usual-looking girl from the Midlands.'

He scrawled his signature several times. 'What's she been doing?'

It was very unlike him to remember any remark she had made more than a few hours ago.

'It might be better for everyone . . .' she said, her voice scarcely audible now.

Her Director stared at her coldly.

'I think that Miss Asra is alone in the world, except for an aunt,' she went on resolutely. 'The girl must feel lonely, and her aunt must miss her a great deal.'

'Is her aunt alone in the world too?' enquired Sam. 'There can't be as many people in Birmingham as I thought.'

Mrs Milne tried again.

'Of course, Miss Asra won't be due for any annual leave until she has been with us for a year, but, in view of the emergency and her special circumstances we might make an exception in her case, a kind of prolonged compassionate leave, if you follow me.'

'I don't follow you in the least. If you're interested in Annie's aunt you have my full permission to get in touch with her.' He shovelled the heap of letters towards her. 'Has Annie said she wanted to go away?'

'Not exactly.'

'Tell me when she says so exactly.'

Annie had various methods, besides the control of her imagination, for maintaining proper pride. Sometimes she spoke to herself in the third person, as the organist at St Martin's used to speak, when flustered, to the choir. 'Asra, are you with me?' 'Dobbs, you've no need to glance so frequently as Asra.' Asra, she said to herself, running for the Hammersmith bus, you don't mean any more to him than the furniture does. And that was really a good comparison. He'd subside and lean against you and tell you all those difficulties about the European and Far Eastern sections, and you could feel his weight lying there, just as if you were the back of a chair. She'd no call to be surprised at this, Vi had told her about it when she came, only at first he hadn't taken to her, now he had, but it was no one's fault but her own if she was cut to the heart. If you can't face living your life day by day, you must live it minute by minute. At least, thank God, her aunt had gone overseas with the ATS and she'd no obligation to leave London. She was free to stay here and be unhappy, just so long as she didn't become ridiculous; for that she didn't think she could forgive herself.

'Your nose is cold,' said Eddie Waterlow, pressing it with his forefinger as she sat listening to music, his touch light as a fall of dust. 'That is a sign of health in pets, so you are not actually out of condition. Something is amiss, however. How are you getting gon?'

Mr Waterlow was the only person she had ever met who imitated her voice, the scrupulously fair intonation of Selly Oak, neither rising nor falling, giving each syllable its equal weight, as though considering its feelings before leaving it behind, and lingering over the final one so that it is given the opportunity to start the next word also. With so many more obtrusive voices around him, so many much more decisive accents, he was fascinated, as a connoisseur, by the gentle transitions, said to be the most difficult in the English language to imitate exactly, getting gon, going gon, passing gon. Curiously enough, she did not mind this at all.

'I'm getting on very nicely,' she said.

'No, no, you are not. You are not wanted as you should be, not appreciated as you wish, in this like me, in this very much like me.'

'My God, Mr Waterlow,' said Annie sadly. 'Does everybody in Broadcasting House know how daft I am?'

He told her that she was betraying herself, and of course at the same time indulging herself, by playing Tchaikovsky. They had to adjourn to one of the canteen store-rooms where there was an old upright piano, long since retired from the struggle to divide the air into music, and a whole tone flat in the middle register. There it was Satie again, and to oblige him she tried one of the little cabaret songs, but could hardly make herself heard above his instructions.

'Ah yes . . . *modestement* . . . for the nerves . . . just let it be a simple occurrence, no logic, just let it happen, however strangely . . . a little incongruity, please, "owl steals pince-nez of Wolverhampton builder" . . . sing, Annie, sing . . . like a nightingale, a nighting gale, with toothache... "I command removal from my presence sadness, silence and dolorous meditation"...'

'I can't imagine how you get through the day without anything to do, Mr Waterlow,' Annie said, when he had reverently shut the lid of the dejected piano, 'I've never met a man before who didn't have to work hard.'

Eddie spread out his arms, as one who was ready at any time for the call.

'Surely the BBC can find something for you?' she asked gently. He looked forlorn.

'The BBC is doing gits bit. We put out the truth, but only contingent truth, Annie! The opposite could also be true! We are told that German pilots have been brought down in Croydon and turned out to know the way to the post-office, that Hitler has declared that he only needs three fine days to defeat Great Britain, and that there is an excellent blackberry crop and therefore it is our patriotic duty to make jam. But all this need not have been true, Annie! If the summer had not been fine, there might have been no blackberries.'

'Of course there mightn't,' said Annie. 'You're just making worries for yourself, Mr Waterlow. There isn't anything at all that mightn't be otherwise. After all, I mightn't have... what I mean is, how can they find anything to broadcast that's got to be true, and couldn't be anything else?'

He gestured towards the piano.

'We couldn't put out music all day!'

'Music and silence.'

After she had gone back on shift, Eddie thought for a while about Sam Brooks. There was something magnificent after all, in the way he squandered young people and discarded them and looked round absent-mindedly for more. It implied great faith in his own future. But should his attention be drawn, perhaps, to Annie's case?

By the end of August the heavy raids had begun. Vi and Annie were both out when the Simmonses' house in Hammersmith was knocked down. Mrs Simmons and the children were quite all right, having taken shelter under the hall table, a half-size billiard table really, which was of a quality you couldn't get nowadays if you tried. Mr Simmons had to stay to look after the shop, but the family left London, and Vi went with them. Annie got accommodation at the YMCA hostel opposite Westminster Abbey; Mr Simmons brought up her things in his van, and she knew he was kindly using some of the petrol ration which he got for the business. It was only her clothes, really, covered now with flakes of plaster. It was just as well that she had brought so little with her in the first place.

Vi wrote to say that her wedding day was fixed, she was going up to Liverpool some time in September to marry Chris and to be his till the end of Life's Story. She wished she'd been able to invite them all, but they'd have a reunion after the war when the lights went up again, they must all swear to make a note of it, August the 30th by the Edith Cavell statue off Trafalgar Square, the side marked Fidelity. The letter did not sound quite like the Vi they had known, and made her seem farther away.

9

AFTER THE first week of September London became every morning a somewhat stranger place. The early morning sound was always of glass being scraped off the pavement. The brush hissed and scraped, the glass chattered, tinkled, and fell. Lyons handed out cold baked potatoes through one hole in their windows and took in the money through another. The buses, diverted into streets for which they were not intended, seemed to take the licence of a dream, drawing up on the pavements and nosing against front windows to look in at the startled inhabitants. A number 113 became seriously wedged against DPP's taxi in Riding House Street and volunteers were needed to dislodge it. They returned to Broadcasting House white with dust. The air in fact was always full of this fine, whitish dust which was suspended in the air and settled slowly, long after the buildings fell.

More menacing than the nightly danger was the need to find a willing listener for bomb stories the next morning. Little incidents of the raids, or of the journey to work, were met and countered at the office by other little incidents, and fell back rebuffed. But all new societies are quick to establish the means of exchange. After Mrs Staples had described how the contents of her handbag, keys, throat lozenges and all, had been sucked, rather than blown, away from her, and how she'd not been allowed to smoke all evening because of the broken gas mains, Mrs Milne felt entitled to a question of her own; if things were going on like this – and she had several anecdotes in reserve – wouldn't it be wise to send one's nice things away to some safer part of the country?

'I'm sure it would,' said Mrs Staples, 'if you can find someone you can trust to look after them.'

'I can't get RPD to consider the question at all. He doesn't even seem to know whether he *has* any nice things or not.

I daresay Mrs Brooks took most of them away with her when she left Streatham. I don't think we shall hear very much more from that quarter,' she added.

Mrs Staples considered. 'You mean specimen glass and china, and that sort of thing?'

'Yes, the irreplaceables, the things you never use – those are what really matters. I've got a damask tablecloth, you know, and napkins to match for twenty-four people. I've heard it said that a woman's possessions are part of herself. If she loses her things, her personality undergoes a change.'

'It's just that one has to be careful when living alone,' said Mrs Staples. 'When one's children are grown up or in the Forces and the flat is empty I find that one talks to certain pieces of furniture quite often, and to oneself, of course.'

'The thing is not to be too hard on oneself,' Mrs Milne replied.

DPP's economy in the matter of staff made it possible for him to avoid the morning stories and almost all discussion of the raids. Placed, as he now was, with the responsibility of making a clean sweep of the programmes at any given moment in favour of battle instructions and of the Prime Minister's new slogan 'You can always take one with you', which was to resound through every home and place of work in Great Britain as soon as the first German landed on this soil, Jeff wished that he had not run out of cigars. Mac might bring some, and he was due over in England pretty soon. He had cabled that he wanted to broadcast direct from the roof of BH, in the thick of the raids, instead of being confined with the rest of the overseas correspondents to the basement studios. There was little or no chance, however, of the Director General giving way on this point, and Jeff idly pictured himself wrestling with Mac on the stairs, as in a silent film, to prevent him going any higher, while Nazi assault troops pounded out of the lifts. Perhaps we all ought to be in the movies, he thought.

Barnett, on one of his regular calls, told Jeff that America was drawing nearer to the brink of war. Lines of exhaustion showed clearly on his face, which was creased like the dry bed of a river. 'The way I look at it is this. The day the United States declare war on Nazi Germany, the Central and South American republics will follow suit. Well, excluding British Guiana and British Honduras, that gives you by my reckoning fifteen independent countries that are going to come in on our side. Now, Mr Haggard, all of them are going to want representation at the BBC. That in its turn means fifteen new sections, and although the standards of living in those places varies, I believe, and their governments are none too stable, they'll all of them want carpets, chairs, desks, typewriters adapted to the Spanish alphabet and steel filing cabinets. If you can tell me where to get any more steel filing cabinets measuring up to our specifications, Mr Haggard, I'm prepared to go to bed with Hitler's grandmother.'

'I hadn't thought of the position exactly in that way,' Jeff replied.

'I daresay you hadn't, very few have. Decisions are made, as you know, with very little thought as to how they're to be carried out.'

'You have my sympathy.'

'But what do you suggest I should do?'

'Pray for a negotiated peace,' said Jeff.

'Now, Mr Haggard, you don't mean that, we all know you don't mean half of what you say.'

'I don't at all mean that it would be desirable. I'm simply saying that it's the only solution for the problem of the steel filing cabinets. If you don't like the idea, you'll have to find a new approach to the whole question.'

On the night of September the 7th the BBC received the signal for 'Invasion Imminent' from the C in C Home Forces, who now had priority over the Ministry of Information. This signal was followed by another: 'No bells to ring till advise.' By an understandable confusion, however, there were church bells which did start ringing in scattered parishes all over the country. Not one was recorded.

'We missed the lot,' Sam protested, at white heat. 'A false alarm, well, what if it was? When the real thing comes there may not be time to ring them.' He set out in search of Dr Vogel.

Hard to track down, the doctor was sometimes to be found in the Monitoring Section, where he had a relation of sorts, said to be his nephew, although he appeared rather the older of the two. The atmosphere of this section was deeply studious. High up in the building, refugee scholars in headphones, quietly clad, disguising their losses, transcribed page after page of Nazi broadcasts in a scholar's shorthand. When they broke for coffee, Beethoven's last quartets were played. Even Sam, fuming energetically into the room, was checked for a moment. Then he recollected himself and shouted: 'Heinz Vogel! Is there anyone here called Heinz Vogel? I'm looking for Josef.'

A bent figure lifted its head. 'Unfortunately my uncle has died.'

Dr Vogel, killed by a piece of flying drainpipe, had been one of the BBC's first casualties. And after all he had not been trying to record. Standing among the debris, he had been courteously persuading an ARP warden, on behalf of a complete stranger, that it was legal under the emergency regulations for a house-holder to return twice to his ruined dwelling, once for his mattress, and once for his personal effects. 'The citizen has this right very clearly laid down,' he explained patiently. 'That is English law.'

Laid to rest in Golders Green, Dr Vogel had wished to be buried in his native Frankfurt. Jeff, not easily surprised, was a little taken aback when he was required to sign papers under-taking to see to this, as soon as hostilities ceased. The nephew, painfully accurate and humble, pointed out that there would be no financial obligation, indeed nothing for DPP to do at all. It was only that he himself was not a British citizen, and needed the signature and authorisation of someone of a certain standing.

'What about RPD?' Jeff asked. 'He worked a good deal with your uncle, whereas I only knew him very slightly.'

'Unfortunately he was too busy.'

'Did he tell you to try me?'

'Yes, Mr Haggard, he suggested that I should make this application to you.'

Jeff, writing more carefully than usual, signed at the foot of the numerous pages, which trembled in the nephew's hand.

'Would you like a drink, Vogel?' he said. 'We all valued your uncle's work. I'm very sorry.'

Heinz Vogel thanked him profusely, but did not drink.

For some time Jeff's meditations had been following a certain course, which he felt less and less inclined to check. A few weeks at most would show whether the invasion was ever likely to take place. If it didn't, and the war expanded in quite other directions, might it not be possible to leave the problems of Sam, as well as schedules of the Home and Forces Network, to other hands? Among the documents he might hand on to a successor would be a chart of the rescue operations, great or small, necessary for getting Sam through a given period of time. And 'necessary' was not an exaggeration. Sam's methods might be improved, but his knowledge could not be replaced. It would have to be explained, for example, that this helpless and endearing expert in self-indulgence, seemingly unhinged at times, was the man who had established the apparent decrease in the proportion of higher and lower frequencies with respect to the middle range as loudspeaker level is decreased. While the war lasted, if the BBC wished to record itself, it needed Sam.

Someone must support him, then – perhaps a new Director of Programme Planning, so that the transition would be less noticeable. Meanwhile, Jeff considered whether it was too late to save himself. Helping other people is a drug so dangerous that there is no cure short of total abstention. Mac had warned Jeff of this, and indeed he had said more; 'You're weakening these people.'

But the possibility of his doing something else had, as it happened, been manifested to Jeff like an emanation from

various quarters, sometimes clear, sometimes muted, in the
form of soundings-out, hints and suppositions, always guarded,
because he was a linguist, and to know foreign languages can
never be quite creditable, but tending steadily towards a certain
point. This point was his knowledge of Turkish and Russian.
There might be employment for him outside this country and
outside the BBC, comparable in importance with the post he
now held. It was being assumed that his Turkish was as fluent as
his French.

'Well?' said Jeff.

That was the way things were done, or were put forward to
be about to be done, in those days. Jeff had very little to leave
behind – that too was well understood – not much to gain,
either, and no embarrassments beyond a possible encounter
with his former wives. He could go anywhere. He admitted
that he might make better use of his detachment. A natural
tendency to extravagance had prompted him to waste it, and to
watch the waste with amusement. I can't change, he thought,
but I can begin to withdraw.

Under a star-powdered sky the Recorded Programmes Department set up an open microphone on the roof of BH, which
caught every sound of the raids until the last enemy aircraft
departed into silence. On the roof, too, the parts of the rifle
were named to Teddy and Willie by Reception from the main
desk of BH, who told them frequently, as he looked down at
the pale pink smoke of London's fires, that it reminded him of a
quiet sector of the line in the last show. Most of the staff juniors
attended, and sometimes Reception would sit and play poker
with them for margarine coupons, while the Regent's Park
guns rocked them like ship's boys aloft.

It felt odd to go down from the roof, during that cloudless
autumn, into the interior of BH, where the circulation had
become even more complex now that on receipt of the second,
or purple, warning all personnel had to leave their rooms and
proceed by the quickest route to the basement. It was only the
fact that very few of them actually did this that kept the

administration going. The Monitoring Section, for example, never raised their heads from their grave task.

Establishment had expected that as soon as Vi Simmons had gone, they would get an application for a further supply of RPAs, but none came. There was extra work, which Annie was quite prepared to do. But time, as though in revenge for the minute watch that was kept on it, from the early news till *Lighten Our Darkness*, behaved oddly, so that she felt much older than she really was, and as though she had been with the BBC much longer than she really had. And yet Willie and Teddy, veterans of nearly eight months, spoke of epochs which she had never known. Once, when the engineers were testing the line from Manchester, a succulent voice cut in, singing an approximation of *Look for the Silver Lining*.

'That's Della!'

In the middle of the second refrain the singer was abruptly switched off. 'Well, at least she's been recorded,' said Willie.

In spite of herself Annie could not help asking: 'Did she get on well with RPD?'

Willie thought not. They were too much alike, he told her.

With only three of them left, the concept of the Seraglio seemed lost. Sam no longer sent for Annie to come and sit with him, but wandered about the building, when the need arose, until he found her. Then, of course, she was rarely alone. It was impossible to maintain the old shifts, and they got through the work as best they could.

'There's something wrong with these,' she said to Teddy, as they sorted out the discs of *Children Calling Home*. These were recorded by line from families evacuated to Canada and the United States. The children's bewilderment, they remembered, had often made Vi feel like crying.

Teddy wearily put one of them onto the turntable. A deep bass voice, hoarsened with smoking, began: 'Hullo, Mum and Dad and Juicy Nelly . . .'

'They're mixed up with Forces Messages again,' said Annie.

They looked dolefully at each other. It was wrong to admit, no matter what the subject, that you were losing heart. And then, when RPD bounded in, as he did at that moment, giving the effect of a trajectory fuelled by indignation and landing exactly where he had intended, their lives expanded and glowed and they knew they were too important to the Corporation ever to feel tired.

'What are you complaining about now, Mr Brooks?' asked Annie, speaking a good deal more bluntly than Vi had done, but with a radiant smile. Diverted, apparently, from his original intention, Sam looked at her and complained that her hair was ragged.

Teddy, watching him, thought: 'Perhaps I ought to break it to him that Annie fancies him.' Jeez, though, it would have to be done tactfully.

Sam twisted one of the outlying curls round his finger. 'Who's been hacking at this?' he asked.

'Willie Sharpe,' said Annie.

'He's made a mess of it.'

'He'll get better with practice.'

'You ought to have asked me about it. I'm very good at cutting hair.'

'Where did you learn, Mr Brooks?' Teddy asked in amazement. 'In the trenches?'

'No, my mother taught me when I was about ten. That meant I could trim my father's beard for him. I imagine the idea was to save money. We weren't well off.'

The two juniors looked at each other, silenced by these impossibilities.

Then Annie felt something stronger than herself take her by the throat and said: 'Do you cut Mrs Brooks's hair?'

'You mean my wife?'

'Yes.'

He was not in the least perturbed. 'I don't think the question ever arose. She was quite self-sufficient.' The enormous moment passed without leaving a trace.

He sprang to his feet and began to pace the stuffy mixer room. 'Teddy, I ask you as man to man, do we appreciate Annie enough? Quite apart from her resemblance to that picture of a small French boy, or girl, in white which none of us seem able to identify, she is tranquil, she is steady, she isn't carried out of herself, as I am, not only by the ludicrous administrative errors of the Corporation, but by the sheer injustice of life's coincidences. I don't suppose either of you realise that Vogel, Dr Josef Vogel, was a casualty in last Saturday's raids?'

'Yes, we did know that, Mr Brooks,' said Teddy. 'He went when there was all that damage round the Highgate Cat and Bells. We had a whip round the Department, you know, for some flowers.'

Sam ignored this. 'You understand, Annie, I think, even if no one else does, that in his professional capacity Vogel was indispensable to me, I'd put it as strongly as that, in the whole business of catching the sound of history as it passes. I must have discussed with him a hundred times what we'd do if German troops landed. In what archives, I put it to you, will you find a recording of the first wave of an invading tank division moving up a sand and shingle beach? I'd told him I was bringing him with me on the unit and we'd place ourselves on the foreshore, or, better still, perhaps, a mile or so up the London road. I can read you the application I've made to Coastal Defence. Of course, they're trying to make needless restrictions of all kinds. . . . '

'RPD struck me as a bit heartless,' said Teddy, when they were left with *Children Calling Home*.

'I don't think so,' said Annie. 'Dr Vogel would have felt just the same.'

Teddy sighed. 'You won't listen to a word against him, will you?'

'I can't help myself, Teddy. I know the style he carries on, but I can't help it.'

'He gets round you. He gets round everyone.'

Annie could not explain to him why she felt no resentment. Her feeling for Mr Brooks was so much the most important part of her life that it seemed like something which did not belong to her, but which she had to carry about with her, at work or in her room, there was no difference. She had a kind of affection, too, for the love itself, which was so strong, but maintained itself on so little. There had been a time, not at all long ago, when she hadn't had this responsibility, but it was hard for her to remember how she had felt then.

Eddie Waterlow, meeting her in the corridor, looked at her sharply.

'Fly with me!' he exclaimed.

'What from, Mr Waterlow?' Annie asked, not pretending to misunderstand him.

10

ON SEPTEMBER the 15th the RAF announced that they were no longer making School Certificate a requirement for flying duties and advertised for volunteers. Willie Sharpe read this on the ticker-tape after he had done his last job for that day, delivering the recordings for *London After Dark*. It was a very bright moonlight night outside, a bad night, as it turned out, in more ways than one.

He had a ticket to sleep in the concert-hall, and a meal allowance in the canteen. On the wiped counter, stale with its twenty-four-hour service, nothing was left but herrings in mustard sauce; they were the week's Patriotic Fish Dish. At separate tables, two messengers and a Czech professor of philosophy were picking quietly over their heap of bones.

Willie remembered Tad (who had recently sent Teddy a photograph of himself with a moustache, and a Polish fiancée), and then the outing to Prunier's. Soon I shan't be here, he thought. I can pass for eighteen easily. With a bit more experience of life's testing moments, I shall look eighteen and a half. He imagined himself in training, in the Mess, listening to *London After Dark*, and wondering whether anybody would be interested then if he said he'd once worked in the Corporation.

The Czech professor approached his table, and asked whether it would be possible to borrow a torch. Evidently he too was going to venture into the concert-hall.

'I'm sorry, I never carry one. As a matter of fact I'm training myself to do without a light, to make myself more useful in case of night combat.'

Willie, however, was too tired for once to expatiate on this. As the professor, resigned to refusal, moved away to ask elsewhere, he handed in his voucher and left.

The first heroic or primitive period of the concert-hall had only lasted a very short while. The grades quickly reasserted themselves, although the structure was complicated, as always, by the demands of time. Just inside the entrance, the old dressing-rooms had been turned into separate cubicles for executives and senior news readers, but junior news readers (after one o'clock in the morning) and administrative assistants (on programmes of special importance) could claim to use any that were vacant.

Tonight they all seemed to be standing empty.

Willie had quite often managed to take half an hour's unentitled sleep in one of the cubicles. He hoped that it was right to regard this as training in initiative. The mattresses were really the same as all the others, but there were single beds, and even small tables. In front of each hung a curtain of a material half-way between felt and sacking, which had once been used to deaden sound in the drama studios.

He paused and listened acutely to the great ground swell of snoring. Pitched higher, pitched lower, came the familiar snatches of coloratura, swearing, and pleading, but everybody seemed safely stowed. Almost reassured, he felt his way behind the rank-smelling curtain into the thick darkness, trusting that he was in the cubicle next to the door, the best, of course, if you had to leave later in a hurry. He was frightened when he heard someone moaning in the corner.

'Who is it?' he whispered.

'Strike a match. There's some by the bed.'

He thought he recognised the voice. The match lit up part of a mottled, damp and livid face. He had always thought Lise rather pretty, she looked frightful now.

'What are you doing in there?'

There was blood on the floor, on the standard green lino which the BBC also used to deaden sound.

'Lise, have you met with an accident?'

The girl suddenly heaved over, crouching under the regulation blanket on all fours, and swaying like an animal fit to drop.

'Shall I get you a cup of tea?' Willie asked in terror. He knew very well what was happening. Make me wrong, he prayed.

'Is this cubicle occupied?' murmured a voice, a man's voice, a foot away behind the curtain. Only an Old Servant could maintain such correctness, only a trained baritone could produce such a resonant *mezza voce*.

Willie peeped out. It was, as he well knew, John Haliburton, the Senior Announcer.

'I rather thought I heard a woman's voice in here. But if it's empty....'

The Halibut was carrying a kind of dark lantern, and wore the correctly creased uniform of the BBC's Defence Volunteers. Everybody knew, although he himself never mentioned it, that he had been wounded at Le Cateau and should be allowed to rest whenever possible. Willie steeled himself.

'I'm afraid you can't come in, Mr Haliburton.'

Lise began to make a prolonged low sound that was not a groan but an exhalation, like a pair of bellows pressed and crushed flat to expel the last air in a whimper. Willie retreated towards her.

'Willie...can you count? You can help me if you can count...you have to tell me how many minutes between each contraction.'

'What's that?' he whispered, struggling to recall his Red Cross Handbook.

'It's a sort of pain.'

'Where do you feel the pain?'

'In my back.'

'Oughtn't it to be in the front?'

'If you are in any difficulties,' suggested Haliburton from outside, 'I advise you to report to the First Aid Posts, or to fetch someone competent. I believe Dr Florestan, at the European News Desk, has medical qualifications.'

In spite of his predicament, Willie did not really want Mr Haliburton to go away. Whatever it was that supported the Senior Announcer, his four years at the Western Front, his training under Sir John Reith, his performer's vanity – all these together gave him a superb indifference to the tossing and

snoring shambles around him, and an authority which made
Willie plead: 'Just a minute, Mr Haliburton.'

Lise groaned again, and this time the noise rose above the
permitted level of sounds in the darkened hall. Willie thought
he could hear a faint tick, as of liquid splashing onto the floor in
small quantities. Meanwhile the Halibut, who had, as he remembered too late, a Deaf Side, passed sedately on.

It's too bad he couldn't rest his leg a bit, Willie thought
confusedly.

The prospect of looking after them both – the correct Old
Servant and the agonising girl – side by side under the same too
narrow blanket, flashed upon him like a nightmare. Without
trying to work things out any further he felt for Lise's damp
hand and held it.

'Strike some more matches.'

'I'd better save them, I think.'

'Are you still counting?'

'I can hold my watch to my ear and count the sixty
seconds.'

Lise heaved, and now once again she was like a young beast
wallowing, and marked out for destruction. While Mr Haliburton had been there, the sleepers nearest to them had
remained relatively tranquil, soothed by his familiar voice,
reassuring even in a whisper. But now that he was gone they
became restive. I must calm her, he told himself.

'I'm not criticising you, Lise,' he said, bending close to her. 'I
believe every human being should follow their own bent, and I
assume that's what you've been doing. Probably you didn't
envisage this situation.'

She clung on, yet he felt separated from her by many miles.
He wouldn't have believed that a girl could grip like that, so that
his hand felt numb, with the tarsus and the metatarsus, was
that right? – crushed together. The British character was at its
finest in adversity. Lise, though, was half-French, if he'd got
that straight. In any case, there mustn't be pain like this after the
war was over. Everyone, people like himself, must carry a range
of simple medication, then you'd be able to be of real help to

anyone you happened to meet in a situation like this during the course of the day.

His palm was stuck to hers with sweat like glue.

'Don't leave me,' muttered Lise. 'Go and fetch somebody. Stay here. Don't tell them in First Aid. Go and get somebody straight away.'

What was needed before anything else, in Willie's view, was something to mop up the floor with. He knew every room in the building, as part of a comprehensive survey he'd made of the defence facilities. The nearest cloths and hot water would be three doors to the left, where there was a messengers' room, and they would be off duty now. As he edged out of the concert-hall he saw Mr Haliburton, propped against the wall to ease his leg, and talking quietly to a small group.

'Sir John always expected us to wear dinner jackets to read the late news . . . on the other hand, informality can, I think, be carried too far. . . .'

In the harsh overhead light of the messengers' room Willie felt sick. There was a bath in there, round the inside of which Accommodation had painted a red line, to remind the staff not to use too much hot water. For some reason this red line also made him feel sick. When he looked down and saw that there was blood on his shoes and trousers it became clear to him in an instant that he couldn't carry on any longer on his own responsibility. He had no hestitation at all about where to go for help.

'Mr Haggard, sir.'

DPP looked up from his desk without hope, alarm, or irritation. He could see that the juvenile who had just come into the room was bloodstained here and there, and that as he was not apparently bleeding himself, the blood must have come from somewhere else.

'I don't think you remember me,' said Willie, grasping the back of the visitors' chair.

'I do remember you,' said Jeff.

'You may think it very queer my coming up here to see you like this.'

'Queer, but not very queer. You'd better sit down. I don't think you gave me your name when we last met.'

Willie gave his name. 'Junior Recorded Programme Assistant,' he added.

He felt it would help him not to be sick if he attempted a measure of formality. 'It's Lise, sir, I mean Miss Bernard, really perhaps I mean Mrs Bernard.'

He glanced down at the knees of his grey trousers.

'Perhaps the thought's passing through your mind that I've murdered her.'

Jeff saw that he was in a bad way.

'Never mind what I think. We can discuss that later. Who is Miss Bernard?'

'Well, she's having a baby, Mr Haggard. I suppose she may have had it by now, but these things take some time, you know. That is, she's giving birth to a child, in the concert-hall.'

Jeff paused before replying, but scarcely any longer than usual.

'In the concert-hall, you say?'

'It's one of those curtained-off bits, just as you go in. I just happened to be passing. I had a ticket for tonight, that was all in order. No, sir, I'm not telling you the exact truth, I hoped perhaps if it was free I might go in there myself. It's the one next to the door, so usually it's kept for the Senior Announcer.'

'But at the moment it's occupied by Miss Bernard, who is in an advanced stage of labour?'

Willie nodded.

'Is the Senior Announcer in there as well?'

Willie shook his head, but with an expression which made DPP ask him whether he was actually going to be sick. Willie thought not yet, and perhaps not at all if he kept his head still.

'Look, William, there are three First Aid Posts on floors one, five, and seven of Broadcasting House, with nurses on permanent duty, and there is also a Home Guard dispensary. I'm only employed here in the capacity of planning the Corporation's programmes. What made you come to me?'

'I thought you didn't really remember me, sir. We were on the Red Cross course together, for all staff without consideration of status. We all thought it good of you to come along, considering you must have seen a lot of casualties already in World War One. In the end we both had the same special chapter for our certificates, sir – frostbite, sunstroke, and sudden childbirth.'

DPP rang through to RPD's office and told him that he had reason to be concerned about two of the junior members of his department. William Sharpe had been made to lie down in the fifth-floor First Aid Post. Lise Bernard had been sent along the road to the Middlesex Hospital. It was fortunate, since of course there were no ambulances free to fetch her, that his taxi had, once more, been available.

'I don't understand you, Jeff. Have you been knocking them about?'

'Bernard was in the second stage of childbirth, Sam. You remember telling me on a number of occasions that your junior staff, past and present, were a particular responsibility to you.'

'Of course they are. What has that got to do with it?'

'Naturally enough they weren't at all anxious to take her in at the Middlesex, they've got emergency beds two deep in the corridors. We just have to be grateful that hospitals, like the rest of us, enjoy feeling powerful. They allowed themselves to be persuaded.'

'I still don't see why you should have been involved in all this.'

'Nor do I. The matron told me some people made the war an excuse for everything.'

Sam appeared to reflect for a while.

'Do you know I'm very glad you told me about this?' he said at last, with warmth. 'I'm very glad indeed that it happened. These two programme assistants, a girl and a boy, who you've never met, who in fact you've never seen or heard of before come to you with their problems, problems, too, of an unfamiliar kind, and although you must have been somewhat bewildered by the part you were called on to play, you did your very best for them – I believe that, Jeff. And that shows that all this appearance of coldness and of not caring a shit for what other people suffer is just what I've always suspected it was, a pretence. I congratulate you, Jeff. You tried to help.'

'That's quite enough,' Jeff replied. 'The time is now 1.47. I'm occupied in sorting out the difficulties of Religious Broadcasting, who want a full-length service of praise and thanksgiving if the unexploded bomb outside St Paul's is removed, but not if it isn't. I rang you because this young woman, as I said, is or was a member of your Department. I think she joined you in May.'

'I wish you wouldn't call my juniors young women, Jeff. They're just girls.'

'Not when they give birth on the premises.'

'I must say I can't see why she should have wanted to do that.'

'You remember the name, I take it.'

'Bernard. Yes, yes, she's been on extended sick leave.'

'Which has now happily drawn to a close.'

'No...well...she's been away for some time...I'm not sure why it was exactly...I admit I've rather lost track there...you see, Jeff, it's my opinion that the memory has only a certain capacity. The model would be, let's say, a brief-case, where the contents are varied, rather than a sandbag. Under pressure of work, and hindrances, and total misunderstanding, and emotional stress, the less essential things simply have to be thrown out....Something does come back, though...I think she was partly French.'

He had forgotten about Willie Sharpe's plight. Lack of curiosity about anyone not actually in the room protected him to an astonishing degree. He might, perhaps, given this protection, last, like some monstrous natural formation, for hundreds of years.

'Sam, are you human?'

'If I'm not, I can't see who is. That reminds me, I don't think I've ever talked to you about a new assistant who's joined my

Department, really rather an exceptional person, I don't know that I've ever met anyone exactly like her.'

'Have you got her there now?'

'She's gone to get me a sandwich. By the way Jeff, it's just struck me that all this business, arranging about the hospital and so on, must have been a bit of an inconvenience for you.'

'You mustn't give it a thought.'

11

LISE HAD always felt that she was particularly unlucky, and furthermore that being unlucky was a sufficient contribution to the world's work. Other people, therefore, had to deal with the consequences. This system worked well, both for herself and her offspring.

There was nothing deliberate, however, in what she had done. After a few nights' and days' drifting, the charitable nuns had taken her in again, as a victim of war's cruel chances, and had arranged for her to go to a good Catholic nursing-home. But on her way back from the cinema she had felt queer, and remembering that she still had her concert-hall ticket she had gone into Broadcasting House for a lie down. The nuns had not liked her going out during the air-raids, or even to the cinema at all, and she was glad not to have to face them again.

Mrs Milne had looked forward to talking over Lise's disaster with Mrs Staples, and had been ready to amalgamate the whole incident, as a narrative, with the bomb stories; morals were relaxed, hearts were broken, while outside the old landmarks fell, and now Harrods Repository had been reduced to dust. But to her amazement Mrs Staples met her braced and poised, as though for a personal attack. When Mrs Milne began by saying that she had no idea where the unfortunate girl was to go to, as her parents seemed unwilling to have anything more to do with her and she could hardly return to the convent, Mrs Staples replied: 'She is coming to me.'

'But what about the infant?'

'They are coming to me.'

'What did they say at the hospital?'

'They were pleased to have somewhere to send her to. I have a good deal more room in my flat than I need. I think I told you that I found myself talking to the furniture. I shan't have to do that now. Lise is perfectly healthy and I imagine that they'll discharge her soon.'

'You'll never get rid of her!' cried Mrs Milne.

'She didn't stay long at Broadcasting House,' said Mrs Staples calmly. 'However, since I suppose she has received basic training in the work of your Department, I see no reason why she shouldn't eventually return to you as an RPA.'

'And who would look after the child then?'

'I should not mind doing so,' said Mrs Staples. 'He looks quite a little Frenchman already,' she added, and Mrs Milne perceived that she was in the grip of a force stronger than reason.

Willie, without RPD having to be disturbed over the matter, was given a day's sick leave. He went straight to the RAF recruitment centre, but failed to persuade them that he was even as much as seventeen. After that he borrowed an old bicycle from the married sister with whom he lived, and biked furiously up to the heights of Hampstead. It might have been more sensible to get off and push when he got to the last and steepest hill, but such a course did not occur to Willie. By the time he reached the summit, close to the Whitestone Pond, his breath came as painfully as a hacksaw cutting through his ribs. However, he had earned the right to get off and sit on the ground.

He found himself looking for wild plants among the coarse flat grass, just as they'd been made to do on outings from Primary School. Some dusty-looking clover flowers were still out, and two kinds of cudweed, besides the daisies. He collected the hooked pods from a trefoil almost too small to see, took out the tiny black peas, and planted them. Then he lay on his back for a couple of hours in the sunshine. The sky was a limpid blue from one horizon to the other, with no condensation trails, without a cloud, without one aircraft. It seemed to Willie that he was beginning to see things in rather better proportion. Perhaps he might recommend Annie to come up here one day.

*

Annie, although she had never met Lise, and only knew Mrs Staples from her first interview at BH, was asked round to tea. This was the result of a delusion that Lise needed cheerful company; in fact it made her cheerful to be unhappy.

The RPA rota was improvised from day to day, with un-specified breaks, and Annie had just enough time to get there and back from the address she had been given in Maida Vale. The large flat had certainly been tidy once, but never would be again while Lise was there. Everything seemed to be tempor-arily out of place, although Lise herself was perfectly motionless on the living-room sofa. The baby, wrapped in a silky white shawl belonging to Mrs Staples, breathed gently, as though simmering, in a wicker basket by her side.

Annie had brought a small pair of socks, knitted while waiting for talks producers. Lise received them indifferently. She let Annie hold the baby, said to weigh eight pounds. Annie could hardly credit that, he felt very warm but light as a doll, staring at her without blinking.

'What'll you call him?'

'I haven't thought.'

'His father was Freddie, wasn't he?'

'Who told you about him?'

'Vi.'

The conversation appeared to be running into silence.

'Do you think you'll return to BH?' Annie asked. She was trying for no more than politeness. Lise, suddenly glowering, burst out: 'That RPD was supposed to look after us all.'

Annie's heart jumped and sprang.

'I can't see what he could have done,' she said. 'From all I've heard, you left without telling anyone.' She added, with an effort, 'Would you like him to come and see you, then?'

'What good would that do?'

'I thought you might find it a comfort.'

This wasn't the right word, as she saw at once. She was beginning to sound like the Parish Visitor.

'Comfort!' Lise said. 'He'd only talk about himself.'

'Did you get to know him well, then?'

'He told me I looked like some portrait or other. He was very great on the personal contact. But it wasn't him that took me round to hospital, and he never did remember which portrait it was, either.'

Lise was making an unusual effort. As always, even the thought of Sam Brooks generated energy in unlikely places.

'Someone ought to tell him, Annie.'

'Tell him what?'

'Tell him that he can't deal in human beings the way he does. Mind you, that's what men are like,' she added.

The effort was altogether too much for her, and she began to doze.

Mrs Staples came in with the tea. 'I've brought some of my ration,' Annie said, in the subdued voice appropriate to the subject. Mrs Staples took the little packet and nodded in the same respectful way. Just a cup each, she murmured. The milkman must have been puzzled out of his wits when she'd suddenly begun to order three pints a day, and National Dried as well. Annie reflected that milkmen were hard to surprise, but she didn't say so, for fear of spoiling the drama of the situation.

Annie had to be back at Broadcasting House at 5.30, baby's bottle was due at 6, the bombing, now that the evenings were drawing in, started at about 7, Mrs Staples, who was having a day off, wanted to be in early tomorrow, and for all of them there was the imperative of the nine o'clock news. As long as one was always a little ahead, the battle with the incessant minutes could be called a truce. 'When does he wake?' Annie asked, putting the somnolent baby back in the basket. 'Oh, about ten minutes from now,' said Mrs Staples. He was quietened then with some boiled water from a teaspoon, which he sucked, like an old man with a sweet, contemplatively, and then returned in the form of a fine spray.

Teddy told Annie that it was a known fact that women of every age became broody during a war, and for several years afterwards. There was a straightforward biological explanation of that. Annie was prepared to believe him. But she had only described the baby's activities to conceal her own bewilderment at what was happening to her. She had expected to feel indignant, as always, at any criticism of RPD, she had waited for her indignation to come like the return of hunger or sleep, but when she thought of Lise's remarks, it was missing; without it she was at a loss, and then, worse still, its place was taken by a stranger, a kind of fury, a furious warm urgency to show Lise that she was wrong, but, also, to show RPD that she was right. How was it possible, though, to want to confront a man and tell him that he talked too much, and that he dealt in human beings, and so forth, and still love him? It is possible, her body prompted her. The only trouble is that you're afraid it'll be the end of all things, and then you're ignorant, and don't know how to go about it. But it is possible.

Jeff Haggard resigned himself to being considered the baby's father by most of Broadcasting House. After all, it was generally believed that when the morning mail came in he speeded up business by throwing away every third letter, also that when the French General Pinard had come to the studio DPP had said a few words to him which had caused him to fall down dead. When Barnett asked him, however, whether the Planning Department was to be held accountable for the damage to two blankets and a mattress in Cubicle 1 of the concert-hall, Jeff referred him to Recorded Programmes. The account duly came in, but this annoyance was of the kind from which Mrs Milne protected RPD. She dealt with the matter herself.

Precisely at this point, Mac came through on the blower to Jeff to say he had set foot once more in this country to have a look round.

'Still satisfied with your work?' he asked.

If there were any rumours about his resignation, Mac could be trusted to have heard them within a few hours. But Jeff did not reply, because he had no words, even to instruct himself, for the bitter loyalty he owed to the noble, absurd, ungrateful and incorruptible truthtellers whose survival, when peace came, must be precarious indeed. He didn't flatter himself that his withdrawal would be received with anything but relief. Structurally he was a load-bearing element, but one that didn't fit. Everything must look more reassuring when he had been replaced. The BBC, perhaps, counted on his being faithful enough to go. Jeff had a sure feeling for beginnings and endings. It could never be easy to leave, therefore it would be sensible to get into practice. He resolved, as the first break, not to help Sam again with any request, reasonable or unreasonable, or undertake any of the business of Sam's department, private or public, at least for the next ten days. More than that would be unrealistic. But to set a time limit would define his resolution.

This time Jeff came across Mac not in Broadcasting House, but in the darkened street, at the end of Portland Place. The sky was calm that night, with stars and shells high up. At the end of the road the guns in Regent's Park fired intermittently.

Mac was reading the *Evening Standard* by the light of a small fire on the pavement caused by an incendiary bomb. He wore a tin hat and his blue formal suit with a Press arm-band, and had drunk a certain amount of bourbon.

'Who lives in all these places?' he asked, looking at the tall faintly glimmering blocks which curved away like a stage set towards the park.

'One of them's the Chinese Embassy,' said Jeff. 'Sun Yat Sen threw rescue notes out of that window.'

They waited until the whole panorama was lit up by a shower of white magnesium flares, but all the blocks looked much alike. A little later the ground shuddered and they caught the sour smell of bursting gutted rooms as a terrace collapsed two or three streets to their right. 'I'm here to do Britain: the Last Ditch,' Mac observed. 'Every night, twenty forty-five. CBC have booked their circuit at twenty-one hours. Anything they can do, I can have done it better.'

'I've always wondered about your methods of news-gathering, Mac,' said Jeff, accepting a cigar. 'I see you do it in the most economical way possible. I admire you for that.

You're preparing to walk straight into LG13, wait for the call-sign, and read them the front page of the *Standard*.'

'You've never appreciated me,' said Mac equably. 'You just want to talk me into making sacrifices. I'll tell you what my network are paying me to do. I'm not broadcasting from the roof of BH because your people won't let me. I'm not doing street interviews because they won't let me do those either. But straight after the lead story I'm giving a summary of opinions from anyone I've talked with in the course of the day.'

'My taxi-driver.'

'You've never let me get near him, chief.'

'He wouldn't help you if you did,' said Jeff. 'He'd probably want your job. He asked me for an audition yesterday.'

Firemen approached to extinguish Mac's small blaze. No longer able to see his paper, he folded it up and put it in his suit pocket. Jeff lit the cigar, which proved in the cordite-heavy air to taste as strong as the canteen's tea. They turned away together.

'Primarily I'm here to find out the reaction of the British people to attack from the air,' Mac continued.

'They don't like it.'

'Then how come they're all hurrying back to London?'

'I don't know,' said Jeff. 'My Listeners' Habits charts show the population of London as down by a third. That's statistics.'

'Statistics can prove sweet Brer Rabbit,' said Mac. 'I toured the stations this morning and you couldn't move for people arriving with their baggage.'

'Well, after all, it doesn't need explaining. We're only really at home in the middle of total disaster. You'll have to speak up for us, Mac. We're mad, and, if we win this war, we're going to be very poor.'

'Where do we go?' Mac asked. The Devonshire Arms, which he favoured, had been knocked down on the previous night.

'Is there anyone you've got to see?'

'I don't need any personalities, I told you, only the ordinary man.'

'Mac, you don't know any ordinary men. You're a correspondent, you don't have time to meet any. You wouldn't
recognise one if you did.'

'I have and I could,' Mac insisted.

'When and where?'

'Want to bet?'

'Five pounds.'

'We're in business.'

Mac thought it best for them both to have a drink on it. 'I'll
take you to see an ordinary man now,' he declared, with great
intensity.

'What time are you through to New York?' Jeff asked,
feeling that he ought to be absolutely sure on this point.

'Twenty forty-five. But I'm not going on the air unless you
come with me to see the ordinary man.'

'I'll come with you to see the ordinary man.'

Mac observed that he had made a mistake in looking so often
at the flashing sky. Never much good at seeing in the dark, he
was considerably worse after tracing the net of searchlight
beams and the scattered brightness overhead. However, he'd
sent out a stringer the night before to count exactly the number
of steps from his flat to Broadcasting House, from Broadcasting
House to the Langham, down Regent Street to the Ritz bar.
'We'll head for Trafalgar Square,' he said, and while the night
crackled and droned around them he steered Jeff forward,
earnestly counting the paces.

They took five hundred and sixteen down Regent Street,
where the buses, caught in the raid, waited patiently for a
green light. 'I knew a poet once,' said Mac, coming to a halt.
The remark had no connection with anything that went
before.

'There are poets here too,' Jeff pointed out. 'T. S. Eliot is
here. You can see him going to firewatch at his publishers most
nights. He moves in measure, like a dancer.'

'He's successful, he's a Harvard man. The one I knew
wasn't.'

'In what way?'

'He lost the will go to on. He found he hated to write. Finally he didn't go any farther than the middle of Brooklyn Bridge.'

'These are hard times for poets,' said Jeff. 'Poetry has suffered its fate. Let's only hope that music doesn't follow it.'

'Every man writes poetry once in his life, did you know that?' said Mac. 'Look,' he added, 'we can find some girls later.'

'Keep counting,' replied Jeff.

Down Coventry Street they passed doors with tiny slits of light, just enough to catch the eye. These were the rendezvous for Europe's Free Forces, soldiers who were sad and poor. They turned right and the area of starry sky widened out, showing that they had entered an open space.

'One thousand two hundred and sixteen. Trafalgar Square.'

'I'd say there was a crowd gathering over there,' said Mac. 'Round that truck.' His sight seemed to have improved.

Discreetly shaded lights were moving round a parked lorry, which seemed to be loading up. The men and women concerned moved gravely, pointing their torches towards the ground. If it was a ritual, then it was surely a funeral rather than a celebration. On the lorry was a single huge dark wrapped object, impossible to identify, the centre of all their coming and going. Patiently they were trying to secure the canvas with pieces of string that were several inches too short. Two policemen stood leaning against an empty stone plinth, evidently in two minds whether to help or not.

'What's happening?' said Jeff, speaking to what he could glimpse of an elderly man.

'We have come to move the king.'

He walked slowly off, as if spellbound.

'How come they didn't do this by daylight? asked Mac in amazement. 'When they could see what they were doing?'

'I daresay they've been at it for ages. They're amateurs, and that has its disabilities, advantages too, of course.'

'What amateurs? What have they got on the truck?'

'If this is the south-east corner, it's got to be the Charles the First statue. That makes them some kind of Royalist society. I suppose they're taking him out of harm's way.'

A woman in the darkness confirmed this, saying mournfully: 'The king is going into hiding.'

'Next thing you know you'll have a republic,' said Mac, and then, stepping forward, 'John McVitie, representing the National Broadcasting System of America. Speaking as a sympathetic onlooker, I'd be grateful if you cared to tell me how you set about packaging King Charles.'

'Sawdust,' said another man, this time a very young one. 'But it was a long time coming, so we waited.'

'That's a lot to do for anyone. Can you tell me where you're thinking of taking him?'

Silence, except for London's outer defences, pounding away like a distant ring of drums.

'And naturally you can't say when you expect to bring him back?'

'There will be omens,' said the melancholy woman. The lorry-driver was cautiously trying his engine. 'White birds will fly, as they did before the martyrdom.'

'Why not?' said Mac.

Jeff made him sit down beside the boarded-up fountains. 'There's no justice in this thing. Some attract all the love and care. Milton's statue in Cripplegate went on the very first day, but he got no co-operation.'

Mac reminded him that he had said these were hard times for poets. 'I'll tell you something, though, it's upset me that these people should be taking away the king when we're committed to go and see this ordinary man.'

'That's perverse of you, Mac. One thing leads to another.'

Jeff was pretty sure that he'd no idea where to go next; in any case, they only had twenty minutes before studio time. Mac, however, seemed to rally, and they patrolled the square again as far as the mouth of the Underground, marked by a faint glow.

'This is where we go down,' said Mac, counting the steps out of habit, and blinking in the frowsty yellowish light.

On the platform it was difficult to walk freely, since the LPTB's bunks occupied the walls in tiers, and other shelterers had arrived to take possession of their marked areas, bringing with them folding chairs and tables, and in some cases cooking-stoves. Others were waiting until the live rail was switched off at midnight to spread out their mattresses on the line itself. Meanwhile, the trains were still running, and those waiting to travel in them were confined to the extreme edge of the platform, nervously clinging to their bags and newspapers, aliens, where they had once been the most important people there. The shelterers, though friendly, crowded up to them, nudging them with kettles, and apologising with the air of those in the right as they set up the evening's games of cards and chess. When a warm block of air preceding a tube's arrival was pushed out of the tunnel, the travellers recovered their dignity for a few moments. The doors opened and they were carried out of reach, while the alighting newcomers got ready to pick their way through occupied territory. Then the night world, created by the violence above ground, settled down, without dispute, to nine hours of their own devices.

At the far end of the platform four men, wearing macin-toshes much like everybody else's, were sitting on the ground on a rug. They were playing nap. Each of them had a hand of cards and some of the tricks appeared to have been made, but they sat quietly, waiting. The nearest man, whose face and hair were both between brown and grey, looked up at Mac.

'Glad to see you.'

'How did it come, Mr Brewster, did you win?'

'We're starting the hand where we left off last night. The all clear went at a quarter to five, just after you left. All right, so you're back. What do you advise me to play?'

Mac looked round at the others. 'Any objections?'

They shook their heads amiably. Mac considered, then selected the ten of diamonds and laid it on the platform. Brewster nodded in cautious admiration.

'Just ordinary play,' Mac said.

Jeff wondered whether he had five pounds on him.

When they got back to Broadcasting House Mac went straight to the studio and gave a news talk which was remembered long afterwards, and which in fact was quoted at length in his biography, *According to Mac*. They had counted their steps all the way back, and arrived with twenty seconds to spare.

JEFF, WHO had gone back upstairs to his office, observed the door-handle give an apologetic rattle, or two, then burst open, while the walls curved inwards towards each other with elastic force, and, when it seemed quite impossible, sprang back again. Shortly after this came the sound of water cascading through the intestines of the building.

He was a few minutes late in going down to the basement for the late night Deputy Director General's meeting. To say that he had been for a walk, however, was a sufficient excuse. 'Very hazardous,' ADDG declared. 'It's said there are parachute bombs falling on North London. We've been discussing whether they ought to be called aerial torpedoes on the Nine O'clock. Defence wants that, but the news readers say they can't get the words out. Nobody in the building seems to be able to pronounce "aerial".'

'Ayeerial torpedoes... airial torpedoes... ayereeal torpe-does...' murmured Director (Talks), Director (Public Relations) and Director (Home).

'Who's reading?' asked Jeff.

'It's the Halibut again. We can rely on him.'

'Certainly we can. He started in opera. It takes more than a few bombs to make a singer give up his part.'

The subject of the meeting was the familiar one of how to carry on. Engineering had skilfully ensured that the BBC, switching from one transmitter to another, need never go off the air. Maintenance was probably at work already on the broken pipes, Catering brewed away remorselessly in the basement, but the problem remained: what should the voices say?

ADDG sighed. 'You can't make "Heavy damages and casualties have been reported" sound reassuring.' He wore a kindly, puzzled, clerical frown. 'More encouraging music, I think, and

talks from serving airmen, if the RAF will let us. We really look
to DPP to shift the next few evenings about, as usual.'

When she felt the building shake Annie went straight along to
RPD's office.

'Did I tell you to come?' he asked, slightly lowering the
volume of *The Teddy Bears' Picnic*.

'I came to see whether you were all right.'

'Why shouldn't I be?'

'The whole building shook just now.'

'I was testing.' He looked vaguely about him. 'But you can
sit down, Annie, I did want to see you, as it happens. I've had
something of a disappointment. Let me tell you about it. At
certain stages of my work I've been in the habit of consulting a
colleague who joined the Corporation at the same time as I did,
and might, I suppose, as he's much less specialised, be thought
to represent a broader outlook. Now, about half an hour ago,
when a totally unnecessary difficulty came up – the Post Office,
with ludicrous obstinacy, refused to give me any more land
lines – this colleague, who I've regarded hitherto as my oldest
friend, wasn't available. He'd gone out with some American or
other.'

'Mr Brooks, you can't expect him to sit here night and day
just waiting for you.'

The raid was at a low ebb, but there was a curious tension in
the air, as though electricity had leaked like water.

'But don't you see, Annie, that some people are born to be
deserted? I've tried to put off thinking about it, but this evening
it's become quite clear upon me that this kind of failure to help
me is part of a pattern, it must be. It can't be chance that it recurs
so often. My wife left me, you know... I don't know whether
you, from your short experience, have formed any definite
opinion of what I'm like?'

'Yes,' Annie said. 'I've formed a definite opinion of what
you're like.'

She saw that he was waiting, and there was no reason why she
shouldn't answer him as she had often done before. Certainly

there was no call for her to drop all the cautious devices which had enabled her to go through each minute of every day without letting on to him what she felt. Not to give way, not to make a fool of herself, had been such reliable guides that to go forward without them was terrible to her. She felt herself pushed into an unknown country, not, curiously enough, by love, but by anger. Her relief at finding him safe and sound had turned into a kind of rage, which confused her at first, and then left her determined.

'Aren't you going to tell me?' he asked confidently.

'Honest, do you want to know?'

'Honest, I do.'

He was making a joke of it then. She collected her forces.

'You're selfish.'

Still holding *The Teddy Bears' Picnic*, he looked furiously up at her.

'I don't understand you.'

Annie felt giddy, as when a great weight goes sliding.

'There's two ways to be selfish. You can think too much about yourself, or you can think too little about others. You're selfish both ways.'

No one can calculate the impact of a blow on a man who has never been struck before. Annie lost a little courage as she looked at him, but she went on:

'Take Mrs Milne. She works out her heart on your account. She'd stay longer than half-past five for you if she wasn't a Permanent. Those matches she leaves for you, for instance. There's not many her age would think of a thing like that. But you don't take the trouble to know how she feels.'

After a pause Sam said: 'I do know how Mrs Milne feels. But I don't care.'

His humble tone disconcerted her. He seemed dismayed. Ready to stand up to him without giving an inch, seeing herself given her cards or even thrown out of the office neck and crop, she was caught off balance. He continued mournfully: 'I don't know why it was, Annie, but it never occurred to me that you would be likely to turn against me.

I was foolish there, I daresay. We were talking just now about desertions.'

'But I'm not deserting you!' Annie cried. 'It's useful to know yourself!'

'It's painful. That's not the same thing.'

He raised his wounded head. Annie felt beside herself.

'I wish I'd not spoken now. Or at least I needn't have said quite so much. Less is more, sometimes.'

'That doesn't sound like you,' said Sam sharply. 'Who told you that?'

'Mr Waterlow did, when he was explaining to me about Satie.'

'Why are you always listening to music with Waterlow? It's ridiculous. Waterlow is ridiculous. No one pretends that he isn't, not even he does. It's my belief that you're always hanging about listening to commercials with Eddie Waterlow when you're in fact being employed and paid to do something else. I don't like Satie, either. Hell, I can't stand him. You can listen to music inside your own Department. You can listen to it here in this room if you want to. I played you some Holst once.'

'It was flat, Mr Brooks.'

'I remember your saying that!' Sam roared. 'I nearly fired you on the spot when you said that.'

'There'll be no need to terminate my contract,' said Annie, with a sudden inspiration. 'I'm about to leave anyway.'

'So that's it! Everything you've said so far is leading up to a petty complaint about your hours. I'm well aware that you're all working overtime. As it happens, I'm sending in an application tomorrow for four more juniors.'

Now that he was fuming to and fro between his desk and his turntables, as he often did, she felt rather steadier.

'I'm not leaving because of the overtime, Mr Brooks. I'm leaving because I love you.'

Halted on the half turn, he looked almost frightened.

'Do you mean you're in love with me?'

'No, I didn't say that. I said I loved you.'

So deep was his habit of demanding and complaining that

he scarcely knew what to do with such a gift. Something had to
be done, of course. 'You're very young,' he attempted. 'For
some reason Establishment never bothered to tell me anything
about you when they took you on, but I know you're very
young. In a few years' time you'll meet someone your own age –'

'You've read that some time in some book or paper,' Annie
interrupted. 'You can't just quite think which one it is at the
moment, but it'll come back to you sooner or later.'

He took off his glasses. It was capitulation. He stood re-
proved now by a delicate blur, the mere shape of a girl.

'I had no idea,' he said.

'That's what I was getting at. You've no idea about others,
and you don't notice what makes them suffer. Do you remember the ring with the red currant?'

Sam floundered. 'Did you have one? I think I remember
your having one.'

'You gave it me.'

'Have you kept it, then?'

'I would have done, if it hadn't begun to go off.'

She almost felt like asking him to put his glasses back.
Otherwise, she wouldn't be able to go on much longer without
touching him.

'Dear Annie,' he said to her, 'I don't think I can talk to you
here. I want to take you out with me somewhere. There's only
one café open now, that's the Demos. We'll go and have a drink
and start from the beginning.'

Her happiness was greater than she could bear.

'That'll be very nice.'

'It won't be all that nice,' said Sam, feeling compunction, and
amazement at himself for feeling it. Annie, for her part, knew
that unlike many in BH he wasn't given to feeling he needed a
drink. Their lives were shaking into pieces. 'What are we going
to do, Annie?' he asked in bewilderment. She put her arms
round him. Goodbye, Asra, she thought. God knows what's
going to become of you now.

*

The ADDG's meeting did not last long, and Jeff felt the tenderness of what might perhaps be a last occasion as he ascended to the outer air. On his way up he met Willie Sharpe, carrying a pile of new recordings for War Report.

'Have these,' he said, offering a handful of cigars.

'I don't smoke, Mr Haggard.'

'I didn't think you did. They might come in useful as bribes.'

He was conscious of Willie's round blue gaze, rejecting the word. 'Tell me, do you consider that either myself or your present Head of Department are likely candidates for your new society?'

'Not just as you stand, perhaps,' Willie admitted. 'But a good society transforms its members. By the way, sir, were you expecting to see RPD this evening?'

'Quite the contrary. I don't even know where he is.'

Willie looked faintly troubled.

DPP walked out past Reception, who seized the opportunity to ask him whether he wasn't put in mind of Ypres, passed a word with the sentries, and stood outside, looking up at what he could hardly make out, the carvings of Prospero and Ariel on the stony prow of Broadcasting House. He could very well remember Eric Gill at work on those graven images, high up on the scaffolding, his mediaeval workman's smock disarranged by the breeze, to the scandal of the passers-by. The sculptor and the figures had both appeared shocking then. Now very few people ever bothered to look at them, and that was reassurance in itself.

Prospero was shown preparing to launch his messenger onto the sound waves of the universe. But who, after all, was Ariel? All he ever asked was to be released from his duties. And when this favoured spirit had flown off, to suck where the bee sucks, and Prospero had returned with all his followers to Italy, the island must have reverted to Caliban. It had been his, after all, in the first place. When all was said and done, oughtn't he to preside over the BBC? Ariel, it was true, had produced music, but it was Caliban who listened to it, even in his dreams. And

Caliban, who wished Prospero might be stricken with the red plague for teaching him to speak correct English, never told anything but the truth, presumably not knowing how to. Ariel, on the other hand, was a liar, pretending that someone's father was drowned full fathom five, when in point of fact he was safe and well. All this was so that virtue should prevail. The old excuse.

Barnett came out for a breath of air and stood at DPP's side for a minute, looking up not at Broadcasting House, but at the stars.

'You know, I'd give a good deal to be able to read the heavens like a map, Mr Haggard. It'll be my hobby, when we get to the end of all this.'

I don't know why I'm leaving this place, Jeff thought, or these people.

Reception emerged just then, and said that DPP was wanted on the telephone.

'It's an outside call, not a very good line, I'm afraid.'

'Where from?'

'That I'm afraid I can't say, sir.'

'Well, who is it?'

'It sounds like RPD, sir.'

'Jeff, I've been trying to get you. Listen, you know how often I've felt that I needed one human being to rely on, just one, I mean, out of all those millions on millions, someone who'd be prepared to listen when I wanted to talk and perhaps have some kind of understanding, not of my own troubles, but of the troubles other people create for me. You know how often I've said that.'

'Well?' said Jeff.

'And how often, too, I've been disappointed.'

'I know that too. As a matter of curiosity, where are you speaking from?'

'That's what I've rung up to tell you. I want you to come to the Demos Café, the Greek place in Margaret Street, D-E-M-O-S, Demos.'

'I'm familiar with the word,' said Jeff. 'I just don't want to go there.'

'Listen. I'm here with one of my RPAs, I think I've told you about her already, I mean Annie Asra. We're very happy. Something rather unusual has turned up, in that she told me not long ago that she was in love with me, no, that she loved me.' Sam rattled the receiver violently. 'Are you following me?'

'I follow you, but I don't quite see how it concerns me,' Jeff said.

'I've told you, I want you to come here at once.'

'No, Sam.'

'Why not?'

'I'm going home.'

'You haven't got a home,' Sam replied. 'Your presence here is essential.'

'Look here,' said Jeff. 'Have you left this girl all this time sitting by herself at a table?'

'She's not by herself. The head waiter is complimenting her on having found a lover. We explained everything. They're all Greeks here, you know.'

'You're intending to live with this girl?'

'I shall take her back with me to Streatham. I've got a house there, you know. With some nice things in it,' he added more doubtfully.

'In that case, there's nothing more that I can contribute,' said Jeff. 'All I can do, like the head waiter, is to offer my congratulations. Kiss her white hand and foot from me, as Petrarch puts it.'

'My God, I don't need Petrarch to tell me to do that,' shouted Sam. 'You haven't even begun to get my point. I want you to come here and talk so that you can put my case to DDG in the morning.'

Jeff waited.

'I'm leaving the Corporation, Jeff.'

'Sam.'

'I've handed in my resignation as from tonight.'

'Do you mean that you're seriously contemplating leaving because you're going to sleep with one of your RPAs? Everyone thinks you do anyway.'

'Jeff, you're not trying to understand me. But you have to grant me one thing, whatever else goes I've always prided myself on this one thing, I mean that I've got a proper attitude towards my staff. You were reproaching me only the other day, I can't remember exactly how it arose, but you suggested that I couldn't even remember the name of one of my girls. Well, you see now that you got it wrong. Annie and I want each other, but that unquestionably means that I can't stay in my Department. I can't stay for as much as another week. If I did, what kind of example would that be for my juniors?'

The silence lasted so long that Sam began to rattle again at the telephone. Through the din Jeff could hear the clashing of dishes and even a service lift in the background, also, he thought, protesters anxious to get at the telephone themselves.

'You're my oldest friend!' Sam roared.

'No, I'm not.'

'I want to talk to you!'

'You can't.'

Nevertheless he hesitated.

The BBC never had time to keep any formal archives. There is no adequate account of the deaths of General Pinard, or of Dr Josef Vogel, or of DPP. Everyone who saw DPP that night, however, agreed that his moment of hesitation before he left BH was quite uncharacteristic of him.

The parachute bombs had been coming down soundlessly for some time, and it was later established that one of them was resting, still unexploded, against the kerb in Riding House Street. In size and shape it approximately resembled a taxi, and passers-by in fact mentioned that they had thought it was a taxi. It was understandable therefore that DPP, who appeared anyway to have something on his mind, should walk up to it, and, confusing it in the darkness, try to open what might have been, but was not, a door. Anyone might have done this, but it was tragic that it should have been an Old Servant, and within a few yards of Broadcasting House.

The Assistant Deputy Director General, when doing the obituary, was doubtful, however, as to whether he should describe Jeffrey Haggard as an Old Servant, in spite of all that he had done for the Corporation. Even after so many years, he seemed hardly that. 'His voice in particular,' he finally wrote, 'will be much missed.'

THE BEGINNING OF SPRING

I

In 1913 the journey from Moscow to Charing Cross, changing at Warsaw, cost fourteen pounds, six shillings and threepence and took two and a half days. In the March of 1913 Frank Reid's wife Nellie started out on this journey from 22 Lipka Street in the Khamovniki district, taking the three children with her – that is Dolly, Ben and Annushka. Annushka (or Annie) was two and three-quarters and likely to be an even greater nuisance than the others. However Dunyasha, the nurse who looked after the children at 22 Lipka Street, did not go with them.

Dunyasha must have been in the know, but Frank Reid was not. The first he heard about it, when he came back from the Press to his house, was from a letter. This letter, he was told by the servant Toma, had been brought by a messenger.

'Where is he now?' asked Frank, taking the letter in his hand. It was in Nellie's writing.

'He's gone about his business. He belongs to the Guild of Messengers, he's not allowed to take a rest anywhere.'

Frank walked straight through to the back right-hand quarter of the house and into the kitchen, where he found the messenger with his red cap on the table in front of him, drinking tea with the cook and her assistant.

'Where did you get this letter?'

'I was called to this house,' said the messenger, getting to his feet, 'and given the letter.'

'Who gave it to you?'

'Your wife, Elena Karlovna Reid.'

'This is my house and I live here. Why did she need a messenger?'

The shoe-cleaning boy, known as the Little Cossack, the washerwoman, who was on her regular weekly call, the maid, and Toma had, by now, all come into the kitchen. 'He was told to deliver it to your office,' Toma said, 'but you have come home earlier than usual and anticipated him.' Frank had been born and brought up in Moscow, and though he was quiet by nature and undemonstrative, he knew that there were times when his life had to be acted out, as though on a stage. He sat down by the window, although at four o'clock it was already dark, and opened the letter in front of them all. In all his married life he couldn't remember having had more than two or three letters from Nellie. It hadn't been necessary – they were hardly ever apart, and in any case she talked a good deal. Not so much recently, perhaps.

He read as slowly as he could, but there were a few lines only, to tell him that she was off. Coming back to Moscow was not mentioned, and he concluded that she hadn't wanted to tell him what was really wrong, particularly as she had written at the bottom of the page that she wasn't saying this in any way bitterly, and she wanted him to take it in the same spirit. There was also something about keeping well.

They all stood watching him in silence. Not wishing to disappoint them, Frank folded up the page carefully and put it back in the envelope. He looked out into the shadowy courtyard, where the winter's stack of firewood was down by now, to its last quarter. The neighbours' oil lamps shone out here and there beyond the back fence. By arrangement with the Moscow Electrical Company, Frank had installed his own twenty-five-watt lighting.

'Elena Karlovna has gone away,' he said, 'and she has taken the three children with her, how long for I don't know. She hasn't told me when she will come back.'

The women began to cry. They must have helped Nellie to pack, and been the recipients of the winter clothes which wouldn't go into the trunks, but these were real tears, true grief.

The messenger was still standing with his red cap in his hand. 'Have you been paid?' Frank asked him. The man said he had not. The guild were paid on a fixed scale, from twenty to forty kopeks, but the question was whether he had earned anything at all. The yardman now came into the kitchen, bringing with him a gust of oil and sawdust and the unmistakable smell of cold. Everything had to be explained to him all over again, although it must have been his business earlier on to help with Nellie's luggage.

'Bring some tea to the living room,' said Frank. He gave the messenger thirty kopeks. 'I'll have dinner at six, as usual.' The thought that the children weren't there, that Dolly and Ben would not return from school and that there was no Annushka in the house, suffocated him. This morning he had had three children, now he had none. How much he would miss Nellie, and how much he did miss her, he couldn't tell at the moment. He put that aside, to judge the effect later. They had been considering a visit to England, and with that in mind Frank had cleared the family's external passports with the local police station and the central police department. Possibly when Nellie signed her passport it had put ideas in her head. But when had Nellie ever allowed ideas to be put into her head?

Reid's, when Frank's father had set up the firm in Moscow in the 1870s, had imported and assembled printing machinery. As a sideline he had acquired a smallish printing business. That business was pretty well all Frank had left. You couldn't do anything with the assembly plant now, the German and direct import competition was too strong. But Reid's Press did well enough and he had a reasonably satisfactory sort of man to do the management accounting. Perhaps, though, 'reasonable' wasn't, in connection with Selwyn, quite the right word. He had no wife and appeared to have no grievances, was a follower of Tolstoy, still more so since Tolstoy died, and he wrote poetry in Russian. Frank expected Russian poetry to be about birch trees and snow, and in fact in the last verses Selwyn had read to him birch trees and snow were both mentioned pretty frequently.

Frank went now to the telephone, wound the handle twice and asked for the Reid's Press number, repeating it several times. Meanwhile Toma appeared with a samovar, the small one, presumably suitable for the master of the house now that he was left on his own. It was just coming to the boil and gave out a faint chatter of expectation.

'What are we to do with the children's rooms, sir?' Toma asked in a low tone.

'Shut the doors of their rooms and keep them as they are. Where's Dunyasha?'

Frank knew she must be about the house somewhere but was lying low, like a partridge in a furrow, to avoid blame.

'Dunyasha wants to speak to you. Now that the children are gone, what is to be her employment?'

'Tell her to set her mind at rest.' Frank felt he sounded like a capricious owner of serfs. Surely he'd never given them much reason to worry about their jobs?

The call came through, and Selwyn's light-toned, musing voice answered in Russian: 'I hear you.'

'Look, I didn't mean to interrupt you this afternoon, but something's happened which I didn't quite expect.'

'You don't sound altogether yourself, Frank. Tell me, which has come to you, joy or sorrow?'

'I should call it a bit of a shock. Sorrow, if it's got to be one of them.'

Toma came out into the hall for a moment, saying something about changes to be made, and then retired to the kitchen. Frank went on: 'Selwyn, it's about Nellie. She's gone back to England, I suppose, and taken the children with her.'

'All three?'

'Yes.'

'But mayn't it be she wants to see...' Selwyn hesitated, as though it was hard for him to find words for ordinary human relationships, '...might one not want to see one's mother?'

'She didn't say so much as a word. In any case her mother died before I met her.'

'Her father?'

'She's only got her brother left. He lives where he's always lived, in Norbury.'

'In Norbury, Frank and an orphan!'

'Well, I'm an orphan, for that matter, and so are you.'

'Ah, but I'm fifty-two.'

Selwyn had a reserve of good sense, which appeared when he was at work, and unexpectedly at other times when it might almost have been despaired of. He said, 'I shan't take much longer. I'm checking the wage-bill against what the pay clerks are actually handing out. You said you wanted that done more often.'

'I do want it done more often.'

'When we've finished, why don't you dine with me, Frank? I don't like to think of you sitting and staring, it may be, at an empty chair. At my place, and very simply, not in the heartless surroundings of a restaurant.'

'Thank you, but I won't do that. I'll be in tomorrow, though, at the usual time, about eight.'

He put the mouthpiece back on its solid brass hook and began to patrol the house, silent except for the distant rising and falling of voices from the kitchen which, in spite of what sounded like a burst of sobs, had the familiar sound of a successful party. Ramshackle, by Frank's standards, and roomy, the house consisted of a stone storey and on top of that a wooden one. The vast stove, glazed with white tiles from the Presnya, kept the whole ground floor warm. Outside, towards the bend in the Moscow river, a curious streak of bright lemon-yellow ran across the slate-coloured sky.

Someone was at the front door, and Toma brought in Selwyn Crane. Although Frank saw him almost every day at the Press, he often forgot, until he saw him in a different setting, how unusual, for an English businessman, he looked. He was tall and thin – so, for that matter, was Frank, but Selwyn, ascetic, kindly smiling, earnestly questing, not quite sane-looking, seemed to have let himself waste away, from other-worldliness, almost to transparency. With a kind of black frock-coat he wore a pair of English tweed trousers, made up by a Moscow tailor who had cut them rather too short, and a high-necked Russian peasant's blouse, a tribute to the memory of Lev Nikolaevich Tolstoy. In the warm room, with no ladies present, he threw off the frock-coat and let the coarse material of the blouse sink down in folds around his lean ribs.

'My dear fellow, here I am. After such news, I couldn't leave you by yourself.'

'That's what I would have preferred, though,' said Frank. 'You won't mind if I speak out. I'd rather have been by myself.'

'I came on the twenty-four tram,' said Selwyn. 'I was fortunate enough to catch one almost at once. Rest assured that I shan't stay long. I was at my desk when a thought came to me which I knew immediately might be of comfort. I got up immediately and went out to the tram-stop. The telephone, Frank, isn't the right way to convey such things.'

Frank, sitting opposite, put his head in his hands. He felt he could bear anything rather than determined unselfishness. Selwyn, however, seemed to be encouraged.

'That's the attitude of a penitent, Frank. No need for that. We are all of us sinners. The thought that came to me didn't concern guilt, but loss, supposing we think of loss as a form of poverty. Now poverty, or what the world calls poverty, isn't a matter for regret, but for rejoicing.'

'No, Selwyn, it's not,' said Frank.

'Lev Nikolaevich tried to give away all his possessions.'

'That was to make the peasants richer, not to make himself poorer.' Tolstoy's Moscow estate was only a mile or so away from Lipka Street. In his will it had been bequeathed to the peasants, who, ever since, had been cutting down the trees to make ready money. They worked even at night, felling the trees by the light of paraffin flares.

Selwyn leant forward, his large hazel eyes intensely focused, alight with tender curiosity and goodwill.

'Frank, when summer comes, let us go on the tramp together. I know you well, but in the clear air, in the plains and forests, I should surely come to know you better. You have courage, Frank, but I think you have no imagination.'

'Selwyn, I don't want my soul read this evening. To be honest, I don't feel up to it.'

In the hall Toma appeared again to help Selwyn into his sleeveless overcoat of rank sheepskin. Frank repeated that he'd be at the Press at his usual time. As soon as the outer door was shut Toma began to lament that Selwyn Osipych hadn't taken any tea, or even a glass of seltzer water.

'He only called in for a moment.'

'He's a good man, sir, always on his way from one place to another, searching out want and despair.'

'Well he didn't find either of them here,' said Frank.

'Perhaps he brought you some news, sir, of your wife.'

'He might have done if he worked at the railway station, but he doesn't. She took the Berlin train and that's all there is to it.'

'God is not without mercy,' said Toma vaguely.

'Toma, when you first came here three years ago, the year Annushka was born, you told me you were an unbeliever.'

Toma's face relaxed into the creases of leathery goodwill which were a preparation for hours of aimless discussion.

'Not an unbeliever, sir, a free-thinker. Perhaps you've never thought about the difference. As a free-thinker I can believe what I like, when I like. I can commit you, in your sad situation, to the protection of God this evening, even though tomorrow morning I shan't believe he exists. As an unbeliever I should be obliged not to believe, and that's an unwarrantable restriction on my thoughts.'

Presently it was discovered that Selwyn's briefcase, really a music case, crammed with papers, and stiffened by the rain of many seasons at many tram-stops, had been left behind on the bench below the coat rack, where the felt boots stood in rows. This had happened a number of times before, and the familiarity of it was a kind of consolation.

'I'll take it in with me tomorrow morning,' said Frank. 'Don't let me forget.'

2

Up till a few years ago the first sound in the morning in Moscow had been the cows coming out of the side-streets, where they were kept in stalls and backyards, and making their own way among the horse-trams to their meeting-point at the edge of the Khamovniki, where they were taken by the municipal cowman to their pasture, or, in winter, through the darkness, to the suburban stores of hay. Since the tram-lines were electrified, the cows had disappeared. The trams themselves, from five o'clock in the morning onwards, were the first sound, except for the church bells. In February, both were inaudible behind the inner and outer windows, tightly sealed since last October, rendering the house warm and deaf.

Frank got up ready to do what he might have done the evening before, but still hoped wouldn't be necessary, to send off telegrams. Then, at some point, he had better go to the English chaplaincy, where he could see Cecil Graham, the chaplain, and count on his saying, out of embarrassment, very little. But it would also mean an explanation to Mrs Graham, who in fact, did both the seeing and the saying. Perhaps he might wait a day or so before going to the chaplaincy.

At a quarter to seven the telephone rang, jangling the two copper bells fixed above a small writing-desk. It was the stationmaster from the Alexandervokzal. Frank knew him pretty well.

'Frank Albertovich, there has been an error. You must come to collect at once, or send a responsible and reliable person.'

'Collect what?'

The stationmaster explained that the three children were deposited at his station, having come back from Mozhaisk, where they had joined the midnight train from Berlin.

'They have a clothes-basket with them.'

'But are they alone?'

'Yes, they're alone. My wife, however, is looking after them in the refreshment room.'

Frank had his coat on already. He walked some way down Lipka Street to find a sledge with a driver who was starting work, and not returning from the night's work drunk, half-drunk, stale drunk, or *podvipevchye* – with just a dear little touch of drunkenness. He also wanted a patient-looking horse. On the corner he stopped a driver with a small piece of resigned, mottled face showing in the lamplight above his turned-up collar.

'The Alexander station.'

'The Brest station,' said the driver, who evidently refused to give up the old name. On the whole, this was reassuring.

'When we're there, you'll have to wait, but I'm not sure for how long.'

'Will there be luggage?'

'Three children and a clothes-basket. I don't know how much more.'

The horse moved gently through the snow and grit up the Novinskaya and then turned without any guidance down the Presnya. It was accustomed to this route because the hill was steep and so a higher fare could be charged both down and up, but it was not the quickest way to the station.

'Turn round, brother,' said Frank, 'go the other way.'

The driver showed no surprise, but made the turn in the middle of the street, scraping the frozen snow into grey ridges. The horse, disconcerted, braced itself, crossing its legs and moving with the awkwardness of a creature disturbed in its habits. Its guts rumbled and it coughed repeatedly, sounding not like a horse, but a piece of faulty machinery. As they settled into a trot down the Tverskaya, Frank asked the driver whether he had any children himself. His wife and family, the driver said, weren't with him, but had been left behind in Rovyk, his village, while he did the earning. Yes, but how many children? Two, but that they had both died in Rovyk when the cholera came. His wife hadn't had the money, or the wits, to buy a certificate to say that they'd died of something else, so they'd had to be buried in the pest cemetery, and no one knew where that was. At this point he laughed inappropriately.

'Why don't you send for your wife to keep you company?'

The driver replied that women were only company for each other. They were created for each other, and talked to each other all day. At night they were too tired to be of any use.

'But we weren't meant to live alone,' said Frank.

'Life makes its own corrections.'

They would have to pull up at the back of the station, in the goods yards. The driver wasn't one of the smart ones, he hadn't a permission to wait at the entrance.

'I'll be back soon,' Frank said, giving him his tea money. The words meant nothing except general encouragement, and were taken in that spirit. Snow was lightly falling. The driver began to drag a large square of green oilcloth over the horse, whose head drooped towards the ground, dozing, dreaming, of summer.

The yard was served from the Okruzhnaya Railway which made a circle round the entire city, shuttling the freight from one depot to another. The sleigh had arrived at the same time as a load of small metal holy crosses from one of the factories on the east side. Two men were painstakingly checking off the woven straw boxes of a hundred and a thousand.

Frank walked past the coal tips and the lock-up depositories through the cavernous back entrance of the station. Inside the domes of glass a grey light filtered from a great height. Not many people here, and some of them quite clearly the lost souls who haunt stations and hospitals in the hope of acquiring some purpose of their own in the presence of so much urgent business, other people's partings, reunions, sickness and death. A few of them were sitting in the corners of the station restaurant watching, without curiosity or resentment, those who could afford to order something at the gleaming rail or the buffet.

The stationmaster was not there. 'The *nachalnik* is in his office. This is the refreshment room,' said the barman. 'Quite so,' said Frank, 'but didn't his wife come in here earlier, with three children?' – 'His wife is never here, this is not her place, she is at his house.' The waitress, tall and strong, elbowed him aside as she lifted the flap of the bar and came out. 'Three little English, a girl with brown hair and blue eyes, a boy with brown hair and blue eyes, a little girl who was asleep, her eyes were shut.' – 'Did they have a clothes-basket?' 'Yes, when the little one sat down she put her feet on it, her legs were still too short to reach the ground.'

'Where are the children now?'

'They were taken away.'

The waitress folded her arms across her bosom and seemed to be challenging Frank, or accusing him. Her accent was Georgian, and it was folly, he knew, to think of Georgia as a land of roses and sunshine only. But Georgians pride themselves on their rapid changes of mood. Frank said, 'In any case, you are not to be held responsible. In no sense was it part of your work to keep a check on everyone in the refreshment room.' Immediately she yielded, becoming anxious to please.

'They're not your children, I can tell that. You wouldn't let them arrive like this in the city without anyone to take charge of them.' Frank asked where the stationmaster lived. His house was in the Presnya, between the cemetery and the Vlasov tile works.

He recrossed the swept and wheel-crushed snow of the coal yards. The horse was standing, entirely motionless, in the white distance, the driver was coming out of the urinal. He agreed to wait while Frank walked the short distance to the Presnya.

Along a side-road patched with clinker, carriage springs, scrap iron punchings and strips of yellow glazed tin which once advertised Botkin's Tea and Jeyes' Fluid, wooden houses stood at intervals. They were raised by two wooden steps above the ground and Frank saw that the entrance, as in the villages, would be at the back. At No. 15, to which he'd been directed, the back door, in fact, was not locked. He shut it behind him, and was faced with two doors.

'Who is at home?' he called out.

The right-hand door opened and his daughter Dolly appeared. 'You should have come earlier,' she said. 'Really, we have no business to be here.'

Inside, the table, covered with oilcloth, had been shoved into the right-hand corner so that no one could sit with their back to the ikons and their glimmering lamps. Annushka was asleep on the clothes-basket, Ben was at the table looking at a newspaper, the *Gazeta-Kopeika*, which dealt entirely with rapes and murders. He looked up, however, and said, 'When you're on a main line, the distance between posts is a twentieth of a verst, so if the train does that in two seconds you're going at ninety versts an hour.'

'What happened?' Frank asked. 'Who's looking after you? Did you get lost on the way?'

A dark woman in an overall came in, not the stationmaster's wife, if indeed there was such a person, but, as she explained, a kitchen-mother, called in to help as required.

'She only gets eighty kopeks a day,' said Dolly. 'It's not much for all this responsibility.' She put her arm round the woman's waist and said in caressing Russian, 'You don't earn enough, do you, little mother?'

'I'll settle up with everybody,' said Frank, 'and then straight home to Lipka Street. We shall have to wake up Annie, I'm afraid.'

The children's outdoor clothes were airing above the stove, along with the stationmaster's second uniform, and a heap of railway blankets. Hauling down the birchwood clothes frame was like a manoeuvre under sail. Annushka woke up while she was being crammed into her fur jacket, and asked whether she was still in Moscow. 'Yes, yes,' said Frank.

'Then I want to go to Muirka's.'

Muir and Merrilees was the department store, where Annushka scarcely ever went without being given some little extra by the astute floor manager.

'Not now,' said Dolly.

'If it hadn't been for Annushka,' said Ben, 'I think Mother might have taken us on with her. I can't be sure, but I think she might.'

The whole house began to shake, not gradually, but all at once, from blows on the outer door. The kitchen-mother crossed herself. It was the sledge-driver. 'I shouldn't have thought you were strong enough to knock like that,' Frank told him.

'How long? How long?'

At the same time the stationmaster, perhaps taking the opportunity to find out what was going on in his house, came in through the front. Probably he was the only person who ever did so. This meant that the whole lot of them – Frank, the children, the kitchen-mother, the stationmaster – had to sit down together for another half-hour. Annie's coat had to be taken off again. She fell asleep again instantly. Tea, cherry jam from the cupboard which could be opened now that the stationmaster had brought his keys. The kitchen-mother suddenly declared that she couldn't bear to be parted from her Dolly, her Daryasha, who resembled so much what she had been like herself as a child. The stationmaster, still wearing his official red cap, lamented his difficulties at the Alexandrovna, where he was besieged by foreign travellers. His clocks all kept strict St Petersburg time, 61 minutes in advance of Central European time and two hours one minute in advance of Greenwich. What was their difficulty?

'You might ask to be transferred to the Donetz Basin,' suggested Ben.

'How old is your boy?'

'Nine,' said Frank.

'Tell him that the Alexandervokzal is the top appointment. There is nothing higher. The state railways have nothing higher to offer me. But it's not his fault, he's young, and besides that, he's motherless.'

'Where's your wife, for that matter?' Frank asked. It turned out that, trusting no one in Moscow, she had gone back to her village to recruit more waitresses for the spring season. They prepared to go, the sleigh-driver pointing out, for the first time, that the horse was old.

'How old is he exactly?' asked Ben. 'There are regulations, you know, about how old they're allowed to be.' The sleigh-driver said he was a young devil.

'They're all young devils,' said Frank. 'Now I want to get them home to Lipka Street.'

They might have been away several years. The whole household, the house itself, seemed to be laughing and crying. From the carnival – that was what it felt like – only Dunyasha was absent. Almost at once she came to Frank for her internal passport, which was necessary if you were going to make a journey of more than fifteen miles, and had to be handed over to the employer. She wanted to leave, she was no longer happy in the house, where criticisms were being made of her. Frank took it out of the drawer in his study where he kept such things locked away. He felt like a man with a half-healed wound who would do better to leave it alone, for fear of making bad worse. Nellie had sent no message to him by the children, not a word, and he saw it would be best not to think about this, or he might not be able to stand it. His father had always held that the human mind is indefinitely elastic, and that by the very nature of things we were never called upon to undertake more than we could bear. Frank had always felt doubtful about this. During the past winter one of the machine men from the Press had gone by night to a spot a little way out of the Windau station, and lain down on the tracks. This was because his wife had brought her lover to live in their house. But the height of the train's wheelbase meant that it passed right over him, leaving him unhurt, like a drunken peasant. After four trains had passed he got up and took the tram back to his home, and had worked regularly ever since. This left the question of endurance open.

While the rejoicing went on and spread to the yard and, apparently to the yard dog and to the hens, locked up for the winter, Dolly came in wearing her brown uniform from the Ekaterynskaya Gymnasium, and asked him to help her with her homework, since after all, she had to be at school by nine o'clock. She spread out her atlas, ruler, and geography exercise book.

'We're doing the British Isles. We have to mark in the industrial areas and the districts largely given over to keeping sheep.'

'Did you take those with you on the train?' asked Frank.

'Yes. I thought they might come in useful, even if I didn't ever get back to the Ekaterynskaya.'

'It was lonely in the house while you were away, somewhat lonely, anyway.'

'We weren't away for very long.'

'Long enough for me to see what it was going to be like.'

Dolly asked: 'Didn't you know what Mother was doing?'

'To tell you the truth, Dolly, no, I didn't.'

'I thought not,' she added rapidly. 'It was hard on her. After all, she'd never had to look after us before, Dunyasha did everything. Annushka wouldn't sit still. Mother asked the attendant for some valerian drops, to calm her down, but he hadn't any. We should have brought some with us, of course, but I didn't do the packing. You shouldn't have expected her to manage by herself. She had to send us back, we weren't a comfort to her. I think you asked too much of her.'

'I don't agree, Dolly. I know my own mind, but so does your mother.'

3

FRANK'S FATHER, Albert Reid, had looked ahead – not quite far enough, perhaps, but to see too clearly in Russia is a mistake, leading to loss of confidence. He was aware that the time was coming when British investors, ironmasters, mill-owners, boiler-makers, engineers, race-horse trainers and governesses would no longer be welcome. Either the Russians would take everything into their own hands or the Germans would, but he thought that the good times would last a while yet. All that had really been needed, when he started out in the 1870s, was a certificate to say that the articles of association of your company were in accordance with British law and another form in St Petersburg to say that your enterprise was advantageous to the interests of the Russian Empire. Besides that, though, you had to have a good digestion, a good head for drink, particularly spirits, a good circulation and an instinct for how much in the way of bribes would be appropriate for the uniformed and for the political police, the clerks from the Ministry of Direct Import, Commerce and Industry, and the technical and sanitary inspectors, to get anything at all. These bribes, too, must be called gifts, and with that word you began your study of the Russian language. All the other formalities – sending the balance sheets, for example, to the central government and the local Court of Exchequer – were just paperwork, which he'd done himself, with his wife's help, by lamplight, in the old wooden house on the works site in the Rogoznkaya. Like the Russian nobility and the Russian merchants, foreign businesses were given ranks, according to their capital and the amount of fuel (soft coal, birch-bark, anthracite, oil) that their factory consumed. Reid's (Printing Machinery) was of moderate rank. Frank's father and mother were the only partners. Both of them had come from long families, that was why Bert had been sent out in the first place to make a living in Russia, but they only had the one son. Frank was sent over to England once or twice as a boy, to stay with his relatives in Salford. He enjoyed himself in Salford because, given half a chance, he enjoyed himself anywhere. When he was eighteen he went back for much longer, to train in mechanical engineering and printing, first at Loughborough Polytechnic, then for his apprenticeship with Croppers of Nottingham.

It was while he was at Croppers, doing quite reasonably well, and playing football for the first time in his life, that his father wrote to him to say that, as a kind of subsidiary to the business, he was going to start his own printing press, quite near the centre of Moscow, in Seraphim Street. There was nothing legal at the moment against foreigners buying property, as long as it wasn't in Turkestan or the Caucasus or anywhere where they were likely to strike oil, and he thought the place could be got fairly cheap. He'd start with hand presses only, jobbing machines, and see how they went along. It was an old warehouse, this place, and there was room to expand. Even though the deal wasn't concluded yet, the men were already calling it Reidka's – dear little Reid's.

There was a photograph enclosed of Seraphim Street, looking like most of Moscow's side-streets, almost past repair, blank, narrow, patched and peeling, with children crowded around a horse and cart selling something unidentifiable. Above was a white sky with vast, even whiter clouds. The shop-signs made Frank feel homesick. Perlov's tea-bricks, Kapral cigarettes 20 for 5 kopeks, and a kabak with a name that looked like Markel's Bar.

His father usually gave the date Russian style, thirteen days earlier than the date in Nottingham, so that there was some adjustment to be done, but it must have been in March that year that there was mention of Selwyn Crane, who'd been taken on, not at the works, but to do the accounting at Reidka's. A few weeks later it seemed that Crane was becoming very religious. 'I've no objection to that, though on the whole I think religion is of more use to a woman than a man, as it leads to content with one's lot.' In the next letter, Bert doubted whether 'religious' was quite the right word. 'Spiritual' would be better. 'Crane has now proclaimed himself a vegetarian, which I do not think is enjoined anywhere in the Bible, and he tells me he's several times been in quite lengthy conversations with Count Tolstoy. Tolstoy is a very great man, Frank,' he continued. 'Fortunately, though, one doesn't have to judge of great men by the oddities of their disciples. The truth is, though, that Crane has a knack with figures and has been up to now a pretty fair man of business – he came to me from the Anglo-Russian Bank. I asked him whether it was not rather surprising that he should have saved a reasonable sum of money, as I fancy he has done – he is not a married man – and continues to live off the said sum and the salary I pay him, while giving it out as his opinion that buying or selling of any kind or description is a sin against mankind. It's rather, he said, that wealth shouldn't be used for the benefit of individuals. Then, you consider me a wrong doer, Crane, I said, determined to treat the whole matter in a spirit of joke, the next thing will be that you'll refuse to shake me, your employer, by the hand. I thought I'd caught him there, but what he did was to kiss me, first on one cheek and then on the other – a Russ habit, as you well know, but this was on the shop floor, Frank, not even in the counting house.'

His father, however, had no hesitation about the chief compositor he'd engaged, a capital fellow, a very steady worker, it would take a revolution to dislodge Yacob Tvyordov. Frank thought, when the time comes, I'll see whether I want these people or not. I'll make up my own mind when it comes to it.

In 1900 he transferred himself to Hoe's of Norbury to get experience with more up-to-date machines. It was in Norbury that he met Nellie Cooper. She lived with her brother Charles, who was a solicitor's clerk, and his wife Grace, at 62 Longfellow Road. It was a nice, substantial house, two entrance doors, the inner one with a stained-glass panel, good new glass in art shades from Lowndes and Drury, representing the Delectable Mountains from the Pilgrim's Progress, dining room and kitchen downstairs in the basement, sitting room opening on to a flight of green-painted iron steps which led into the garden, a bit of fencing to screen off the vegetables, three bedrooms on the first floor, one of them spare as Charles and Grace didn't have any children. Frank had a room in a boarding house where the landlady, probably unintentionally, as it seemed to him, was gradually starving him to death. He joined (as he had done in Manchester and Nottingham) the local choral society. At refreshment time (they were rehearsing, perhaps over-rehearsing, *Hiawatha*) he had to excuse himself to Nellie, who was helping to serve out, for taking more than one fish paste roll. Nellie asked him what his job was, whether he had to heave things about in the open air and couldn't help getting up an appetite. Then, without listening very attentively to his answer, she said she had been teaching for four years and was due to take her qualifying exam for the certificate.

'I'm twenty-six,' she added, as though it might as well be said now as later.

'Do you like teaching?'

'Not all that much.'

'You oughtn't to go on with it then. You oughtn't to try for the certificate. You ought to train to do what you want to do, even if it's sweeping the streets.'

Nellie laughed. 'I'd like to see my brother's face.'

'Does he worry about you?'

'He's doing all right, anyway. I suppose there's no real need for me to work at all.'

'I don't know why you do it, then.'

'It gets me out of the house, so I'm not under my sister-in-law's feet and she doesn't have to see me all day.'

'Did she say that to you, Miss Cooper?'

'No, she wouldn't say anything like that. She's a sufferer.'

Frank was struck by her way of looking at things. There was a tartness about it, a sharp flavour, not of ill-nature, but of disapproval of life's compromises, including her own. The introduction meant that he was entitled to see her home from the draughty Jubilee Hall where the rehearsals had been called. Nellie had to help put away the Choral Society's crockery. Then she came back in her coat, with her shoes in a water-proof bag. Frank, to establish his claim, took the bag from her. He always did everything quickly and neatly, without making a business of it.

'If we were in Moscow now it would still be all frozen up,' he said, going down the steps beside her.

'I know,' said Nellie. 'But when you do things at school in geography you know them, but you don't believe them.'

'No, you have to see them for yourself. It makes you want to do that.'

'Were you at school in Russia, then?'

'Yes, I was,' he said.

'Well, if you'd read about Norbury while you were there, tell me honestly, would you have wanted to come and see it?'

'I would,' Frank answered, 'if I had known I was going to be in such good company.'

She ignored this, but Frank felt satisfied. He asked her what she thought of *Hiawatha*. She told him that the composer lived in Croydon, not so far away, and this was supposed to be his favourite among all his pieces. 'He christened his son Hiawatha, you know.'

'But what's your opinion of the music, Miss Cooper?'

'To be honest, I don't care so very much for music. I can hold a part all right, but only as long as I'm with a lot of others. I don't know how I got through my sight-singing test when I came to join the society. I've often wondered about that. Dr Alden, that was the old choirmaster, didn't hardly seem to listen. Perhaps he'd been drinking.'

'Well, but there you are again. Why do you come to re-hearsals, if you don't care about them?'

It was the same reason – to get out of the house, to get out of the way of her sister-in-law, who, when Frank met her, seemed harmless enough, but harmlessness, as he knew, could be a very hard thing to bear. When he went to Longfellow Road to call for Nellie, Grace Cooper would fuss over him and ask him whether his landlady was treating him right. She told him to leave his shaving mirror in the bed during the day and if by the evening it was clouded over that meant that the bed was damp, and he had a right to complain about it at the Town Hall. Better take the mirror along with him, to show to the authorities. Frank got the notion that Grace always talked about damp.

Several times he was asked to stay to supper, and they sang hymns afterwards at the piano. Frank realised then that Nellie had told the truth about her voice, and he admired her for telling the truth.

The trouble was that he was still only training. His lodgings and laundry cost him twelve shillings and fivepence a week, and by Saturday he was hard up. 'I know how you're placed,' said Nellie, 'I'll pay my share.'

'I'm not sure I could agree to that,' Frank said.

'You're afraid I'll take out my purse and lay it on the table and rattle it about, getting out the money. Don't get that idea into your head. Just as we go out, before we ever get out of the house, I'll give you something for my half. That way there can't be any awkwardness. It's called Dutch treat, you know. What's that in Russian?'

There was no Russian word for it. 'Students, perhaps,' said Frank, 'I've seen them empty out their pockets at the beginning of the evening and put all the money they've got in the middle of the table.'

'That's not Dutch treat,' said Nellie.

Once he had his training certificates, he had reasonably good prospects to lay before her. He felt that he could assume that she wouldn't be too distressed at leaving her family and friends, still less at getting out of Norbury. If he wanted to go ahead with it, he ought to speak to Charlie, explaining in more detail about the firm and his prospects. He did want to go ahead with it, and after fixing things up with Nellie, he did speak to Charlie. No worry about a ring, because he had brought with him a ring belonging to his mother which his father had bought for her at Ovchinikof's in Moscow. It was a Russian triple knot, in three different colours of gold, made so that the three circlets were separate but could never be taken apart. They slid and shone together on Nellie's capable finger. At the choral society it was thought pretty, but foreign-looking. 'When your mother gave it you, she must have expected you to find someone,' said Nellie. 'Was she ill?'

'I don't think so, she certainly didn't say so.'

'What were the girls like in Nottingham?'

'I can't remember. Very moderate, I think.'

'I daresay they fancied you because you were tall?'

'They might have done.'

'Did you fall in love with any of them when you were in Manchester, or when you were in Nottingham, and offer them this ring, and get turned down?'

'No Nellie, I didn't.' They were walking in Norbury Park. The air and the trodden earth and grass breathed out moisture. Grace had warned them that they would find it very damp.

'You might have had to take the ring back to Moscow, then, and tell your mother it was no go.' They sat down on a bench, from which an elderly man tactfully got up as they approached.

'Look here Frank, do you know a lot about women?' He was undaunted.

'I think you'll find I know quite enough for the purpose, Nellie.'

There was no need to wait a long time for the wedding. Frank's parents had to arrange to come from Moscow, and it was never easy for them to leave the business, but all his relatives from Salford were singlemindedly devoted to attendance at weddings and funerals, and would let nothing stand in their way. The preparations made Frank resolve never, until he came to be buried, to let himself become an object of attention at any kind of religious ceremony again. He knew, however, that he ought not to grumble. Both Charlie and Grace, who were going, after all, to considerable expense, told him that it would be Nellie's day. He felt deeply tender towards her because of this and because of her practical good sense and the number of lists she was making and the letters which were answered and crossed off yet another list. He was startled when she said: 'I'm doing all this as it should be done, because I owe it to both of us. But I'm not going to be got the better of by Norbury.'

'They wouldn't dare,' Frank said. 'Which of them would?'

'You don't think I'm marrying you, Frank Reid, just to get out of Norbury?'

'I don't put myself as low as that,' he said, 'or you either.'

'I don't just mean the people here,' she went on earnestly, 'I mean all the people we've invited, those cousins of yours from Salford, and those aunts.'

'They're not so bad.'

'People always say that about their aunts,' said Nellie. 'The wedding will bring out the worst in them, you'll see. I'm not a dreamer. I have to look at things quite squarely, as they really are. That's one of the things you like about me. I know it is.'

She had no doubts. Even her curling hair seemed to spring up from her forehead with determination. Frank kissed her, but not in such a way as to interrupt her. She asked him whether he'd given any thought as to what the wedding would be like.

'It's best to take things as they come,' he said.

'Well, I'll tell you what it's going to be like. I'm not talking about the church service. I mean afterwards, when we're back here. We're going to have ham and tongue, cucumber sandwiches, vanilla shape and honeycomb mould, nuts, port wine and Madeira. The port wine will be a bit much for Charlie and after a bit it'll be too much for the lot of them, and they'll all take some, because teetotallers always say that port doesn't count, and the older ones, they'll draw together a bit and lower their voices and say to each other, she doesn't know what she's in for. She's twenty-six and he's the first boy she's ever been out with seriously. He's a decent sort, you can see that, so they won't have been up to anything yet, and she hasn't any idea what she's in for.'

'I was hoping they'd have confidence in me,' said Frank, 'they've no reason not to.'

'Oh, they won't have anything against you personally. But they have to make out that it's a tremendous thing – the only thing that ever happens to a woman, really, bar having children, and change of life, and dying. That's how they see things in Norbury. There's a certain expression they have, I've noticed it so often. They'll say that if they'd known what it was going to be like nothing would have dragged them to the altar.'

Frank felt rather at a loss. He kissed her again and said, 'Don't be discouraged.' She remained rigid.

'What does it matter what all these people think, Nellie? If you're really right, we ought to pity them.'

Nellie shook her head like a terrier.

'I'm not going to be got the better of. They may not know it, they won't know it, but I'm not going to.'

It was a brilliant day, a moment when a Norbury's dampness justified itself in bright green grass, clipped green hedges, alert sparrows, stained glass washed to the brilliance of jewels, barometers waiting to be tapped. They were alone in the house. Nellie said: 'Would you like to see my things? I mean the things I'm going to wear for the wedding. Not the dress, they'll bring that later. It's not lucky to have it in the house for too long.'

'Yes, of course I would, if you feel like showing them to me.'

'Do you believe in luck?'

'You've asked me that before, Nellie. I told you, I used to believe it was for other people.'

They went up past the half-landing and into a bedroom almost entirely filled by the wardrobe and various pieces of furniture which looked as though they'd come to rest there from other rooms in the house. The morning sunlight, streaming through the one window, caught the wardrobe's bright bevelled glass. On the white bed some white draper's goods were laid out, turning out to be a petticoat, a chemise, drawers and corsets. These last Nellie picked up and threw on the ground.

'I'm not wearing these. I've given up wearing them. From now on I'm going to go unbraced, like Arts and Crafts women.'

'Well, it's always beaten me how women can stand them,' said Frank.

'Don't think I'm going to pay for them, though. They can go back to Gage's.'

'Why not?'

'They make ridges on your flesh, you know, even with a patent fastener. You'll find I don't have any ridges.'

She began to undress. 'I'm twenty-six.'

'You keep telling me that, Nellie.'

'All the same, even at my age, when I've got these things off I'm not sure what to do next.'

It was a moment's loss of confidence, which Frank knew he mustn't allow. Under his hands her solid partly naked body was damp with effort. She was recklessly dragging off something or other whose fastenings seemed to defy her. Her voice was muffled. 'Go on Frank. I'm not going to let them stand about knowing more than I do. I won't be got the better of.'

4

THE YOUNG Reids did not go straight to Moscow. One of the things that Frank's father had told him at the Norbury wedding was that he'd better have a look at what they were doing in Germany, and so for three years he worked with Hirschfeld's printing machinery in Frankfurt. Dolly was born there, and so was Ben. Then came the miscarriage. It was summertime, the hot, landlocked German summer. They were living in the suburbs, and in those days there were still barrel organs playing in the streets. From the pavement below their room an organ repeated the same tune *Schön wie ein engel*. Again and again it tore into the sentimental music with steel teeth. Nellie lay flat on her back, losing blood, hoping to save the baby. She told Frank to throw some money out of the window to the organman to bring them luck, but they had no luck that day.

In the winter of 1905 Bert Reid died in Moscow – not in the uprisings, although that was a year of strikes and violence, almost a revolution against the Russian war with Japan. The German and English papers showed pictures of the streets barricaded with wrecked trams. The electricity had been cut off and the snowy, tomb-like barricades were lit by kerosene flares. Five batteries of artillery arrived to shell the factories in the Presnya and the Rogoznkaya where the men held out. Then they pumped in water through the gaps with equipment borrowed from Moscow's fire services. The water turned to ice on impact. When the strikers came out to try to escape back to their villages, the soldiers overturned their sledges and scattered their possessions in the snow. The assembly plant was taken over and the Reids moved to the nearest hotel, Sovastyanov's. There, after a week during which he had no occupation, since the army wouldn't let him on to his own site, Bert complained of heart pains. These pains were the symptoms of bacterial endocarditis. Pieces of inflamed tissue were making their way from the walls of the heart into the bloodstream. The Greek doctor who was called in – their usual doctor, a German, had left for Berlin when the light and water in his surgery was cut off – had nothing to prescribe except rest and valerian drops and warm water. He told Mrs Reid that in his opinion her husband's heart had given way from grief at the sad happenings in St Petersburg and Moscow. But Dr Weiss, if he had been there, though he might have diagnosed more accurately, would not have been able to save Bert.

Mrs Reid, perhaps, really did die of grief. She collapsed in the study of the Anglican chaplaincy, where she had gone to see about the funeral arrangements. Summoned by cables, Frank arrived at the Alexander station with Nellie and the two children, who wanted to start playing immediately in the deep snow. He remembered – though she had left no will and indeed had nothing of her own – that she had expressed a wish to be buried in Salford. All that had to be put in hand, and he had to find somewhere to live. The wooden family house on the site had been half burned down and then swamped with water. Without much difficulty he took a lease on 22 Lipka Street. Some of the men got together to help him rescue what furniture they could. The piano, oddly enough, his mother's Bechstein, came out undamaged from the ordeal by fire and ice. Everything else he got from Muir and Merrilees, which had remained open during what the manager called the disturbances, its dark blue flag with the golden M & M flying frozen above the shop's façade.

It wasn't a time for risk-taking, because Frank was determined that Nellie shouldn't have to worry about money. A look through the books showed that the import and assembly business would have to be wound down, or better still, sold as it stood. That was a pity, because Reid's main suppliers, Hoe's of the Borough Road in south-east London, were as reliable as the day and the night. The trouble seemed to have been two things which Frank hadn't known anything about. In the first place, although his father had got his letters, giving him some idea of the German competition, he hadn't acted on the advice, or had acted on it eccentrically. He'd set his heart on expansion, and, worse still, become fascinated by the idea of the Mammoth Press which Hoe's were putting into production for Lloyds Weekly News at a cost of eighteen thousand pounds. Another Mammoth, not for any definite customer, but most unwisely ordered on spec, had been delivered to the site, and was lying prone under tarpaulin, colossal, unassembled, unpaid for, looking, as it lay under many inches of snow against the pale green sky, like an ominous relic of the past rather than the machinery of the future. By Bert Reid's bedside when he died, among the letters he was drafting to the Ministry of Interior to plead for those of his people, his 'hands', who had been arrested, was an illustrated booklet from Hoe's describing, in heroic terms, the Mammoth. Now, with the sheds, the plant and the site itself, it must find, even in its dismembered state, a purchaser, probably one of the merchants of the second grade, with whose sons Frank had gone to school. Once it was gone, he could strike a balance, and concentrate on Reidka's.

Frank's affection for Moscow came over him at odd and inappropriate times and in undistinguished places. Dear, slovenly, mother Moscow, bemused with the bells of its four times forty churches, indifferently sheltering factories, whore-houses and golden domes, impeded by Greeks and Persians and bewildered villagers and seminarists straying on to the tram-lines, centred on its holy citadel, but reaching outwards with a frowsty leap across the boulevards to the circle of workers' dormitories and railheads, where the monasteries still prayed, and at last to a circle of pig-sties, cabbage-patches, earth roads, earth closets, where Moscow sank back, seemingly with relief, into a village.

Nellie, too, very much preferred Moscow to Germany. She enjoyed putting 22 Lipka Street in order. The village habits of the great manufacturing city didn't disconcert her at all. She was at home there, it seemed to Frank. This threw a new light on her hostility to Norbury, which had been neither town nor country.

5

THEY HAD had to move to Moscow in the dead of winter, and as they came out of the Alexander station the whole Tverskaya seemed to be drifting with smoke and steam, everyone, men and women alike, rolling and smoking their own cigarettes, their breath condensing heavily in the frost, like cattle in a pen. Selwyn had met them, anxious for their welfare and unmistakably grieving, to be forgiven everything for his sincerity. What had to be forgiven was his inability to help in any way with the children, the porters and the luggage, not so much through incompetence as inability to grasp the kind of thing that might be needed. Frank had met him before on short trips to see his parents in Moscow, Nellie not at all. 'How do you do, Mr Crane. This is Dolly, our eldest. This is Ben.' Selwyn bent down towards them, wrapped as they were like bundles against the cold.

'Both of them bereaved!'

'They've never met their grandparents, so they're hardly likely to miss them,' said Nellie. 'Perhaps you'd help Frank to check the items.'

At that first meeting, she told Frank, she'd thought that Mr Crane was only elevenpence in the shilling. But Selwyn, though he would probably have been at a loss in Frankfurt, managed well enough in Moscow. He didn't oppose his will to the powerful slow-moving muddle around him. What he did not like, or could not change, he guilelessly avoided. The current of history carried him gently with it.

Before his first visit to Reidka's Frank asked Selwyn to sit down with him and give him an accurate idea of what he'd find when he got there. Selwyn began, as his nature was, with reassurance. 'Of course, your chief compositor will be there, Yacob Tvyordov will be there, as always.'

303

'What happened to him last year? Wasn't he out on strike with the others?'

'He is the Union Treasurer, and he was out for six days. I believe those are the only six days he's ever missed.'

'Where did my father find him?'

'He came from the Flying Swan Press when it closed down. They only did hand-printing, of course.'

'And Tvyordov?'

'Only hand-printing.'

'How old is he?'

'I don't know. We've got his particulars, I suppose. Some people are ageless, Frank.'

'What about the overseer?'

Selwyn never liked to speak ill of another human being. He hesitated.

'Korobyev. Well, it's his business, of course, to collect the fines for mistakes, spoiled work, laziness, drunkenness, absence and so on. An unenviable task, Frank! But there it is, the Printers' Union agreed to the scale of fines, and we keep to the agreed scales. But since your father died, I fear Korobyev may have instituted a collection of his own whenever he feels the need for ready money.'

'Who does he collect from?'

'Well, perhaps from anyone who is not quite strong enough to object. Perhaps from Agafya, our tea-woman, perhaps from Anyuta, our cleaning-woman. Perhaps a few kopeks from the errand-boys.'

'Have you spoken to him about it?'

'Your father may have told you that I don't believe in direct resistance to evil. The only way is to put it to shame, to put it to flight, by good example.'

Frank thanked him, went to the press, shook hands with the entire staff, and called a general meeting to discuss the conduct of the overseer. This meant the three hand-compositors and their two apprentices, the pressmen, the readers, the three machine-men, the putting-on and taking-off boys, the gatherers, the folders, the deliverers, the storekeeper, the warehouseman who also entered the work in the account books and checked deliveries, the paper-wetting boys, the errand-boys, the doorman and Agafya and her assistant Anyuta. There was only one place where there was room to address them all at the same time and that was the shed which served both as the paper warehouse and the tea-kitchen. Once they were assembled the men complained that the boys, some of whom were only just fourteen, were incompetent to judge the question, and they were sent home. This cleared a good deal of space. Meantime Korobyev had not arrived, he had not been in at all that day, and was feeling faint.

'Well, we'll proceed without him,' said Frank, taking up his stand on the tea-counter. 'I'm speaking to you, not as a stranger, because as you know, I'm a child of Moscow, but as a stranger to this press which was my father's last enterprise.' Some crossed themselves. 'Because he died, I have come back to you. I think I may say that during my time in England and Germany I've learnt the business pretty thoroughly. Tonight we have to decide between ourselves what is meant at Reid's Press by fair dealing.'

It was the shortest meeting that Frank had ever attended. It appeared that there was no one in the room who did not want to get rid of their overseer. Korobyev did not insist on working out his time, or accept Frank's invitation to explain himself. All he asked for was his internal passport, which allowed him to travel more than fifteen miles from his place of birth, and which an employer, if he thought fit, could refuse to give back. Frank gave it back. As Korobyev left the building, the compositors hammered him out by knocking their sticks against their cases. The battering sound seemed to excite itself and to work itself into a metallic frenzy, splintering the ears. The din stopped as suddenly as it had begun, and outside, at the tram-stop, Korobyev could be heard shouting: 'Listen to me! Let everyone hear what has been done to the father of a family!'

Suddenly Agafya, her head covered with a white handkerchief, went down on her knees before Frank and implored him to have mercy on Korobyev.

'That's all rubbish, Agafya. He was taking forty-seven kopeks a week off your wages.'

'I'm on my knees to you, Frank Albertovich, sir.'

'Yes, I see you.'

'You heard him say he's the father of a family.'

'It's a disgrace if he is,' said Frank. 'He's not married.'

Agafya, satisfied with the dramatic effect she had made, returned, like an old sentry to his post, to her samovars and to her campaign, in which no settlement seemed possible, with the storekeeper, over the issue of tea. The tea came, not in leaf form, but in tablets. These were charged as Consumables, but Frank thought they might just as well go down under Maintenance Materials. Forbidden to smoke, everyone at the Press was impelled to drink black tea not only at the stated hours, but if they could, all day.

From that morning Frank took on the job of overseer himself, or you might say there was no overseer at Reidka's, only a manager who worked rather harder than most. Even so, the change would not have been possible without Tvyordov.

This man was the only compositor to be employed year in year out, on a weekly wage. The other three were on piece work. He had a broad, placid face, and the back of his head, covered with short greying stubble, gave the same reassuring impression as the front. Work started at Reidka's at seven, and at one minute to seven he was in the composing room. It took him a minute exactly to get his setting rule, bodkin, composing-stick and galley out of the locked cupboard where they were kept. These were his own, and he lent them to no one. Tvyordov did not take any tea at this time. He put on a clean white apron which hung from a hook by the side of his frame, and a pair of slippers which he brought with him in a leather bag. Then he stepped into his frame and put his German silver watch on the lower bar of the upper case into a clip of his own construction, which fitted it exactly. The watch had a second hand, or sweep. Tvyordov spent no time in distributing the type from the reserves of the thirty-five letters and fifteen punctuation marks, that had always been done the night before, but started straight away on his copy, memorised the first few phrases, filled his composing-stick, adjusted the spaces and took a sounding from his watch to see how long this had taken and to set his standard for the day. This was not an absolute measure. It depended on the weather, the copy, the proportion of foreign words, but never on Tvyordov himself. If at any point later on in the day he found that he had pushed down his last space a few seconds too early he would wait, motionless and untroubled, then shift his setting rule down at the watch's precise tick. When the stick was lifted into the galley he grasped the letters lightly as though they were a solid piece of metal. This was difficult, the apprentices trying it were often reduced to tears, but during the past four hundred years no easier way had apparently been discovered of doing it. In this way he could set one thousand five hundred letters and spaces in an hour.

At three minutes to ten Tvyordov took a cup of tea, which necessitated going down to the canteen, and went to the washroom. This was one of the breaks made compulsory by the unions during the brief period after the government had been frightened by the disturbances, when they were allowed to negotiate. It was said that when Tvyordov had taken to the streets he had been wounded, or damaged in some way. A great many shots had hit people for whom they were not intended. There was certainly no sign of any damage now.

After his tea, at ten o'clock, Tvyordov took his lunch, and at eleven he lifted his type again, his head and body sympathetic to the ticking watch. At twelve he went home for his dinner, and in the afternoons was less silent, but only marginally. There was something indescribably soothing in the proceedings of Tvyordov. There was nothing mechanical about them. There were many minute variations, for instance in the way he washed the type free of dirt and, while it was still just moist enough to stick together, lifted a small amount on to his brass slip, resting it against the broad middle finger of his left hand. No one could tell why these variations occurred. Perhaps Tvyordov was amusing himself. What would he consider amusing? On Saturday nights, when Agafya was seeing to the

oil lamp in front of the composing room's ikon, Tvyordov
wound up the office clock. On his way home, on Saturdays
only, he stopped for five minutes exactly at Markel's Bar for a
measure of vodka. On Monday mornings he arrived thirty
seconds earlier than usual, to clean the clock glass for the
week. No one else was trusted to do that.

There was no mystery about Tvyordov's attitude to the
machine-room. Linotype, he felt, was not worthy of a serious
man's carefully measured time. It was only fit for slipshod work
at great speed. To make corrections you had to reset the whole
line, therefore you had orders not to do it. The metal used was a
wretchedly soft alloy. Monotype, after some consideration, he
tolerated. The machine was small and ingenious, and the letters
danced out as they were cast from the hot metal, separate and
alive. They weren't as hard as real founder's type, still they
would take a good many impressions, and they could be used
for corrections in the compositors' room. When, or even
whether, Tvyordov had been asked for his views was not
known, but Reidka's did monotype, and no linotype.

Probably the very fact that Tvyordov was known to work
there had attracted commissions to Reidka's. There was plenty
of small work, for which hand-setting was still necessary.
Reidka's printed parcel labels, auctioneers' catalogues, hand-
bills of rewards for information leading to the arrest of thieves
and murderers, tradesmen's cards, club cards, bill heads, bottle
wrappers, doctors' certificates, good-quality writing paper,
concert programmes, tickets, time sheets, visiting cards, circu-
lars of debts, posters (in three colours, if wanted, at a third more
per 100). Frank also accepted leaflets and some magazines and
school books, but no newspaper work, and no poetry. There
was one exception here, Selwyn's poems, entitled *Birch Tree
Thoughts*, which would soon be ready for the press, and where
could they be printed but Reidka's? *Birch Tree Thoughts* was at
the censor now, and since all poetry was suspect, would perhaps
be more carefully read there than it ever would be again. But
Frank didn't expect requests for printing from revolutionaries
or politicals. These people seemed to be able to produce,

almost at will, the illegal manifestos and threats that livened the bloodstream of the city. Frank wondered, and even sometimes tried to calculate, how many printing presses were hidden away in students' garrets and cellars, in cowsheds, bath houses and backyard pissoirs, hen coops, cabbage-patches, potato-stacks – small hand-presses, Albions probably, printing on one side only, spirited away to another address at the hint of danger. He imagined the dissidents, on Moscow's a hundred and forty days a year of frost, warming the ink to deliver one more warning. Printer's ink freezes readily.

When he judged he had the feel of things at Reidka's, Frank made a call on all the other shops and offices in Seraphim Street. There was a regulation imposing tax on new businesses according to the amount of nuisance they caused to the neighbours. To circumvent this, Frank suggested that he should contribute to the street's welfare by paying the wages of a nightwatchman, to patrol the street up to the point where it joined the Vavarkaya. There was a room over Markel's Bar where he could sleep during the day.

'But Frank, there's a hint of bribery here,' said Selwyn.

'Put the wages down to overheads,' Frank told him.

6

IN 1911, then, Dolly was eight, and wore a sailor suit with a pleated skirt, banded with rows of white. Ben was seven, and also wore a sailor suit, with buttoned boots. Both of them had sailor hats made for them at Muirka's, bearing the name of a British ship, HMS *Tiger*. Dolly was preparing for her entrance to the Gymnasium. She was almost a schoolgirl, but was not afraid to grow older, because she knew that there was in store for her some particular greatness. Towards autumn, Annushka was born. She was delivered by the midwife, the babka. Dr Weiss, long since back in Moscow, came in later, competent, carbolic-scented, eager to talk to Frank about his personal investments. When he had gone, the babka sprinkled Nellie and the baby with holy water and brought tea brewed from raspberry leaves. She had already told Frank to buy a small gold cross and chain, and this was put round Annushka's neck, to remain there for the rest of her life. Dolly and Ben, who had no gold crosses, demanded them.

'Shall I get them?' he asked Nellie anxiously. She was a woman and had the heavy end of the whole business to carry. She answered that he'd better, if he didn't want to be plagued. This struck him as not really fitting the case. Dolly never plagued, it was her habit to ask for things only once.

Charlie wrote regularly, to Frank rather than to Nellie, who was much less likely to answer. He gave a good many details about his health, about the funeral of King Edward VII, and about the Choral Society's monthly concerts, regularly enclosing the programmes. When Annushka was born he wrote at length, enclosing a five-pound note. His letter went on:

> You say that the situation is uncertain in Russia and that you believe you ought to be ready to pull up stakes if necessary,

but that you must not grumble at that, well, Frank, I would say that at this moment you must be the better off of the two of us – it continues to be a bad winter here, a black frost last night, and I've been told by several acquaintances here that in their houses the contents of the chamber-pots froze, which I believe is very rarely recorded in the South of England, cap that if you can. Then there's the political aspect. Whereas from what you say you have a passable set of workpeople at the Press and a steady foreman, England is now a place of nothing but trouble and strife, which they call popular agitation. We have now eight hundred miners on strike, and if you can tell me how Old England is to be kept running without coal, and how coal can be spirited out of the ground without miners, then I'm not the only one who would be obliged to you. Then the railwaymen are out again, there are troops standing by this time, very different from twenty years ago. You will ask me, are not their grievances very real? Well, what will you say to this, the Printers, too, not only going on strike as far as their daily work is concerned but producing their own sheet, which is dignified by the name of a newspaper. Yes, I am being asked to read with my second cup of tea, instead of my *Daily Mail*, this revolutionary sheet, for I consider it no less. When all this began, *The Times* said that 'the public must be prepared for a conflict between Labour and Capital, or between employers and employed, upon a scale such as has never occurred before', or it may have been 'such a scale as', I have not the exact words in front of me.

Nellie said that it was quite enough if one person in the household read Charlie's letters. 'He used to talk like that, too. You can't have forgotten that.'

'I suppose he's got time on his hands since poor Grace died,' Frank said. 'His letters do seem to be longer. Well, he sends his love.'

'We don't know him,' said Dolly. 'We don't know our Uncle.'

'I'll send him a message in general terms from the lot of you.'

'You can borrow my Blackbird, if you like,' said Ben. This was his new fountain pen, which troubled him. It was guaranteed not to leak, but writers and schoolchildren knew better. Ben wished to be relieved of the responsibility of the Blackbird, without losing his own dignity.

To Selwyn also Frank had made it clear that he might have to sell Reidka's, and take his family home, in the next few years or so. Opinion in the British community was divided. The British consul, who was only in Category 3, had no opinion to give. Frank thought the chances of having to leave Russia were about fifty-fifty, but wanted to know how Selwyn would be placed. Selwyn replied that he considered himself as a stranger and a pilgrim, who ought always to be ready to move on. There were Tolstoyan settlements, he believed, everywhere in Europe, there was one, for example, at Godalming.

'You have to bring your skills to such places, of course, but that is all that is asked.' He'd bring management accounting, Frank thought, poetry, music, spiritual advice, shoe-making. In summer, he knew, Selwyn wove his own birch-bark shoes before he took to the roads. They just about lasted the trip. He came back through the Sukhareva Market to the north of Moscow, bought himself a pair of leather boots there, and went back to Reidka's.

Long before his death last year Tolstoy had fallen hopelessly out of fashion with thinking Russia, but not with his foreign disciples, and certainly not with Selwyn. What Tolstoy had thought of Selwyn, Frank was not too sure. Selwyn had been welcome at his Moscow house in Dolgo-Khamovnicheski Street, and Frank believed that he had first met Tolstoy at the Korsakov private lunatic asylum which adjoined the property. Tolstoy had forbidden any repairs to the fence, so that the patients could put their hands through gaps and pick the flowers if they felt like it. There were regular concerts at Korsakov's, got up by the innumerable charities of Moscow.

Selwyn had a fine tenor voice, a reasonable tenor voice anyway, which was what passed for a fine one in Russia, the land of basses, and – never having been known to refuse an appeal to his kindness – he had given a recital one evening. What he had sung Frank didn't know, but some of the patients in the audience had become restless, and others had fallen asleep. Selwyn, who told the story without a hint of vanity or resentment, had sung on, but afterwards, since there was no applause, he had taken the opportunity to apologise to Tolstoy, who was sitting in one of the back rows. At the time Tolstoy made no reply, but a few days later he had said: 'I find you have done well. To be bored is the ordinary sensation of most of us at a concert of this kind. But to these unfortunates it is a luxury to have an ordinary sensation.'

'Are you going to sing for them again?' Frank had asked.

'Of course, if Dr Korsakov invites me. But he thinks the experience shouldn't be repeated too often.'

Frank didn't in any way contest the greatness of Lev Nicolaevich, but his hopes for the immediate future of Russia lay with the Premier, Piotr Stolypin. Something about Stolypin's neatness, quietness and correctness, his ability to keep his head, his refusal, when Rasputin tried to hypnotise him, to be affected in the slightest degree, his decision to accept the premiership even though his enemies had tried to dissuade him from politics by blowing him up in his own house and crippling his young daughter, who had lost both her feet – something about all this suggested that Stolypin might, in Nellie's phrase, not be got the better of. Stolypin asked for ten years in power. He gambled on ten years. By offering government loans to Russia's one hundred and seventy-nine million peasants, so that they could buy their own land, he intended – if he was given ten years – to prevent revolution. Stolypin, however, had, as part of his official duties, to accompany the Tsar to a gala performance at the opera house in Kiev. He was in disgrace with the Imperial family and so was not invited to the royal box, but given a seat in the stalls. When he stood up in the interval he presented an excellent target to a terrorist agent in the theatre, who had been unwisely hired by the police as a security man. Stolypin was shot through the lungs and liver, and died four days later.

A memorial fund was opened, but foreigners living in Russia were not allowed to contribute. Frank was sorry about this.

'But would you call him a just man?' Selwyn asked anxiously.

'No, not at all, he fixed the elections and he fixed the members of the Duma, but then the Duma wasn't designed to work in the first place. He didn't make any profits for himself, though, and he saw there was a way for the country to survive without a revolution.'

'A man of courage.'

'Certainly, or he wouldn't have stood up in the theatre.'

Stolypin had asked for ten years, and had been allowed five. In the September of 1911 he was lying in state in an open coffin in Petersburg, just at the time when Nellie felt recovered enough after the birth of Annie to get up and go out a little. She leaned heavily on Frank's arm. They walked a short distance.

'How does it feel being a mother of three?' he asked, not able to contain his love and pride for the new child. 'It'll take up all my time,' Nellie said. 'Still, it took up all my time when I only had Dolly.' 'I hoped Dunyasha would be useful to you. That's all she's supposed to be doing, being of use to you.' 'That Dunyasha!' said Nellie.

They took a taxi to a café on the edge of the Alexander Gardens. There was not a breath of wind, and under the glowing white sky tinged with pink from the horizon which seemed to fume with a warning of frost, the scant leaves were hanging motionless from the lime trees. The waiters who had to serve the tables outside the café were wearing their overcoats over their long aprons. It was the first sting of autumn. In two weeks the statues in the gardens would be wrapped in straw against the cold, all doors would be shut and all windows would be impenetrably sealed up until next spring.

7

THESE SUDDEN decisions of Nellie's – but Frank could really only remember one, in her bedroom in Longfellow Road, that hot afternoon, with just enough breeze, after Frank had drawn the blinds, to make the tassel at the end of the blind-cord tap against the window. And she'd accounted to him then for what she felt. In the two years since Annushka was born, had she grown unaccountable?

At first it seemed to him that Nellie must be coming back, and he wired to all the railway stations between Mozhaisk and Berlin. After that he wired to Charlie every six hours. After three days Charlie wired back – Nellie not here, but guaranteed safe and well. Then, as though offering a respectable substitute, he added, shall be coming to Moscow myself shortly. In the confusion, which rapidly became the monotony, of loss it was something to have a fixed point when things must change or be changed, if only by the arrival of Charlie. That was not quite the same thing as wanting him to come, but it meant that Frank had to make arrangements and give instructions, two ways of bringing time to order.

How could Nellie be safe and well without them, the four of them? He wrote to her by every morning post.

'If you want proper envelopes and paper, they're in the right-hand drawer of my desk,' he said to Dolly.

'I know they are.'

'It's locked, but you've only got to ask me.'

'I know.'

'In case you want to write to Mother.'

'Do you mean to ask her why she went away, or to ask her when she's coming back?'

'You don't need to ask either.'

'I shan't need the paper,' said Dolly, 'because I don't think I ought to write. I can only write properly in Russian, in any case.'

'Why not, Dolly? Surely you don't think she did the wrong thing?'

'I don't know whether she did or not. The mistake she probably made was getting married in the first place.'

'Is that what you're going to put in your letter?'

'I told you it would be better if I didn't write one.'

Obviously for a few days at least, perhaps for a few weeks, something would have to be done by way of looking after the children. Annushka had been removed from him, and by her own consent was totally under the doting protection of the cook and kitchen-maid, but he needed help with Ben, and still more with Dolly. With an impulse to avoid the English chaplaincy and the English community for as long as possible, Frank thought of the Kuriatins. Their home was always open to him.

Arkady Kuriatin was a merchant of the second grade. The dues he paid weren't high enough to allow him to export; all his trade was within the Russian empire. He dealt in timber, wood pulp and paper, and Frank had done business with him for some time. Arkady had children – how many, Frank couldn't say, because extra ones, perhaps nephews and nieces, perhaps waifs, or even hostages, seemed to come and go. His wife, Matryona Osipovna, was always at home. Frank had heard her say, 'What is there better outside than in?' Nellie had always admitted Mrs Kuriatin's kindness, but couldn't be doing with her. It was true that she had recommended Nellie to be sure that Dolly and Annushka always had their eyes washed out with their own urine, as this would preserve their bright glances.

Kuriatin had no telephone. Like most of the second-grade merchants he maintained an elaborate pretence, which, however, was a reassurance as well as a pretence, of keeping up the old ways. Sometimes he would indulge himself with the latest improvement. He had a motor-car, a 6-cylinder 50-horse-power Wolseley, of which he was proud, for there were only fifteen hundred cars or so in Moscow. But there was no electric light in his house, and you could not telephone him there.

Fortunately, he chose to live in an unpretentious street – though the house was large – not far from the Press, and Frank was able to go round there in the middle of the morning. He knocked at the outer street door, although he was perfectly well aware that unless it was a special occasion, and the Kuriatins were giving a dinner there would be no one in the front rooms at all. He waited, and, as he expected, a ferocious-looking servant in a peasant smock appeared round the side of the house, with the air of a gaoler paid to discourage charitable visitors. He could not pretend not to recognise Frank, but shouted, as though to the deaf, the master was away.

'I'll see Mrs Kuriatin,' said Frank.

To the right, as you went in, was a vast salon, the shutters closed, the chandeliers wrapped in canvas, the furniture hidden like corpses under white cotton shrouds, the whole floor covered for protection with spread-out sheets of the *Trade Messenger*. On the left the door was shut, but Frank knew it was the dining room. Here, when Kuriatin played host, the table clinked and clashed with imported silver and glass and the fierce servants were forced out of their smocks and felt boots and into black coats, shoes, and white gloves. The minor gentle-folk who had accepted the Kuriatins' hospitality were not likely ever to invite them in return, but Kuriatin seemed smilingly to relish this impoliteness. As soon as the guests had gone, the family migrated to where they really lived, children, servants, dependants and relations on top of one another, in a couple of low-ceilinged, smoky rooms at the very back of the house.

Mrs Kuriatin, who had been lying on a shabby ottoman, flung down her cigarette and heaved herself towards him.

'Ah, Frank Albertovich, if you had come yesterday, when I was feeling poorly, I should not have been able to receive you.'

'Let's be glad that didn't happen, Matryona Osipovna.'

A number of young children were milling about, the tribe of Kuriatin, all of them well-grown, but broad, rather than tall, as though they had adapted themselves to the shape of the room where they spent so much of their time. Two very old women who nodded appeasingly were probably poor relations. One woman he knew – she was the wife of one of Kuriatin's partners, or rather accomplices, in the timber business; the other, in black silk, he didn't know.

'This is my sister, Varya,' cried Mrs Kuriatin. 'Her husband couldn't accompany her, he died not long ago.' Frank took the sister's hand. It was difficult not to feel that he was on a visit to a harem. The air was thick with the smell of lamp-oil and cigarettes from the Greek-tended tobacco gardens of the Black Sea. Mrs Kuriatin now varied her sentence of welcome to: 'If you had come yesterday you would not have been able to see me, and I should not have been able to help you in your trouble.'

Frank looked round the crowded room.

'You're among friends here, Frank Albertovich, and my sister and I are as one person. They say, if Vera slips, Varya falls.'

'Well, let's not call it trouble,' said Frank, 'it's only that as a friend, I'm asking you to do something out of friendship.' Mrs Kuriatin was more than ready. He explained that he did not want Dolly ('That angel!' Mrs Kuriatin exclaimed, rather to his surprise) and Ben to have to be at home by themselves after school. He wondered if, perhaps for a few days only, he hoped, they could come to the Kuriatins instead. He would be able to call round and take them away himself when the Press closed at five o'clock.

Mrs Kuriatin and her sister both shook their heads at the idea of a few days. Out of sheer tenderness of heart they liked every emergency to go on as long as possible. But at least the difficult time had started, and a messenger must be sent at once to Dolly's school and to Ben's, so that they could come that very afternoon. Mitya (Mrs Kuriatin's eldest, referred to as though, like the Crown Prince, his movements must be known to everybody) was coming home early this afternoon, because a special present had been sent to him, for Shrove Tuesday. As to the others – she looked round her with an air of doubtful proprietorship – yes, all, or most, would be there to welcome Dolly and Ben.

Frank sincerely thanked her, and asked her, out of civility, what Mitya's present was. It was a tame bear-cub, or perhaps not tamed, sent down from the North. The prices of ordinary brown bear fur, for rugs and coats, had gone down terribly since they had put proper heating into the Trans-Siberian railway. Still, this one's mother had been shot for sport by one of Arkady's business contacts and generously he had ordered them to box up the cub and put it on the train for Moscow. They knew it had arrived alive, they had been notified from the Yaroslavl station. Only of course it must be fetched. The words, spoken in chorus by Mrs Kuriatin and her sister, gave Frank an uneasy sensation.

When he was a boy he had sometimes been to New Year treats, in Moscow and out in the country, where a performing bear was brought in as an entertainment. There was usually an argument with the door keeper and another with the cook when the animal was brought in through the kitchen. It wore a collar and underneath the bright lights, looked drowsy. First it shifted a little from foot to foot, as though to put them down was painful, then it gave, after a good deal of prompting, what was said to be an imitation first of a Cossack dance, then of an old peasant carrying a heavy load and falling down on the ground, then, as it was led out of the room, of an English governess simpering and looking round over her shoulder at the men. The fur under its collar was worn away, perhaps from doing this particular trick so often. Sometimes it was rewarded with an orange, but, as a joke, the bear-man would take the orange away so that everyone could enjoy its disappointment.

Frank had never been much amused by the dancing bear, nor, as far as he could see, was anyone else. This was only a cub, though. When he got back to Reidka's he told Selwyn what he had arranged, largely for the relief of repeating it aloud. At least he can't make it have anything to do with Tolstoy, he thought. But it turned out that at the New Year Lev Nicolaevich had himself taken the part of the performing bear, wearing a skin which had been lined with canvas. According to Selwyn, this enabled him to give a more spiritual turn to the whole occasion.

8

THE BEAR-CUB at the Kuriatins' was disappointingly small, and its head looked rather large for its body and seemed to weigh it down. The skin was very loose, as though the cub had not quite grown into it. The dense fur, dark, golden and ginger, grew at all angles, except along the spine which was neatly parted, and on the glovelike paws and hind feet. The protruding claws looked as if they were made of metal, and the bear itself was a dangerous toy. Both front and back legs were bent in an inward curve. The total effect was confused and amateurish, openly in need of protection for some time yet. Planting its feet on the ground in a straight line required thought from the bear, and was not always successful. When Mitya Kuriatin hit it with a billiard cue it turned its torpedo-shaped head from side to side and then fell over.

'Is that all it can do?' asked his sister Masha. 'You said it would dance.'

Mitya, humiliated in front of the English guests with whom he had intended to cut a dash, and by the presence of an animal when at the age of thirteen he would have so much preferred something mechanical, shouted 'Well then, music!' Masha went to the pianola, which Kuriatin had bought in Berlin with the idea that it would save the trouble of having his children taught to play the piano. Perhaps rightly, they took very little interest in it, and although they knew how to start and stop it they did not know how to change the music rolls. Now when Masha turned the switch the idiot contrivance began halfway through. Masha flung herself across the brocaded piano stool and pressed the key down to loudest. The bear withdrew to the farthest corner of the room. Turning round with a loud scratching of claws on the floorboards beyond the carpet, it faced all comers.

'It won't dance, it won't do anything, it's imbecile.'

They tried throwing cold water over it. The bear sneezed and shook itself, then tried to lick up the sparkling drops on the surface of its fur.

'It's thirsty,' said Dolly coldly. After glancing at it for a moment she and Ben stood together in isolation behind one of the curtains.

'What are you two talking about?' Mitya called out.

'We're saying that you should give it something to drink.'

'Yes, it's one of God's creatures,' said the treacherous Masha.

Mitya blundered out of the room, and came back with a bottle of vodka and a pale blue saucer of fine china with a gilt rim.

'Where did you get those?' asked Dolly.

'From the dining room. It's all laid out for some reception or other.'

'Are you allowed in there?' said Ben.

'My father's in Riga. I'm the master here!' Mitya's face was red with senseless excitement. He poured the vodka into the saucer and, slopping it over, carried it to the bear's far corner. For the first time its mouth opened and its long dark tongue came out. It tilted its head a little and licked the saucer dry. Mitya poured again, and this time screwing its head round the other way, the little animal drank again.

'Dance now,' shouted Mitya.

The bear got on to its hind legs and was as tall, suddenly, as Mitya, who retreated. Losing its perilous balance it held out its paws like small hands and reeled on to the carpet where its claws gave it a better hold, while a gush of urine sprayed across the pattern of red and blue. For some reason one of its ears had turned inside out, showing the lining of paler skin. It rolled over several times while the dark patch spread, then sidled at great speed out of the door. All the children laughed, Dasha and Ben as well, they were all laughing and disgusted together, the laughter had taken possession of them, broke them in half and squeezed the tears out of their eyes.

'It's gone into the dining room.'

Then they were silent and only Mitya went on grossly laughing as they followed clinging to each other to the front of the house and heard a tearing and rending, then a crash like the splintering of ice in the first spring thaw as the bear, and they could see it now reflected in the great mirrors on every wall, lumbered from end to end of the table making havoc among glass and silver, dragging at the bottle of vodka which stood in each place, upending them like ninepins and licking desperately at what was spilled. The service door flew open and the doorman, Sergei, came in, crossed himself, and without a moment's hesitation snatched up a shovel, opened the doors of the white porcelain stove and scooped out a heap of red-hot charcoal which he scattered over the bear. The tablecloth, soaked in spirits, sent up a sheet of flame. The bear screamed, its screams being like that of a human child. Already alight, it tried to protect its face with its front paws. Mitya was still doubled up with laughter when from the passage outside could be heard the roar of Kuriatin, pleased with himself because he had come home early as his wife had implored him. 'Devils, do I have to let myself into my own house?' He was at the door. 'Why is that bear on fire? I'll put it out of its misery. I'll spatter its brains out. I'll spatter the lot of you.'

Frank, quietly removing Dolly and Ben from the uproar, would have liked to know where Mrs Kuriatin had been all this time and why Sergei, half idiotic as he was, hadn't thrown water at the wretched animal instead of red-hot cinders. This was the only one of his questions that the children could answer. Sergei had known that bears were lovers of water. Water would never have stopped a bear.

'You told us you thought we could go there every day after school,' said Ben, 'as long as we were reasonably quiet.'

'I don't think that now.'

'What will you say?'

'I shall go round to Arkady Kuriatin's office tomorrow and offer to pay for some, not much, of the damage.'

'Will you ask him what happened to the bear?' asked Dolly.

'No.'

'Its face was burning.'
'I shan't ask him.'

At Kuriatin's absurdly old-fashioned counting-house, almost next door to his home, as though he wanted to keep watch over both at once, Frank was told once again, this time by a clerk, that the master was out. 'I haven't seen him all day, Frank Albertovich.'

The clerks still used pen and ink and were allowed a fixed number of nibs every week. Their calculations were done on an abacus, whose black and white beads clicked at great speed, fell silent, and then started to click again.

'Well, I've something to say to him, but I shan't take long.'

'What am I to say if I'm asked why I admitted you?' said the clerk.

'Say you haven't seen me all day.'

Not long ago Frank had found that the floor of the machine-room at Reidka's needed strengthening, and Kuriatin had agreed to supply the wood for the new joists. Four days before Frank was due to take delivery, he sent a message that he was ill and couldn't discuss business. Two days later he was surprised that Frank didn't know that he'd given up supplying timber as there was no profit in it for an honest man, and the next day he was said to have gone on a pilgrimage. A week later he was back, but sent word that he couldn't see Frank either then or perhaps ever, because of certain misunderstandings between himself and Frank's father. As to the wood, that was in one of the store houses. That very evening, meeting Frank by chance in the steam-room of the Armenian baths, Kuriatin, very much the worse for drink, embraced him tearfully and asked his forgiveness for having been unable to fulfil the order. The next morning he said sharply that he could have made the delivery some time ago if the percentage tax had been paid to the Ministry of Commerce and Industry, and, of course, some-thing allowed for Grisha, Grigory Rasputin, who was certainly in regular receipt of bribes, though never from Kuriatin, who avoided Petersburg and conducted his business in cash. When the cash was put into his hands he went through it minutely to make sure that there were no 1877 notes, or 100-rouble notes issued in 1866. Neither of these were legal tender. Probably he would have rather been paid in poultry-food, or benzine. Finally, Frank had got his timber, only a few hours later than he had actually allowed for. His calculations had not been far out.

Kuriatin's private office was as dark as the rest of the establishment, and not much more comfortable. On seeing Frank, he opened his arms wide. He was wearing a black kaftan from which came a strong, healthy human odour. An unfortunate incident? The children left to themselves? Damage? Broken china, pissed carpet, fire, destruction, twenty-three and a half bottles of the best vodka? Did Frank think his credit wasn't good enough to bear a little loss, a little trifle? Did he think there was some shortage of tablecloths? All that he'd had to do, on returning, was to dismiss Sergei and some of the women servants, give Mitya a beating, hire sledges, tell the guests when they arrived not even to take off their overcoats and galoshes and drive off with the lot of them to Krynkin's Restaurant.

'I was wondering where your wife could have been at the time,' said Frank. 'I understood that she would be with the children.'

'She was lying down, as all women do. She's terrified of animals, can't stand them in the house.' But why, Kuriatin continued, why did Frank himself not come to his home that evening, no formality, just to share what God provided?

'No thank you, not this evening, Arkady Filippovich.'

'You won't partake of our simple fare?'

Frank knew the invitation wasn't meant to be accepted. It was out of the question for him to come round like that, as a guest on the spur of the moment. Merchants of the second grade did not entertain in such a way. Preparations would have had to be made. Without them, he would have caused almost as much trouble as the bear.

Kuriatin took Frank's arm and escorted him down the bare wooden stairs, both of them, from long practice, avoiding the weak places.

'Why don't you get something done about these stairs?' Frank asked. 'And why don't you let your clerks have a telephone? The Germans will get ahead of you.'

'Why don't you get your wife to come back to you?' shouted Kuriatin, exploding with laughter, as the doorman came out of his cupboard-like room and ushered them, deeply bowing, into the street. For Kuriatin life, like business, was a game, but not a gambling game. On the contrary, it was one in which he had arranged to win, although the rules were peculiar to himself. Knowing that the children had been put at risk in his half-savage household, he had felt Frank's visit as a reproach. But by insulting Frank – of whom he was genuinely fond – he had restored himself to a superior position. It almost compensated him for the loss of his tablecloth, glass and china, to which he had been insanely attached.

9

FRANK WENT straight to the English chaplaincy off the Marosseika, where he should, perhaps, have gone in the first place. Evening tea-time was one of Mrs Graham's visiting hours. He was not afraid of Mrs Graham, or at least not as afraid as some people were. In any case, in taking his predicament to her he was doing her a service. She was a scholar's daughter, brought up in Cambridge, and not reconciled to living in Moscow. Although she hadn't, Frank knew, attended college herself, she might be called a student of a kind, a student of trouble, or rather of other people's troubles.

'Mr Reid?' she called out in her odd, high, lightly drawling voice. 'This is an expected pleasure.'

'You knew I was going to come and ask you something?'

'Of course.'

Restless as a bird of prey which has not caught anything for several days, she nodded him towards the seat next to her. There were no comfortable chairs in the chaplaincy, except in Mr Graham's study.

Mrs Graham was not alone, indeed she rarely was. Opposite her sofa there sat a woman of about her own age, somewhere between forty and fifty, wearing a grey skirt of stout material, a grey blouse that did not quite match it, a grey spencer with pink bits about it somewhere and a felt hat, put on quite straight. The total effect was that of gallantry in the face of odds. She was introduced as Miss Muriel Kinsman. Frank remembered now that he had been told she was coming to Moscow from the depths of the country, where she'd been a governess, and that she had been unjustly dismissed from her employer's estate and, as usual, a collection was being taken up to help her with her fare home. 'Not only does she look like a dismissed governess, but it's clear that she was born looking like one,' Mrs Graham had told him. 'And that I consider unusually hard on her.' Now he shook hands, saying 'It's a pleasure to meet you, Miss Kinsman. I'm only sorry you're not staying longer in Moscow.'

Miss Kinsman fixed him with her great melancholy eyes in her weatherbeaten face. 'I'd stay here willingly if there was anyone who took the least interest in whether I did or not.'

'But you'll be going home to your family?'

She made no answer, and Frank feared he'd been impolite. Bad luck if he was to be reproached for that when in fact he cared amazingly little whether she went home or not.

Mrs Graham said, 'I'm inclined to think sometimes that it's a pity there's such a thing as a postal service. The pain of waiting for letters which don't come very much exceeds the pleasure of getting them when they do. I hope I've said that the right way round. Miss Kinsman hasn't heard from anyone in England for some years.'

'I should like you to call me Muriel, Mrs Graham, even if only once. I should just like to hear that name again.'

'What did they call you out at Vladislavskoe?'

Miss Kinsman explained that although the German governess (who was admittedly younger, or anyway a few years younger, than herself) had always been called Fräulein Trudi, she herself had never been been anything but Missy.

'Whatever did that matter?' asked Mrs Graham. 'I shouldn't mind being called Missy.'

'Everything matters when you get out to one of those places. Nothing arrives without your seeing it come out of the forest two versts away, and down the dip, out of the dip, up the road so that by the time it gets to the house, cart or carriage or motor-car or whatever it is, you're sick of it already, so you're driven to brood all day about what's going on in the house itself, and I suppose that gets magnified, every little thing that's said, every bark and shout, every tick and tock. Perhaps one loses one's sense of proportion. Yes, one certainly does. One incident gets added to another, and it's the sum total of them all that weighs one down.'

The matter of the lost key to the clock. The matter of the lost key to the wine-cooler. The matter of the valerian drops.

The matter of the Giant's Stride. The matter of the cigar case. The matter of the pickled cucumber. The matter of the bath house. The matter of the torn photograph...she's drifting, thought Frank, and presumably she's come here to drift, for a length of time which would be decisively fixed by Mrs Graham. He felt sorry for her.

'Wasn't it quite what you expected?' he asked.

'There shouldn't be such a state of mind as expectation,' interrupted Mrs Graham. 'One gets too dependent on the future.'

She offered a box of Crimean cigarettes. Frank refused, but not Miss Kinsman, who said, 'I'm afraid I've formed the habit since I came to Russia.'

'So have I,' said Mrs Graham, 'my husband wishes I hadn't. But I smoke the *mahorka*.' Not always, thought Frank, but she did on this occasion, rapidly rolling up the coarse workman's shag in a piece of yellow paper. She lit it and tossed back her head. The cigarette hung from the corner of her mouth, where it looked quite in keeping with her wild grey Cambridge knot of hair, her peasant sarafan worn with a tweed skirt and her bead necklaces. 'Tell!' she cried, puffing.

Miss Kinsman rambled on, in a low voice, not always easy to follow. Although it seemed that some object, always the same one, perhaps the cigar case, perhaps the cucumber, had repeatedly made its appearance in her room and had suggested to her that the whole household was hostile to her and was showing this in petty ways – 'in pranks' Miss Kinsman said – the main trouble had been a noble one, her high concept of education. The Lvovs themselves appeared to take no interest in their children's lessons, that was left to Pavel Borisovich, an unmarried Uncle who was installed in the house, with not much to do except interfere. This Pavel Borisovich had been intended for the College of Pages, but had been sent to school in Berlin, and thought it right to impose an absurdly strict regime on the children. His enthusiasm wouldn't have lasted, of course, nothing did, he just had one craze after another – languages, psychology, gymnastics. It was during his gymnastics mania that he'd got one of the estate carpenters to instal a Giant's Stride in the garden after the last hay had been cut. She had thought it her duty to say that it wasn't, in her opinion, a safe piece of apparatus. You stepped out, holding one of the six ropes, into the air and whirled faster, even faster, from one landing-place to another. It was certain to lead to broken bones. But it isn't always a good thing to be in the right.

'It's good, but it's hardly ever safe,' said Mrs Graham.

She was, or probably was, a kind-hearted woman, but she was too sharp, Frank thought. All sharp people, no matter whether they were men or women, were tiring.

The matter of the Giant's Stride. The matter of the Lvov children's timetable. Learning should not be associated with enforcement, but with freedom and joy. The matter of the bath house. Nakedness was not an important thing in Russia. The coachman had not intended any disrespect. The Uncle, Pavel Borisovich, had probably not intended any disrespect. The matter of the torn photograph.

'What about the Fräulein, the German governess?' Mrs Graham asked. 'How did this Uncle Pavel get on with her?'

Miss Kinsman paused. 'They got on together very well.'

It was nearly time for Vespers. No church bells were allowed to ring in Moscow except from the Orthodox church itself. Mrs Graham was aware of the exact time, apparently without looking, as she sat with her back to the carriage clock. At three minutes to six she began to stir, and Frank said, 'I'd better be off now, Mrs Graham. There was something I'd wanted to talk to you about, but it can very well wait till another time.'

'I shouldn't have thought it could,' said Mrs Graham. She said goodbye to him in her distinctive manner, looking down for a moment at his hand in hers as though wondering where she'd got it from, then pressing it and looking into his eyes with an assurance that he would not be forgotten.

In the hallway a door opened and the Anglican chaplain, the Reverend Edwin Graham, came out.

'Ah, Reid. You're here, Reid. Nice to see you.'

A servant brought him his galoshes and his hat and cloak. The chaplain put them on, went back into his study, came out with a few sheets of typed paper fastened with a paperclip, waved away the servant, who appeared again, thinking something more was wanted, looked round at Frank to see if he was coming to the service, waved the sheets of paper at him in ironic invitation, and made off across the square to the chapel. Frank too went off into the darkness.

He meant to go up to the Novinsky Boulevard and take a tram. That was the quickest way home, quicker, at this time in the evening, than a sledge. A senseless fear had come over him that if he stayed away too long, the children, once again, would be gone by the time he got back. Turning right up the Nikits-kaya he looked round, for no very definite reason, and saw that Miss Kinsman was behind him, threading her way efficiently between the many pedestrians. There were no drunks on this respectable street, and she made rapid progress. In Frank's opinion, she ought to have gone to Vespers. But it struck him now that Mrs Graham, who could act very quickly if she thought fit, had told Miss Kinsman, during those few minutes while he was in the hall, about his difficulties. She had tipped Miss Kinsman the wink. Everyone knew that Nellie had gone, and on this delicate subject all, apparently, were experts. With the ruthlessness of the timid, Miss Kinsman was coming after him now to suggest that she would be suitable for the post of governess at 22 Lipka Street.

And perhaps she was right, but Frank didn't feel able to think about the whole thing, much less make up his mind, at the moment. He remembered that he had given something, twenty-five roubles in fact, to the collection for her expenses and her fare to Charing Cross. He didn't grudge that at all, but, all things considered, shouldn't it have let him off? He was known in Moscow, in both the Russian business community and the English one, as a just man. He hadn't anything, quite the contrary, against Miss Kinsman. But if she had it in mind, or had had it put into her mind, to move into his house and take charge of the family, there was Dolly to be thought of. Dolly's word was not 'just' but 'fair'. She would not think it fair of him to make any arrangement with Miss Kinsman. Miss Kinsman was dowdy, another of the words that couldn't be translated into Russian, because there was no way of suggesting a dismal unfashionableness which was not intentional, not slovenly, not disreputable, but simply Miss Kinsman's way of looking like herself. Frank had never pretended to be able to answer Dolly's objections, but he knew, for the most part, what they would be. On the other hand, what was there to stop him from letting Miss Kinsman overtake him and finding out from her quite clearly – for he could, after all, be wrong, – exactly what she wanted?

There was nothing to stop him, but he turned into a side-street. He might as well go to the Povarskaya and catch his tram lower down the Boulevard. In that way he'd avoid Miss Kinsman, and would never have to speak to her at all. She wouldn't have to brood on the matter of Mr Reid's odd behaviour. Really it would be sparing her distress.

Everyone took short cuts in Moscow. The tram numbers, except for the line round the boulevards, were frequently changed, and unless you felt like paying for a sledge or a cab you were bound to spend a good deal of time on foot. But once you were off the main streets you had to know (since it could scarcely be explained) the way. Street names soon ran out. You were faced by towering heaps of bricks and drain-pipes, or a lean-to which encroached on the pavement, or a steaming cowshed whose rotten planks seemed to breathe in and out under their own volition. All these things, which had no legal right to be there and were unknown to any map, had to be imagined away if you wanted to steer a true course. There might be no alternative to walking through one door of a temporary building and out at the other. The turning Frank had reached was, he knew, Katsap Pereulok, although there was no trace of a sign. The passageway was filled, like a gully, with pearly darkness. There was a light on the corner, though not a municipal one, only a kerosene lamp fixed low on the wall. He looked back; Miss Kinsman, in her felt hat and winter overcoat, was just turning into the passage.

Not only good sense, but ordinary politeness told Frank that he must speak to this woman and offer to take her back to Povarskaya. She looked lamentably out of place in this unsavoury lane, struggling to put up her umbrella, although no snow was falling. But if she'd come as far as this, she must know the way back, and if she couldn't catch up with him, she could go back to the chaplaincy. I shouldn't like to try and give a connected account of what I'm doing, he thought. I shouldn't, for example, like to give an account of it to Tvyordov. But I'm being hunted. She's hunting me down, like a bill-collector. Instead of turning right, back to the boulevards, he went left, through a narrow opening, towards the Kremlin. He was going twice as far as he needed to, because of this hunting process. But poor woman, surely she can't come much farther.

Kolbasov Pereulok. The name was painted up, but ahead of him access was narrowed down by towering piles of sacks on either side, as if the two houses opposite each other, dimly lighted, were in competition to block out each other's windows. There was a reek of tar and frying buckwheat pancakes (Frank sighed with hunger). Once into the lane, the ground floors of the houses became shops, with windows half below the pavement level. There was no way of telling what they dealt in. Very likely they were repair shops, there was nothing you couldn't get repaired in Moscow, a city which in its sluggish, maternal way cared, as well as for the rich, for the poorest of the poor. Bring me your broken shoes, your worn-out mattresses, your legless chairs, your headless beds, and in some basement workshop or hole in the wall, I will make them serviceable, at least for a few months or so. They will be fit to use, or at least fit to take to the pawnbroker's.

On the corner there was a Monopoly, a government vodka shop. It was small, but brightly lit. Inside, a woman of great size and strength, wrapped in a black knitted shawl, sat on a stool behind a wooden partition with a small window in it, wired in, like a ticket office. There was nowhere to sit down. Men and women waited with empty bottles or leaned uncertainly against the wooden walls. The exact money had to be counted out before the taps behind the partition were unlocked.

Miss Kinsman, Frank was convinced, and the conviction came with a rush of relief, would never risk walking past this place. If she did she was an impostor, with no right to her felt hat and her dowdiness and the touching stories she had told at the chaplaincy. And it came to him that, more than anyone else he'd ever encountered in Moscow, Miss Kinsman was like his second cousin Amy in Nottingham, younger, but like cousin Amy, who crossed the road rather than go past a public house because she believed that if she did, the doors might open and men would stumble out to piss and inside she would glimpse women stabbing each other with hat-pins. Whether this really ever happened to his cousin he didn't know. He usually wrote to her regularly, as he did to all of them, but hadn't this month, and the slight physical sensation, not of guilt, but of feeling he ought to feel guilty, turned into a considerable irritation. Still he was almost in the clear now. The Monopoly, as usual, was on the corner of the main street, in case people started drinking on the premises, and the police had to be called in. He had come out on Znamenkaya, which when you considered that he ought to be home by now, was ridiculous. But he was free now and his mind went back to his own troubles, or rather let them rise from where they had been waiting to the surface.

He was heading towards the river, and the air was full of the vast reverberations of the bells from the five golden domes of the church of the Redeemer, not at anything like their full power, but like the first barrage of artillery before the main attack. The attack did not come – it was Lent, and they chimed only once, but they were answered from across the river by a hundred others, always with one chime only. He stood listening to the bells in the open starlight. From the cathedral square a ramp went down to the water. The river ran darkly, still choked with the winter's majestic breaking ice and the debris carried along with it, an inconceivable amount of rubbish – baskets, crates, way-posts, wash-tubs, wheels, cradles, the last traces of the traffic the ice had carried while, for four months, it was a high-road. Watching the breaking ice from the bridges was one of Moscow's favourite occupations. The *Gazeta-Kopeika* said that a pair of dead lovers, clutched together, had floated by, frozen into the ice. The *Gazeta* repeated this story every spring.

There was no bridge here, but from the towpath someone, at some time, had fenced off a piece of the river with wooden stakes. A dilapidated gangway led out from the towpath to a raft, floating on empty kerosene drums. It had a roof of sorts, and people fished there. Frank had often fished from it himself, without a permit, when he was a schoolboy. Up till March, of course, you had to make your own hole in the ice. Although he was in a hurry, the relief from tension made him slow down, and he walked down to the platform to watch the ice for a while. You had to get through the piled snow at the river's edge and then there was just a two-foot drop on to the sodden platform which oozed and creaked beneath you. He stood there, with the half-frozen wooden slats vibrating beneath him, and the church bells sounding more clearly, a kind of distant hum, as the Redeemer fell silent. Then he walked the length of the gangway. When he stopped he heard another, lighter creaking as Miss Kinsman jumped down behind him.

She came purposefully towards him, not out of breath, her umbrella folded now. Frank reflected that he was caught. The place was a kind of fish-trap anyway, he'd known that since he was ten, and now he was trapped himself and must put the best face on it he could.

'Have you been trying to catch up with me, Miss Kinsman? I'm afraid I didn't see you.'

The frosty night air was as keen as a needle. She stood there, and answered him mildly, without a hint of complaint.

'Yes, I have. I think you did see me.'

They were standing together under the ramshackle roof, and she was settling down like a fowl in a fowl-house, brushing off first one shoulder of her overcoat, then the other, although snow had not been falling.

'I'm afraid it must have meant coming through some rather rough-looking streets,' he said.

'Poor, but I shouldn't call them rough.'

'There was the Monopoly.'

'Oh, I don't mind the Monopolies. They're not like English public-houses. They're not allowed to drink on the premises, you know. They have to take the vodka at least a hundred metres away before they start drinking. And it's such stuff, have you ever tried it?'

Frank had. 'It does what it's always said to do, and what it's manufactured to do. That's the trouble, perhaps.'

'And the woman in there, she was a Tatar woman, that means she's a Muslim, you know, she's forbidden to drink by the Prophet. The Prophet, you know,' she repeated, nodding emphatically.

'But did you want to speak to me?' he asked, and added, 'about anything in particular?'

She looked at him closely and said 'No.'

'You've nothing to say to me?'

'Oh, you needn't have been afraid of that,' she added. 'I didn't want to talk to you, I wanted to talk to Mr Frank Reid.'

'Who did Mrs Graham say I was?' Frank asked.

'I didn't quite catch. So often one doesn't quite catch! And then she had to go to Vespers. But, you see, it's a matter of some urgency. Really, my passage for England is booked for tomorrow, if I can't find any other employment here, that is. All I need is his address, Mr Reid's address. That, of course, you must have, as you're one of the business community here, even though he must be a younger man than yourself.' She looked at him from the deeper shadow of her hat. 'I wouldn't have troubled you, only I should have to speak to him tonight.'

'What makes you think he's younger than I am?' Frank asked.

'He has young children, I know that. Otherwise I shouldn't need to speak to him.'

Frank considered for a moment.

'I'm sorry to disappoint you, Miss Kinsman, but I'm sure that this wouldn't be a good moment to speak to Frank Reid.'

'Is he out of Moscow, then?'

'Well –'

'Ultimately, you see, nobody is interested in me but myself. Certainly you, a total stranger, can't possibly be. But I have to make do with the material I have.'

'Miss Kinsman. I'm quite sure that if you did see Frank Reid, it wouldn't lead to anything. I know him quite well enough for that.'

She looked at him searchingly. He offered to see her back to the nearest tram-stop. She shook her head, and trudged off across the gangway and up the slippery ramp, towards the Redeemer. Until she was out of sight all he could do was to stand there like an idiot, pretending to watch the ice.

10

THE NEXT morning, as Frank discovered from ringing up the chaplaincy, Miss Kinsman left very early for the Alexander station. Mrs Graham said, 'Really, I expected to read something about you in the *Gazeta-Kopeika*. Everyone thought you were going to push her into the river.'

'Who's everyone? There was no one there.'

'Oh, people on the towpath, you know.'

'What were they doing?'

'Watching the ice.'

'Mrs Graham, I got the impression that Miss Kinsman wanted to have a post with me in Lipka Street, as governess to my children.'

'Oh, I should never have suggested that myself. After all, I know why she had to leave her other place. The matter of the bath house.'

At lunchtime, at Reidka's, he tried to put his case – largely to put it to himself – to Selwyn, who said, 'I don't remember a fishing-place like that near the Redeemer. I thought the banks were supposed to be kept clear.'

'It's surprising what the police will overlook if there's no trouble. It's been there for twenty-five years at least, I expect they've got used to it. But it doesn't matter about the place. I can show it to you anytime you like. It's just that I feel I haven't behaved even reasonably well to this woman, but I don't know where she's going when she arrives in England, and if I did I shouldn't know what to do about it.'

'You're thinking of sending her money.'

'Money isn't such a bad thing as people make out.'

'It doesn't heal the spirit, Frank.'

Frank shifted his ground.

'I suppose she must be getting on for fifty. It doesn't seem a good time for disappointment. I suppose, I mean, if you're younger, there's more chance of things getting better.'

'How old are you, Frank?'

'That's another thing, she seemed to think I looked older than I am. Perhaps I do, I don't know.'

It was five o'clock. Selwyn locked the safe and the cupboard where the account books were kept and, although he was always due at some meeting or concert or other, sat down again to give counsel.

'Your difficulty in making up your mind what to do about Miss Kinsman is a reflection of your difficulty in deciding what to do about Nellie. Am I right in thinking that you don't know all her motives? And will you let me say that you would reach a conclusion more quickly if you considered yourself less – if you thought, as each solution presented itself – who will be wounded by this? and whose heart will be made lighter?'

'I'm thinking about my children,' said Frank. 'I was thinking about them when Nellie left. I thought about them when this woman tracked me down through the back streets of the Tverskaya. Who else is going to think about them?'

'Frank, give me your hand.'

Selwyn's hand was lean and spindle-fingered, the palm hardened by grasping his pilgrim's staff through hundreds of versts of summer tramping. He sighed, and gently let go again.

'Frank, not so very long ago I acted in a manner which I had never, up till then, considered excusable. I have known a number of people who acted in the same way, and though I would not have thought it right to condemn them, I would never have approved of what they did, and I would have done all I could not to act in a like manner. The strange thing is that, as you know, I've been for a number of years now under the influence of Lev Nicolaevich, and have made up my mind, and indeed my whole being, towards a worthier mode of life and one which would be of more use to my fellow creatures. Yet now I was apparently reverting to a former attitude, one that

I held when I was a younger man. I'm speaking of the sexual impulse, Frank, and its gratification.'

'Well, I thought you must be,' said Frank.

'At that time I thought that both men and women benefited from a multiplication of joyous relationships. But I had come to see how wrong that is. My predicament was, then, how to act in order to cause as little pain as possible and, above all, what I should tell the human beings concerned.'

'I don't know what you had to tell them,' said Frank.

'You would have been as puzzled as I was?'

'I'm puzzled as it is.'

'But I haven't distressed you by what I've been saying? You haven't taken offence?'

'How could anyone take offence at you, Selwyn? You might as well take offence at a drink of cold water.'

Selwyn gave a melancholy smile. 'We must go back to the subject later.' He seemed reluctant to leave, a symptom which Frank recognised at once. At length he said, in a lowered voice, almost a reverent voice, 'How is it going, Frank? Has it been set up?'

He meant, Frank knew, the *Birch Tree Thoughts*. 'I'm trying to get the loan of some European type, Selwyn, you know that. Sytin's have some, but they won't lend it. We may have to try in Petersburg. Tvyordov will set it up for you, he won't mind what language it's in, and of course the boy won't be able to read the proofs, but I can leave that to you. We can hand-print it on the Albion.'

'The punctuation may give trouble, I know that. It happens that I –' he took a manuscript notebook out of his breast pocket, opened it – but it seemed to open itself at the required place – and handed it to Frank, who, aware that he hadn't been grateful enough for Selwyn's ready sympathy over Miss Kinsman, took it and read aloud:

'Dost feel the cold, sister birch?'
　　'No, Brother Snow,
I feel it not.' 'What? not?' 'No, not!'

'Are you sure that's right, Selwyn?'

'What would you say is amiss?'

'I'm not quite sure.'

'Wasn't I successful in conveying my meaning?'

'It seems a bit repetitive.'

Selwyn took back the notebook, as though he did not like to see it in less expert hands, and Frank, saying that he'd lock up, was left alone in the darkened building, to look through the various offers of his paper suppliers. Paper from Finland was the cheapest by far, but the Tsar might decide to legislate against it. There was another offer, too, for the Mammoth, this time from Kuriatin, who thought he had discovered a purchaser in Tokyo, but as he had no licence to export, everything would have to be done through a third party.

This brought Frank's mind, for a moment, back to the ruined crockery and tablecloths. He had discovered why Kuriatin set so much store by them. Like more important merchants than himself – Tretyakov, Kutzenov, Botkin – he had put aside part of his possessions to give to the People if necessary, thus showing his goodwill towards them.

'All for them, and the embroideries, and the pictures, and the portrait of my wife by Bogdanov-Belsky. Let the people treasure them, and let them remember Kuriatin!'

But there were other things he had earmarked to take with him if history turned against him and the family had to go into exile – the damask tablecloths, in particular, although there were only twenty-three of them. Before he came from his village in Orel, Kuriatin had never seen such things, not even on the altar at Easter.

11

'CERTAINLY SOME woman must come into your house to care for your children,' said Selwyn, calling round that evening. 'When a woman leads a little child by the hand she ensures your future, just as when she serves you food and drink she bids you live.'

'She hasn't got to do that,' Frank said, 'but I want them kept happy, and they won't be happy running riot. And I want someone who'll speak good Russian to them. Their life is here in Moscow, for the time being anyway.'

'The young woman I have in mind speaks very pure Russian, Frank, in spite of everything.'

'In spite of what?'

'She has had some education, at one time they wanted to make a teacher of her. I'm sure she's capable of a responsible position. But she is unfortunate.'

'I don't want anyone too unfortunate about the place. What went wrong?'

'She is young –'

'How young?'

'I would say she is nineteen or twenty, and she is poor. There can be no higher claim on any of us, surely, than youth and poverty.'

'Where does she come from?'

'Vladimir.'

'Where they're mostly carpenters.'

'Yes, Lisa Ivanovna is a joiner's daughter.' Selwyn moved his head very slightly from side to side, as though in time to music.

'Did you meet her in Vladimir?'

'No, I met her in Muir and Merrilees, at the handkerchief counter. Yes, she is in charge of the gentlemen's handkerchiefs. I told you that she could manage a responsible position.'

'You picked her up at Muirka's.'

'She was shedding tears. That was enough for me, as it should be for us all, for us all.'

'You mean she'd been fired?'

'Not at all, it was simply that she's not used to living in a great city, and she feels oppressed, like any other child of nature.'

'Did she tell you that?'

'No, that is what I sensed.'

'They pay them quite fairly at Muirka's,' said Frank. 'That's to say, as wages go here. And they get a discount on staff purchases. But I think I ought to try and find someone older and perhaps a bit more fortunate. She sounds as though she'd need looking after herself.'

'But you mustn't think of it as a question of your own convenience.'

'What else is it?'

'Try to put aside this consideration of self.'

Soothe him, Frank thought. 'Well, it wouldn't be for very long, in any case.'

'You've heard from Nellie, then?'

'I haven't heard.'

'You're expecting her back, though?'

'I'm always expecting her.'

'What am I to say, then, to Lisa Ivanovna?'

'The worst thing about you, Selwyn, is that you make everyone else feel guilty. I feel guilty now. You'd better bring this girl to see me.'

'And when shall I do that?'

'Well, when does Muirka's shut? Half-past six. Bring her to the house, when she gets off work. I don't want her in the office. We'll have to see what she thinks of the children.'

'You have a good heart, Frank. Many men, most men I fancy, would have said, "We'll have to see what the children think of her," or even "We'll have to see what I think of her." '

'I don't want to have to think about her at all,' said Frank. 'I'm at the end of my wits.'

He had the impression that they were avoiding an important aspect of the subject, but felt too tired to work out what it was.

When Selwyn brought Lisa into the living room at 22 Lipka Street, Frank thought that she looked less unpromising than he'd expected. How unjust (or unfair) that was, to ask someone to live up to a promise about which they knew nothing, and yet that was what interviewing usually came down to. It was her hair that surprised him. As a shop assistant, she must have worn it rolled up. Old Merrilees would never permit anything else behind the counters. But her hair now, her thick fair hair, which gleamed in the electric light, pale blonde on one side, palely shadowed on the other, was parted in the middle and fell in two flaxen pigtails like a peasant's or rather like a peasant in a ballet. He didn't think he'd be able to put up with this.

She had the pale, broad, patient, dreaming Russian face, and it struck him that it reminded him of another face which he had seen recently, though he couldn't remember when or where. She wore her black shop assistant's dress with a lilac-coloured shawl over it, and plain gold rings in her ears. Selwyn's description of her had suggested that she might turn up fainting, possibly in rags, but when she took off her shawl she looked like any other employee at Muirka's.

Selwyn proposed that they should all sit down. Lisa Ivanovna looked astonished, then her expression became serene and, once again, calmly receptive. She sat in the armchair nearest to her, which had always been Nellie's. But Lisa was taller, as well as broader, than Nellie, so that her head came almost to the top of the chair-back. She sat, not at all stiffly, but absolutely still, all, so to speak, in one piece. Nellie had never been much of a sitter-still. She was a jumper-up and walker-about.

When Frank spoke to Lisa directly she turned politely towards him, but her self-possession produced a curious effect, as though, in spite of the politeness, she was listening to something else a little beyond his range.

'Are you used to looking after children?' he began, but Selwyn, leaning forward, interrupted rapidly in English.

'Frank, I work as your accountant, as I did for your father before you, and I do my best in that capacity, but in the present matter you must think of me as an older brother.'

Lisa was not embarrassed by these remarks which she could not understand. Evidently she had the gift of quiet. She waited without any particular expression, but not with the passive air of someone about to be disposed of.

'All I ask,' Selwyn went on, 'is that you should make it clear that the atmosphere is one of hope, and that you have no shadow of doubt that you will soon be reunited with your own wife. I'm speaking to you freely.'

'I should have thought we could have taken that for granted.'

Selwyn subsided. Now that he saw everything was going well, his mind was turning to his next charitable enterprise. With the terrible aimlessness of the benevolent, he was casting round for a new misfortune.

Frank tried again. 'Lisa Ivan'na, are you used to looking after children? Have you ever done it before?'

'Yes, I have younger brothers and sisters.'

'Did you find it hard work?'

'It's hard work looking after one child. It's quite easy if there are several.'

'Is that so?' asked Selwyn, his attention caught. 'I should have thought the opposite.'

'Well, I've got three of them,' Frank persisted. 'You'll see them in a minute. My wife has been called away urgently to England. The youngest one needs looking after sensibly while the others are in school, and I suppose she might be taught a few letters and numbers. When they come back from school, at midday, they'll want to go skating, if the ice is holding anywhere, or a walk in the Prechistnaya.'

'Should you want me to live in this house?'

'Where are you living at the moment?'

'I'm in the female assistants' dormitory, on the top floor of Muir and Merrilees.' She added, 'I should prefer to live in your house.'

'We shan't need to go for a walk in the Prechistnaya,' said Ben, coming into the room. 'Dolly won't walk unless she's going somewhere, and there's only one place I want to go, and that's the Nobel garage in the Petrovka.'

'Go and fetch Dolly.'

'And Annushka?'

'Yes, and Annushka.'

Ben disappeared, and Selwyn got to his feet. 'Your decision is as good as made,' he said. 'I'll be on my way.' He was going to the Foundling Hospital. Wrong, of course, to feel impatient with him or to criticise him as he hurried, on errands of mercy, to the hidden rooms of the poor, the unlucky, and the bereaved into which he could pass, although a foreigner, with charmed steps. This, to be sure, was partly because he was often thought to be touched by the finger of God.

As the three children came back, Annushka silent under Dolly's stern control, it struck Frank that they should be showing, so much more than they did, the effect of motherlessness. They ought either to be quieter or more noisy than before, and it was disconcerting that they seemed to be exactly the same. He would have been heartbroken if they had shown the least symptom of unhappiness, but was disturbed because they didn't. Annushka was, perhaps, wearing too many shawls and too many layers of clothing in the efficiently-heated house, and she had two holy medals round her neck now as well as her gold cross, but she looked pampered rather than neglected, and as if she were enjoying herself.

'This is Dolly,' he began.

'Dolly is Darya?' Lisa asked.

'Yes, Darya, Dasha, Dashenka. But I'm English, and I'm Dolly.'

'Dolly, this is Lisa Ivanovna. She's coming to look after you for, I don't know how long for, as long as is necessary, perhaps a few weeks, it might be longer than a few weeks.'

Dolly and Lisa, as was correct, shook hands, and the two self-contained creatures stood for a moment opposite each other, in the green-shaded lamplight, reserving judgement.

'Ben, shake hands with Lisa Ivanovna,' Frank said.

'Are you going to live in our house?' asked Ben.

'I think so.'

'It would be better if you made up your mind.'

'You don't know what would be better for me,' said Lisa equably. 'You've never seen me before.'

'Yes, I have. I've seen you at Muirka's.'

'At the handkerchief counter,' Dolly added.

'Have you ever noticed us?' Ben asked. 'We go there quite often.'

'No, I haven't. I'm sorry if I'm disappointing you.'

'You're not disappointing us,' said Dolly. 'We want to know whether you're observant or not.'

Frank felt that Lisa would find looking after the children easier if she got used to the way their minds worked. Nellie had said to him often that she didn't know where they got it from and that although she didn't want them to grow like her own family, she hoped that at least they'd grow less unlike other people's children. And yet she had left them, she had sent them back on the train from Mozhaisk, like parcels.

He suggested that Lisa should go and give notice to Muir and Merrilees, and take up her duties in Lipka Street next Monday.

'Yes, I must work my week out.'

'Bring all your things on Monday. You'll have a room to yourself here.'

She looked, for the first time, appalled, and he realised that she had never, either in her village or in Moscow, slept in a room by herself before.

The children had gone off to the kitchens, where he knew they would be demanding bread dipped in tea and joining in a discussion of Lisa Ivanovna. Voices could be heard, louder and softer as the kitchen doors opened and shut to admit more people. Perhaps children were better off without a sense of pity. And then again perhaps Lisa didn't need pity, and he remembered that Selwyn had been about to tell him, but hadn't reached the point of telling him, why he had said she was unfortunate, and why she had been in tears behind the counter at Muirka's.

They had settled her wages at four roubles, sixty-seven kopeks a week, the same as she'd been getting at the store, but with no deduction, of course, for board and lodging. Although he did not feel particularly proud of the offer, he could see that she thought it more than fair.

'There's only one other thing, Lisa Ivanovna. Your hair.'

'Yes?'

'I'd rather it wasn't in plaits.' He wasn't compelled to give a reason, and he didn't give one. She nodded to show that she understood. 'Is there anything more you want to ask me?'

'Yes, do you have a dacha?'

'Yes, we do have one, at Beryoznyk. The children like it, of course, but I don't go there much myself. I'd really prefer to get rid of it, it's so damp, but I don't have to think about that yet, it's still winter.'

'It's nearly spring.'

He hoped she wasn't going to start contradicting him, also that she might smile occasionally. What he couldn't imagine was her shedding tears, in Muirka's or anywhere else. The outside world didn't seem to make enough impression on her for that.

12

FRANK RANG up Kuriatin to ask him whether there was any further news of the Japanese offer for the Mammoth. 'If you can't get an export certificate I'll have to look elsewhere. I have to clear the land, then let the site and the workshops together. There's been an opportunity cost of three thousand roubles a year on that site ever since my father died. I'd rather sell, of course.'

'And the trees, what about the trees?'

'They go with the site, of course, but they're not much, a few willows and alders.'

'More than a few, Frank Albertovich.'

Like all merchants, and all peasants, Kuriatin was obsessed with the chance to cut down trees. A dream of buying the site had begun to torment him. As to the Mammoth, Frank had not expected a direct reply quite yet. But neither had he expected Kuriatin to change the subject abruptly, and to say, with a laugh which seemed to blast the fragile telephone system, 'And so you are suited? No more English governesses, no more old women.'

'I've found a girl, yes. She's not a governess.'

'Let me tell you a story from the district of Orel, from my part of the country,' shouted Kuriatin. 'What does it show? Why, simply the necessity of ruling in one's own house. A peasant took a young woman to wife...'

Kuriatin frequently told these stories, though, to do him justice, Frank had never heard him tell the same one twice. This might simply be because they weren't, as he always claimed they were, from the district of Orel, but invented to suit the occasion.

'With a hundred other women to choose from he took a lazy one, a lazy girl who did everything in the house as badly as possible, and made him sell his horse to buy her fine clothes. Meanwhile the bread she made was so heavy that it had to be thrown to the pig, and the pig died in great pain. And the linen she spun was so coarse that when the husband got into bed with his wife the sheets tore off his skin. In the end he said to the woman, "You have caused me to sell the horse, the pig is dead and you have borne no children. So now you can get between the shafts and live on oats and rye, and do a horse's work." In this way he showed he was master in his own house. Remember that story, because there's a great deal of benefit to be got from it.'

'There's no benefit at all,' Frank replied. 'I object to it in principle and in detail.'

'You don't understand it. You have no peasants in England, and therefore no stories.'

'We have plenty of stories,' said Frank, 'but the woman always comes off best.'

'All the more reason to remember this one.'

At the Press the work went forward with a satisfactory lack of incident, making a pattern of its own, from the entries in the order book through to the finished orders, checked, counted and stacked for delivery. There was only one problem, he told Tvyordov, and that was the European type for the hand-printing of *Birch Tree Thoughts*. Still, there were several places he hadn't tried yet.

Tvyordov was distributing, and went on rattling back the type, without looking at the labels, while the difficulty was put to him. Apparently it did not interest him, or rather there was something else which interested him more. Still rattling away, he said, 'A man lives under the rule of nature. He can't look after children, and he can't live alone.'

'Why not?' Frank asked. 'Selwyn Osipych lives alone.'

'Perhaps, but he's a man of God.'

'I can't see why a man shouldn't live alone, whoever he is, as long as he stays sober.'

'That's what you say, Frank Albertovich, but your wife left only a few days ago and you've taken a woman into your house already.'

Tvyordov said this in no spirit of reproach. When you looked at it, his opinion was not very different from Kuriatin's.

Far more important, as far as Frank's peace of mind was concerned, was the judgement of the household in Lipka Street. This depended on Toma and the cook, and to some extent on the yard dog, Blashl, a loyal but very foolish animal whose attachments were intense. The yardman had no opinion apart from Blashl's. Toma, speaking for all, but without explaining how they reached their conclusions, reported to Frank that they would be glad to welcome Lisa Ivanovna next Monday.

'Well, did she come?' Frank asked that evening. The children were waiting round the supper table, which was already laid with several kinds of bread and a dish for cold boiled cabbage dressed, as it was Lent, with sunflower oil instead of butter. Ben was complaining that Annushka wanted, against all precedent, to say grace. 'Oh Lord Jesus, who with five loaves and two fishes,' gabbled the stoutly-built little girl.

'She doesn't understand what she's talking about,' said Ben.

Frank was overcome with the same uneasiness that he had felt when the Chaplain had waved his sermon at him, amiably enough, but without expectations. Lukewarm, but not quite cold, unbelieving, but not quite disbelieving, he had fallen into the habit of not asking himself what he thought.

'It won't do any harm if she says grace,' he said.

'It doesn't mean anything,' said Dolly, looking up for the first time. 'My teacher says there is no God.'

'I never heard anything about this before.'

'Oh, Lord Jesus, who with five loaves . . .' persisted Annushka.

'I have a different teacher this year,' said Dolly. 'Last year, we had Anastasia Sergeevna, this year we have Katya Alexeevna.'

'She's ugly,' said Ben, 'she's got enough black hair on her arms to stuff a mattress.'

Dolly ignored him. 'She's thought about everything for a long time, and she says there is no God.'

Lisa came into the room. She turned towards Frank, simply to make sure who was supposed to be keeping order, but the gesture seemed to be enough in itself, and the children, who had really wanted to fall silent, fell silent. So too did Frank, because Lisa had cut off her hair. Perhaps she had got someone else to cut it off for her, because it seemed to have fallen acceptably into shape.

'That's how my teacher's hair is cut,' said Dolly. Frank was not sure whether the resemblance frightened her, or not.

Quiet had descended, the room was at peace, and everybody sat down to eat. Frank tried to avoid looking at Lisa. Cutting her hair had made a great difference to her appearance. Her great beauty was her eyes, which were not particularly large and quite close together, but a long oval in shape and dark grey in colour, with dark lashes, the lower lid raised a little, as though she was always expecting to look into a bright light. It must be awkward for her at first, with all of them sitting round. When he did take a glance at her, though, it occurred to him how much a person's face changes at mealtimes. Lisa's face, so pale, so placid, so undisturbed even by speaking and smiling, was distorted now by the large piece of white bread she had crammed in, and her right cheek jutted out while her fine young jaws moved mechanically to and fro and her white throat dilated in the task of swallowing potato soup. 'Well, the girl's got to keep alive,' he thought. And it might be that she was hungry. Certainly Lisa wasn't worried by what he might be thinking of her. Perhaps she thought that he ought to be satisfied with her as she was, or more likely she wasn't thinking of him at all. After all, she had been hired, on a temporary basis and for an agreed weekly wage, to look after the children. And with her beautiful hair gone, she ought to look less interesting. He wished that this was so.

Toma brought in a platter of the fish from which the soup had been made, and set it on the sideboard. Like the soup tureen, it was one of the set Nellie had brought with her, first to Germany, then to Moscow – Staffordshire, given to them by Charlie. It had been held up at the customs for goodness knows how long, because the removal people had wrapped it in English newspapers, and they'd had to wait until the Russian censors had read, or said they had read, every line and every word.

Off came the lid of the tureen with a wild escape of steam, smelling of fish like a wharf at sunset. Each of them had a plateful except Annushka, who had a small saucer, not part of the set. She began to wail.

'You oughtn't to be here at all,' Dolly told her. 'We love you, but you're superfluous.'

Annushka cried more loudly, and Lisa got up silently and led her out of the room.

'Keep something hot for Lisa Ivanovna,' said Frank.

When they were out of the room he took the opportunity to ask Dolly about her new teacher.

'Doesn't the priest come round classes?'

'Oh, Batiushka!' said Dolly. 'Yes, he comes round, but he's afraid of women politicals. He's afraid of my teacher.'

'If she was a political she wouldn't be working at your school.' It seemed, however, that this teacher had spent some time the year before in exile, as a suspected person, in a village somewhere on the river Yemtsa. 'The government allowed her thirteen roubles a month, and a grant for extra winter clothes, but she didn't buy any.'

'She's dowdy,' said Ben.

'You only get eight roubles as an exile if you're of peasant origin,' Dolly went on. 'But then, of course, you can earn money working in the potato fields.'

'Lisa Ivanovna's of peasant origin,' said Ben. 'That's her status. It's on her papers.'

'Have you been looking at them?'

'No, we asked her.'

'That's enough,' said Frank.

'It'll be all right when she comes downstairs again,' said Dolly. And indeed a curious peace entered the room with Lisa, curious to Frank because he felt it, at the same time, a disturbance. She had put Annushka to bed, and as she began to eat her fish, Frank saw that he was right, and she had been hungry. 'But there's no need for that,' he thought. The assistants had to pay for their meals at Muirka's, but the staff restaurant was subsidised, like his own canteen at the Press. If she hadn't had enough to eat there, whose fault was it but hers, and what had she spent her wages on? To keep the conversation going, he said, 'I see you've had your hair cut, Lisa Ivanovna.'

'We all of us wish you hadn't,' said Ben.

'Well, if I made a mistake, it will grow again,' said Lisa.

She ought to look at him, it seemed to Frank, with some kind of bewilderment or reproach, or at least put her hand up to the back of her head which was what all women did when their hair was mentioned.

'You look like a student,' said Ben. 'All you need is my gun.' He produced a toy revolver, made of wood and tin. 'It's a Webley, that's what all the students have now. I got it at the Japanese shop near the Kuznetsky Bridge.'

'I thought they sold kites there,' said Frank.

'They do,' said Ben. 'I don't want a kite.'

'Lisa cut off her hair because you didn't like it the way it was when she first came here,' said Dolly. 'You ought to say something about it.'

'I imagine Lisa doesn't want to sit here and listen to these remarks,' said Frank. 'Who would? I certainly shouldn't.'

'I don't mind being told that I look like a student,' said Lisa. 'I should like to have studied. But I shouldn't want to look like something that I'm not.'

– How could you look like something that you aren't? – Frank wanted, not to cry out, but to observe quite calmly. – What you are, Lisa Ivanovna, is solid flesh inside your clothes, within arm's length, or nearly, in all the glory of solid flesh, lessened a bit by your idiotically cutting off your hair – you must have known that wasn't what I meant, so why did you let them take the scissors to you? – lessened a bit perhaps, but solid still. But I can only recognise what's solid by touching it, which in this particular case, to be honest, would be by no means enough.

'What did you do with it?' asked Ben. 'Did you sell it? You have to have it off if you've had typhoid, but then it isn't worth anything.'

Before he shut up the house for the night Frank took the opportunity to say to Lisa, 'I'm sorry you never managed to study, if that's what you wanted to do. If you need help, or if you need anything else, anything at all, please ask me.' He expected her to reply with the well-tried phrases 'You're very good,' or 'You're a good man, Frank Albertovich,' but instead she said that there were people who needed help more than she did. That's unquestionably true, he thought, and perhaps I'm one of them. But he felt disconcerted.

13

THERE WAS nothing wrong, nothing that you could lay a finger on, in the way Selwyn did his work at Reidka's, but the imminent birth of his first volume had unsettled him. Middle-aged poets, middle-aged parents, have no defences. When the *Birch Tree Thoughts* were printed, sewn, bound, pressed and distributed to the better-class bookshops on the Lubyanka, he would have anxieties, but at least they would be different ones. Meanwhile, however, he had begun to speak of a German version – which would mean borrowing yet another set of type – and a Russian one. It was these two projects which had driven Frank to the idea of taking on a second accountant. The profits at Reidka's would just about bear the additional salary. He had had to do this without hurting Selwyn's feelings, but Selwyn was not a vain man.

'You understand that Bernov will be the costing accountant, something we've never had. He won't be concerned with the management, though we'll have to listen to his advice.'

'Yes . . . yes . . . where did you find him, Frank?'

'He's coming to us from Sytin's, a very small firm after a very big one, but I daresay that'll give him more opportunity.'

'From Sytin's! He'll find it another world. When is he coming to the Press?'

'I've got him down for the 27th of March, Russian calendar.'

'Excellent, excellent . . . But, Frank, that's the Feast of St Modestus. There'll be the blessing of the office ikon.'

'Not till the afternoon, they've agreed to work normal hours till four. It's not a church holiday. We'll have all day to show Bernov how we do things.'

Frank knew that Selwyn ought to have been present when he interviewed the alert, ambitious, bright-eyed Bernov, and he felt a pang of shame when Selwyn put only one more question: 'Would you say that this young man has been touched to any extent by the teachings of Tolstoy?' He had to say that he didn't know, but thought it unlikely.

'But you wouldn't call him a quarrelsome fellow?'

'He didn't quarrel with me when I saw him.'

All that had been fixed before Nellie went away, in what, if time were space, would be a different continent. Every day he sent her a letter which, for 8 kopeks, included a blank reply form. He had mentioned that there was a girl now, a Russian girl, to look after the children. He had, of course, no address for Nellie except Charlie's, where he imagined the envelopes piling up in the hall under the multi-coloured light from the stained-glass window above the front door. Dolly and Ben also wrote once, and Annushka added a wavering Russian A. Frank did not know what Dolly had put, and thought it dishonourable to try to find out. She had asked him how 'irresponsible' was spelled. But this letter, too, would come to rest in the hall, in Charlie's brass dish.

'You lose your wife, you take on a new clerk,' Kuriatin shouted down the telephone, to which he'd never got accustomed. 'Why do you need more staff?'

'You'd be just as suspicious if I got rid of the lot of them,' said Frank.

'It's only that I understand the printing business. The great ones are expanding, the little foreigners like you have to watch out for themselves.'

'You don't understand printing in the least, Arkady Filippovich. You'd have been exactly the same if it had never been invented.'

'I want to see you. We will speak of all these things at Rusalochka's.'

'We can speak, if you like,' said Frank. 'But at Rusalochka's we shan't be able to hear each other.'

During the forty-nine days of Lent entertainments were supposed to be cut down, and some of Moscow's restaurants were closed, but not Rusalochka's, the tea-rooms attached to the Merchants' Club. 'Come to Rusalochka's,' repeated Kuriatin, 'we will settle our business there once and for all.'

Frank tried as far as possible to avoid this place, which conflicted with his idea of what was sensible and his preference for a quiet life. Since it was supposed to be devoted to tea-drinking, the walls were frescoed from smoky ceiling to floor in red-gold and silver-gold and painted with dancing, embracing and tea-swilling figures overlapping with horses, horse-collars with golden bells, warriors, huts prancing along on chickens' legs, simpering children, crowned frogs, dying swans, exultant storks and naked women laughing in apparent satisfaction and veiled, to a slight extent, by the clouds of a glowing sunset. Service at Rusalochka's was in principle a simple matter, since nothing was served but tea, cakes, vodka and *listofka*, *slievanka*, *vieshnyovka* and *beryozovitsa*, the liqueurs of the currant-leaf, plum, cherry and birch-sap. But the great silver teapots, each like a kettle-drum on its wheeled stand, crossed and recrossed the aisles between the tables, which became smaller and smaller as the room filled up, only avoiding collision with each other and the trollies of strong alcohol through the manipulation of the waiters, who seemed to be chosen for strength rather than skill, and as a result of the threats and warnings of the customers bellowing either for further orders or, as it seemed, to encourage the racing teapots, as in a sporting event. The customers registered only as the opening and closing of mouths, all sound and sense being drowned by Rusalochka's mighty Garmoni-phon, the great golden organ which with its soaring array of Garmonica pipes occupied the whole of one wall of the demonic tea-rooms. A German in a frock-coat played it, or perhaps a series of Germans in frock-coats, closely resembling each other. At home, the merchants preferred the old Russian songs, but not here, not at Rusalochka's, a very expensive place, by the way, where one saw and was seen, and where first Grieg and then Offenbach's *Belle Hélène* were now being played at the pitch of a dockyard in full production. And yet Kuriatin, if he wished to, was able to make himself heard.

'I've come here because you asked me to,' said Frank, drawing up a massive gilded chair. 'But I hadn't forgotten what it was like.'

He was well aware that Kuriatin had invited him to Rusalochka's partly as a joke, a joke which would be allowed to develop according to its natural direction. At the same time, he had genuinely intended a treat, believing that Frank, in his ordinary business day, never encountered anything as over-whelming as the Garmoniphon. But Kuriatin could not rest easy with this, because business intruded, and even if he made or negotiated an offer for the Mammoth he would feel he had missed something if he had no option on the Reid site, and its buildings, and its trees. Above all he had the suspicion that Frank was not, after all, impressed by Rusalochka's (although many of the decorations had been carried out in real gold leaf), and pity for Frank on account of this and, warring with the pity, envy.

What, in heaven's name, was Selwyn doing at Rusalochka's? The premises were barred against anyone but merchants and their guests, and yet there he was, making his way, wavering but unchallenged, towards their table. 'I wanted to have a few words with Frank Albertovich. I asked at his house and they told me that he had an engagement here.'

'Sit down, sit down, Selwyn Osipych,' Kuriatin cried, 'sit down, my dear friend,' then as Selwyn smiled and looked round him vaguely, but did not sit down, 'You don't want to sit with me!' Selwyn, whose appearance was just as bizarre as ever, could be of no possible importance to him, financially or socially, and yet Kuriatin trembled from head to foot with eagerness. 'You don't want to sit with me, it distresses you to see a man spend money at Rusalochka's. You'll tell me that in the villages the peasants have been taking the thatch off their roofs this winter to feed their cattle, and no doubt that's true. But in Russia who is happy?'

'No, no, you're wrong,' said Selwyn mildly, 'I don't criticise what you're doing. How can I criticise a life I don't understand? And surely you are happy.'

'It's true, it's true. When I die, God will say to me, well, I gave you a life on earth, Arkady Filippovich, and what's more, a life in Russia. Did you enjoy it? And if not, why have you wasted your time?'

'What did you want to talk to me about, Selwyn?' asked Frank, as quietly as possible. 'Couldn't it wait? For God's sake sit down, in any case, if you're going to stay here.'

But Selwyn, looking round at the golden and copper walls, the threatening organ-loft, the perilous circulation of the waiters, the bloated, steaming and streaming customers to whom an attendant was now bringing hot towels, in the Chinese style, to wipe their drenched foreheads, gently shook his head. The effect on Kuriatin was immediate. Laying his hand on Selwyn's arm he began to plead, almost to wheedle.

'A nice glass of something . . . a samovar, a samovarchik, a dear little samovar . . . I can call for anything here, there is currant cake, Dundeekeks, as in Scotland . . . ' Lumbering up from his seat he folded Selwyn in his arms and kissed him as high as he could reach, on the chin, while one of the mobile teapots, on a straight course past the table, swerved and missed him narrowly.

Disengaging himself, Selwyn nodded at Frank and made his way out of Rusalochka's. Kuriatin subsided.

'You sounded like a rich man in the Bible when the prophet comes in,' said Frank. 'I know you're doing quite well, but you're not rich enough to carry on like this.'

'Selwyn Osipych was like a reproach to me. He didn't intend it, of that I'm sure, but, yes, he has acted as a reproach. Now I feel I don't want to withhold anything from you.' At this point the organ redoubled its volume and even Kuriatin had to raise his voice. 'I shall withhold nothing!'

How could Selwyn, in a couple of inconclusive minutes, have raised, quite unintentionally, such trust and repentance? It was a gift that would have been of inestimable value to him in business, if Selwyn had ever done any.

'I invited you here,' said Kuriatin, still in tears, 'in the way of business, without good intentions. I was lying to you when I said I couldn't obtain permits to export the Mammoth. I saw that delay was likely to bring me increased profits.'

'Of course you were lying,' Frank replied. 'I came here mainly to tell you that I've managed to negotiate the permits from the Ministry of Internal Affairs and the Ministry of Transport myself. I'd have been happy for you to do the job, but I can't wait any longer, I've got to have the site clear, either for rent or sale.'

At the words 'rent or sale' Kuriatin looked for a moment like his usual self, but then his eyes filled with tears again and he declared that the details no longer mattered to him.

'Just because Selwyn Osipych came in, and wouldn't sit down at the table?'

'Ah, you don't know what I was like in childhood, Frank Albertovich. The thought of a man's childhood can touch his soul, even when it's hard as flint. I've got photographs of myself as a child, poor faded things, but they show me as I was then, sitting in a little goat-cart.'

'How long do you think your change of heart will last?' Frank asked, thinking of various other dealings outstanding between them.

'Who can tell?' Kuriatin pushed the bottles on the table away from him.

Frank went downstairs, retrieved his overcoat, and escaped from the overpowering heat and noise and the improbable sight of the merchant's repentance. As he reached the Redeemer, a down-and-out of some kind moved up to him out of the shadow of one of the porches in the southern wall. Near the great churches the police never moved the beggars away, nor did anyone want them to. Frank stopped to take out his reserve of twenty-five-kopek pieces, which were always at the ready. It was Selwyn, however, in his tattered sheepskin.

'I have been waiting for you Frank. I couldn't speak to you in the presence of Kuriatin.'

'In that case I can't think why you turned up at Rusalochka's at all.'

'I hoped you might come away with me.'

'Well, I was there on business. Is there anything wrong?'

Their breaths rose together as steam into the bitterly cold lamplit air, Selwyn's fainter than Frank's.

'I went back to the Press, Frank, after it closed. I had the keys, as you know, this evening, as you had to leave early for your appointment. I went back because I hadn't had the opportunity during the day to see how far they'd got with . . .'

'With your poems.' He could, of course, have asked Tvyordov, but Selwyn, Frank knew, was in awe of Tvyordov.

'Yes, yes, with *Birch Tree Thoughts*.' Selwyn pronounced his title, as always, in a different and sadder tone, which in England would be reserved for religious subjects.

'The *Birch Tree Thoughts* are all right,' said Frank. 'You can have the first printing when you go in tomorrow. I told them to leave seventy-five copies in the compositors' room, to keep them separate from the deliveries. You could have taken them away tonight if you'd gone in there. I can't see why you didn't.'

'Ah, that was what I came to tell you, Frank. There were lights on in the building.'

'Didn't you see that the lights turned off when you left?'

'Let me be more specific. There was one light on, Frank, one light in the building, I think the light of a candle, moving from one window to another.'

'Well, who was it?'

'That I fear I can't tell you. I didn't go in to see.'

'Do you mean you left them to it, whoever it was?'

'I didn't know who it was carrying the light, Frank. It might have been a man of violence. I am a man of peace, a man of poetry.'

Selwyn seemed to be murmuring something, perhaps a blessing. 'Every single man that's born into this life, Frank, writes poetry at some time or other. Possibly you may not have done so yet.'

'Listen, Selwyn. Are you taking in what I'm saying?'

'Yes, indeed.'

'In the first place, give me the keys.'

'The keys to the Press?'

'The keys to the Press.'

Selwyn hesitated, as though struck by doubt or inspiration, and then handed them over.

'Now, either go round to 22 Lipka Street, or telephone them, and tell them I'll be late back, later than I said I would. Is that clear, and are you sure you won't forget to tell them?'

'Yes, yes, I'll speak to Lisa Ivanovna.'

'Just tell her what I've said.'

It was the worst season of the year in Moscow to hurry anywhere. The sledges were off the streets, there was still too much ice for taxis, nothing for it but a cab. It was the eve of a Saint's Day, so that all fares would be doubled. What Frank expected to find at the Press he didn't know. In the cab he tossed up, Tsar or Eagle, with one of his twenty-five-kopek pieces. Eagle, and he'd stop at a police station and get hold of an inspector to come with him. Tsar, he'd go on by himself. He went on by himself.

14

At REIDKA'S, a glimmer of light still showed in the window of the compositors' room. Frank negotiated the rows of trolleys waiting for tomorrow's delivery boys and tried the main entrance door. It was unlocked. He went upstairs, not troubling to walk either quietly or noisily.

A young man, still wearing his overcoat, was sitting with his back to the room on one of the compositors' stools with a lighted candle in front of him. He might almost have been asleep, but he suddenly pulled himself up straight and turned towards Frank a pale reproachful student's face. His blond eyelashes gave him a bemused look, as of something new-born, but he wasn't too dazed, as the electric light came on, to blow out the candle. Probably he had always had to economise.

'You have found me.'

'I wasn't looking for you, though,' said Frank. 'Who are you?'

The young man pulled out of his overcoat pocket an automatic about six inches long which might, like Ben's, be a toy, or might be a Webley. That's what students have these days. There was nowhere to hide a gun in a student's regulation high-buttoned jacket, they had to keep them in the right-hand coat pocket. He got to his feet and fired twice. The first shot went far wide of Frank into the opposite wall, where it dislodged a quantity of plaster. The second, wider still but at closer range, struck the upper wooden case of Tvyordov's frame, smashed it to bits, discharged the small capitals in a metal cascade on to the floor, then ricocheted off through the very centre of his white overall where it hung ready and buried itself behind the frame.

'You see! You see I didn't mean to hit you!'

'I don't know whether you meant to or not!' said Frank. He walked forward, put his forearm under the young man's chin and against his throat, and pushed. He had learned to do this as a boy in the yard of Moscow 8 School (Modern and Technical). Then he took the automatic out of his hand, shut the safety catch, and looked at it.

'You want to keep these properly cleaned,' he said. 'Otherwise the trigger spring breaks and it goes on firing until it's empty.'

The student, doubled up, was coughing. Frank fetched him a glass of water from the tap at the sink in the corner.

'Is this water safe?'

'It's what my staff drink.'

'I feel better. My name is Volodya Vasilych. My last name I don't give.'

'I didn't ask for it.'

'These are your premises, Frank Albertovich. You want to know what I'm doing here.'

'I'm sure you'll tell me in time. I take it you're a student?'

'Yes.'

'A student of what?'

'Of political history.' Frank wondered why he'd bothered to ask. He said, 'Meanwhile I shall have to account for all this mess and destruction to my chief compositor when he comes in the morning.'

Without any awkwardness Volodya dropped on to all fours and began to pick up the type.

'No, leave it,' said Frank. 'It has to go in the right place or not at all. What I really want to know is how you got in here.'

'The door wasn't locked.'

'Didn't that surprise you?'

'Nothing surprises me.'

From downstairs a voice called out: 'Sir, shots have been heard coming from your premises.'

It was the nightwatchman. Nothing on earth would bring him upstairs if there was a chance of being fired at. Altogether he was a sensible fellow.

'Everything's all right, Gulianin.'

'Good, sir. Very good.'

Gulianin retreated. 'Doubtless he'll fetch the street police,' said Volodya.

'Doubtless he won't. He'll wait to see how much I give him in the morning.'

Volodya, who seemed to have prepared what he had to say, repeated, 'My name is Volodya Vasilych.'

'So you told me.'

'I only shot at you to demonstrate that I was serious. Let me explain. You are a printer, Frank Albertovich.'

'I don't deny that. Did you want something printed?'

'I'm used to working a hand-press, but I no longer have access to one. I thought that if I could find a hand-press here I could get what I needed, only a couple of pages, done in a few hours. But you have no shutters here and I can't work without light, which means I can't conceal myself.'

'I can see that's awkward for you. But you could have come and given us an order, you know, in the usual way. However, I must warn you, that we don't do anything political.'

'What I have written is not political.'

'What's the subject?'

'The subject is universal pity.'

Volodya's expression was strained, as though he had entered his remark for an important prize, and could hardly believe that he wouldn't receive it.

'Well, then, you could have asked us for a quotation,' said Frank, 'I mean, just for the two pages. It would have saved a good deal of time and damage, and I don't think you'd have found our price unreasonable.'

'Prices...I don't know anything about that,' Volodya murmured, and then, after a pause for reflection, 'it's possible that what I wanted to print might be considered as political.'

'I suppose that would depend on who's being universally pitied,' said Frank. 'Have you got your copy with you?'

Volodya hesitated. 'No, I have committed it to memory.' Then he made a wide gesture with both arms, as if he was scattering food for hens, and cried: 'But after all, what can that matter to you? You're a foreigner, the worst that you could

suffer, if things didn't go right, would be expulsion from
Moscow back to your own country. A Russian can't live
away from Russia, but to you it's nothing.'

Frank had long ago got used to being asked, usually by
complete strangers, for assistance. They were convinced that,
as a business resident in good standing, he could help with their
external passports or with permissions of some kind, or else
they wanted him to delay their military conscription or to
threaten their college superintendent into giving them better
marks, or to sign a petition to the Imperial Chancery about a
relative who had fallen into disgrace. Sometimes they wanted
to borrow small sums of money to tide them over, or larger
ones to help them train as a doctor or an engineeer. He had a
reputation for doing what he could, otherwise these people
wouldn't have gone on coming to him, but all of them, at one
point or another, reminded him that he was a foreigner who,
even if things didn't go right, had nothing to lose.

'What makes you think it wouldn't matter to me if I had to
leave Russia?' he said. 'I was born here, I've lived here most of
my life, I love Moscow at all seasons, even now at the beginning of the thaw, and I'm a married man with three children.'

'Yes, but your wife has left you.'

Volodya spoke confidently, but seemed to realise that he was
not making exactly the impression he had intended.

'Where do you live?' Frank asked him.

'A long way out. In the Rogozhskaia.'

'Go back there.'

'But my property...'

'Not the gun. Here's the candle, if you brought it with you.
Don't come here again.'

As Frank took a last look round the room, he noticed the
seventy-five copies of *Birch Tree Thoughts*, still neatly piled and
undisturbed by Tvyordov's frame.

'Take this as a souvenir,' he said to Volodya, handing him the
top copy.

Volodya put the book in his now empty pocket and loped
away down the stairs. Frank switched off and locked up.

Impossible to repair Tvyordov's upper case, or the bullet-hole in his apron. Impossible, too, to estimate the effect on Tvyordov, when he reported for work next day, of the defilement and disturbance. That was a problem for the morning, and there were likely to be others. Open the doors, the Russians say, here comes trouble.

On the way back he went down to the iron bridge, the Moskvoryetszkevya, where passers-by were still watching the ice, and threw the little gun into the river. Then he walked home with a reasonably clear conscience.

In the living room Dolly and Ben were still, apparently, finishing their homework. A twenty-five-watt bulb, the strongest that could be bought in Moscow, hung over their table, Dolly's brown exercise book, Ben's pink one. Dolly was tracing a map, a mildly hypnotic process. Her nickel-plated nib scratched industriously. Outside the circle of light, Lisa was sewing. Frank would have thought that the light wasn't good enough there and that all this sewing might have been done by somebody else in the house. There was a little room fitted up with a Singer off the kitchen passage. Perhaps Lisa wanted to show that she wasn't quite a governess and not quite a servant. Perhaps she didn't want to show anything, and they were all passing a peaceable evening without him.

'You're late,' Dolly said.

'Didn't Selwyn Osipych telephone you?'

'Yes,' said Dolly reluctantly, 'but Lisa answered, and she didn't tell us how long you'd be.'

'He didn't tell me either, Dolly.'

'Well, we were waiting,' Dolly said. 'Ben got rather restless.'

'I'll tell you why I'm late, it's nothing to worry about. There was someone at the Press, someone hanging about who shouldn't have been there. I went to see what was going on. Don't worry, it wasn't a thief.'

Dolly seemed mildly disappointed.

'If it wasn't a thief, who was it?'

'He was a student, I think.'

'Don't you know?' Dolly asked. 'You never used to be like this.'

'He said he was a student.'

'What did he want?'

'I'm not quite sure.'

'What was he called?'

'Volodya something-or-other.'

'Where has he gone?'

'Back home, as far as I know.'

'Will he come back?' Lisa asked. Frank met her clear, blank gaze. He felt pleased to have aroused even this much interest.

'I think it's very unlikely. I'm afraid the whole outing must have been a great disappointment to him, and I don't think he'll have any further business at the Press.'

'I can't see why he had to come so late anyway,' said Ben. 'Were you angry with him?'

'Not at all, I gave him a present.'

'Do you think he's got a gun?'

'Not now.'

15

When FRANK had been a small boy and they had lived on the site, the first sign of spring that couldn't be mistaken had been a protesting voice, the voice of the water, when the ice melted under the covered wooden footpath between the house and the factory. The ice there wasn't affected by the stoves in the house or the assembly-shop furnace, the water freed itself by its own effort, and once it had begun to run in a chattering stream, the whole balance of the year tilted over. At the sound of it his heart used to leap. His bicycle came out of the shed and he oiled it out of a can which was no longer frozen almost solid. In a few weeks the almond trees would be in flower and the city would be on wheels again.

The day after the break-in, he allowed himself, as he had done then, to expect the spring. He knew he had an awkward day ahead, although he'd always thought, until the last week or so, that he enjoyed difficulties. Perhaps he still did. What kind of day it would be for the new cost accountant seemed uncertain. Before that began he had to think of Tvyordov, for whose sake he was coming in early through the snow-patched streets.

Outside the Press he found two fourteen-year-old apprentices who had, until work began, nowhere else to go. They were arguing over a boat-shaped piece of wood in the gutter and as to which direction it would be swept in when the current unfroze.

'Listen,' said Frank. 'I'm sending both of you with a message to the chief compositor.'

He had decided what to do while he was having a shave at one of the many barbers who opened at five o'clock in the morning. 'Look at this letter. Read me the address on the envelope.'

The smaller boy read out, 'Chief Compositor I. N. Tvyordov, Kaluga Pereulok 54.'

'Do you know where that is?'

'Yes, sir.'

'Go together, keep an eye on each other, knock at the door, take a message if there is one from the chief compositor, and come back here within the half-hour.'

In the letter he had told Tvyordov that there had been a break-in at the Press during the night, so that the work would be interrupted, and there would be no need for him to check in until the next day, when everything would continue as usual. Pay for the missed day would be maintained. On the whole, Frank considered his message as untruthful – there had been no break-in, it was quite clear that Selwyn had forgotten to lock up – and cowardly, since it was only deferring an awkward moment. On the other hand, to confront Tvyordov, without any warning, with the ruin of his apron and his upper case would be inhuman, and at the same time Frank had to bear in mind that it was the feast of St Modestus, the patron saint of printing, and it was his duty to see that the blessing of Reidka's ikons went through, if possible, without disturbance. He had also to consider the nightwatchman, Gulianin, who had heard shots, but must be persuaded that he hadn't. With this in mind Frank had brought a reasonable sum of money in notes.

The nightwatchman, however, couldn't immediately be found. He lived over Markel's Bar, a few doors down from the Press, slept there all day, and was said to be asleep now. Back at Reidka's, the delivery boys had arrived, and, by the time Frank had unlocked, so had the two apprentices.

'We gave your letter to the chief compositor. His wife came to the door, but she fetched him and we put it into his hands.'

Frank knew Tvyordov had a wife, because she came to the dinner he gave to the whole staff and their families on his name-day. He couldn't have said exactly what she looked like, and very probably she couldn't have recognised him. There had been no answer for the apprentices to bring back from Tvyordov.

Selwyn and the number 2 and 3 compositors came in together, and, while they were still hanging up their coats downstairs, the police were announced. For this Frank blamed himself. If he'd insisted on seeing the nightwatchman earlier and had given him a hundred roubles – somewhere between tea-money and a bribe – Gulianin wouldn't, as he evidently had done, felt the need to take his information to the police. From them he would have got considerably less, but very likely he needed ready money immediately. Probably he was caught in the tight network of small loans, debts, repayments and fore-closures which linked the city, quarter by quarter, in its grip, as securely as the tram-lines themselves.

Frank said that he would see the police in his office. Only a captain and an orderly and to Frank's relief, in uniform. That meant the nightwatchman couldn't have seen Volodya leave the building, or he would have recognised from his cap that he was a student, and trouble with a student would have meant the plain-clothes section, the Security. Tea was brought, the captain, though not the orderly, unbuttoned his jacket. Just a few questions, a little interrogation, a dear little interrogation. Why had Mr Reid come back here so late on the previous evening? A light in the window, who had reported that?

'My accountant, Selwyn Osipych Crane.'

The inspector smiled. 'Well, we know Selwyn Osipych.' From one end of Moscow to the other, Frank thought, when they hear Selwyn's name they either laugh or weep. In its way it was a considerable achievement. Now Selwyn himself came into the office through the connecting door, stricken and haggard. 'Frank, strange things have been happening. Ah, good morning, officer.'

The captain looked at him indulgently. 'If you saw a light here last night, sir, that should have been reported to us at once.' He turned to Frank. 'And you, too, sir, should have reported it.'

'I left that to the nightwatchman,' said Frank.

'Gulianin very correctly came to us. He also heard shots.'

'Is he sure he heard them?'

The police captain stirred some jam into his tea. 'Not al-together sure. This is a very noisy street. You have a blacksmith here, and a motor-car mechanic, and up to midnight you've got the noise of the trams. Let's say he thought he heard something.'

This was a fairly strong hint that the inspector was prepared not to take things any further. He accepted a glass of vodka flavoured with caraway seeds, which was kept in the office exclusively for the police. How he could drink it so early in the morning, or indeed at all, Frank couldn't fathom. But it preserved a distinction of rank, since the orderly, knowing his place, refused it.

'Now, sir, did you find any property missing?'

'No, nothing at all.'

'Pardon me,' Selwyn broke in eagerly, 'when I came in just now I counted the first run of *Birch Tree Thoughts*. There are only seventy-four copies there. Yes, seventy-four. One has been purloined.'

'What are *Birch Tree Thoughts*?' the inspector asked.

Frank explained. In the ordinary way, poetry was suspect and, once again, might have been a matter for the Security. But this was something written by the harmless Selwyn Osipych, and the captain only said, 'Well, sir, what do birch trees think?'

Selwyn, who believed all questions should be answered, replied that they thought in the same way as women. 'Just as a woman's body, inspector, moves at her heart's promptings, so the birch tree moves in the winds of spring.'

Frank could see that the captain and the orderly were not listening, being in the genial grip of inertia and greed. He took an envelope out of his drawer, and, conscious of taking only a mild risk, since the whole unwieldy administration of All the Russias, which kept working, even if only just, depended on the passing of countless numbers of such envelopes, he slid it across the top of the desk. The inspector opened it without embarrassment, counted out the three hundred roubles it contained and transferred them to a leather container, halfway between a wallet and a purse, which he kept for 'innocent income'.

'Selwyn, take the police officers downstairs and out through the back way,' said Frank. 'They'll want, I'm sure, to have a look at the rest of the premises.'

After giving them five minutes he went to confront his No 2 and No 3 compositors, who were surrounding, like dazed mourners, Tvyordov's broken frame and scattered type and the white apron which, with its single bullet-hole hung, a victim, from its hook. The inspector could only have missed the disorder, or overlooked it, because it suited him to.

'Put the covers on,' he said.

The covers were put on the frames only on Saturday nights and on the eve of feast days. Each compositor did this for himself. The frames were sacrosanct, and the two men moved like trespassers.

Frank told them there had been an incident, a little incident, a little break-in during the night, and that he had asked Tvyordov personally not to come in today. There must have been an intruder, but he must have managed to get away. It wasn't a thief, nothing had been stolen, or nothing – Frank corrected himself – that couldn't be replaced. They were to get on with the current orders, in the first place with Muir and Merrilees' Easter catalogue, all of which had to be hand-set. This was popular with the compositors because they were paid by the page, and most of the pages were taken up with illustrations. But what had become of the open discussions, Frank asked himself, the joint decisions between management and workers which he had set his heart on when he took over Reidka's?

'The police are satisfied,' he said. 'As you've seen for yourselves, they came and they went. All we have to do is a day's work.'

But they could not adjust themselves to Tvyordov's absence. Hand-printing, whose rhythm was still that of the human body, went adrift with the disappearance of the pace-setter, assumed always to be on duty as the given condition of the whole process.

16

AT NINE o'clock, as had been arranged for his first day, the new costing accountant came to take up his duties. As Frank had told Selwyn, Aleksandr Alexsandrovich Bernov had been with Sytin's, the giant print works beyond the Sadovaya Ring. Clean-shaven, sharp-glancing, quick on the uptake, he had been impatient with his place there as head clerk, but his ideas – if they were his – were geared, perhaps irretrievably, to a large firm. He saw the business, any business, as an un-declared war against every employee below the rank of cost accountant.

Frank wanted to discuss the possibility of paying something for distributing the type, a payment compositors had been asking for, but had never been given, since the days of Guten-berg. Bernov admitted that at Sytin's, until they went over to machinery, the men used to take away the type and throw it into the river on the way home rather than distribute it in unpaid time.

'But, Frank Albertovich, I want to make this clear from the start – one mustn't encourage the survivals of the past. Hand-printing is associated now with Tolstoyans and student revolutionaries and activists in garrets and cellars. The future belongs to hot metal, of course.'

'It's still useful for small jobs and essential for fine work,' said Frank. The image persisted of Tvyordov's ruined possessions, only a few yards away, and his murdered apron. Bernov, however, urged that Reidka's should give up the small jobs altogether. Rent more warehouses, instal linotype and print newspapers.

'There's a new paper or a new journal starting up every day. And with a newspaper you're printing so many identical units that you can go straight into large-scale unit costing.'

'I don't want to print newspapers,' said Frank. 'This firm has to be kept on a very delicate balance, so that it can be sold without loss and at short notice if the international situation gets worse.'

'Or if your wife, Elena Karlovna, doesn't return,' said Bernov, nodding energetically. Evidently this was discussed even at Sytin's. With quiet tact, Selwyn leaned forward.

'How do you see our future, Bernov?'

'Very simply. I'm glad you asked me. More pay for more efficiency. English and German firms have a system of merit rating for their workers. I don't know if we shall ever accept that here. But you can start by increasing the fines for drunkenness, lowering the agreed payments for waiting time when the paper runs out and so forth, and, above all, no special cases, no humanitarian allowances. That's what prosperity means. You're giving everyone the money they deserve.'

'But we mustn't consider what money they deserve,' said Selwyn. 'Consider only whether we, the men of business, deserve to have money to give to them.'

Bernov's face, so much more expressive than was good for him, crumpled up a little.

'Of course, I'm only here as your cost accountant. Decisions are for the management only. Perhaps I ought to say, though, that the question of whether the management deserve their profits has no relevance to their economic performance.'

'I'm sorry to hear you say that,' Selwyn murmured. 'Yes, truly sorry.'

Frank saw that Bernov looked bewildered, and sent out to the Bar for something to eat. *Zakuske* were brought on a covered tray by the proprietor himself, anxious to discover what kind of scandal had been reported, or not reported, by his lodger, the nightwatchman.

'Has he woken up?' Frank asked.

'He spoke of hearing shots when he was about his duties last night,' said the proprietor.

'Remember it's a very noisy street.'

Bernov ate rapidly and immediately began on a new proposition. At Sytin's, and perhaps during the whole of his life, he must have been deprived of proper attention. 'Look at the government expenditure this year! A hundred and ten million roubles on railways, eighty million roubles on education. Education means cheap printed books. They could be produced and even bound on the premises, using strong cartridge paper.' Frank reminded him that in times of emergency cartridge paper was liable to run very short. Bernov began to tap with a silver pencil he'd got. In 1915, the year after next, there was to be an international printing fair in Berlin, the largest in history. These industrial fairs, in his opinion, were the guarantee of continuing peace in Europe. Russia must not be outdone. The small printing shops of Moscow, places like Reid's, employing thirty to sixty people, must come to an agreement with the giants like Sytin's and prepare a joint exhibit. By that time, Frank thought, he'll have fretted himself to death.

At four o'clock two old men, two of the oldest in the place, came up to the compositors' room. They were collators, checking the order of the sheets, and seeing them, with the help of two boys and a bucket of water, through the hydraulic press. They had done the same work with the old screw press, and were never likely to do anything more difficult. Now they had an air of authority.

They had exchanged their felt slippers, which they wore at work, for leather shoes, and in these they creaked across to the ikon corner and dragged out a table to stand in front of it. A third, even older man, this time from the store room, brought in a white cloth, two candles and two tarnished silver candlesticks. They spread the cloth, adjusted the creases, crossed themselves and bowed. Frank, coming out of his office, was asked to light the candles. As he struck a match he thought uncomfortably of Volodya, who must have brought his matches with him.

The candlelight would have been more impressive if they'd turned out the electric light, but this was not important to the staff of Reidka's, who had had a service of blessing when their electricity was installed, and were proud of it. With the lighting of the candles, however, they began to come silently in, not crowding, not touching each other, and all these people who would have fought fiercely to get ahead at the tram-stop, or on the bridges watching the ice, took their stand as though their places were marked out for them. As they faced the ikon they crossed themselves, striking the forehead, each shoulder in turn, then the breast.

The men stood on the right, the tea-woman and her assistant on the left, Frank and Selwyn, as usual, in the centre. Bernov had excused himself from the ceremony, and gone home, carrying quantities of paper-work.

The whole assembly were turned to the right, with their eyes on the candles, which, like the oil for the ikon-lamp, were paid for by a voluntary weekly subscription from everyone over the age of sixteen. The ikon was not an old one. It was an example of a new photographic process which was said to be an exact simulation of oil painting, in reds and blues of excellent quality which neither time nor lamp-smoke could darken, while the glittering halo of St Modestus and the letters of the alphabet in his bound book far outshone the ancient silver of the candle-sticks. Those had come from the old house on the works site. Even there, Frank remembered, it had been thought unlucky to clean them.

The yardman threw the door open and the familiar heavy-treading, heavy-breathing parish priest came in, followed by a deacon and a subdeacon. From the doorway he gave his blessing. They were taken into Frank's office which, on these occasions, became a vestry. The priest came out in his stole, the deacons in their surplices. The censer was lit with a piece of red-hot charcoal from the canteen samovar. The fragrance of the smouldering cedar of Lebanon reached every corner of the room where men, women and children stood motionless.

Some of them, Frank knew, were agnostics. The storekeeper had told him that, in his opinion, soul and body were like the steam above a factory, one couldn't exist without the other. But he, too, stood motionless. The priest offered a prayer for the

God-protected Tsar and his family, for the Imperial Army, that it might put down every enemy of Russia beneath its feet, for the city of Moscow and for the whole country, for those at sea, for travellers, for the sick, for the suffering, for prisoners, for the founders of the Press and the workers there, for mercy, life, peace, health, salvation, visitation, pardon and remission of sins.

Because I don't believe in this, Frank thought, that doesn't mean it's not true. He tried to call himself to order. Thomas Huxley had written that if only there was some proof of the truth of religion, humanity would clutch at it as a drowning man clutches at a hencoop. But as long as mankind doesn't pretend to believe in something they see no reason to believe, because there might be an advantage in pretending – as long as they don't do that, they won't have sunk to the lowest depths. He himself could be said to be pretending now, still more so when he had attended the Anglican chapel, with the idea of keeping Nellie company. Why he had felt alarmed when Dolly told him that her teacher said there was no God, he didn't know. The alarm suggested that as a rational being he was unsuccessful. Either that, or he had come to think of religion as something appropriate to women and children, and that would be sinking to a lower depth than Huxley had dreamed of. Perhaps, Frank thought, I have faith, even if I have no beliefs.

The priest was giving a short address. 'You are workers, and you are not only called upon to work together, but to love each other and pity each other. How can that be? You will say that you didn't choose to work next to this man or that man, he happened to be there when I first arrived, it was accidental. But remember, if that thought comes to you, that there are no accidental meetings. We never meet by chance. Either this other man, or this woman, is sent to us, or we are sent to them.'

The final blessing began. At the words 'guard this place and this house and the souls of those who dwell there' the doors opened again, and Tvyordov walked in. Every head turned towards him, and then back again. He crossed himself and went to stand in silence, with his back to his frame.

The priest held out a double-barred silver-gilt cross, the lower arm slanted to the right, representing the fates of the good and the bad thief. The congregation filed forward to kiss the cross, the men first, the two women after them. The tea-woman and her assistant kissed the priest's hands also. Although they were probably the most devout souls in the congregation, they hurried away in a state of agitation. The *pyerchestvo* for the blessing of the ikon was entirely their responsibility, and while they were upstairs the glasses might somehow have been disarranged, or supplies of small cakes and pies put out which were supposed to be kept back till later. Tvyordov also kissed the cross, but not the priest's hand.

'Go on,' Frank said to Selwyn. 'I'll be down later.'

Selwyn nodded, and escorted the priest, the deacon and the subdeacon, towards the stairs to the tea-place. They would expect to be entertained, as usual, in the office, but there was no way, at the moment, of explaining the unwelcome change in the arrangements. The congregation followed, with the exception of Tvyordov, and the room filled with that peculiar silence, as though it was stretching itself, which follows when a great number of people have recently left. Frank confronted his chief compositor.

Tvyordov did not speak to him at once. As though he was starting on his day's work, he took the covers off his frame and looked in pain, rather than in bewilderment, at the disorder. He picked up one or two letters from the violated upper case, and from habit let them fall into what would have been their right places. Then he took down his white apron, looked at the bullet-hole, put his finger through it and folded the apron neatly.

'You sent word to me not to come. But I've never missed the service of blessing.'

'You've never missed anything,' Frank replied, 'not since my father started this place, and all the work was hand-set.'

He could hardly tell Tvyordov what he hadn't told the police. He might, perhaps, have risked it if he had known what Tvyordov felt about students and about student activities, but he didn't know.

'I owe you some kind of explanation,' he began at last, 'for the state of your frame. It all happened yesterday evening.'

'It's not my frame,' replied Tvyordov, 'the frame belongs to the Press. The tools were mine, the sponge was mine, the apron was mine.'

'Anything that was damaged will be replaced.'

'That won't be necessary. What happened doesn't interest me. I shall never work in this room again. You'll have to find someone to continue instructing my apprentice, and someone to wind the clock on Saturday evenings, and clean the glass on Monday mornings. Tomorrow I shall start downstairs with the monotype.'

Onto the folded apron he put his composing-stick, his setting-rule, his shears, the sponge, and the bodkin in its cork for removing wrong letters, and with two movements of his hands made them into a compact parcel. He was on his way out.

'What are you going to do with those?' Frank asked.

'I shall throw them in the river.'

17

CHARLIE'S TELEGRAM said that he would arrive on the 31st of March. In Moscow that would be the 18th. The thaw would be nearly over, but the city's sealed windows hadn't yet been opened to let in the spring. Certainly he wouldn't be seeing the country at its best. Frank's hospitable instincts were disturbed. No shooting, no skating, but then Charlie didn't shoot and couldn't skate. No horse-market, but then Charlie wasn't interested in horses. The light would still be too poor for decent photography, but then he never had any luck, anyway, with his snapshots. But how would Charlie compare Moscow in spring-time with Norbury, where every green front hedge and back lawn must, by now, be shooting and putting out leaves? He might think, perhaps, that Nellie never ought to have been brought to Russia.

The servants asked what must be prepared for their English visitor. Frank reminded them that he was English himself.

'Yes, but you are Russian, you are used to everything Russian,' said Toma, 'you make mistakes, and you don't mind our mistakes. God has given you patience, to take the place of your former happiness.'

'Karl Karlovich will need plenty of hot water at all times, and a boiled egg every morning.'

The 18th of March, the Feast of St Benjamin, was a general holiday. In a sense, this was convenient, as the Press would be shut, and there would be no difficulty about meeting Charlie.

'Which of us are you going to take with you to the station?' asked Dolly. 'Our uncle will expect a warm welcome.'

'I'm not taking any of you. He'll have had a tiring journey, and when he gets here he'll want a few quiet moments to take everything in.'

He was making his brother-in-law sound like a sick man, and in fact Dolly asked whether Uncle Charlie was quite right in the head.

'Of course he is, but he might find it a bit confusing at first. He's never gone in for travelling. Anyway, there's nothing odd about wanting peace and quiet.'

'Is he bringing Mother back with him?' Ben asked in a perfectly level voice.

'No.'

'If Mother does come, will you have to get rid of Lisa?'

Frank knew, rather than saw, that Dolly was sitting with her head turned away, as still as if she had been frozen.

'I don't much like that expression "get rid of",' he said.

'Why not?'

What did you get rid of? Frank thought. Epidemics of cholera, draughts, mice, political opponents, bad habits. Ben had meant no harm, of course, quite the contrary. 'Get rid of' had been a favourite expression of Nellie's.

When Lisa came, a little after the rest of the household, for her weekly wages, he asked her how long she was going to stay with them.

'How can I answer that?' she said, counting her money carefully. 'I can't answer it.'

'You might say "as long as I want to".'

'It would have to be "as long as I'm wanted". That I don't need to tell you.'

Frank unlocked another drawer in the desk. 'Look, here are your papers, here's your internal passport. I'm supposed by law to keep them here, but I'm giving them back to you. You're free to go when you want to, when you need to. You can say now, "I shall stay as long as I want to." But I very much want you to stay, Lisa Ivanovna.'

Charlie, wrapped in plaids and mufflers, expected, perhaps understandably, to be taken straight from the station to Lipka Street, but Frank put the luggage in charge of a porter, and avoiding the stationmaster, whom he felt he couldn't face just at the moment, propelled Charlie into the refreshment room.

'Do they have tea here?' Charlie asked.

'Charlie, I want you to tell me about Nellie.'

'What, immediately? I haven't had much opportunity to wash, you know, since we crossed the border.'

'How's Nellie?'

Charlie sighed. 'I've got bad news for you, but no, wait, you're rushing me a bit, I haven't expressed myself rightly, there's nothing to be alarmed about. As far as I know, Nellie's perfectly well, it's only that she's not with me, she's not in Norbury.'

'You mean you've come all this way to tell me you don't know where she is?'

'She's not in material want, Frank, that I do know.'

'I should hope not. I sent off some money straight away.'

'Yes, that arrived by post, before she did. I gave it to her pretty well as soon as she arrived. I thought she was just back for a visit, you see, although I'd heard nothing from her for quite a while. She only stayed the night, stowed away her bags in the attic, where they still are, by the way, then she was off again.'

Frank ordered some tea. 'Where is she now?'

'She's school-teaching, Frank. She'd still have her certificate, of course. Don't ask me where, because I don't know. I mean that she wrote me that she was at a school, and she can't be learning at her age, so she must be teaching. No address, she sent the letter poste restante to the tobacconist at the end of the road. Perhaps you remember him?'

'Can't you make the tobacconist say where it came from?'

'It wouldn't be right to persuade him to break a confidence. That's what he's paid for, really, to destroy the covering envelope. Besides, he's a Wesleyan.'

'I see.'

'I've brought her letter, if you want to look at it.'

'No, Charlie. It wasn't written to me.'

Charlie straightened himself in his chair, stirring the lemon in his tea, determined to get used to foreign customs. Well, he'll have to say it right out now, thought Frank, feeling sorry for him.

'Frank, was there any kind of disagreement between you and Nellie?'

'Did you ask her that?'

'Yes, but I didn't get an answer. She wasn't short with me, like she often used to be, I don't mean that. If I had to describe her, I'd say she was half-asleep, like a woman dreaming.'

'Did she say anything about the children?'

'I did, but she didn't.'

'What did you say?'

'I asked her what arrangements she'd made about the kiddies. She didn't answer that, either.'

'Did it strike you that, if she was like a woman half-asleep, she might have lost them?'

'No, Frank, it didn't, or I'd have been terror-struck. And after all, she hadn't lost anything else.'

Charlie had come sixteen hundred miles to give what, after all, had turned out to be very little information. He had had to disturb the habits of a lifetime, take the London, Brighton & South Coast Railway into London, get his visa from the Russian consulate, change his money into marks and roubles, confront the border inspections, lose his books (*Raffles* and *Sentimental Tommy*) and his pack of patience cards, both of which had been confiscated by the customs at Verzhbolovo. 'Surely there couldn't have been much harm in a pack of cards?' Frank explained that playing cards were a state monopoly, and the proceeds went to support the Imperial Foundlings Home. 'Well, that shows the Tsar's heart is in the right place,' said Charlie.

What had propelled him, as far as Frank could make out, had been shock. He had been unsettled when Bertha died, aghast when Lloyd George had introduced National Insurance (though relieved when it turned out that there wouldn't be pensions for criminals), worried – as he had told Frank – by the recent behaviour of Englishwomen and English railway-men and printers, but none of these had constituted the kind of distress that Nellie had caused him when, supposed to be in Moscow, she had rung the bell at Longfellow Road, and worse still, disappeared the next day. Perhaps, too, there was a wish, long unrecognised, to go one better than his much-travelled sister. Who would have believed that Charlie Cooper would ever get as far as Russia? But there was no practical object in his journey whatever. The only idea that had come to him, he said, was that 'they might advertise'. Frank pointed out that advertisements were for lost and missing persons, and Nellie, properly speaking, was neither. Charlie, however, had been thinking of something on the lines of the Lost Boys in *Peter Pan*, who appealed to their mothers to come home. Frank was rather surprised at this stroke of imagination, but Charlie said it had been suggested by the vicar.

'So you've been discussing my troubles quite extensively in Norbury.'

'Not extensively, Frank. Only to sympathetic ears.'

Once they were back in Lipka Street, Charlie explained that he intended to stay about a week or ten days, to see whatever there was to be seen, and to broaden his mind a bit, because that was what travel was for. He'd been afraid that it might be inconvenient, but he could see that he needn't have worried about that – Frank was very well able to manage, and the whole place, he could also see, was something like. The warmth of a Russian household and the excitement of the servants' greeting to a distinguished relative from a foreign country powerfully affected him, so that he was much less like a man on an awkward and distressing mission than a tripper on a day-outing.

'My word, Frank, you don't do yourself badly. Plenty of everything, people to look after you, the house kept warm all the time, almost too warm for comfort, I'd say. I can't call to mind a single house in Norbury with anything more than coal fires.'

'I should be careful of the vodka if I were you, Uncle Charlie,' said Ben anxiously. 'It doesn't taste of anything but it's quite strong.'

'Uncle Charlie needs something quite strong,' said Dolly.

'Well, I'll take a little,' Charlie said amiably, 'if your father thinks it's good for me.'

'It's not at all good for you,' said Frank. But the vodka, pliant, subtle, and fiery, eased the moment, as it had done for so many millions of others.

Charlie was not deaf, but he didn't always entirely take in what was said to him. In this way, although he was sometimes taken off guard, he was spared a good deal. He helped himself freely at table, remarking, 'I hope I'm not overdoing it.'

'You can't overdo it,' said Frank, 'the cook will be disappointed if you don't take plenty.'

'She needn't worry. It's excellent, and then there's all these little touches, these slices of cucumber, I mean, that's what I call little touches. I'd never have believed that the housekeeping would go ahead like this while you were managing on your own, so to speak.'

'He isn't managing on his own,' said Dolly. 'He has Lisa.'

'There's a Russian girl who looks after the children,' said Frank. 'I don't know why she isn't here now.' He had expected her to be there, and although she was presumably only a few yards away he was not able to prevent himself from feeling the deprivation as a physical pain.

'You were a very long time at the station,' Dolly said. 'Lisa had supper upstairs with Annushka.'

'Well, I hope I shall meet your Miss Lisa tomorrow, then,' said Charlie. 'A good thing she's got an English name, isn't it? Just for a chat, then tomorrow.'

'I'm afraid Lisa won't be able to chat to you,' said Dolly. 'She doesn't know any English.'

'Dear me, that's a pity. You'll have to see if you can teach her any. Just "how do you do?" and "thank you" and "A was an apple-pie" – just useful phrases to be going on with.'

Dolly and Ben both left the room.

'They're unusual kiddies,' said Charlie. 'They've got a quaint way with them. You can't tell what's going on in a child's mind, of course. Those two join in the conversation quite freely, but that doesn't mean you can tell what they're thinking. I'm not sure that Nellie and me were ever permitted to join in quite as freely as that. There was rather rigid discipline in our home, you see.'

The tea came in, and Toma, who wanted a closer look at the brother-in-law, took up once again with Frank a grievance of long standing about the necessity of buying a fifth samovar. One was upstairs now with Lisa Ivanovna and the two large ones were in the kitchen. The argument was not a formality and went on for some time, while Charlie sat perspiring in the warmth of the room, turning his head from one unintelligible speaker to the other. The door, meanwhile, was left open, and Lisa came in.

Charlie got to his feet, was introduced as Karl Karlovich, and could only smile. Lisa also smiled, and said to Frank in Russian, 'Please don't think I intended to sit down here. I know you want to talk to your brother-in-law.'

'No, I don't want to talk to him,' Frank answered in English. 'Stay here, I'm in love with you.'

'Pardon, I didn't quite catch that,' said Charlie.

Lisa went silently away.

'She looks like a very refined type of young lady, Frank. A pity she's had her hair cut short, as it's quite a nice colour. At home I'd have thought she was a suffragist.'

'She's employed here on a temporary basis,' said Frank. 'I mean while Nellie's away.'

'Oh, I see, she's not a young lady, she's a young woman.'

'I'm sure her hair will grow again quite quickly,' said Frank.

18

CHARLIE CONTINUED to show an unexpected readiness to enjoy himself. This began, conventionally enough, with a call at the chaplaincy, where Frank himself, since the departure of Miss Kinsman, had felt himself coldly received. If this was so, Charlie didn't notice it. He repeated to Mrs Graham his amazement at the housekeeping at 22 Lipka Street.

'That's Russia, I suppose. You'll feel the difference, you and your husband, when you come to the end of your ministry here and go back home again. I tell Frank that in his house it's more like the Arabian nights.'

'I'm glad, Frank,' said Mrs Graham, lighting one of her horrible cigarettes, 'that your house has become like something out of the Arabian nights.'

'Someone to open the door,' Charlie went on, 'someone to shut it for you, someone to bring anything you're in want of. With a smile, you know! And then the kiddies are no trouble at all.'

'Ah yes,' said Mrs Graham. 'I heard that Frank had engaged a girl to look after them.'

'Of course, when she does say anything it's in Russian and I can't make head or tail of it,' said Charlie. 'But you've only got to look at her to see that she's the right sort. She's "just the sort of creature that Nature did intend". Do you know that song, Mrs Graham?'

'No, I don't,' said Mrs Graham, afraid, perhaps, that Frank's brother-in-law might begin to sing.

'It's an Irish song,' he told her. 'It's called "I met her in the garden where the praties grow". But you can't draw a hard and fast line between the nationalities. It describes her to a T.'

'Lisa used to work as an assistant in Muir and Merrilees,' said Frank. 'I hope –'

'In which department?'

'The men's handkerchiefs, I think.'

'Ah, yes.'

'I hope that when you and the Chaplain next come to see us, you'll have a talk with her.'

'Oh, you mustn't trouble yourself about invitations,' said Mrs Graham, 'until your wife comes back.'

Mrs Graham struck Charlie as a gracious, friendly woman, who seemed to have a kind word for everyone. He was also impressed by Selwyn, a clever chap, he thought, who'd read a lot. He was surprised that Nellie hadn't mentioned him more in her letters home.

'He told me he was a poet, Frank. I wonder if you knew that?'

'Yes, I did know it.'

'And he's a vegetarian, too, like George Bernard Shaw. But Shaw isn't a poet. It must be easier for him, writing prose, to sustain himself on vegetables.'

'Selwyn doesn't eat much at any time,' said Frank.

'It seems an odd thing for a management accountant. But you can't argue with genius, it strikes where it will. When he took me yesterday to hear that pianist, you know, Scriabin, yes, at that concert hall, and we were walking back together, he suddenly told me to stop, and we stopped dead in the middle of the tram-lines.'

'What for?'

'He didn't give any reason. He just threw back his head and looked at the stars, and we moved on almost immediately.'

Selwyn had also given Charlie a copy of *Birch Tree Thoughts*. There it was, in its familiar buff paper cover. 'It would have been more of a keepsake, of course, if it had been in Russian, but then, if it hadn't been in English I shouldn't have been able to follow it. I've had a glance through it. This one is a kind of lullaby, I think, to make a child drop off to sleep. I didn't know Crane was a married man.'

'It isn't the poet speaking,' said Frank. 'If I'm thinking of the right one. It's a birch tree.'

'Well, I consider it a privilege to meet a poet on equal terms like that. You must feel it too, in the day-to-day running of the business.'

While Selwyn and Charlie had been at the conservatoire Frank had taken the opportunity to call on Mrs Graham again. He had telephoned to ask her if he could have another word with her; it hadn't been possible, he said, the other evening, but at the moment his brother-in-law was out.

There was no one else in the drawing room, evidently she'd thought it worth while to keep it clear for him. He began at once, 'I wanted to ask you if you'd heard from Miss Kinsman. To tell you the truth, I haven't been altogether easy about her.'

'Did you expect to be?' asked Mrs Graham.

'I'm not sure that I have any special responsibility towards her. But I know that she'd lost her job and needed another one, and perhaps she expected ... I mean that if she was disappointed, I'm very sorry.'

'Ah, but are you?' Mrs Graham said. 'Would you consider me old-fashioned to an absurd degree if I said that a man's duty to a woman, even an older woman, or perhaps I should say particularly to an older woman, in a strange city, is to escort her safely to wherever she happens to want to go?'

'No, I don't think you're old-fashioned, Mrs Graham. I find you confusing, but that's a different matter. I find all women confusing, even Dolly. It's because you use a different manner, if I may put it that way, according to who you're with. Now your husband would never do that.'

'He should be able to, it was part of his pastoral training,' said Mrs Graham briskly. 'I admit I didn't need training in it myself. But in any case, you didn't find poor Muriel Kinsman confusing?'

'Yes, I did. But even so, I wasn't sufficiently polite to her, or even reasonable.'

'Well, she arrived safely at Harwich. She was completely harmless, or as harmless as a penniless person can be. The poor always cause trouble, my father was a country curate and we were poor as dirt. Where did she go? Well, I gave her a note to the Distressed Gentlewomen, and Mr Crane knew of a Tolstoyan settlement somewhere near London, with running water, of course. But that isn't really what you came here to talk about, is it? My husband wouldn't have been able to advise you, because it wouldn't have been his business. It isn't my business either, but then I don't care whether it is or not.'

'I haven't any secrets,' said Frank. 'Everyone in Moscow knows everything I do.'

'Perhaps you've been in Moscow too long.'

'I hope not.'

'I won't say "let's get to the point". We arrived there a long time ago. This young woman. She, also, was recommended by the great recommender, Mr Crane. He's an idealist. I don't accuse him of anything worse than that. He's not of the earth, earthy, he's of the clouds, cloudy. But what does your brother-in-law think?'

'Charlie thinks very highly of Lisa Ivanovna,' said Frank. 'He's told you that already.'

'Of course he thinks quite highly of her!' Mrs Graham cried, raising her voice to a pitch that Frank had never heard before. 'Show me a single man in this city who wouldn't! Quiet, blonde, slow-witted, nubile, docile, doesn't speak English, hardly speaks at all in fact, sloping shoulders, half-shut eyes, hasn't broadened out yet though I daresay she will, proper humility, reasonable manners, learned I suppose behind the counter at Muirka's.'

'I don't think her eyes are usually half-shut,' said Frank.

'You're all of you serf-owners at heart! Yes, this brother-in-law too! Fifty years after Emancipation, and you're still chasing them into the straw-stacks!'

'Don't let yourself be carried away, Mrs Graham,' said Frank. 'They've never had serfs in Norbury.'

'Still you haven't answered what I asked you. The brother-in-law. Over here, presumably, in distress at his sister's disap-pearance. What does he think of the situation he finds in your house?'

'There's nothing to think. If Lisa had come to work for us, and Nellie had left the house in consequence, there might have been some objection, but it was quite the other way about.'

'Yes, quite, quite the other way about,' said Mrs Graham hoarsely. She blew out quantities of smoke. Frank felt dismayed.

'You're distressing yourself unnecessarily. I'm sorry it should be on my account.'

'Do I irritate you?' Mrs Graham asked, gallantly trying to regain her usual manner.

'Not yet.'

'There's something else. I find your Lisa difficult to place. We were saying that Selwyn Crane is an idealist, by which we meant, or at least I did, that he's easily taken in. How much did he know about her? I'd say she was probably a deacon's daughter, or a psalm-singer's, or a bell-ringer's – some church official, anyway.'

'I think her father was a joiner.'

'You've seen her documents, of course.'

'Of course.'

'I'm only asking you the questions you ought to have asked yourself. Very likely you have. After all, you were brought up here. You must see a lot of young Russians, a lot of students, but after all Russians can be young without being students – many more of them, I mean, than we do here at the chaplaincy. A joiner's daughter! Well, I don't know that I've ever spoken to a joiner. Milkmen, sewing-women, photographers – terrible people! – German dentists – but not joiners. I'm glad to say that so far the woodwork at the chaplaincy has held up, and there's been no need to call a joiner in.'

'We were talking about Lisa Ivanovna,' said Frank.

'Well, let me put it quite plainly. Perhaps I'm quite on the wrong tack in thinking there's anything mysterious about her. But do you think it's possible that she's connected with any kind of revolutionary group?'

'Mrs Graham, what I think is this: your imagination's running away with you a little. I can't help feeling that you're

determined to find something wrong with Lisa, however unlikely. Politics need spare time, and anyone who looks after my
three children for twenty-four hours of the day and night won't
have much spare time left.'

'But, my dear Frank,' said Mrs Graham, leaning forward, 'is
she sleeping in the house?'

It was the first time she had ever called him 'my dear'. He
went on rapidly, 'And then, political activity needs a certain
temperament, I think. For example, Dolly's teacher –'

'Oh, the godless one!' said Mrs Graham. 'Yes, I've heard of
her. But I'm sure you need have no fears about Dolly. Never did
I meet a child of her age whose head was screwed on more
firmly.'

Frank wondered exactly what Dolly had been saying when
she came to tea, as she sometimes did, at the chaplaincy. Mrs
Graham rolled another handful of rank shag, and squared her
thin shoulders. She's going to pieces, Frank thought. 'No hard
feelings,' he said, and in her contempt for such a commonplace
remark, she began to feel better, so that they parted almost on
friendly terms.

19

'YOUR WIFE and her brother must be close, very close!' exclaimed Mrs Kuriatin.

'I don't think so,' said Frank. 'They haven't seen each other for some years.'

'No tie is as strong as that between a brother and a sister, none. Only prison and hunger are stronger, that's what's said. What do I know of what Arkady is doing? But I know what's in the heart of all my six brothers in Smolensk.'

Kuriatin, too, seemed extravagantly delighted at the arrival of the brother-in-law, whom he insisted as regarding as a lawyer, perhaps as a public prosecutor from an important district. 'Norbury. What is the significance of that in Russian?'

'Northern city, I suppose,' said Frank doubtfully.

'The same meaning, then, as Peking,' said Kuriatin in triumph.

He must show, he said, this newcomer how a Russian enjoys himself, in a way quite unknown to the West. Ordinarily he would have done this by taking a taxi to the gipsy brothels in Petrovsky Park. Were there good gipsy brothels in Norbury? Frank reassured him on this point. But these places were all compulsorily shut during Lent, and Frank stipulated that Charlie who, after all, was musical, shouldn't be taken to Rusalochka's. The motor-car, then. They could go in Kuriatin's Wolseley Star – a 50 h.p. model, with detachable wheels, which Frank felt was a wise precaution – to, let's say, the Merchants' Church, between Kursk and Ryazan, about twelve miles out of Moscow. The roads, though, were still covered with only half-melted snow.

'No matter, I have Columbus tyres from Provodnik's. Provodnik sells only the best, and makes me a special price. They will go over any road, and in the worst weather.' Ben confirmed this, although Mikhailo, Kuriatin's chauffeur, promoted from head groom, had never let him get a proper look at the engine and hadn't, Ben thought, really got the proper hang of it himself.

Kuriatin was in high spirits. He knew Charlie couldn't understand anything he said, but treated this as a jest, to be overcome by noise and persistence. 'You'll come back deaf,' Frank said. 'I shall be responsible for you to Nellie, you know.' He told Bernov, who as part of his own plans for advancement had taken a course in commercial English, that he'd have to go along as interpreter.

'You surprise me, Frank Albertovich. A day's work at the Press will be lost if I go on this expedition, and if they want to attend Vespers at the monastery we shall have to stay the night.'

'You won't get as far as that.'

'You anticipate a breakdown?'

'If that happens, get Mikhailo to check the carburettor. This Russian petrol is very low on benzine.'

'What is a carburettor? I wish you were coming with us,' said Bernov, and Frank felt a surge of affection for him, which was replaced when he got to work by remorse. Reidka's had settled down at once into its new arrangement, giving him an indescribable sense of quietened anxiety and present satisfaction, such as he had had as a small boy when watching a bee-hive or a top. During the day, new official regulations arrived, requiring that henceforward all fines for absence or drunkenness should not be held back by the firms concerned, but should be paid into an account under government control, where the Ministry of the Interior would decide, eventually, how the money could best be spent for the benefit of the workers. The fines didn't amount to much, but Frank knew that Bernov would have enjoyed deciding whether the small amount of lost income was an overhead, a variable cost or an abnormal cost. Anxious detail was a relief to him from the large-scale schemes which he was already beginning to see would never, alas, find a place at Reidka's. And now, instead of a day of delicious close evaluation and adjustment, he had to rattle, in deep embarrassment, through the chilly landscape on Kuriatin's outing. But Frank knew he couldn't have asked Selwyn to go. Although Kuriatin's change of heart hadn't lasted long, only, indeed, until the next working day, there was no knowing when, in Selwyn's presence, it might return, and Frank couldn't see how a change of heart would fit in to a day out in the Wolseley.

He was late home, having helped to read over the proofs of *Three Men in a Boat*. He had something to eat, of sorts, in Markel's Bar. When he got back, Lisa brought in the children to say goodnight, something which had never happened to him before, and which he thought only happened in other families. It was most unusual, to begin with, for them all to agree to go to bed at the same time.

'Is Uncle Charlie back?' asked Dolly

'No, he isn't back yet.'

'Do you think they've had a puncture?'

'Very likely,' said Frank. 'All cars have punctures.'

'They ought to make them all with solid wheels, like Trojans.'

'Perhaps, but people want to be comfortable.'

'I don't see that Uncle Charlie ought to stay here much longer,' said Dolly. 'He hasn't brought Mother back with him, and he can't tell us when she's coming, either.'

'Don't you care anything about your uncle?' asked Frank, with a straightforward desire for information. Annushka, born to take life in the way easiest to herself and to extract from any situation only the aspect which did her most credit, shouted, 'I love my Uncle Charlie!'

'He seems to like everything so much,' said Ben, trying to render justice, 'we're not used to that.'

'And his visit hasn't led to anything,' said Dolly. 'He isn't supposed to be here just to enjoy himself.'

Frank pointed out that Charlie's train tickets to London, via Warsaw and Berlin, were booked for the 28th of March, Russian calendar, and it was the family's business to see that he enjoyed himself till then. He would rather have liked Dolly to give him a hug, but she had apparently decided against this. All day, ever since he could remember, Frank had been used, in Moscow, to physical human warmth, and not only when he was a child. Even now, his Russian business contacts frequently threw their arms round him, so did his servants and his employees, while the tea-woman and the yardman, if he didn't manage to stop them, kissed his hands. All that Dolly gave him was a fearless, affectionate glance.

Frank sent all the servants to bed and said that he would sit up for Karl Karlovich himself. At half-past ten Kuriatin and his party came back, not in the Wolseley, which had started to pour out smoke and had been abandoned, with Mikhailo, a few miles out of Moscow, but in a broken-down horse and carriage which was all they'd been able to hire on the spot. Kuriatin was noisy and anxious to show that everything had been a success, Bernov looked tired, shrunken and sober, Charlie was his usual self. He saw nothing amiss with their day. He hadn't, he explained, taken any vodka as he thought it might be affecting his bowels, but he had had a few glasses of kvass, the Russian beer made, they told him, out of bread, which was just as remarkable, when you came to think of it, as if they'd made bread out of beer. Clever people, the Russians. It didn't matter that they'd never reached the church. When you'd seen one Orthodox church, you'd seen them all. And at the traktir they'd had a special dish, a fish-pie with a hole in the top, into which you crammed caviare.

'Mr Kuriatin's treated me very liberally all day,' he went on. 'I'm beginning to see that over here the expression "friend of the family" means just what it says.'

'So it does in England,' said Frank.

'I shouldn't have understood, of course, without Mr Bernov here, and his useful gift of tongues. He was explaining to me on the way back what Mr Kuriatin was saying, I mean about how much he felt for you and how he'd like to do something more for you.'

Kuriatin, who had caught his name, nodded, laughed, rolled his eyes and emitted sounds, though not quite at the same time.

He was like a mechanical figure in a second-hand toy shop, slightly out of kilter.

'He wants to take the three children into his household, Frank, for as long as need be, so that you'd be free of all responsibility. What do you think of that? It seems his wife is a motherly soul who can't have too many kiddies in the house. And it wouldn't cost you anything. He held out his arms wide, just like he's doing now, and said, "Let them regard me as their second father." Didn't he, Mr Bernov?'

'Yes,' said Bernov. 'He repeated that more than once.'

'What's he saying now?' asked Charlie.

'He's saying that a man who has drunk vodka is like a child: what is in his heart comes straight to his lips.'

'Is that a traditional saying?'

'It may be,' said Bernov, 'I've never lived in a village and I'm not familiar with traditional sayings.'

'It doesn't matter anyway,' said Frank. 'He doesn't really want to adopt my children. It's just a general expression of good-will, or more likely the opposite.'

'Surely, as a businessman, he'll be as good as his word!' Charlie cried. 'Surely he's the soul of hospitality.'

'Of course he is.'

Suddenly bored, Kuriatin got off the sofa with a plunging motion and, not waiting for the samovar, made his way out, yelling for his coat and boots. The carriage had been kept waiting in the drizzle. He drove off, without offering Bernov a lift.

'It's of no importance, Frank Albertovich, I'd prefer to take a tram in any case.' Bernov struggled into his galoshes. 'This time, however, you've asked too much of me. I'm your cost accountant and I should prefer to confine myself to my daily duties.'

Charlie was tired and went straight to bed, still praising and approving. This damp weather was so much healthier than a hot, dry climate. A good thing, really, that the Wolseley had broken down, because up to then it had seemed to make Mr Bernov a bit unwell. But Mr Kuriatin had known what to do, and at the traktir he'd made him take a special remedy, a draught of mothballs dissolved in vodka.

'It's a useful tip, really. One ought to write all these things down somewhere handy. Well, Frank, I'll say goodnight.'

20

IT SEEMED, on the day before Charlie was due to leave, as though he had been there for as long as they could remember. He had taken to eating kasha, two or even three bowls of it, at breakfast, with a lump of butter in each. 'I shan't get this at home,' he said. He had, he felt, got a pretty good general look at Russia. On his drive with Kuriatin and Bernov he hadn't been far out of the city, but far enough, he thought, to see what the rest of the country and its agriculture must be like.

'I saw cabbage stumps everywhere. There's too much reliance on the cabbage in Russia, Frank. If I have any criticism, it's that these people aren't like our allotment-holders at home. A farm or a factory can make a loss, but an English allotment, never. And that brings me to my other point.'

The other point had to be left for the time being, because it was a fixed principle in Norbury that nothing of importance must be discussed in front of the servants.

'Even though they don't understand me they might gather the sense of my gestures and facial expressions. You don't want them to know your business.'

'Everyone knows my business,' said Frank.

Charlie walked with him as far as the tram-stop. 'I'm sorry I haven't seen your place of work. But I daresay a rest will do me no harm. And Dolly has promised to come with me to the Rows after school and interpret for me to the shopkeepers, so that I can get a few little presents to take back home. Now, that brings me to the point I was unable to make at breakfast.'

'What was that?'

'It's about the kiddies. That offer of Kuriatin's – there's a rough diamond for you, if you like – it set me thinking. You turned that down, but how does this strike you – suppose I were to take the three of them with me tomorrow when I go back to England?'

'Look, Charlie –'

'I've surprised you, haven't I, Frank? But it's a grief to me that your kiddies don't know their native land. We were talking about allotments – well, they've none of them ever seen one. I daresay they've never even seen a vegetable marrow. And then, you know, I find it a bit lonely in the house at times.'

'You want them to live with you permanently?'

'Think it over, Frank. I know you're not having an easy time, even if we haven't talked much about it. Think it over during the day, and see how it appeals to you.'

'Your father looked quite put out,' Charlie said to Dolly, as they walked into the Trading Rows. 'I hope I didn't speak out of turn.'

'Don't worry about it now,' Dolly told him. She was in tearing spirits, wearing her new fur-lined overcoat over her school uniform, and totally in charge. 'We'll get your presents first. Then you can give me some tea, and I'll tell you what I think.'

They climbed to the Upper Rows, the top storey of the great market, intersected in each direction by glass-covered corridors from which the moving mass of shoppers, also under glass, could be seen swarming forth and back. The middle storey was for wholesale. Upstairs, they faced half a mile of merchandise, laid out for ready spenders. Dolly's eyes shone.

'Just a few items,' said Charlie feebly. 'There are neighbours who've been good to me, there's the vicarage, and I suppose the Choral Society and one or two people at work.'

'What are you taking back for Mother?'

'I'm not sure of her whereabouts, Dolly dear. Otherwise, you know, I should have –'

Taking his list away from him, Dolly dragged him rapidly forward. 'This is the grocery section. Not the imported groceries, the Russian things. Tinned sturgeon in wine, potted elk, dried elk, caviare of course, but this isn't the best kind, partridges in brandy. Then down this way there's the *galanterya*, amber beads, kid gloves, silk fans with pearl handles, velvet babies' boots, all that sort of thing, or you can get peasants' feast day dresses, you don't have to buy the whole dress, you can just get a *kokosnik* or a *shugai*. Now we're getting on to the gold and silver and jewellery and the religious objects.'

'I can't afford these things, Dolly. Can't we take a short cut? In any case, they wouldn't do for presents, religious objects would look quite out of place at the vicarage.'

'They've got pearl ear-rings here. They're only river pearls, though.'

As she spoke she turned her head towards him. Charlie was taken aback to see, what he'd never noticed before, that her ears were pierced in an altogether foreign way, and that she was wearing a pair of gold sleepers.

'When did you have that done, dear?'

'Oh, when I was two weeks old, I suppose. Annushka's are just the same.'

He said awkwardly, 'Perhaps you'd like me to get you some of these pearls, then?' Dolly laughed. 'I've got plenty of them at home. We're not allowed to wear them at school.'

Taking pity on him, she turned left at the crossing point of the next glass corridors, and they bought a number of small birchwood objects and a cigar-case. She counted his change and recovered, without argument, another thirty kopeks. Charlie had to be careful with his purchases, all of them wrapped by now in coarse paper, or, said Dolly, they might break.

To get a glass of tea, they had to go down to the restaurant, which was in the basement of one of the sandstone towers of the Rows. But the place was dismayingly full, the air thick as gas and thronged with customers' elbows on the shove.

'We won't stay here, we'll go and have tea with Selwyn Osipych.'

'I don't know where he lives, Dolly, and surely he'll be working at the Press.'

'No, he won't. My father goes in every day, except some times not on Saturday. Selwyn doesn't go in on Thursdays. They're both in on Fridays because it's pay-day. No one's allowed by law to be paid on Saturdays or the eve of feast days, to stop them getting drunk the next morning.'

'That's all very well, but it may not be very convenient to call if he's not expecting us,' Charlie pleaded.

Selwyn lived in the east Miasnitskaya, just where it changed from a prosperous to a doubtful quarter. One street further and you were among the brothels, male and female, the Khitrovo market which was not much like the shops in the Rows, and the lodging houses where job-seekers, cholera suspects, military deserters and wanted criminals hid themselves by day. Dolly would not, in the ordinary way of things, have been allowed so far to the east of the Miasnitskaya. But she knew the house, and brazenly rang for the doorman.

'See if Selwyn Osipych is at home.'

'He has rooms in this house, but he is scarcely ever here.' Selwyn, however, came down himself to greet them.

'You should have told me –'

'I know,' said Charlie. 'But I'm not at the helm this afternoon. We couldn't get tea at the Rows.' Behind the other two on the stairs, he persevered with his explanation. 'Well, you're both of you very welcome,' Selwyn insisted. Dolly raced up first. Selwyn's room was lit only with paraffin lamps and the red glow of the stove.

'I don't have electricity here,' he said, 'or tea, I mean tea as such. I make an infusion of the nine herbs of healing – buttercup, rattray, marguerite, dead nettle, wild parsley, St John's Wort, clover, balsam and grass. I gather them in summertime, and dry them out on my return.'

'Those herbs of healing are for sick cows,' said Dolly.

'Healing knows no barriers, Dolly.'

'Dead nettles, ugh! Send the doorman out for some tea and a lemon.'

The doorman, however, was at the ready to sell some of his own supply. Indeed, he'd got it out as soon as he saw that Selwyn Osipych had visitors. Few wanted to drink an infusion of the nine herbs. Charlie felt that perhaps they were being difficult guests, and said that the grass and buttercup mixture sounded very interesting, and he'd been recommended something like that for asthma.

'Each plant is under the patronage of a different saint,' said Selwyn. 'These things aren't purely medicinal.'

The room had a ceiling of carved wood, which repeated the pattern of the gables. It was painted white, and Selwyn had got a carpenter to put up row after row of bookshelves, which held not only his books but his shoe-making tools, his needle and thread and his jars of herbs. The same carpenter had made the plain wooden chairs and table, jointed without a single nail. Charlie looked round for something to praise, but was reduced to, 'Nice place you've got here.'

'I'm not sure that it's nice,' said Selwyn, quietly. 'I looked for somewhere to live here because it's on the edge of the Khitrovo market.'

'Is that a good place to shop?'

'Yes, if you want to find whatever's been stolen from you during the last six months, or have yourself tattooed, or get an abortion.'

Charlie frowned, glancing towards Dolly. 'Say no more. I suppose the rent is pretty reasonable, then.'

'Selwyn Osipych doesn't mind so much about the rent,' said Dolly. 'He lives here because he likes to walk about at night among the unfortunate.'

'It's quite true that I don't need much sleep,' Selwyn said. 'And there are times late at night when the souls of men and women open naturally, as is the case with certain plants.'

'Shall I put on the kettle?' Dolly asked. Selwyn had one of the very few kettles in Moscow. There was no word in Russian for it. He had brought it back several years ago from a visit to his home town, Tunbridge Wells.

'You don't have all these servants, then?' asked Charlie.

'No, the relationship seems to me a false one.'

'Well, our Dolly seems to be very handy in the kitchen.' Selwyn explained to him what Tolstoy had told him; if grown men and women live simply, and do tasks of which the need is obvious, the children will soon wish to share them.

'Do you think Nellie lived simply?' Charlie asked.

After Dolly had seen to the tea she sat down and said abruptly: 'Uncle Charlie wants to take us back with him to Norbury. How he got such an idea into his head I can't think.'

'Now, my dear,' said Charlie, 'you're speaking more sharply than you intend, I'm sure. I made the offer to your father, as I told you, in all good faith. I was only surprised that it upset him so much.'

'I think I understand it,' said Selwyn leaning forward, all interest and concern. 'Dolly doesn't want to leave her father.'

'We don't want to leave Russia,' said Dolly. 'It's the beginning of spring. We want to go to the dacha.'

Sucking the last slice of lemon, sitting in the tender lamplight, she looked at them tolerantly.

'We don't want to leave Lisa Ivanovna.'

21

THAT EVENING Charlie, to Frank's amazement, repeated his offer.

'You're not going to start on about that again?'

'Yes, Frank, I am, because it's come to me that you were against the whole idea because you thought I wouldn't be able to manage on my own on the journey, and it's true, I haven't much experience of looking after kiddies. But now I can see a way round that, and it'll have another benefit too, because I mentioned to you that I was rather lonely at times in Long-fellow Road. Now how would it be if I got Miss Lisa to come with me? I mean at the same wages you're paying her here, which I take it are fair ones.'

Frank stared at him, but saw that he was obliged to believe him. 'I don't know, Charlie,' he said. 'How would it be? Have you asked her?'

'You're forgetting that I can't make myself understood in Russian. The thing, naturally, would be for you to speak to her on my behalf.'

In silence, Frank set himself to compose a short speech. 'Dear Lisa, please consider the following three possibilities, which I've been asked to put before you by my brother-in-law. First, Karl Karlovich wants you, although he doesn't know it himself. He would like you to go to England with him to look after the children on the journey, at the same wages I pay you (which he takes it are fair ones), and then later, when he realises what he really feels, to go to bed with him, to the disgust, disapproval, and envy of all his neighbours in Norbury. Second possibility: Karl Karlovich wants you, &c. &c., but he's sharper than I thought, and he *does* know it himself. The results would be the same, and at the same wages I pay you (which he takes it are fair ones), but would take place a good deal sooner. A third possibility: Karl Karlovich doesn't want you, but he suspects that

I do. This distresses him, partly on his sister's account, partly, I think, on mine, as I'm sure he has my moral welfare at heart, and it's come to him that if he can get you away to England (still at the same wages), he'll deliver me from temptation.'

'I don't quite know how I'd explain it to her,' he said aloud. 'But are you sure the children want to go to Norbury?'

Charlie looked disheartened. 'Not quite sure,' he said.

Frank decided that after all his brother-in-law was a more honourable man than himself, but he also realised that he didn't care, and the relief of admitting this combined, to some extent, with the relief of seeing Charlie off with his hold-all, his portmanteau, the presents which he had bought with Dolly in the Rows and the dozen bottles of vodka and fifty cakes of green tea which Kuriatin, at the last moment, had sent to the station. Although it was only ten days since he'd arrived, Charlie seemed largely to have forgotten the practical details of the journey. Customs regulations, time zones, warning bells, were all scattered in his mind, all muddled. Certainly he seemed to have forgotten the main object of his visit. Nellie wasn't mentioned between them.

'I'll let you know when I get back safely, Frank, you can count on that. I feel I haven't thanked you half enough. And I'm more than sorry if I've caused any unpleasantness by suggesting. . . . I mean, if you think there's any kind of cloud between us, I'm quite prepared to tear up the return half of my ticket here and now and go straight back to Lipka Street with you.'

To emphasise what he meant he took out his wallet, but the return ticket was not there. A search followed, Frank going through Charlie's coat, feeling like an amateur pick-pocket, and finding the ticket at last, after all, in the wallet. The third bell rang. Charlie clambered up the high steps of the carriage and, as the train moved out of the station, tried to look back out of the window, but too many of the other passengers crowded in front of him and he was lost to sight.

*

'Has he gone?' asked Dolly.

The same room, the same soup, the same bread, but no Charlie. It seemed, as they all sat down together, as though a threat had been removed. The day settled down, once again, without a ripple. Lisa still chewed energetically, and still spoke only when she was spoken to, she still created a sense of repose without tedium, as though the natural condition of life was peace. I've got to disturb her, Frank thought, at all costs.

'I don't think I shall ever get married,' Dolly went on. 'Lisa, too, probably won't ever get married.'

'Lisa, why did you tell Dolly that?' Frank asked.

'What I told her was that once, perhaps even ten years ago, it was considered a terrible thing in the villages for a woman to be single.'

'That's not the same thing at all.'

'No, not the same.'

'My teacher isn't married,' said Dolly. 'Miss Kinsman wasn't married.'

'None of you children ever met Miss Kinsman,' said Frank. 'I didn't know you'd ever heard of her. Lisa, I give you my permission to reprove Dolly if she oppresses me, as all women, without exception, seem to be impelled to do.'

'Why is it better now for women than it was ten years ago?' asked Ben.

'It is better,' said Frank. 'But perhaps Lisa would explain why.'

Lisa never changed colour, but now she put down her spoon and said, 'I haven't much practice in explaining. It's unkind to ask anyone for more than they have to give.'

'Unkind!' said Frank, aghast.

Next day, at Reidka's, as soon as Bernov was out of the way, he asked Selwyn whether he'd ever thought of him as an unkind or inhuman person. While Selwyn, instead of denying it immediately, was thinking the question over in his gentle, irritating way, Frank said, 'You told me it was my duty to try to understand Lisa Ivanovna.'

'I don't know that I used the word "duty",' said Selwyn, recalled to himself. 'That necessarily suggests something that you don't want to do. I envisaged a moment somewhat like entering the warmest room of the bath house, the steam room, where desire and duty become one. Do you follow me?'

'Quite well, as a matter of fact,' said Frank. 'But the trouble is that I can't do much when there's so little time. I only see her in the morning and again in the evening.'

'That's more, to be honest with you, than I should have expected. I don't think you ought to reproach yourself on that score. It's possible, though, that Lisa Ivanovna's life is, to some extent, joyless. If that is so, I'm quite prepared to take her out some evening, as I did your brother-in-law. All large meetings are banned, of course, particularly for young people, but we might try a Temperance group, or a gathering of the Russian Pilgrims of the Way of Humility, or a literary circle. All these events are free, or cost very little, and all, as long as the numbers are kept small, are approved by the political police.'

Frank let this pass. 'When she first came – you know, when you brought her to the house – I noticed how quiet she was.'

'Certainly she was quiet. One would hardly notice she was in the room.'

'I do notice when she's in the room. But I'd thought that when she'd been with us a little longer, she'd talk more.'

'Of course, as I understood it, she was never expected to stay with you very long.'

'That's my point. I think I ought to know what she intends to do when she leaves here, and whether she has anywhere to go.'

'One could ask her about that, of course. But, Frank, why not leave that task to me? I was responsible, I own, for bringing Lisa to your notice, as I have brought so many unfortunates before her, in the quest for material help. This time, perhaps, you don't feel inclined to thank me.'

'I'm not sure yet whether I do or not,' said Frank. 'I'll tell you later.'

'To return to what you asked me in the first place: do I consider you to be unkind, or to have the potentiality for unkindness? That, Frank, must be a question of the imagination, I mean of picturing the sufferings of others. Now, you're not an imaginative man, Frank. If you have a fault, it's that you don't grasp the importance of what is beyond sense or reason. And yet that is a world in itself. "Where is the stream," we cry, with tears. But look up, and lo! there is the blue stream flowing gently over our heads.'

'I'm not sure whether she trusts me,' said Frank. 'On the whole, I hope not.'

22

On the eve of Palm Sunday the servants, in preparation for their Easter confession, went round the house and to the neighbours' to ask forgiveness for any sins they had committed, knowingly or unknowingly, against them. There was no need to specify the sins.

Frank was taken aback when Lisa told him that she also needed forgiveness from him, for actions, for words, and for unspoken thoughts.

'What could you possibly have done wrong?' he asked. 'I don't know what your unspoken thoughts are, but I've got no complaints about what you do.'

'Who is there who can go through a single day without doing wrong?'

'Well, if it's going to be a competition, my conscience isn't clear either.' She waited silently. 'I forgive you, Lisa,' he said.

On Palm Sunday she put on her black shawl and took the children out to see the crowds. 'I'll join you later, I'll look out for you,' he told them. Almost as soon as they were gone, he was wanted on the telephone. It was the Ministry of Defence, political division, or more precisely, the Security police.

'We are holding Vladimir Semyonich Grigoriev, a student, who has confessed that he broke into your premises on the night of the 16th of March. Can you identify this man?'

'There are six thousand students in the University,' said Frank.

'But only one of them broke into Reid's Press on the night of the 16th of March, with the aim either of printing subversive matter or of stealing type and other materials in order to print it elsewhere.'

'Nothing was stolen.'

'Why did he go there then? He had the whole of Moscow to choose from. In any case, we are requesting you to come round to Nikitskaya 210, and fetch him away.'

'Fetch him away! It's Palm Sunday: I don't want him!' Frank said. 'I'm always being asked to fetch something or somebody. I'm a printer, not a common carrier.'

'The streets are crowded. You won't be able to get a taxi today. We'll send one for you in six minutes.'

Frank had never been before to the security headquarters on the Nikitskaya, which had nothing to distinguish it from the other four-storey blocks on either side of it. On the third floor, which had none of the carpet-slippered, tobacco-stinking ease of the district police station, he found three men, of whom one did the talking, one took down shorthand notes, and one remained standing by the door. Volodya, looking pitiable, was sitting the wrong way round on a wooden chair, his chin resting on the back. He was wearing his crumpled dark green student's uniform.

Asked to identify the detainee, Frank said he'd never known his surname or his address.

'Well, we do know it,' said the interrogator. 'Can you confirm that your household at 22 Lipka Street consists of yourself and your three legitimate children, a general manservant in charge of opening the door, a cook, an assistant to the cook, a temporary nursery governess whose native village is Vladimir, a yardman, and a boy who formerly cleaned the lamps but now that electricity has been installed, cleans the shoes and does odd jobs of various kinds?' Frank did confirm it, wanting to protest that in spite of the enormity of the list he didn't live as grandly as all that. But it was the way he was expected to live, otherwise he'd be falling short as an employer, just as he was when he shaved himself, instead of going to the barber on the corner of Lipka Street. The interrogator, who had been reading from a card, turned it over and added: 'Your wife, Elena Karlovna, has temporarily left you.'

'I don't contest any of this,' said Frank.

The man made a mark on the card, and went on, 'When Grigoriev intruded on your premises, what was it that he intended to print?'

'I don't think it existed, except possibly in his mind.'

'My mind is my own,' cried Volodya, lifting his head from the chair-back. 'You can't touch it.'

No one paid him the slightest attention, a disappointment to Frank, who'd hoped he might be taken away for good.

'Frank Albertovich Reid, we know that you're trying to dispose of your business with the intention of returning to England. During the past eighteen months you have acquired a declaration, made before a notary, that you have no outstanding debts, a police permit declaring that there is no obstacle to your leaving the empire, and a special permit from the Governor General covering the sale of a printing establishment. These documents have been translated into English and you have paid the specified charges for certifying the correctness of the translation and for attesting that it was made by someone authorised by the law of the land to translate it.'

'I don't contest any of that either,' said Frank. 'I'm not leaving Russia at the moment, but I think it's right to be ready to go. All these documents were legally obtained and paid for.'

'And they can be legally invalidated. It won't be so easy to get them a second time.'

'I trust that won't be necessary,' said Frank.

'We are making you a surety for the good behaviour of Vladimir Semyonich Grigoriev. He will be under our surveillance, naturally, but it will be your responsibility to see that he doesn't become involved in any subversive or politically objectionable activity.'

'You haven't forgotten that he broke into my premises?' asked Frank. 'I hadn't pictured myself providing a reference for him.'

'You told me you wished me well,' said Volodya, in a broken voice.

'We shall notify you if Grigoriev changes his address. To recapitulate, if there is any further scandal we shall have to see about the withdrawal of your exit permits, and in any case while Grigoriev is still at the University you will not be in a position to leave Moscow. If you have no further questions, you're free to go now.'

The third officer, who seemed to be there only to open and shut the door, opened it.

23

No one had suggested providing a taxi to take them away again, and they walked together through the streets which, after the morning Mass, were emptying themselves towards Red Square. High up and on the edges of the horizon the mists, born of the last snows, became transparent and vanished. The bells rang the entry of Christ into Jerusalem. Frank looked far and near for a sight of Lisa's black shawl. There were hundreds, perhaps thousands of black shawls, and a great many young women in charge of children. She must be there, but she was lost to him.

'Why I didn't turn you in to the police in the first place, I don't know,' he said. 'You've caused me an amazing amount of inconvenience. By the way, who gave you away in the end?'

'I don't understand you,' said Volodya. 'I went to the police myself, I confessed myself, I made a clean breast of it and told them I had broken into your premises.'

Among the crowds, the pedlars of pussy-willow, up from the country, traversed every street, or stood at every street-corner. By tradition they said nothing to their customers, and, as they held out the red-stalked willows, named no price. These were grave confrontations. Frank thought it unlikely that Volodya had any money, and bought willows for both of them. There was no question of their going any farther without them.

'Let us forgive each other!' cried Volodya.

'I assure you I'm doing my best,' said Frank.

'You think I'm cracked, perhaps.'

'No, I don't think you're cracked.' Volodya, however, seemed unwilling to give up the idea. 'At your age, you were cracked like me.'

'I didn't have time to be cracked,' Frank said. 'It would be awkward if I were to start now.'

Along the Kremlin wall there were trestle tables, set out in rows and covered with white cloths. The stall-holders offered plenty, but not variety. All of them were selling the same things, and the crowds pressed on, apparently in amazement at the repetition of barrels and jugs of kvass, strings of bread rolls, kvass, rolls, rolls, kvass. Frank bought a string of rolls and, not feeling at all hungry, gave them to Volodya, who began to eat, dangling them from the forefinger of his left hand. He suggested once again that they ought to forgive each other.

'I only want you to remember that to some extent I'm dependent on your behaviour,' said Frank. 'Let's leave it at that. I don't think you're dangerous. I'm sure, for example, that you didn't mean to kill me the other night at my office.'

'Oh, but there you're quite wrong, Frank Albertovich,' said Volodya eagerly. He was still young enough to speak clearly with his mouth full. 'I did mean to kill you. That's what I hadn't explained. I meant to shoot you, but unfortunately there was something wrong with the automatic.'

'I don't know what you mean by "unfortunately" in this connection,' said Frank, but Volodya rushed on. 'You took Lisa Ivanovna into your house. That was why I tried to kill you.'

'So you're not connected with any political group?'

'No, no.'

'And you didn't want to print anything?'

'No, nothing.'

'Not even a few pages on universal pity?'

'What is universal pity?' asked Volodya doubtfully.

'But you feel responsible for some reason for Lisa Ivanovna, and you wanted to get rid of me. Why didn't you come round to the house and take a shot at me there?'

'That would have caused scandal. For Lisa to be living in the house of a foreign merchant when he was shot might have made things very difficult for her.'

'Lisa works in my house, just as she did at Muir and Merrilees. You never went round there and fired at the manager. Do you seriously think she'll come to any harm with me?'

'I don't know, perhaps not, it makes no difference, I feel like shouting aloud that it's too much for me to bear. Listen, please, I should prefer you to understand. It isn't bearable that she should be approached, spoken to, breathed upon, quite possibly touched by a man such as yourself, Frank Albertovich.'

Volodya was, in fact, shouting aloud, as though addressing one of the forbidden students' meetings. 'Have you ever spoken to her yourself?' Frank asked. Yes, it appeared that Volodya had spoken to her several times, but always in public. He had met her on three separate occasions in the Prechistenskaya public library. He went there because the University libraries were closed during the periods of student unrest, which had become longer and longer. Lisa, after her day behind the counter, went there to read the magazines and newspapers. Speaking in low tones wasn't forbidden in the library, although presumably, Frank reflected, the rules made breathing upon and touching very difficult.

Volodya's eyes were full of unshed tears, which gathered brightly and increased, as Annushka's sometimes did, without a sound. Without warning, dropping the willows and what was left of the bread, he threw his arms round Frank's neck.

'Did you believe what I said? Did you?'

Frank felt outnumbered.

'I didn't want to kill you. When I said that, I wasn't telling the truth. My intention was only to frighten you.'

'What made you think I'd be frightened?'

'I thought you were a coward,' said Volodya, 'but wrongly, wrongly.'

'Why did you think that?'

'Because you ran away from the English governess.'

Frank unhitched Volodya's long clinging arms. He had seen Lisa, Dolly, Ben and Annushka, walking away from him, with their backs to him, past the Inverskaya chapel. Pigeons were threading their way through the press of bodies and legs to retrieve Volodya's fallen bread. Frank hurried across the square, against the human current, towards Lisa. When he caught up with them (which was not so difficult, after all, since the pavement outside the Inverskaya was laid out in pink and grey granite setts, and Annushka would walk only on the pink ones), the children, with their arms full of willow branches, besieged him. He must agree to their going to the dacha with Lisa for the school holiday, from Easter Tuesday until the Tsaritsa's name day. Frank pointed out that the snow would still be on the ground in the woods, while in Moscow even the windows hadn't been opened yet, and he himself would be wanted at Reidka's, which would not be on holiday. He asked what he was supposed to do without them. Dolly said that she was sure Mrs Graham would ask him round pretty frequently to the chaplaincy.

'Swear by the health of His Imperial Majesty that you'll let us go,' shouted Ben.

'But your mother might come back while you're away.'

'Are you expecting her?' Dolly asked.

'No.'

Annushka said she wanted him to carry her. Lisa said nothing. They would, after all, only be away for a few days. However wet and cold they got, it would be unkind not to let them go.

24

THE SKY was of a blue so pale that it could hardly be distinguished from white. On Good Friday the churches stood
dark and silent. On Easter Saturday, cheesecakes were brought
out in their tens of thousands in every parish, to be blessed.
On Monday the house-cleaning began. Every blanket had
to be taken outside and beaten, the rugs must come up,
the curtains down, fur-lined coats had to be stowed away, the
mattresses had to be ripped open and remade, feather by
feather. Frank was consulted by Toma as to whether the
windows should not be opened. I leave it to you, he
said. And the poultry let out? I leave it to you. No post was
delivered on Easter Monday, so he went across to fetch it
himself from the General Post Office on the west side of
the Miasnitskaya. There was nothing from England except
an Easter card from Charlie, with a hand-coloured photograph of chickens, lambs and young children, and a printed
quotation:

> 'The world would be a dreary place
> Were there no little people in it.'

There was also a letter from Volodya, correctly stamped, which
read:

Honoured Frank Albertovich
In my haste on Palm Sunday I am afraid I may not
have made myself clear on one point. I may have
suggested to you that there was in fact, as well as in
possibility, a sexual relationship existing between you
and Lisa Ivanovna. Let me say now that having thought
more deeply on the subject, and on your reputation in

the foreign business community here in Moscow, and
particularly on your age, I realise that my suspicions
must be groundless. I wish therefore to withdraw them.
On every other point in discussion between us my
opinions remain the same. Indeed, they are unalterable.
        With sincere respects,
                                Vladimir Semyonich Grigoriev

Although it was not his habit, Frank read the letter through
twice. The handwriting, for a student, was wretched.

At 22 Lipka Street packing had already begun for the few
days' visit to the dacha. None of the servants were going,
though they would have liked to, and to indicate this they
had thrown themselves into unnecessary activities, sewing up
the children's clothes in rolls of sacking and loading the china
into crates of straw. 'We shan't want all these,' said Dolly. It was
quite unlike the long summer holiday, when everyone came,
and they stocked up as though for a siege. 'There'll be no one
there except Egor and Matryona.' She meant the old couple
from the nearest village who were supposed to act as caretakers.
Toma agreed that there was no point in taking cups and saucers
for those who were not able to appreciate them. Those two
were born ignorant, he said, and if you boiled them in a kettle
for seven years, you wouldn't boil that out of them. 'That's not
what I meant at all, Toma, and you know it,' said Dolly. The
china remained in the hall, half unpacked again, when night
fell.

Frank asked Lisa not to go to bed. 'There's something I want
to ask you, and if you're going away for five days I'd better ask
you now.'

She stood by the door, untroubled.

'Lisa, do you know a man, a young man, that is, called
Volodya Semyonich Grigoriev?'

'Yes, I do. Is he in trouble?'

'Why do you ask that?'

'He's a student,' she said, shrugging her shoulders a
little.

Frank wanted to ask her where she had met Volodya, to see if she would tell the same story, but felt this would be base and undignified.

'Where did you meet him?' Lisa asked.

Taken aback, Frank shifted his ground. 'You're quite right, he has been in trouble. I should be ready to help him, though, if he's a friend of yours.'

Lisa seemed puzzled.

'Would you, Frank Albertovich?'

'No, to be quite honest, I shouldn't.'

'I can't tell what he's been saying about me. What did he say?'

'He told me that he'd only met you three times.'

'Perhaps you could count it as three times, I'm not sure. He used to come into Muir and Merrilees, to the counter, and hang about the department. The students couldn't afford to buy anything. But it was warm in there, and it was also warm in the Prechistenskaya.'

Volodya had written a note, she went on, and put it in the magazine she was reading, then waited while she turned the pages until she got to it. 'That's not such a strange thing in a public library. But you have to write in pencil. When I opened it, it said: "You're alive. I too am alive."'

'I didn't ask you what it said.'

'What kind of trouble is it? I think he's only twenty.'

'And I'm not. That, too, he's pointed out to me.'

Lisa looked at him with polite concern. She seemed, however, as always, to be listening only enough to grasp what was said and to respond to it correctly and efficiently, while compelled to hear, by some inner secret conspiracy, another voice.

'Listen to me, Lisa,' Frank said, gripping her by the forearms, 'since we're telling each other what was in our private correspondence, let me go a bit farther. This Grigoriev told me it wasn't bearable that you should be breathed on, touched, gone near to, spoken to, no, spoken to, breathed on, gone near to, touched, that's it, by a man like me. What do you say to that, Lisa? You're alive. Is it bearable? Is it?'

For the first time he had all her attention, or, if he was deceiving himself there, and I daresay I am, he thought, at least more than he had ever had before. It was the first time, too, that he'd ever made love to a woman with short hair. What an advantage, none of that endless business with the hairpins. And with all the blood in his body he knew that she was not taken by surprise.

'Don't regret this, Frank. If you're sure, if you know beyond any doubt that what you're doing is helpful, then go on, go on with a stout heart.'

It was Selwyn, who must have made his way through the straw and clutter of the front hall. As Frank turned to confront him, Lisa disengaged herself quietly and was out of the room.

'You're angry with me, Frank. But, my old friend, the fathers of the Russian church saw anger itself as "black grace". It helps to remember that. All strong emotions, Frank, may be worthy of grace.'

'Selwyn.'

'Frank, yes.'

'Selwyn, get out of here, if you don't want your teeth down your throat.'

Presumably Selwyn had had some reason for calling, but he had no chance, at that particular moment, to say what it was, while he retreated rapidly towards the front door. Frank went up the dark stairs in to the back of the house and knocked at the door of Lisa's room. He had not expected it to be locked, and it was not locked, but he waited until he heard her bare feet cross the wooden floor to open it.

In the very early morning, they left for Shirokaya. The children said goodbye to him affectionately, but absentmindedly, the leavers commiserating with the left behind. They had March fever. They were going out of the still sealed-up, glassed-up house into the fresh, watery, early spring.

Toma kept repeating that the two taxis which were to take everyone and everything to the station were outside; the drivers had been waiting in the semi-darkness, arguing, for more than an hour. Lisa Ivanovna and the children, Toma said, must sit down for a minute, in the old way, the Russian way, before starting on their journey, to ensure that they'd return safely home. No one took any notice of him. Blashl, who was never allowed into the house, had floundered into the hall and in her terror was wailing, rather than barking, and wagging her tail insanely. Told to leave, she lost her way and could be heard upturning heavy objects in the kitchen. Lisa appeared in her waterproof.

'What are you going to say to me?' Frank asked her, at the foot of the stairs.

Lisa appeared to think a little and then said, 'Until next Saturday, Frank Albertovich.'

'For God's sake stay with me, Lisa,' said Frank. There was no way of telling whether she had heard him. The doorman and the cook were in the hall to say their goodbyes and Blashl, unrestrained, had trundled once again out of the kitchen quarters, sweeping her tail in wide arcs. Annushka, as disturbed as Blashl by the scent of departures, howled and clung. Lisa restored tranquillity, and in five minutes they were gone. He was almost sure that she could not have heard what he had said to her.

25

THE DACHA was not convenient, and not in good repair. The passionate affection which Dolly and Ben felt for it suggested that, after all, children and adults were hardly of the same species. It was true, though, that Nellie, too, had been unwilling to part with it. And Selwyn, who had no dacha of his own, had often come down for Saturday and Sunday. Oddly enough, when he was there, he behaved much more like an ordinary management accountant than he did in Moscow.

Although there was a large industrial town three miles away, with workers' suburbs and dormitories, Shirokaya could only be reached by a woodcutters' branch-line along the edge of the forest. The nearest village, Ostanovka, got its name from the railway halt. From there the quickest way was on foot through the woods, while the luggage went round by carrier's horse and cart. The carrier also came round twice a week to fill the water-barrels. The rye-bread, heavy as a tombstone, was bought in the village. The tea they brought with them from Moscow.

Tea was drunk with pickled lemons, which stayed in the dacha from one year's end to another in large barrels in the store-room, along with the salted melons, the pears in vinegar, the soused apples, the pickled cabbage, the pickled onions and plums, the pickled mushrooms. The mushrooms, strung from the ceiling, were sorted into the slimy buttery ones, the fleshy rusty ones, the white ones, which were in fact brown, the huge pine-tree ones, the red-capped aspen ones, the birch-tree ones, gathered from the north side of the trees, which never dry out. What would have been thought of in Norbury as ordinary mushrooms were despised. They were Unworthy Ones, only strung up and preserved on Frank's account, as he was supposed to like them. The store-room itself was as damp as if it had been beneath the sea. The barrels were made of oak, but they were covered in grey lichen which had never been seen growing on an oak. In Moscow, it was an insult to say of someone that he looked as if he had been scraped off the bath house wall, but moulds and mildews, thicker than in any bath house, spread and flourished among the dacha's stores. Only the strength of the vinegar and vodka, Russia's potent protectors against universal death from poisoning, safeguarded the unseen fruit and fungus as it brewed through the winter months.

There was a bath house, however, half of the lavatory shed. It worked very simply. Underneath a lid of perforated zinc there was a layer of stones from the brook, which could be heated by lighting a brushwood fire. When the fire had died down you went in, shut the door and pulled back the grating in the roof until Egor's face squinted down at you, ready to pour down a bucket of cold water that raised a suffocating cloud of steam from the blistering heat of the stones. The bath house, Frank knew, ought to be raised a good two feet above the ground, but then, so should the whole place. The damaged planks would have to be cut back until you got to a sound edge, and replaced with sound wood. The sight of the derelict, unkempt dacha, half gone back to moss and earth and almost fermenting with its load of preserves and alcohol, would be enough to bring a keen English Saturday carpenter – Charlie, for instance – to the verge of tears.

In front of the dacha, running across its whole length, was a veranda of shaky wooden planks, with a roof supported by fretwork columns. There the day, in summer, when it was hot, could be drowsed away. Courage, though not strength, was needed to raise the loose boards of the flooring. Underneath there was much animal and vegetable life. You could hear a scuttling and rustling, and if you bent down and looked closer you could catch the glint of metal. Some previous tenant (the whole estate, the forest, the village and the dacha, was owned by a Prince Demidov who preferred to live in Le Touquet) had left his knives and forks there for safety during the winter, and had forgotten them, or perhaps had never returned. And there was part of a croquet set, although who could ever have tried to play croquet at Shirokaya? But thirty years or so ago a croquet set had been the right thing to take down to the country, and perhaps the dacha then had had its own piece of grass.

The forest – as the Prince's German agent had explained to Frank when he first took the lease – had been cleared occasionally, but never cut. The trees grew so close to the dacha that they threw shadows, with the first light, through every window. Only a few yards away from the veranda the forest began. The fringes were of hazel and aspen, with green grass in the clearings as soon as the snow melted, and a wealth of cloudberries, bilberries and wild raspberries. The birches were the true forest. They had created for themselves a deep ground of fallen leaves and seeds, dropped twigs, and rotting bark, decomposing into one of the earth's richest coverings.

As the young birches grew taller the skin at the base of the trunks fragmented and shivered into dark and light patches. The branches showed white against black, black against white. The young twigs were fine and whip-like, dark brown with a purple gloss. As soon as the shining leaf-buds split open the young leaves breathed out an aromatic scent, not so thick as the poplar but wilder and more memorable, the true scent of wild and lonely places. The male catkins appeared in pairs, the pale female catkins followed. The leaves, turning from bright olive to a darker green, were agitated and astir even when the wind dropped. They were never strong enough to block out the light completely. The birch forest, unlike the pine forest, always gives a chance of life to whatever grows beneath it.

The spring rain, however welcome, made a complication. The drops ran down the branches as far as the heaviest twig, then hung there perilously, brilliant silver above, dark below. They were tenacious, apparently intending to stay on at all costs. If small birds landed on the branch at the same time, sometimes with the intention of getting at the drops of water, the whole system seemed in jeopardy. Twigs and boughs bent beneath the invasion, sighing, swaying back and forth with a circular motion, crossing and recrossing to settle back into their myriad delicate patterns. And yet quite large birds, starlings and even jackdaws and wood-pigeons, risked the higher branches in the early morning.

In July the fine seed-bracts, pale as meal, were set free from the twigs. The air was full of floating mealy seed. It was useless to try to keep it out of the dacha, all that could be done was to sweep it into weightless mounds in the corner of every room and on the veranda. By autumn, when their aromatic sharpness seemed to have vanished, or rather to have been assimilated into the burial scents of the decaying earth, the birches were hung with yellow leaves, but now the branches seemed too delicate to bear the twigs, the twigs too fragile for the stalks. The long thin fronds seemed to be stretching towards the ground, threatened with exhaustion. In each tree, even in the middle of the forest, there were five or six different movements, from the airy commotion at the top to the stirring of the older branches, often not much thicker than the younger ones, but secure at the dark base. When the heavy autumn rains began the trees gave out a new juicy scent of stewed tea, like the scent of the bundles of birch twigs in the steam-room of a public bath house which the customers used to beat themselves, leaving stray damp leaves on the tingling skin. By early winter the whole forest seemed worn out with the struggle. The clearings were crossed with fallen trunks, here and there, to be stepped over. By the time spring came again they would have sunk into a sepulchre of earth and moss, and beetles innumerable.

There were other dachas in the forest, but they were to the north-west, nearer to the village. At night there was not a light, not a human sound. Egor and Matryona, under their quilt next to the store-room, slept like the dead. There was only the voice of the birch trees.

Sleep walks along the benches, according to the Russian lullaby, and says 'I am sleepy.' Drowsiness says 'I am drowsy.' On the third night, Dolly woke, and knew she had been woken, by the slight noise of a door opening, the door on to the veranda. The noise did not strike her as frightening, rather as something she had been expecting. At home, Blashl would have barked, here there was only the darkness. She put on her boots and school overcoat and went out on to the veranda. Lisa was standing there, leaning against one of the wooden pillars in her waterproof, with her black shawl over her head.

'Are you going out, Lisa?'

'Did you hear the door?'

'Yes, I heard it.'

'It doesn't matter. Yes, I'm going out.'

'Where to?'

'It might have been better if you hadn't woken up, but you did wake up. Now you'll have to come with me.'

She did not take Dolly's hand, or even wait for her, but walked down the veranda steps into the forest. The little girl followed after her, dragging her feet because she had put on her boots without her stockings. She had never been before among the trees at night.

There were paths through the birch forest, made for the autumn shooting. In fact there was a path, which might have been called a ride, almost opposite the dacha. Lisa walked steadily along it, taking the middle of the track, which was raised above the rain-worn hollows on either side. You couldn't say it was pitch-dark. The moon in the cloudy night sky moved among the moving branches. Dolly could see, at first, if she looked back, the light in the dacha front window which was left burning all night. Then, although the path seemed to run quite straight, the light disappeared. The dacha, where Ben and Annushka lay strewn and sleeping, divided from her by sleep, was left behind.

At the point where another track crossed their own, Lisa stood still and looked round.

'Dolly, you're limping.'

'I'm all right.'

'I can't go back with you now.'

'I'm all right.'

Dolly was no longer thinking either of herself or of anything else, being concerned with struggling painfully alone through the plunging half-darkness. The leaf scent pressed in on her. There was nothing else to breathe. They had turned to the left, and walked perhaps almost as far as they had come along the first path from the dacha. Then Dolly began to see on each side of her, among the thronging stems of the birch trees, what looked like human hands, moving to touch each other across the whiteness and blackness.

'Lisa,' she called out, 'I can see hands.'

Lisa stood still again. They were in a clearing into which the moon shone. Dolly saw that by every birch tree, close against the trunk, stood a man or a woman. They stood separately pressing themselves each to their own tree. Then they turned their faces towards Lisa, patches of white against the whiteish bark. Dolly saw now that there were many more of them, deep into the thickness of the wood.

'I have come, but I can't stay,' said Lisa. 'You came, all of you, as far as this on my account. I know that, but I can't stay. As you see, I've had to bring this child with me. If she speaks about this, she won't be believed. If she remembers it, she'll understand in time what she's seen.'

No one answered her, no one spoke. No one left the protection of the trees, or moved towards them. Lisa, in her usual serene and collected manner, turned, and began to take the same way as before back to the dacha. Dolly, tired to death, trudged after her. Halfway down the main path she saw the familiar light again in the window of the dacha. When they reached it, Lisa sat Dolly down on one of the old cane chairs on the veranda, took off her boots, and rubbed her wet feet dry with her shawl. Neither of them said anything about what had happened. Dolly went to her room and lay down in the large old bed which she shared with Annushka. She could still smell the potent leaf-sap of the birch trees. It was as strong inside the house as out.

26

AT LIPKA Street the hallway had been cleared of straw and litter, the china and clothes which should never have been packed were now unpacked, and Blashl was confined uneasily to the yard. Frank suggested that the windows might be unsealed for the spring, but was told that the children would be disappointed if the Opening took place without them. He wondered by what guile or what process of persuasion he had been led to allow them to go to the half-savage, mouldering dacha in charge of the girl whom he pressingly and achingly needed here in his own house.

'I'll go down and fetch them on Saturday,' he told Toma, who had been forbidden to make any more direct reference to the children. 'Not for three more days! Even your brother-in-law would have been company for you!' cried Toma.

The post arrived. Nothing from England, an invitation from Mrs Graham – just a small party and she'd be glad if he liked to stay on after the others had left – and an official letter from the Ministry of Defence. This was to say that F. A. Reid, a foreign resident, printer and former importer of printing machinery, was released from his responsibility towards V. S. Grigoriev, student of the University of Moscow, who had been taken once again into preventive detention. There would now be no objection, since he held the necessary permits, to the departure of F. A. Reid and his family from the Russian Empire at his earliest convenience.

First they'd wanted him to stop, now they wanted him to go. In spite of himself Frank felt a deep pang at his first rejection from the magnificent and ramshackle country whose history, since he was born, had been his history, and whose future he could scarcely guess at. The Security, of course, might well change their minds again. In a country where nature represented not freedom, but law, where the harbours freed themselves from ice one after another, in majestic sequence, and the earth's harvest failed unfailingly once in every three years, the human authorities proceeded by fits and starts and inexplicable welcomes and withdrawals. To try and work out why they had one opinion of him last week, and another this, would be a squandering of time. One thing, though; if he was in disfavour, it would make it easier to arrange matters for Tvyordov.

On the eve of Palm Sunday Tvyordov had told Frank that he wished to displace himself. He wanted to go to England.

'It's mostly machine-work there now,' Frank told him.

'But they print by hand in Russian.'

Tvyordov had brought out a copy of Tolstoy's *Resurrection* – the first complete edition in Russian, without the censor's cuts. It had been printed by Headley Brothers at 14 Bishopsgate Without, in the east end of London.

'I don't know Headley's personally,' said Frank, 'but I could write to them, if that's where you want to go. Have you read this book?'

'I've looked at the half-title, title page, and end-matter,' said Tvyordov, 'the rest I haven't read.'

'It's a new explanation of the gospels. The resurrection, for those who understand how to change their lives, takes place on this earth. But this edition isn't in legal circulation. In your place I think I'd get rid of it.'

Tvyordov put the book, without regret, into the satchel which he now carried instead of his familiar bag. Frank guessed that *Resurrection* would go into the river, following Volodya's automatic, the white apron and the tools, and becoming part of the shoals of murky waste which night and day were making their devious way down to the Volga.

'Do you think, Frank Albertovich, that I shall have any difficulty in getting an external passport?'

'They don't want skilled craftsmen to leave,' Frank said. 'But on the other hand they're glad to be rid of trouble-makers and political dissidents.'

'I am not a trouble-maker.'

'But you were a union secretary in 1905, and you're still the branch secretary. I think they'll let you go, but I don't know if you'll be able to come back.'

Tvyordov's face was not designed to show much expression, but a kind of iron or wooden disapproval could be detected now. His object had been to earn substantially in England and then to go back to his native village, Evnyak, the place of willows.

'Are there willows there now?' Frank asked him.

Tvyordov thought not. The stream, he believed, was dried up, the landlord had got permission to deflect the water. There had been a pretty wooden hump-backed bridge, but it had been replaced by concrete for the Imperial Motor-Car Reliability Trials of 1911, when Evnyak had been on the official route, from the Baltic to the Black Sea. Changes, yes, but it was his village still. It was there that he wanted to lay his old compositor's bones.

'Possibly I could go to Bishopsgate Without and leave my wife behind for the time being.'

'I shouldn't do that,' said Frank.

Silently he had stored up the history of the bridge at Evnyak to repeat to Ben, who was fanatically interested in the Reliability Trials. At the end of the day he had often found himself quite well supplied with facts and incidents which might possibly be of interest to the children or, when she had still been there, to Nellie. If no one wanted to listen to them he put them quietly away.

It occurred to him now, as he read the Security's letter, that he had better sign Tvyordov's application at once, and that Selwyn had better be the second recommendation. He took a taxi to the office and got this done. Selwyn, eagerly writing his signature, glad to be asked for help, suggested that after work they should go to the small hall at the Philharmonia and listen together to a programme of Igor Stravinsky. Frank said that it was kind of him, but he didn't feel much like going out. He found it hard, in point of fact, to concentrate on anything except the first night after Lisa came back to him. Selwyn persisted.

'I thought we could have a serious talk in the interval.'

'Surely it's a mistake to go to the Philharmonia to have a serious talk,' said Frank. 'Why don't you come to the house? You know you're always free to come there, or very nearly always.'

'I'd like the setting to be appropriate for what I have to say.'

'You mean it's something that will only sound right in the refreshment room of a concert-hall?'

'Music always makes its effects, Frank.'

The undefended gaps in Frank's mind allowed for a tormenting image of Lisa and, something he hadn't bargained for, a grotesque Volodya, insisting to the Security, by way of a defence, that he too, was alive. His only resource against these thoughts was the work in hand. 'In any case, I want that *Three Men in a Boat* job finished. None of them will be in tomorrow, it's a compulsory holiday for the Tsaritsa's name day.'

'Ah, Frank, poor woman! Poor woman!'

'I can't worry about the Imperial family now. I'm going down to the paper warehouse.'

He looked doubtfully at Selwyn, who seemed exceptionally pale. 'Come to the house this evening.'

Selwyn said, 'Let me start by saying that we've often spoken, you and I, about the two sides of man, the spiritual and the material, as though they were divided. What a mistake that is! The two should be indistinguishable, or rather there should be a gradual transformation, until what seems to be material is seen to be nothing of the kind.'

'Selwyn, what are you talking about?'

'About Nellie.'

'I don't see how you can be. Nellie and I are practical people. I thought when I first met her that I'd never known anyone act more sensibly.'

'But you brought her to Holy Russia, Frank, a land of great contrasts.'

'That's where my work was. She knew that, and she didn't object.'

'Russia hasn't changed you, Frank, because you were born here. But didn't you find that it changed Nellie? Didn't her whole nature become, as they say here, wider? Didn't she talk less about the household, and go more often to Shirokaya?'

'Perhaps a bit more often, I don't know.'

'Nellie was turning towards the spiritual. Unfortunately she couldn't, as yet, distinguish it from the romantic, which casts a false glow over everything it touches. I tried to explain to you, some time ago now, that I had recently been through a period of sexual temptation and trial. You remember that?'

'I'm afraid I don't,' said Frank.

'Nellie saw me in a false glow, my friend.'

'You're raving, Selwyn. She hardly ever said anything about you.'

'Let me tell you what happened. Before her train drew into Mozhaisk I took a point of vantage where I could see it arrive. You know Mozhaisk, you know the great cathedral there, the Cathedral of St Nicholas. Well, not far from there there's a restaurant on the station, the last opportunity for the passengers to get boiling water for their tea before Borodino. A half-an-hour stop. They all got out. I saw your wife and children get out. They were quite unmistakable. That red tam-o'-shanter! Nellie sent the three children to the refreshment room and began looking up and down the platform. A woman looking for someone who doesn't come is a touching sight, Frank. The little ones came out and she spoke to them again – spoke earnestly. The porter took out their boxes and cases from the guard's van, and a rug, I think a tartan rug. Then Nellie took one long look round, again in all directions – there was resignation in that look! – gave what I suppose was money to the stationmaster, and kissed the children. During all this time I remained where I was. I didn't go forward. I didn't betray my presence. She waited on the platform until the very last moment, the third bell, then she climbed back into her carriage. Still I didn't reveal myself.'

'God give me patience,' said Frank. 'Do you mean you were supposed to meet her there?'

'It was not I, Frank, who suggested it.'

'But did you meet her or didn't you?'

'I've told you what I did. I failed the tryst.'

'What tryst?'

'She wanted to go away with me to some more free and natural place. Perhaps under the sky in forests of pine and birch, where a man and a woman can join body and soul and find out what work they have to do in the world.'

'Why did she send the children back to Moscow?'

'I supposed that, since I had failed her, she didn't want to take them on with her to Norbury.'

'My God, they'd have been better off in Norbury than with you in the middle of a forest of pine and birch. All right, you arranged to meet Nellie off the Berlin train at Mozhaisk. Why didn't you?'

'For many reasons. I had to consider your feelings, the feelings of a true friend. And then, if I left the Press, I was without any definite means of earnings, and I was doubtful about my capacity to support such a large family.'

'I'm beginning to understand it. You got cold feet and left her stranded. Poor Nellie, poor little Nellie, ditched at a hole of a place like Mozhaisk, walking up and down the platform, and you flaming well never turned up. I've put up with a lot this Easter, but I'm damned if I see why Nellie should have to.'

'Frank,' Selwyn cried, holding up his hands in surrender, 'don't descend to violence! Candidly, that was why I thought it would be better to discuss all this in a public place, where you couldn't act violently, even if you wanted to.'

Frank paused. 'Just tell me one thing. Where is Nellie now?'

'She went to Bright Meadows.'

'Where?'

'A Tolstoyan settlement, of which I'd once given her the address. I call it Tolstoyan, although Lev Nicolaievich, I fear, refused to countenance most of such places. But there are handicrafts, vegetable gardening and, I'm sure, music . . .'

'How do you know she went there? Her own brother didn't know her address. She hasn't written, either to me or to her children.'

'Or to me either, Frank.'

'Well then, who told you?'

'I had news from Muriel Kinsman.'

'Miss Kinsman?'

'She undertook to write to me regularly. I recommended her also, you see, to Bright Meadows, as she seemed at a loss, and had very little money.'

'I don't want to talk about Miss Kinsman. What's the address? Come on, what is it?'

'I can give it to you, but I fear it will be of very little use. I heard from Muriel Kinsman this morning, and she tells me that Nellie found she didn't care for the communal life.'

'So she left.'

'Yes, she had left Bright Meadows.'

'Selwyn,' said Frank, with extreme bitterness. 'You could have told me all this before.'

'I did what I could to help you.'

'Yes, you found Lisa for me.'

'I tried more than once to explain my actions to you in detail. I came to your house only a few evenings ago, not criticising you in any way, nature and humanity are the only standards I recognise, but it was hardly a moment for discussion, you were with Lisa Ivanovna, with your hands on her breasts. But Frank, perhaps you don't want to discuss this incident.'

'I don't mind talking about Lisa, as long as you don't say she's like a birch tree in the wind. She's solid flesh. She's not an incident.'

Selwyn shook his head.

27

ON THE following morning Frank was called to the telephone. 'It's very early, Toma.' 'Yes, sir, but it's someone speaking from the Alexandervoksal.'

The time was just before seven o'clock. 'Mr Reid, for the second time your children are here all by themselves at this station. Could you make it convenient to fetch them at once?'

'I should like to speak to the elder of my two daughters,' said Frank. 'Please fetch her to your office.'

He stood listening for what seemed a very long time to the distant surge and grind of the station, pierced once by a warning bell.

'This is Darya Frantsovna Reid. Do you hear me?'

She spoke clearly, but not with her old decisiveness.

'Yes, I hear you. Dolly, what have you done with Lisa?'

'She came with us to Ostanovka. Then she put us in a carriage in the train to Moscow. We were quite all right.'

'But what did she do?'

'She just turned away and walked down the platform, so we couldn't wave.'

'But Dolly, where is she?'

'She was going to take another train.'

'Where to?'

'*Papashka*, I'm here with Ben and Annushka. What am I supposed to do?'

When he arrived at the Alexandervoksal he found at first only Dolly. Ben had gone to the engine-cleaning shed, Annushka was counting the money with the attendant in the first-class ladies' lavatory. Dolly was standing alone outside the stationmaster's office. She clung to him fiercely, sniffing at his spring overcoat, just out of store, like an animal. The two of them clung together.

She would not be parted from him. The two younger ones wanted to go back to the house where they were received like survivors from an earthquake. Dolly came with him to Reid-ka's, and sat all morning in the customer's chair in his office.

Agafya came up from the tea-place, carrying sugar with her, prepared, as in former days, to indulge the office's princess. When she saw Dolly she stopped, with the brownish-white sugar sticks still in her hand. Seeing that the comedy was over, she put them back in their paper wrapping, and nodded to the pale and silent Dolly.

'She's helping me a bit with the letters,' said Frank, not very convincingly.

'God will make her of use to you,' said Agafya.

After a time he asked Dolly one or two questions, cautiously, not being sure himself how much he wanted to know. Had they locked the doors of the dacha properly, and given the keys to Egor and Matryona? – Oh, yes, all that! – Had they been into the woods? – Yes, they had. – Were the paths wet? – Yes, rather wet. – When Lisa Ivanovna told them to stay in the train and get out at Moscow, did she say where she was going herself? Yes, Berlin. She had to go to Berlin. – Frank asked nothing more about the visit to the dacha either then or ever.

Volodya, thought to be a conspirator, had turned out to be nothing more than a lover. Lisa, who, Frank could have sworn, was a lover, had turned out to be heaven knows what. It was clear enough now why the Security were in favour of his leaving Russia. He had dangerous employees, or one danger-ous employee, at least, a dangerous young woman, pretending to be looking after his children. He had let her escape, more likely arranged it. He must, for example, have given her back her papers, without reporting this to the authorities. But what-ever they thought now, they hadn't thought it on Palm Sunday, and Frank couldn't imagine who, in all Moscow, could have suggested it to them since then.

By midday, he saw that he must take Dolly home. He told Selwyn and Bernov to carry on. Selwyn unexpectedly shook his hand.

'Remember that what binds us together is the knowledge of the wrongs we have done to one another.'

Bernov, on the other hand, asked if he could come with them in the taxi, if they were getting one, as far as the Alexander Gardens. It was his lunch hour. On the way he took the opportunity to tell them that he was thinking seriously of going to England. No, not for a visit, to emigrate. He had collected most of the necessary forms.

'Bring them in tomorrow, then,' said Frank, feeling as if he were lifting a heavy weight. 'Have you got an address to go to in England?'

Yes, Charlie had told him that he would always find a hearty welcome in Longfellow Road.

Along the river-banks the grass from last year was showing, indescribably seedy, through the drenched earth, and with it the first patches of new grass. Even in Moscow there was the smell of green grass and leaves, inconceivable for the last five months.

At 22 Lipka Street, Annushka came to the front door with Toma, bellowing 'We're opening the windows!' In the hall-way, Ben was energetically turning the handle of the 'Amour' gramophone, which a moment later out-roared Annushka with the splendid voice of Fyodor Chaliapin.

'We can't wait any longer, sir,' said Toma. 'The ice has been melted for days, the children are back from the country, the fowls must come out of their shed, or they'll become diseased.'

'I left it entirely to you,' said Frank. 'Go ahead.'

The hens, in fact, were already out, stepping delicately about the backyard, alternately stretching out their long necks with dignity and rummaging, with squalid abandon, in the crevices between the brickwork.

It's not true, Frank thought, that she was pretending to look after the children. She did look after them. It's not true that she pretended to make love to me. She did make love to me.

All morning the yardman had been removing the putty from the inner glass, piece by piece, flake by flake. Blashl, frantic at his long disappearance, howled at intervals, but the yardman worked slowly. When all the putty was off, without a scratch from the chisel, he called, lord of the moment, for the scrapings to be brushed away. The space between the outer and inner windows was black with dead flies. They, too, must be removed, and the sills washed down with soft soap. Then with a shout from the triumphant shoe-cleaning boy at the top of the house to Ben, still in the hall, the outer windows, some terribly stuck, were shaken and rattled till they opened wide. Throughout the winter the house had been deaf, turned inwards, able to listen only to itself. Now the sounds of Moscow broke in, the bells and voices, the cabs and taxis which had gone by all winter unheard like ghosts of themselves, and with the noise came the spring wind, fresher than it felt in the street, blowing in uninterrupted from the northern regions where the frost still lay.

A horse-and-cab pulled up outside. There were still a good few of them left, for those who had time to spare or didn't want to spend too much. Toma, still dusty and splashed with soap and water, ran out, buttoning up his grey jacket as he went. He opened the door, and Nellie walked into the house.

ABOUT THE INTRODUCER

JOHN BAYLEY is former Thomas Warton Professor of English Literature at the University of Oxford. His many books include *The Characters of Love*, *The Short Story: Henry James to Elizabeth Bowen*, *Shakespeare and Tragedy* and *Tolstoy and the Novel*. He has written several novels, and is the author of the bestselling *Iris*, a memoir of Iris Murdoch.

CHINUA ACHEBE
Things Fall Apart

THE ARABIAN NIGHTS
(2 vols, tr. Husain Haddawy)

AUGUSTINE
The Confessions

JANE AUSTEN
Emma
Mansfield Park
Northanger Abbey
Persuasion
Pride and Prejudice
Sanditon and Other Stories
Sense and Sensibility

HONORÉ DE BALZAC
Cousin Bette
Eugénie Grandet
Old Goriot

SIMONE DE BEAUVOIR
The Second Sex

SAMUEL BECKETT
Molloy, Malone Dies,
The Unnamable
(US only)

SAUL BELLOW
The Adventures of Augie March

HECTOR BERLIOZ
The Memoirs of Hector Berlioz

WILLIAM BLAKE
Poems and Prophecies

JORGE LUIS BORGES
Ficciones

JAMES BOSWELL
The Life of Samuel Johnson
The Journal of a Tour to
the Hebrides

CHARLOTTE BRONTË
Jane Eyre
Villette

EMILY BRONTË
Wuthering Heights

MIKHAIL BULGAKOV
The Master and Margarita

SAMUEL BUTLER
The Way of all Flesh

JAMES M. CAIN
The Postman Always Rings Twice
Double Indemnity
Mildred Pierce
Selected Stories
(in 1 vol.)

ITALO CALVINO
If on a winter's night a traveler

ALBERT CAMUS
The Outsider (UK)
The Stranger (US)

WILLA CATHER
Death Comes for the Archbishop
My Ántonia
(US only)

MIGUEL DE CERVANTES
Don Quixote

RAYMOND CHANDLER
The novels (2 vols)
Collected Stories

GEOFFREY CHAUCER
Canterbury Tales

ANTON CHEKHOV
My Life and Other Stories
The Steppe and Other Stories

KATE CHOPIN
The Awakening

CARL VON CLAUSEWITZ
On War

S. T. COLERIDGE
Poems

WILKIE COLLINS
The Moonstone
The Woman in White

CONFUCIUS
The Analects

JOSEPH CONRAD
Heart of Darkness
Lord Jim
Nostromo
The Secret Agent
Typhoon and Other Stories
Under Western Eyes
Victory

THOMAS CRANMER
The Book of Common Prayer
(UK only)

DANTE ALIGHIERI
The Divine Comedy

CHARLES DARWIN
The Origin of Species
The Voyage of the Beagle
(in 1 vol.)

DANIEL DEFOE
Moll Flanders
Robinson Crusoe

CHARLES DICKENS
Bleak House
David Copperfield
Dombey and Son
Great Expectations
Hard Times
Little Dorrit
Martin Chuzzlewit
Nicholas Nickleby
The Old Curiosity Shop
Oliver Twist
Our Mutual Friend
The Pickwick Papers
A Tale of Two Cities

DENIS DIDEROT
Memoirs of a Nun

JOHN DONNE
The Complete English Poems

FYODOR DOSTOEVSKY
The Adolescent
The Brothers Karamazov
Crime and Punishment
Demons
The Idiot

W. E. B. DU BOIS
The Souls of Black Folk
(US only)

GEORGE ELIOT
Adam Bede
Daniel Deronda
Middlemarch
The Mill on the Floss
Silas Marner

WILLIAM FAULKNER
The Sound and the Fury
(UK only)

HENRY FIELDING
Joseph Andrews and Shamela
(UK only)
Tom Jones

F. SCOTT FITZGERALD
The Great Gatsby
This Side of Paradise
(UK only)

PENELOPE FITZGERALD
The Bookshop
The Gate of Angels
The Blue Flower
(in 1 vol.)
Offshore
Human Voices
The Beginning of Spring
(in 1 vol.)

GUSTAVE FLAUBERT
Madame Bovary

FORD MADOX FORD
The Good Soldier
Parade's End

E. M. FORSTER
Howards End
A Passage to India

ELIZABETH GASKELL
Mary Barton

EDWARD GIBBON
The Decline and Fall of the
Roman Empire
Vols 1 to 3: The Western Empire
Vols 4 to 6: The Eastern Empire

J. W. VON GOETHE
Selected Works

IVAN GONCHAROV
Oblomov

GÜNTER GRASS
The Tin Drum

GRAHAM GREENE
Brighton Rock
The Human Factor

DASHIELL HAMMETT
The Maltese Falcon
The Thin Man
Red Harvest
(in 1 vol.)

THOMAS HARDY
Far From the Madding Crowd
Jude the Obscure
The Mayor of Casterbridge
The Return of the Native
Tess of the d'Urbervilles
The Woodlanders

JAROSLAV HAŠEK
The Good Soldier Švejk

NATHANIEL HAWTHORNE
The Scarlet Letter

JOSEPH HELLER
Catch-22

ERNEST HEMINGWAY
A Farewell to Arms
The Collected Stories
(UK only)

GEORGE HERBERT
The Complete English Works

HERODOTUS
The Histories

PATRICIA HIGHSMITH
The Talented Mr. Ripley
Ripley Under Ground
Ripley's Game
(in 1 vol.)

HINDU SCRIPTURES
(tr. R. C. Zaehner)

JAMES HOGG
Confessions of a Justified Sinner

HOMER
The Iliad
The Odyssey

VICTOR HUGO
Les Misérables

HENRY JAMES
The Awkward Age
The Bostonians
The Golden Bowl
The Portrait of a Lady
The Princess Casamassima
The Wings of the Dove
Collected Stories (2 vols)

SAMUEL JOHNSON
A Journey to the Western
Islands of Scotland

JAMES JOYCE
Dubliners
A Portrait of the Artist as
a Young Man
Ulysses

FRANZ KAFKA
Collected Stories
The Castle
The Trial

JOHN KEATS
The Poems

SØREN KIERKEGAARD
Fear and Trembling and
The Book on Adler

RUDYARD KIPLING
Collected Stories
Kim

THE KORAN
(tr. Marmaduke Pickthall)

CHODERLOS DE LACLOS
Les Liaisons dangereuses

GIUSEPPE TOMASI DI
LAMPEDUSA
The Leopard

WILLIAM LANGLAND
Piers Plowman
with (anon.) Sir Gawain and the
Green Knight, Pearl, Sir Orfeo
(UK only)

D. H. LAWRENCE
Collected Stories
The Rainbow
Sons and Lovers
Women in Love

MIKHAIL LERMONTOV
A Hero of Our Time

PRIMO LEVI
If This is a Man and The Truce
(UK only)
The Periodic Table

THE MABINOGION

NICCOLÒ MACHIAVELLI
The Prince

NAGUIB MAHFOUZ
The Cairo Trilogy

THOMAS MANN
Buddenbrooks
Collected Stories (UK only)
Death in Venice and Other Stories
(US only)
Doctor Faustus

KATHERINE MANSFIELD
The Garden Party and Other
Stories

MARCUS AURELIUS
Meditations

GABRIEL GARCÍA MÁRQUEZ
Love in the Time of Cholera
One Hundred Years of Solitude

ANDREW MARVELL
The Complete Poems

CORMAC McCARTHY
The Border Trilogy (US only)

HERMAN MELVILLE
The Complete Shorter Fiction
Moby-Dick

JOHN STUART MILL
On Liberty and Utilitarianism

JOHN MILTON
The Complete English Poems

YUKIO MISHIMA
The Temple of the
Golden Pavilion

MARY WORTLEY MONTAGU
Letters

MICHEL DE MONTAIGNE
The Complete Works

THOMAS MORE
Utopia

TONI MORRISON
Song of Solomon

MURASAKI SHIKIBU
The Tale of Genji

VLADIMIR NABOKOV
Lolita
Pale Fire
Speak, Memory

V. S. NAIPAUL
A House for Mr Biswas

THE NEW TESTAMENT
(King James Version)

THE OLD TESTAMENT
(King James Version)

GEORGE ORWELL
Animal Farm
Nineteen Eighty-Four
Essays

THOMAS PAINE
Rights of Man
and Common Sense

BORIS PASTERNAK
Doctor Zhivago

SYLVIA PLATH
The Bell Jar (US only)

PLATO
The Republic
Symposium and Phaedrus

EDGAR ALLAN POE
The Complete Stories

MARCEL PROUST
In Search of Lost Time
(4 vols, UK only)

ALEXANDER PUSHKIN
The Collected Stories

FRANÇOIS RABELAIS
Gargantua and Pantagruel

JOSEPH ROTH
The Radetzky March

JEAN-JACQUES
ROUSSEAU
Confessions
The Social Contract and
the Discourses

SALMAN RUSHDIE
Midnight's Children

WALTER SCOTT
Rob Roy

WILLIAM SHAKESPEARE
Comedies Vols 1 and 2
Histories Vols 1 and 2
Romances
Sonnets and Narrative Poems
Tragedies Vols 1 and 2

MARY SHELLEY
Frankenstein

ADAM SMITH
The Wealth of Nations

ALEXANDER SOLZHENITSYN
One Day in the Life of
Ivan Denisovich

SOPHOCLES
The Theban Plays

CHRISTINA STEAD
The Man Who Loved Children

JOHN STEINBECK
The Grapes of Wrath

STENDHAL
The Charterhouse of Parma
Scarlet and Black

LAURENCE STERNE
Tristram Shandy

ROBERT LOUIS STEVENSON
The Master of Ballantrae and
Weir of Hermiston
Dr Jekyll and Mr Hyde
and Other Stories

HARRIET BEECHER STOWE
Uncle Tom's Cabin

ITALO SVEVO
Zeno's Conscience

JONATHAN SWIFT
Gulliver's Travels

JUNICHIRŌ TANIZAKI
The Makioka Sisters

W. M. THACKERAY
Vanity Fair

HENRY DAVID THOREAU
Walden

ALEXIS DE TOCQUEVILLE
Democracy in America

LEO TOLSTOY
Collected Shorter Fiction (2 vols)
Anna Karenina
Childhood, Boyhood and Youth
The Cossacks
War and Peace

ANTHONY TROLLOPE
Barchester Towers
Can You Forgive Her?
Doctor Thorne
The Eustace Diamonds
Framley Parsonage
The Last Chronicle of Barset
Phineas Finn
The Small House at Allington
The Warden

IVAN TURGENEV
Fathers and Children
First Love and Other Stories
A Sportsman's Notebook

MARK TWAIN
Tom Sawyer
and Huckleberry Finn

JOHN UPDIKE
The Complete Henry Bech
(US only)
Rabbit Angstrom

GIORGIO VASARI
Lives of the Painters, Sculptors
and Architects

VIRGIL
The Aeneid

VOLTAIRE
Candide and Other Stories

EVELYN WAUGH
The Complete Short Stories
Black Mischief, Scoop, The Loved
One, The Ordeal of Gilbert
Pinfold (1 vol.)
Brideshead Revisited
Decline and Fall
A Handful of Dust
The Sword of Honour Trilogy

EDITH WHARTON
The Age of Innocence
The Custom of the Country
The House of Mirth
The Reef

OSCAR WILDE
Plays, Prose Writings and Poems

MARY WOLLSTONECRAFT
A Vindication of the Rights of
Woman

VIRGINIA WOOLF
To the Lighthouse
Mrs Dalloway

WILLIAM WORDSWORTH
Selected Poems (UK only)

W. B. YEATS
The Poems (UK only)

ÉMILE ZOLA
Germinal